SHALLOW GRAVE

SHALLOW GRAVE

A MATT SINCLAIR MYSTERY

Brian Thiem

CROOKED
LANE

NEW YORK

Published in the United States by Crooked Lane Books, an imprint of The Quick Brown Fox & Company LLC.

Crooked Lane Books and its logo are trademarks of The Quick Brown Fox & Company LLC.

Library of Congress Catalog-in-Publication data available upon request.

ISBN (hardcover): 978-1-68331-143-0
ISBN (ePub): 978-1-68331-145-4
ISBN (Kindle): 978-1-68331-146-1
ISBN (ePDF): 978-1-68331-147-8

Cover design by Andy Ruggirello
Book design by Jennifer Canzone

Printed in the United States.

www.crookedlanebooks.com

Crooked Lane Books
34 West 27th St., 10th Floor
New York, NY 10001

First edition: July 2017

10 9 8 7 6 5 4 3 2 1

For

The fifty-one Oakland Police Officers who
have given their lives in the line of duty.

And

For the thousands of officers in Oakland and
around the country who do the job every day
with the knowledge they may do the same.

Chapter 1

The radio in Oakland homicide sergeant Matt Sinclair's unmarked Crown Vic crackled. "Tactical commander to all teams. Execute."

Sinclair pressed the gas pedal to the floor, and his car rocketed down the block. He slammed on the brakes one house shy of their target, flung open his door, and rolled out, pulling a Remington 870 pump shotgun behind him. He racked a round into the chamber, the sound echoing through the early-morning quiet of the residential neighborhood.

He paused a few seconds to allow the officers in the next two cars to catch up. He then jogged down the street and up the house's cracked cement walkway. His partner, Sergeant Cathy Braddock, Officer Kurt Fletcher of the intelligence unit, and four other homicide investigators on the team followed. His eyes scanned the house and yard, looking for movement or something as insignificant as the flutter of a curtain in a window. Nothing.

Two of the investigators peeled off and ran down the side of the house, heading for the backyard where they'd establish a perimeter. Sinclair glanced back and saw Sergeant Jankowski, a huge man of nearly three hundred pounds, cradling a twenty-pound battering ram and jogging to catch up.

The street was quiet. No pedestrians. Morning newspapers were still lying in driveways. Although the sun had risen more than an hour ago, it was still fighting to penetrate the typical morning fog that blanketed the city.

Braddock and Fletcher followed Sinclair up four rotting wooden steps to the small porch and stacked behind him to the side of the door. Sinclair tried the doorknob of the metal security door on the off chance that Animal's wife was careless. She wasn't.

Sinclair pounded on the door with his fist and yelled, "Police! Search warrant. Open the door!"

He heard raised voices. A chair or table screeched across the floor. The radio bud in Sinclair's right ear clicked. "Bathroom light came on in the rear. Toilet flushing."

Although seizing narcotics was not the primary purpose of their warrant, Sinclair wasn't about to let them flush their stash. "Hook—key," he ordered to the two men at the bottom of the stairs.

Jankowski's partner, Lou Sanchez, climbed onto the porch and jammed a pry bar between the steel door and frame. He yanked and the metal cage sprang open. Sanchez pulled it to the side, and Jankowski swung the battering ram, affectionately referred to as "the key to the city," at the doorknob. The door splintered and flew open.

Sinclair followed the battering ram through the door into a tiny living room crammed full with a couch, coffee table, TV, and two occasional chairs. A man about Sinclair's height, dressed in plaid boxer shorts and a wife-beater undershirt stretched tight over a huge belly, shuffled his feet in the doorway of the hallway, unsure if he should retreat or attack.

Sinclair leveled the shotgun at his chest. "On the floor," he yelled. "Now!" The man dropped to his knees, and Braddock rushed forward and shoved him to the ground.

While she was handcuffing the first suspect, Sinclair headed into the hallway. There was a closed door on his right. He grabbed the knob. Locked. Stepping back, he kicked the door. A rail-thin woman in her twenties hovered over the toilet, tearing apart plastic-wrapped bundles of white powder and dropping them in the toilet. Gripping the shotgun with his right hand, he grabbed the woman's arm with his left and pulled her away from her task. She glared at him with bloodshot eyes, grabbed a butcher knife from atop the toilet tank, and slashed at Sinclair.

Sinclair released his grip on the woman. He stepped back as the knife blade swept past his neck, missing by inches. Sinclair grabbed the foregrip of the shotgun with his left hand, pivoted, and swung the butt of the shotgun at her head. The knife clattered to the tile floor, and the woman dropped in a heap beside it.

Chapter 2

Sinclair signed the bottom of the statement form and handed it to the patrol lieutenant. In addition to the three unmarked cars belonging to homicide, a marked patrol SUV and a semimarked lieutenant's car were parked in front of the small, pale-yellow stucco house. They were in a working-class neighborhood in the Melrose District of Oakland, which was seeing revitalization thanks to the booming Bay Area, pricing many people out of San Francisco and into the sketchier parts of Oakland.

"It's not like I don't have enough use-of-force paperwork to handle with my own guys," the lieutenant said.

Sinclair leaned against his car and took a few puffs on his cigar. "My LT would've handled it, but he's tied up at the Simbas' clubhouse," he said, referring to the Savage Simbas Motorcycle Club, the primary target of the three search warrants the department's SWAT team and homicide unit had just executed. The house Sinclair's team hit and another private residence were secondary targets suspected of containing evidence of the murder and ties to the club.

The uniformed lieutenant turned and said to Jankowski, "Are you finished with your supplemental?"

Jankowski, the oldest investigator in the unit with more than thirty years in the department, handed him a sheet of paper. "Not much to it. I stepped into the bathroom, saw the lady meth head swing a knife at Sinclair. He ducked and buttstroked her before she could take another swipe at him. Me—I would've shot the cranked-up bitch."

The lieutenant slid the papers into his notebook and opened his car door. "Hell, ignore my griping. I'm just glad you guys are okay."

The patrol lieutenant drove off with the other marked car behind him, leaving the three homicide cars parked in front of the house. An ambulance had taken the woman Sinclair butt-stroked with his shotgun to the hospital an hour ago, where a patrol officer would guard her until she could be transferred to the city jail. She was the wife of the Savage Simba sergeant-at-arms known as Animal, the man who killed a fellow club member in a biker bar last night. Two other patrol cars had transported a club prospect that they'd found hiding in a closet and Animal's brother-in-law, the man Sinclair encountered in the living room, to homicide.

Braddock and Fletcher came out the front door and walked to their cars carrying armfuls of paper bags. They were dressed in the department's dark-blue utility uniform instead of their normal plain clothes, as was Sinclair. They both wore Kevlar vests, leather boots, and their duty gunbelts. Long-haired and bearded, Officer Kurt Fletcher had been assigned to OPD's intelligence unit for ten years, where he was responsible for tracking gangs and had become one of the nation's foremost experts on the Hells Angels.

"I'm guessing we have close to a kilo of meth," Braddock said. "No telling how much they flushed. And eight handguns. Maybe one of them's the murder weapon."

"I hate giving you the shit work," Jankowski said to Braddock, "but do you mind turning all that stuff in? I need to get over to the clubhouse. They've got Animal and about twenty bikers in custody there and a shitload of evidence."

"No problem," she said, then turned to Fletcher. "Any word from Phil?"

Despite numerous calls last night and this morning to Phil Roberts, the Intel unit sergeant, no one could reach him. Roberts had been both Sinclair's and Braddock's training officer when they came to homicide. He and Sinclair had been partners for four years until Sinclair's drinking caused him to self-destruct and get booted out of the unit. When Sinclair got his sergeant stripes back two years ago, he returned to homicide and took over as Braddock's training officer, and Roberts was given the coveted Intel supervisor job.

"Nothing," Fletcher said. "This ain't like him. He always answers his phone and would never miss out on something like this. If nothing else, he should've figured out something was up when he got to the office this morning and no one was there."

Sinclair grunted. At one time, Phil had probably been his best friend in the world, a man who had his back no matter what. But when Sinclair was tasked with the Thrill Kill Murders six months ago, Phil sided with the Feds to keep an escort service's client list from him. The list was the key to solving his case, and Sinclair still couldn't understand how someone like Phil, the man who taught him there was no cause more noble than investigating the death of a human being, would protect a bunch of wealthy businessmen and politicians over taking down a killer. He wondered what happened to make his old partner change so drastically.

While Jankowski and Fletcher drove to the clubhouse, Sinclair and the other homicide investigators returned to the Police Administration Building, known as the PAB to those who worked there. After cataloging and turning in the guns to the property section and the drugs to criminalistics, he changed out of his uniform in the basement locker room and headed up to the homicide office on the second floor of the nine-story building.

Sinclair hung up his suitcoat and grabbed his coffee cup, which had an outline of a corpse on one side and *Homicide, Our Day Begins When Someone Else's Ends* on the other, weaving through the throngs of plainclothes and uniformed officers who were assisting in one way or another with the motorcycle gang murder. Jerry O'Connor, one of the two homicide sergeants who had covered the back of the house when Sinclair and the others made entry through the front, stood by the coffee station. Sinclair held out his cup, and O'Connor filled it.

He and Braddock had gotten a call from Jankowski at 2:00 AM to assist O'Connor and Sanchez with interviewing witnesses to the shooting in the Iron Horse Bar. Although most club members who were present at the time were long gone by the time the police arrived, investigators were able to get three eyewitness statements from other patrons who saw what had happened. The bar owner gave a statement as well—his establishment may have catered to bikers, but retaining his business license and alcohol permit required his cooperation with the police. Jankowski had also reviewed footage from two surveillance cameras in the bar that corroborated what the witnesses said. According to what they knew so far, Shane Gibbs, a full-patch Savage Simba club member, walked into the West Oakland biker bar with another member nicknamed Tiny. Gibbs got into an argument with the club's sergeant-at-arms, known as Animal, who had pulled out a gun and killed him.

"Here's the game plan from Jankowski," O'Connor said. "They brought about twenty people from the clubhouse, four more from the crash pad the homicide suppression team hit, and our two dudes, all in custody for the drugs and guns that were found. Any who don't cooperate and give a statement get booked."

"Sounds good to me," Sinclair said. He knew the DA wouldn't file charges on people just because narcotics were found in a house they happened to be in, but holding that hammer over their heads might motivate them to talk about the murder or some other illegal activity the club was involved in.

"The guys from HST are guarding the prisoners and keeping them separate in the lineup room," O'Connor said, referring to the homicide suppression team, a squad of officers that located witnesses and suspects and put pressure on hot spots to prevent retaliatory murders from occurring. "When you're ready, grab one, take him into an interview room, and see what he says. If it's 'Fuck you' or 'I don't know shit,' take him back to the lineup room and have HST take him to the jail and book him."

"Anyone in particular we should start with?" Sinclair asked.

"When Jankowski gets back, he might have a different plan, but for now, anyone but Animal and Pops, the club president. We'll save them for Jankowski."

Chapter 3

Sinclair and Braddock wove through the property crimes section and down a hallway to a large room with a one-way mirror along one wall. On the other side of the mirror was a stage where investigators could line up six people to see if witnesses seated on the other side of the mirror could pick out the person who robbed, raped, or assaulted them. But in the sixty-year-old PAB, space was at a premium, so the lineup room was also used for staff meetings, training classes, briefings, file storage, and at times like this, a witness and suspect holding area. Sinclair and Braddock escorted Animal's brother-in-law to an empty interview room.

Sinclair removed the suspect's handcuffs, pulled out a chair, and said, "Have a seat." Sinclair and Braddock sat in chairs on opposite sides of him. Braddock smoothed her chestnut-colored hair, which she wore in a short bob; opened her notebook; and wrote the date and time on the top of her legal pad. She was five foot six and had an athletic build, which she fought hard to maintain at the gym between the hours they worked and her family obligations. Although she came on the department about the same time as Sinclair, she was only promoted to sergeant five years ago, which made her the junior investigator in the homicide section.

Sinclair pulled a legal pad and statement form from his leather folio and asked, "Last name?"

The man glared at Sinclair. Then he said, "Hammond."

Sinclair wrote on the legal pad and then asked, "First name?"

"Tyrone."

"Middle name?" Sinclair asked.

"Ain't got none."

Sinclair glanced at Braddock, who sat there expressionless, jotting down the same information on her legal pad as Sinclair. "What about a nickname—something people call you?"

"T-bone." He smiled.

Sinclair grinned. "Okay, you're obviously a male. What race are you?"

T-bone glared at Sinclair again. "Why the fuck you asking me that? Do I look Chinese or something?"

"Hey, it's just a box I have to fill out on the form," Sinclair said, playing the role of an overly efficient bureaucrat. "I have to ask."

"I'm black, man."

"Date of birth?"

"Five–thirty–seventy-six."

"You just had a birthday, huh?"

"Yeah," T-bone said.

"How tall are you?"

"Six foot."

"Same as me," Sinclair said. "Your weight?"

"About two hundred."

"Really?" Sinclair asked. "I weigh one-seventy. You seem to be quite a bit more than that."

"Okay, maybe two-forty or two-fifty."

"I'll put down two-forty," Sinclair offered. "Is that okay?"

These pieces of information were needed for the statement and arrest report, but Sinclair had learned over the years that they helped with getting a suspect used to answering his questions, which was paramount once he began asking about more difficult topics. He continued with address, phone numbers, occupation, and other identifying information, and then said, "I want to talk with you about what happened today, but before I do, I have to read you your rights, okay?"

T-bone shrugged, and Sinclair read the Miranda rights verbatim from the statement form. "Do you understand each of these rights I've read to you?"

"Yeah."

"Having these rights in mind, do you wish to talk to us now?"

"I don't know nothing about those drugs and guns."

"That's fine," Sinclair said. "And I'll take a statement to that effect, but first you need to agree to talk to us."

"I'll talk, but I ain't admitting to nothing."

"That's fine." Sinclair wrote T-bone's responses on the form and slid it in front of him. "I need your initials here and here and your signature here, saying you agree to talk."

T-bone signed the form, and Sinclair slid it into his folio. Out of sight and out of mind. "Let's first get the stuff about the drugs and guns out of the way. We found quite a bit of methamphetamine in the house. What do you know about that?"

"Look at me. Do I look like someone who snorts crank?"

Meth addicts were usually skinny, but casual users could maintain their weight and health as long as they controlled their usage. "No, you don't. But that doesn't mean you don't sell it."

"Look, man, this is my best clothes," he said, referring to the pair of baggy department store jeans and worn sneakers that the officers permitted him to put on before they transported him. "All I get is six hundred a month for disability. I give most of that to my sister to let me sleep on the couch."

"Your sister looks like a tweaker," Sinclair said. "No disrespect meant, but she's skinny as shit and looks like she hasn't slept in weeks. Are the drugs hers?"

"I won't say nothing about my sister."

"How about Animal? You know, Reggie Clement, your sister's husband. The quantity of drugs tells me someone's selling."

"They're not married. And I won't say nothing bad about him either. For the record, I don't know nothing about no drugs or guns."

Sinclair looked at Braddock. She shrugged. "Actually, I don't care much about the drugs," Sinclair said. "What I'm investigating is a shooting that happened last night. We know that a Simba club member named Shane Gibbs was shot in a bar last night. We don't know exactly what happened, but we know Animal was there, and after the shooting, he came to your sister's house. My guess is he might've ditched a gun there and said something about what happened in the bar."

"What's Animal say happened?"

"Some other detectives are talking to him. I'm thinking that Shane must've done something to get himself shot. If Animal said something that you heard about what Shane did, it might help him."

"I don't know nothing about any shooting, and I don't want to talk about any of this shit anymore."

If Sinclair were only concerned with getting T-bone to confess to possession of narcotics or firearms, he would've stopped the interview, since T-bone's statement would probably be ruled as an invocation of his Miranda rights. But they needed to know what Animal said and did when he came to the house, and Miranda rights only applied to suspects, not witnesses. For the next half hour, he and Braddock worked on T-bone, trying to get him to divulge anything they could use against Animal, but got nowhere.

Sinclair handed him his business card. "Sorry, but the boss says I have to send you to jail. If you change your mind and want to talk, give me a call."

They took him back to the lineup room and brought in a second suspect, a thirty-year-old man with a shaved head, wearing black jeans and a Savage Simba leather vest. The vest displayed the club's patch on the back, an embroidered lion's face with its mouth wide open as if it were roaring. Above the patch was a banner that read, *Savage Simbas*, and underneath was a rocker that read, *Oakland*. Outlaw motorcycle gangs were highly territorial, and Oakland had been Hells Angels territory for decades, so other gangs needed their permission to open a charter in or around Oakland. For years, the Eastbay Dragons, another black gang, was the only motorcycle club the Angels allowed, so when Savage Simbas started a club five years ago, everyone assumed the Hells Angels had blessed it.

As soon as Sinclair read the club member his Miranda rights, he said lawyer. Since this man might've been involved in the murder, either as a principal or accessory, that ended the conversation. The same thing happened with their third interview.

Sinclair and Braddock returned him to the lineup room and were preparing to grab another gang member to interview when one of the officers told them the homicide section commander wanted to see them. Lieutenant Carl Maloney was sitting behind his desk in a glass-walled office that overlooked the homicide room. Dressed in a white shirt and red-and-blue-striped tie, Maloney was in his late forties. He had thinning hair and carried about thirty pounds more than when he was a fit street cop more than two decades earlier.

"Are you two having any luck?" he asked.

"We struck out with the first three," Braddock said.

"Knowing the biker code, I doubt we'll get much," Maloney said. "Have you seen your old partner yet?"

"No," she replied. "When we left the scene of our warrant, the Intel guys still hadn't heard from him."

"I hope he surfaces soon. The media's going crazy over this, and it would sure be nice to have Phil around to talk about the history of the Simbas and other biker gangs." Maloney got up and pulled a slip of paper out of the suitcoat that was hanging on a rack in the corner of his office. "I just got a call from the radio room. Patrol's standing by on a DOA in the Oakland hills.

A hiker or someone came across a body in a shallow grave on the road into the PAL camp," he said, referring to the Police Activities League. "I hate to dump this kind of case on you guys when you're not on standby, but with all the attention on this biker murder, I don't want to divert Jankowski's and Sanchez's full attention from what they're doing."

Investigators in homicide usually prided themselves on handling every callout during their standby week, but sometimes it wasn't possible. Although a body dump in the hills had all the markings of a whodunit that Sherlock Holmes couldn't solve, Jankowski and Sanchez had picked up the slack for them on more than one occasion.

"No problem, boss," Sinclair said. "What's another open case on my desk?"

"Here're the details." Maloney handed him the note. "And Matt, let's hear some optimism. You might go to the vic's house to make a notification and find a spouse just waiting to confess."

Chapter 4

Sinclair stepped out of his car with his notebook in hand. He wrote, *Tue, June 3, 1006 hrs. 10100 Skyline Blvd, approx. 50 yds. from gate to PAL Camp. Clear, dry, sunny, warm, approx. 70°.*

The PAL camp was located high in the redwood forest of Joaquin Miller Park, a twenty-minute drive from downtown Oakland and a world apart. The Oakland Police Activities League was the brainchild of a forward-thinking police captain who commanded the department's youth services division in the early eighties, along with a group of officers and community and business volunteers. With a motto of "Getting to the kids before they get into trouble," the organization reached thousands of youth annually through after-school programs and sports and at the rustic camp in the hills, where inner-city youth often got their first experience with the outdoors.

Several marked patrol vehicles were lined up on the road leading into the camp. A fortysomething blond-haired man with sergeant strips on his short-sleeve shirt approached Sinclair and Braddock. Sergeant Shumaker had come on the department five years prior to Sinclair and had spent all his twenty years in uniform.

"The call came in at nine eighteen," Shumaker said in his best imitation of Joe Friday's just-the-facts-ma'am voice. "A citizen riding his mountain bike down the road from the archery range startled a pack of wild dogs or coyotes in the brush just off the road. He investigated further and observed they had partially dug up a body buried in a shallow grave. He called nine-one-one on his cell."

"Is he still at the scene?" asked Sinclair, noticing a bicycle parked between two police cars.

"Yeah, one of my officers is getting his statement down at one of the camp buildings. We'll transport him back if you want to talk to him."

Sinclair looked at the two single-pole gates, swung open alongside the road. "Was the gate locked when you got here?"

"Yeah, one of the PAL officers showed up with a key. But as you can see, it's not a far walk for someone, even carrying a body. They could've parked right on the other side of the gate at night or even driven into the archery range and walked down a trail or just through the woods. This place is pretty isolated at night, except for occasional security checks by the rangers."

Sinclair and Braddock followed Shumaker and a civilian evidence tech across a soft carpet of pine needles and wood bark that reminded him of the mulch in well-kept suburban neighborhoods. Dirt and debris had been sprayed ten feet from the hole where the body lay, consistent with the reported digging by wild animals. The corpse was lying in a prone position, a heavy-duty green garbage bag covering most of its upper torso. Dirt partially covered the legs, and the flesh of one leg had been ripped apart and partially eaten. The victim wore dark-blue jeans, which appeared to be more expensive than the Levi's Sinclair typically wore off duty, and new-looking Nike sneakers. A two-tone gold-and-stainless-steel watch was on the dark-skinned wrist hanging outside the garbage bag. Sinclair squatted down and examined the watch.

"Rolex," he said. "And it doesn't look like a knock-off."

"Same thing I noticed," said the tall, bearded civilian tech. "Maybe I've been doing this too long, but when I see a black man wearing a Rolex taking a dirt nap in the Oakland Hills, my first thought is some drug gang is wiping out the leadership of its rivals."

Sinclair said nothing, but as hard as he tried to avoid jumping to conclusions before he had the facts, he had to admit that had been his first thought too. The garbage bag was ripped at the bottom, probably by the animals trying to get to their meal, and part of the victim's head was visible. Sinclair walked around the body, looking carefully where he put his feet to ensure he wasn't trampling any evidence, and leaned over to get a closer look. Dried blood surrounded a small hole on the man's shaved head.

"Looks like an entrance wound," said the tech, scrolling through his digital camera photos. "I got good close-ups of it, and I'll get more once the coroner uncovers the rest of the body."

"Any reports of gunshots or suspicious activity out here last night?" Braddock asked Shumaker.

"The dispatcher checked the last twenty-four hours and found nothing," Shumaker said. "Are you ready for the coroner? I already gave them a heads-up that they'd need some shovels and stuff, so they might already be on their way."

"Have them respond and get an ETA," Sinclair said. "Meanwhile, Braddock and I'll go down to the camp and talk with the witness."

They bounced down the narrow, treelined road in their car to a few simple wooden buildings around the perimeter of a clearing. Farther into the trees were the elevated cabins where the kids bunked overnight. A basketball court was at one end of the clearing, which had been a swimming pool badly in need of repair before it was filled in and paved over years ago. Sinclair had been to the camp several times in his first few years in the department, and as much as he loved the mountain setting and programs that kept kids off the street, he'd felt nothing but disdain for the police officers working there. To him, cops were supposed to fight crime and lock up bad guys. If they wanted to be social workers, they should've picked that career. But after fifteen years of banging heads with the worst elements of society in a career that took him from patrol to special operations to vice narcotics to robbery and finally to homicide seven years ago, he was beginning to think there might be more to policing than just arresting crooks. He also wondered how many more years he could endure seeing the most depraved acts people could do to one another before a job spending summers at a camp in this redwood forest would look enticing.

Sinclair parked his car in front of the reporting officer's cabin. The RO was the primary officer on a call and responsible for writing the crime report. Over the years, it became a slang term for any police officer. The RO's cabin was where the PAL officer or the substitute stayed overnight when camp was in session. A heavyset white officer wearing the short-sleeve uniform and a tall, athletic-looking, black female officer dressed in jeans and a navy-blue polo shirt with the PAL patch came out of the cabin, followed by a thirtysomething man dressed in a T-shirt and cargo shorts with black spandex bike shorts poking out the legs.

The uniformed officer handed Sinclair a two-page handwritten statement that didn't say much more than the summary Shumaker had already provided him. After skimming the document, Sinclair asked the citizen, "Do you ride your bike up here often?"

"I ride every day, weather depending, but there's like a hundred miles of trails up here, so I mix it up."

"When were you last up here?"

"Maybe a week or ten days ago."

"Tell me about the wild dogs or coyotes," Sinclair said.

"I didn't really get a good look at them. Just shapes running away, but I've seen packs of dogs and coyotes in these hills before."

Sinclair removed his sunglasses and peered into the dark forest just beyond the cabin. The warm sun coupled with a light breeze carrying the rich scent of the pine trees distracted him for a second. "How can you tell the difference?"

"Some dogs look a lot like coyotes, but when it's a pack of wild dogs, there're all shapes and sizes in the pack. Most look like they have some pit bull in them, but sometimes shepherd mixes too. Coyotes all look the same. You hear them baying and yipping most nights up here."

"Have you come this close to them before?"

"Normally I see them in the distance. Coyotes aren't out much during the day. They're pretty skittish and take off when they see people."

"You know quite a bit about them," Sinclair said.

"I ride in the winter when there aren't many people hiking the trails, and I've run across all kinds of animals, including bears, up here. I try to make plenty of noise when I'm coming around corners to let hikers or animals know I'm around."

Sinclair looked at the man's address on the statement form. "Castle Drive's not far away, is it?"

"About a mile. There's a trail that runs through the woods so I don't have to ride on Skyline Boulevard to get to the park."

"That's your business address also."

"I'm a financial planner, so I work out of my house and see my clients at their offices or homes. I set my own schedule, so I usually ride in the mornings."

"Did you see any suspicious people or activity today?"

He shook his head.

Sinclair turned to the PAL officer. "Doesn't look like much going on at the camp."

"Our first session of the season isn't until next week," she said. "There will be a few dozen volunteers here this weekend to get everything ready. That will be the first real activity since last summer."

Sinclair thanked the citizen and officers and drove back down the bumpy road with Braddock. The coroner's van sat behind the patrol vehicles, and two men dressed in the dark-blue utility uniform of the coroner's investigators were crouched over the body. They were from the Alameda County Sheriff's Office, which had taken over the administration of the coroner's office years ago, and it was only recently that the last of the civilian coroner's investigators had retired. Sheriff's deputies now assumed the role of coroner investigator on all scenes. Although handling dead bodies didn't seem like a glamorous duty assignment, Sinclair figured it beat working at one of the two jails and being locked behind bars with prisoners all day.

The older deputy of the two straightened up when Sinclair and Braddock approached. "Preliminarily, I'd say the victim was killed within the last twenty-four hours," he said. "The body still shows signs of rigor."

"Pretty sloppy burial," Sinclair mused. "Any ID on him?"

"We were just starting when you pulled up." The deputy brushed dirt from the victim's left back pocket with a gloved hand. "This feels like a wallet. I can remove it now if you want to see who he is."

Sinclair moved behind the deputy as he removed a brown leather wallet. He flipped it open and pulled the top card from its slot.

The ID card had the Oakland Police Department logo in the upper left corner. Underneath it read, *Phillip Roberts, Sergeant of Police.*

Chapter 5

Sinclair was no stranger to death. Still, it took every bit of self-control he possessed to maintain his composure when they realized the victim was Phil. Braddock crumbled. He helped her to her feet and walked her to their car with his arm around her waist. He left her there, returned to the body, and rallied the officers and coroner's deputies. "You don't need me to tell you that we need to do this right. If you need a few minutes to get your game faces on, do it now."

Sinclair didn't agree with what psychologists considered the five stages of grief: denial, anger, bargaining, depression, and acceptance. He'd observed people too many times to believe there was one normal response when they learned of a loved one's death. Everyone at the scene displayed a degree of shock—surprise that one of their own was dead. Maybe if Phil's body wasn't right in front of them, there might have been some degree of denial. Looking at the grim faces in front of him, Sinclair saw only pain and sadness. He allowed himself to feel that way for the minute it took to help Braddock to their car, a safe place where she could feel how she needed to for as long as necessary. But now, all he felt was anger—a simmering rage. But he knew from past experience that anger must be controlled and focused. His entire focus had to be finding the killer. Nothing else mattered.

Sinclair looked at the coroner's deputies. "Call your boss on your phone—no radio—and get whatever resources necessary to exhume the body properly. Tell your boss that Sergeant Roberts used to work homicide. And if anyone leaks his name to the media or to anyone who doesn't need to know, I'll have his ass."

Sinclair turned to Shumaker. "Call the watch commander. Tell him I want enough officers for a perimeter twenty times larger than what we have. We need every evidence tech in the city up here. I want this scene processed just like we see *CSI* do it on TV. I'll handle the other notifications and have my lieutenant try to get the lab out here."

Sinclair pulled out his cell and called Maloney. By the time he finished telling him what little he knew, Braddock had returned to his side wearing fresh makeup and a look of sheer determination on her face.

★

Sinclair and Braddock ducked back under the crime-scene tape and crossed the parking lot to a cluster of unmarked Crown Vics in a makeshift staging area. Lieutenant Maloney stood by his car with a phone pressed to his ear.

Within an hour of identifying the victim as Phil Roberts, more than fifty people had descended on the scene. In a perfect world, the full resources of the police department and coroner's office would respond to every murder, but with the sheer number of homicides in Oakland, it was impossible. Sinclair could count on one hand the number of times a pathologist from the coroner's office and a team of criminalists from the crime lab responded to a crime scene, but the murder of a police officer pulled out all the stops.

Being accustomed to solving problems with action, the officers at the scene would have preferred to scour the city for the responsible party and bring him in dead or alive—preferably dead—but Sergeant Shumaker focused his officers on expanding and securing the perimeter.

"The chief will be here in a minute," Maloney said. "Anything new to report?"

"Phil was wearing a holster on his belt, but his gun's missing," Sinclair said. "They didn't find his badge, phone, or any keys on his body."

"Should we put out a comm order on his car?" Maloney asked.

"Already done, Lieutenant," Braddock said.

"If we don't notify Phil's wife pretty damn quick, the word's gonna get out," Sinclair said. "You know everyone in the PAB already knows. Some RO's gonna tell his spouse, who's gonna call Phil's wife."

"There's not much we can do here while they're processing the scene," Braddock said. "Matt and I can take off and see her."

"Hang on a sec," Maloney said as a black unmarked Ford police interceptor sedan, one of the few new unmarked cars the department had received that year, pulled into the parking lot. A man unfolded himself from the passenger seat. Chief Clarence Brown's dark-brown complexion complimented his expensive dark suit. With a shaved head and standing a head taller than Sinclair, Brown could pass for a former MBA star, but Sinclair knew the police chief's athletic ability was limited to political gymnastics, in which he excelled. The department chaplain, a pear-shaped man dressed in an ill-fitting police uniform with dress tunic, got out of the back seat and followed Brown as he strode their way.

"Tell me you have some inkling of who did this," Brown said to Maloney.

Maloney shook his head.

"Do you know if he was on duty last night when the murder occurred?"

"Not that we know of. His officers tried to call him last night about the biker murder," Sinclair said. "But he never returned their calls."

Brown ignored Sinclair and turned back to Maloney. "Which investigator is primary on this?"

"Sergeant Sinclair," Maloney replied. "He was assigned the case before we knew it was Sergeant Roberts." Maloney shuffled his feet, as if to muster the courage to continue. "And I see no reason to change that."

"I can think of plenty," Brown snapped.

Sinclair had butted heads with the chief plenty of times. It was Brown who demoted and suspended him two years ago when he crashed a city car while drunk. Brown was none too happy when the city arbitrator ordered Sinclair's sergeant rank and position in homicide restored six months later. If it hadn't been for the media's love affair with Sinclair, Brown would have pulled him from the Bus Bench Killer investigation, his first case after returning to homicide. And if the stakes weren't so high during the Thrill Kill Murders last year, Brown would've relieved Sinclair of duty for targeting a city councilmember who had an extramarital affair with the victim. But Sinclair had solved both murders, preventing many additional deaths. Even the chief had to admit that although Sinclair ruffled plenty of political feathers and often created a wake of damage in his path, he produced results.

"Wasn't Roberts Sinclair's partner?" Brown asked. "We've pulled investigators previously when there's a personal relationship."

"They were partners over two years ago," Maloney said. "Roberts spent nine years in homicide and partnered with half the unit during that time and worked with everyone at one time or another. If you're looking for a homicide investigator who didn't know Roberts personally, you won't find one at OPD. And I doubt you want to turn this over to another agency."

Brown locked his eyes on Sinclair for a few beats. Then he said to Maloney, "Okay, but I don't want to see any of his Dirty Harry shenanigans this time. Everything by the book."

"Always," Sinclair said.

"What's your first move?" Brown asked Sinclair.

"Talk to the officers in Intel. See if he was working something last night. If nothing pans out, interview his wife and look into his personal life. No matter what, I need to retrace his steps over the last twenty-four hours."

Brown nodded. "The chaplain and I are going to visit his wife now and make the death notification."

"I'd like to be there," Sinclair said. "I'm not saying she did it, but I'd be derelict in my duties if I didn't interview her before she formulates a story."

"A member of my department was murdered." Brown glared at Sinclair. "My top priority is the well-being of his family. No one is going to grill her when she's in shock."

Sinclair saw right through Brown. He only cared about people below him when they could do something for him. But he was all about appearances, and right now, he needed to appear to care about Phil's family because that's what the rank and file, the mayor, and the media would expect. Nevertheless, it was futile to argue. Besides, Sinclair doubted this was the work of Phil's wife.

"Interviewing her can wait," Sinclair said.

"I'll ask the appropriate questions—when she last saw him, if he had any problems with anyone, that kind of stuff. I still carry a badge, in case you forgot." Brown tapped the ornate gold badge clipped to his thin dress belt, a belt that couldn't support the weight of a gun, extra ammo, and handcuffs—the tools real cops carry.

"Yes, sir," Sinclair said and turned.

"And Sinclair," Brown added, "I expect you to keep Lieutenant Maloney fully abreast of all developments."

"Yes, sir," Sinclair called over his shoulder as he continued walking to his car.

Chapter 6

Sinclair and Braddock got out of their car in front of the Savage Simbas clubhouse, located in a multiuse zoned area of West Oakland. The motorcycle club had taken over the property of a tow company that went out of business years ago. The tow company had been one of several with a city contract, and Sinclair had been there often back when he worked uniform. The concrete block building had housed an office in the front and a four-bay garage in the rear, where rudimentary repairs were made to cars that had broken down or been involved in collisions. Outside the rear doors was the tow yard, surrounded by a ten-foot chain link fence topped with concertina wire, where a hundred cars used to sit awaiting pickup by their owners.

A half dozen burly men dressed in ballistic vests, black T-shirts, and utility pants lounged between the SWAT van and the building. One of them opened the door for Sinclair and Braddock as they approached. The counter where the office staff formerly collected tow fees was still there. Sinclair pushed open a waist-high swinging door, squeezed past two old metal desks, and opened a door with the Savage Simbas logo. Heavy wooden blocks, carved with *Pres*, *VP*, *Sgt. at Arms*, and other titles, were scattered about a rectangular conference table. Jankowski, Fletcher, and the three other officers assigned to Intel sat around the table sorting through file folders and stacks of paper.

"Are you done interviewing everyone downtown already?" Jankowski asked.

Sinclair walked across the room to an open door that led to what used to be the repair shop. A dozen officers were photographing and cataloging evidence spread over the pool tables and a rickety bar, made out of two-by-fours and plywood. Sinclair shut the door and faced Jankowski and the Intel officers. "What I'm about to tell you remains in this room. You can't say anything to anyone until his wife and kids have been notified."

Everyone stopped what they were doing and looked up.

"The LT sent me and Braddock to a DOA up in the hills," Sinclair said. "A body buried in a shallow grave. It's Phil Roberts."

No one said anything for a full minute. Sinclair would wait as long as necessary for it to sink in. Finally, Jankowski said, "We're on stand-by. Sanchez and I will take it."

It had been a hundred years since the department had failed to solve the murder of one of their own. Every homicide investigator's worst nightmare was being assigned the murder of a fellow officer and failing to solve it. He could have the most spectacular career, but being the detective that didn't clear a brother cop's murder would become his legacy. And he'd have to live with that failure for the rest of his life.

"I appreciate the offer, Dan," Sinclair said. "But you know that's not how it works. The lieutenant assigned me before he knew any details. It could've been a slam-dunk clearance."

Jankowski shifted his considerable weight, causing the wooden chair to creak. "This dead biker was no altar boy, and he ain't worth all the effort we're wasting on him. I'll get this thing cleaned up and put to bed ASAP."

"Braddock and I have no shortage of investigators willing to help. There'll be plenty to do when you're done with this."

Jankowski nodded his understanding. "I need to get over to the coroner's office. They're starting to cut on my dead dude."

When Jankowski closed the door, Sinclair and Braddock pulled out chairs across from Fletcher and sat down. The other Intel officers put on their best stoic faces and pulled their chairs closer.

"What happened to him?" Fletcher asked.

Sinclair gave him the rundown of the crime scene and what little he knew. "Was Phil working something last night?"

"I was the last one to leave the office," Fletcher said, referring to him and the other three officers sitting around the table. "Sarge was still in his office when I said good night to him, which was nothing unusual. He said he'd see me in the morning. Again, nothing unusual."

"Any idea what he was working on?" Sinclair asked.

Fletcher glanced at his three coworkers, exchanging a meaningful look.

"Listen up," Sinclair said. "I've had enough of your unit's secret squirrel shit to last a lifetime. If there's something you can't tell me that's so fucking top secret, it better be about some goddamn terrorists planning to blow up Oakland with a nuke. Absent that, I need to know everything Phil was working because something he was investigating got him killed."

Finally, Fletcher said, "Don't write any of this down, and please don't ever repeat what we told you. You know how it is in Intel. We're sworn to secrecy, not only on the cases we're working, but on the inner workings of the unit."

Sinclair placed his hands on the table, palms up to show he wasn't armed with a pen.

"We each have an area of specialty," Fletcher said. "Mine is gangs, another's terrorism. That kind of stuff. Sergeant Roberts oversees everything, and he also does special investigations for the chief. Different kinds of sensitive, hush-hush investigations normally involving politics."

"Was he working one of those cases?" Sinclair glanced around the room looking for a response.

Each man shrugged his shoulders.

"Occasionally, he would bring us in on something, maybe to help with a surveillance or work with the Feds on a wire," Fletcher said. "But whatever he's been doing lately, he hasn't told us anything."

"Who would know?"

"The org chart shows Intel reports directly to the chief of police," Fletcher said. "For admin stuff, the assistant chief oversees the unit. When Sarge is on vacation, I'm the senior officer, so I turn in overtime slips and time sheets to the assistant chief."

Normally, a police sergeant reports to a lieutenant, who reports to a captain, who reports to a deputy chief. Reporting directly to the police chief gave the Intel sergeant a lot of power and access. But since the chief was busy managing a thousand other police employees, it also gave the Intel sergeant a great deal of freedom and autonomy. "But the sensitive investigations come directly from the chief?" Sinclair asked.

"To the best of my knowledge," Fletcher said. "A few months ago, Sergeant Roberts was tasked with investigating the deputy director of parks and rec after an audit found some missing money from a fund for aquatics programs. All of us worked surveillance on the number-two guy, and I typed up some search warrants on banks."

"Whatever became of it?"

"We had a strong criminal case, but Sergeant Roberts told us to forget everything after he came back from a meeting with the chief—our investigation never occurred. The next day, the *Tribune* ran a short article about the deputy director resigning for personal reasons."

"So instead of subjecting the city to the embarrassment of a trial of a senior executive, they force him to resign, and everyone keeps their mouths shut about the theft," Braddock said.

"Our job description includes keeping our mouths shut," Fletcher said.

"What happens to the files of these cases?" Sinclair asked.

"You've seen all those file cabinets with the locks in Sergeant Roberts's office?"

Sinclair and Braddock nodded. "What happens when Phil's on vacation and you're the acting?" Sinclair asked. "Do you have the keys and combinations?"

Fletcher shook his head. "He'll give us certain cases to work when he's gone, but there's a lot he doesn't share with us. We all operate on a need-to-know basis in the unit. It's not only necessary for security, but it also gives us deniability if we're ever called before the grand jury."

"Does Phil work with the Feds and other outside agencies?"

The four men again shrugged their shoulders. Fletcher said, "We all work with and swap intel with federal agencies and other PDs, normally the Intel units of other police departments. Different Feds and a few of the DA inspectors from the special investigations unit sometimes visit him at our office."

"Can you guys put together a list of who Phil's seen or talked to over the last few months?"

"Sure," Fletcher said. "But if you're trying to determine what sensitive investigations he's involved in, why not just ask the chief of police?"

"I will," Sinclair said. "But I like to know the answers before I start asking questions."

Chapter 7

Sinclair and Braddock donned disposable surgical gowns, booties, and safety glasses and entered the autopsy room of the coroner's office. The room contained a dozen autopsy tables, two of them occupied. Dr. Gorman, the senior pathologist in the office, stood over a body on a stainless-steel table by the door. Jankowski stood on the other side of the body, taking notes on a legal pad.

Gorman put down his scalpel and raised his splash-protective visor over his gray hair. Unlike some of the pathologists who entered this medical specialty because they had no bedside manner, Gorman was personable and loved talking with investigators who came in to view his autopsies. "Matt, Cathy," he said, lowering his eyes for a few counts. "I'm so very sorry for your loss—our loss. I must have conducted thirty or forty postmortems on Phil's cases when he worked your unit. I remember when he brought you both here to view your first autopsy and how much potential he saw in you."

Sinclair took a deep breath to push down any emotions. "Thanks, Doc. This has to be hard on you too."

"I always considered him a friend," Gorman said. "I didn't want you to undergo any more trauma than necessary, so I started on him before you arrived. Let me finish up with Sergeant Jankowski's case. Then we can get back to Phil."

Laid out on the table, Shane Gibbs looked to be at least six two and a muscular two hundred pounds. His chest cavity was open, its contents arrayed in a stainless-steel pan resting on his thighs. Gorman took one of the lungs in his hands and said to Jankowski, "You saw the three entrance wounds in the upper torso. Two of them went through this lung." Gorman poked an index finger into holes in the dark-red organ.

"Cause of death?" Jankowski asked, as if it weren't obvious.

"Shock and hemorrhaging as a result of multiple gunshot wounds. If I discover anything else, I'll call you." Gorman turned to Sinclair and Braddock. "Give me a minute to change gloves and I'll tell you what I learned about Sergeant Roberts."

"Anything new on your case?" Sinclair asked Jankowski.

"Witnesses said another biker-looking dude named Tiny, who was anything but, came into the bar with Gibbs just before the big hoopla. Other people overheard Animal calling him a stupid motherfucker and yelling, 'You fucked up. You were stupid and put the club at risk.' Gibbs motherfucked him back and shoved him. Then Animal shot him."

"Can't let a man disrespect you like that," Sinclair said.

"Nope. Got no other choice but to kill him," Jankowski replied. "I'd like to know what Gibbs did that pissed Animal off so bad."

"Maybe you can charm him into waiving his rights and telling you."

"Too late for that. Animal's been screaming for his lawyer ever since we put the cuffs on him. The LT said we can't pretend we didn't hear it, so he had O'Connor book him into the jail."

"Are you ready?" Gorman asked Sinclair.

"See you back at the ranch." Jankowski waved as he ambled out the door.

Sinclair and Braddock followed Gorman to a table at the far end of the room. A white sheet covered what Sinclair knew was Phil's body. Gorman glanced at a form on a clipboard and handed it to Sinclair. Sinclair copied the coroner's case number into his notes along with the other identifying information from the form: *Roberts, Phillip, male, African American, 48, 6'0", 190 lbs.* Phil had told Sinclair years ago that when he first came to homicide, he weighed 170, the same as Sinclair. The long, irregular hours cut into his gym time, and he put on twenty pounds in the first two years. Phil warned the same would happen to Sinclair, but Sinclair failed to follow the lead of his senior partner's donut breakfast and fast-food lunch diet. That had been seven years ago.

Sinclair had never seen a body covered with a sheet at the coroner's office before but was relieved they'd done so, whether it was out of respect for a police officer or so the other employees who also knew Phil wouldn't have to see him in that condition. Gorman pulled the sheet down to the neck. They had already made the incision along the top and back of his head to remove the skullcap and examine the brain, but everything had been put back in place. Phil's smooth mocha-colored skin had taken on a grayish pallor. Gorman gently turned his head to the side.

"In the back of his head is the hole that we all noticed at the scene," Gorman said. "It is, in fact, a bullet entrance wound. Notice the extensive stippling around the wound, which would indicate the muzzle was very close, possibly only an inch or two away when the firearm was fired."

Gorman placed Phil's head back on the block, facing upright. Sinclair saw another hole, larger and more ragged, on Phil's forehead, about two inches above his right eye.

"This is the exit." Gorman grabbed the skin where it had been cut at the back of the head and peeled it over the skull, partially covering Phil's face with the bloody inside of the scalp. "Look closely at the skull."

Sinclair leaned in closely while Braddock looked over his shoulder. "I don't see anything," Sinclair said.

"Exactly," Gorman said. "The bullet didn't penetrate the skull. I traced the bullet's path between the skull and the tissue and skin covering the head. There was no penetration. I examined the brain and noticed minimal trauma."

"I've heard of this happening to soldiers in Vietnam," Sinclair said, "but never in a homicide case."

Gorman smiled. "It's not as rare as you might imagine. The thing is, you and I don't see it much because the victims don't make it to us. I spoke to an associate who works at Highland ER. He's seen this several times. This bullet hit the skull at an acute angle. If the skull didn't have skin covering it, the bullet would've ricocheted off it. But it penetrated the skin, which provided enough resistance to prevent the bullet from exiting until the bullet's trajectory, which was still mostly straight, carried the bullet to the front of the head. At that point, the energy of the projectile was greater than the resistance of the skin, so it punctured the skin and exited. Had it been at a slightly lesser angle, it may have never fully penetrated the skin, merely cutting the scalp, which would look a lot like a knife wound. A slightly greater angle and it would've penetrated the skull and entered the brain."

"But this didn't kill him?" Braddock asked.

"I think not," Gorman said. "Don't get me wrong, a firearm going off inches from someone's head with the projectile striking the skull is no walk in the park. It would surely leave someone dazed and possibly unconscious, depending on the caliber and other factors. There could be some degree of traumatic brain injury."

Gorman lectured, enjoying the role of teacher. Had this been another case, Sinclair would've played along as Gorman slowly laid out his findings and led him to the cause of death. "How'd he die, Doc?"

Gorman pulled Phil's scalp back in place and handed Sinclair a large magnifying glass. "If you look in his eyes, you'll note indications of petechial hemorrhage."

Tiny blood vessels in Phil's eyes appeared to have burst, which was a classic indication of asphyxiation. Sinclair handed the magnifying glass to Braddock, who shook her head. With another victim, she would've looked at the body closer—however reluctantly—when suggested by Dr. Gorman. It took every bit of detachment Sinclair was capable of not to think of the body in front of him as Phil. He understood why Braddock wouldn't even try to do the same.

"When we unearthed the body from the grave, the plastic garbage bag was covering his face and upper torso. The torn area at the back of his head was probably done after the fact by animals. An unconscious man would be unable to free himself from the plastic bag."

"If someone wanted to kill a man and the first bullet only stunned him, why not just put another one in his head rather than suffocating him with a plastic bag?" Braddock asked.

"Maybe they thought the shot killed him," Sinclair suggested. "We know how head wounds bleed. He was probably unconscious, so they might've just bagged what they thought was a dead body and transported it for disposal."

Both Braddock and Gorman nodded their agreement.

Gorman pulled the sheet off Phil's body and went back to work. "I want to get a closer look at the lungs and neck area before I confirm a preliminary cause of death as asphyxiation, and of course, nothing will be final until we get the tox screen back in three to four weeks."

"Hey, Doc," Sinclair said, "I know you don't like to do this, but could you estimate the time of death?"

"It's inaccurate. It's more of a guess than a scientific estimate."

Sinclair held Dr. Gorman's gaze but said nothing.

"Since I was at the scene and felt rigor and some body warmth still remaining, I'd say between six PM and midnight, plus or minus a few hours either way."

On their way out of the morgue, Sinclair and Braddock stopped at another examination table where all of Phil's personal effects had been laid out. Sinclair fanned through his wallet, hoping to find a scrap of paper with a name or phone number, but the wallet contained nothing but his ID, cash, and credit cards. Sinclair never suspected robbery as the motive, but the only crooks that would bypass cash and a Rolex watch were those who already had more money than they knew what to do with or those who were in over their head and too distracted to grab it. The garbage bag was draped over the end of the table. Next to it were two cotton rags about fourteen inches square, which looked like the kind of dark-red shop rags that every mechanic used, except in a light-blue color. Both had stains that could have been either grease or blood.

"Hey, Doc," Sinclair said to Gorman, "where'd these rags come from?"

"They were inside the garbage bag. The deputies deduced they might've been trash that was already in the bag when your subjects decided to repurpose it, or maybe the killers used them to wipe blood from their hands and then threw them in the bag along with the deceased."

Sinclair thanked Gorman and walked outside, where he and Braddock stripped off their protective clothing. The last remaining feelings of sadness that he'd been pushing down ever since he saw Phil's ID at the scene suddenly changed. The possibility that some asshole would throw dirty rags into the bag with Phil's body, treating both like trash, really pissed him off.

Chapter 8

On the drive back to the PAB, Sinclair called communications to send the first available tech to the coroner's office to pick up the garbage bag and rags. While Braddock typed up the lab request forms, Sinclair started on a press release.

News From the Oakland Police Department

On June 3, at 1023 hours (10:23 AM), Oakland police officers were dispatched to a report of a citizen who discovered a human body partially buried in a shallow grave in a City of Oakland recreational camp on Skyline Blvd. Responding officers interviewed the citizen, who said he was riding a bicycle on park trails when he made the discovery. Preliminary investigation indicates the victim was shot at another location and transported to this scene. The victim's name is being withheld pending notification of next of kin. Anyone with any information is urged to call Sergeants Sinclair or Braddock of the Oakland Homicide Unit at (510) 238-3821.

Sinclair e-mailed the release to the twenty people on the distribution list and put a hardcopy on the lieutenant's desk and another on the unit admin's desk, while Braddock e-mailed the lab requests to the crime lab and printed out a copy.

Normally, the criminalistics section admin accepted and logged hand-carried forms to insulate the criminalists from constant interruption by investigators begging for priority work, but when Sinclair and Braddock walked to the counter, a fingerprint examiner and a DNA technician came out of the back room and said they'd get right on it. Sinclair had heard that before, but on this case, he believed it.

"Where to now?" Braddock asked, her finger poised over the elevator buttons.

"To Intel." Sinclair was hopeful. When he was new in homicide, Phil had taught him to document every step of an investigation. Phil was as diligent about this as any investigator he'd ever met. He couldn't imagine Phil losing those habits when he left the unit. "We're going through every inch of Phil's office. He's probably left notes or scraps of paper lying around on his desk or tucked into a drawer that might contain some clue about what he's doing. If we have to, we'll get the bolt cutters from property and cut the padlocks on his file cabinets."

They walked down the fourth-floor hallway, and Sinclair pressed the buzzer next to a metal door marked only with the room number. Sinclair looked up at the security camera and winked. A moment later, the door opened, and Fletcher appeared with his finger to his lips. He was back in his plainclothes attire: jeans, black T-shirt, and leather vest. With his shoulder-length hair, he looked like he'd fit in perfectly at a Hells Angels motorcycle rally. He leaned close and whispered, "IAD's here." His breath smelled of cigarettes.

The other three officers were sitting at their workstations. Fletcher leaned against one of the file cabinets that lined a wall in the main room and pointed at the closed door that led to Phil's office. Above him, a red light blinked in the motion detection sensor.

Sinclair opened the door without knocking. A diminutive Filipino woman sat in front of Phil's computer, and a pudgy white man sat at Phil's desk, paging through a stack of file folders.

"What the fuck are you doing in my murder victim's office?" Sinclair said.

Lieutenant Jules Farrington leaped up, knocking the wheeled desk chair in which he'd sat into a bookcase behind the desk. Farrington had been in Sinclair's academy class and, as far as Sinclair was concerned, should've never graduated. He trailed the group on every run, scored the lowest in every pistol and shotgun qualification, and during defensive tactics, got his ass kicked by every other recruit in the class, including two female officers about half his size. He had reddish-blond hair and a complexion the same shade as the reams of printer paper his IAD section churned out daily. After he had spent his mandatory two years in uniform, Farrington bounced from internal affairs to inspector general and back several times, making sergeant and then lieutenant by acing the promotional exams and kissing the ass of everyone above him in the department. "Jeez, Matt, you startled me. You know profanity is a violation of the manual of rules."

"Well, shit, Jules, I'm entering an extension of a murder crime scene, only to find someone ransacking it." Sinclair pointed at the dark-haired woman. "Who's that?"

"She's with the city's IT department."

"She's hacking into my victim's computer, destroying the integrity of what might be evidence." Sinclair glanced at Braddock, who remained stone-faced. "I'll ask again, what the hell are you doing here, Jules?"

"I know we're friends, Matt, but especially in the presence of others, you should address me as 'lieutenant.'"

Sinclair smiled, knowing it probably looked like a smirk. Farrington was a dweeb, but a dangerous one. He definitely wasn't a friend, but Sinclair didn't want to turn him into an enemy. Satisfied he'd put him on the defensive, Sinclair raised his eyebrows and waited for an answer.

"I'm under orders from the chief to go through all files, paper and electronic, to safeguard any sensitive information that might be present. I've also been appointed as the acting commander of the intelligence unit until a new supervisor can be selected and transitioned in."

"It's highly likely that Phil was murdered by someone connected with a case he was working," Sinclair said. "I need to go through all of this before you muddy the waters."

"I'll provide you any information I uncover that's relevant to your investigation."

"How the fuck do you know what's relevant?" Sinclair barked. He then lowered his voice a notch and continued, "At this stage, *I* don't even know what might be relevant. That's how murder investigations begin. But you wouldn't know that because the only people you've ever investigated have been other cops." Sinclair felt Braddock's hand on his arm.

"Sergeant, I'm going to ignore your insubordination and tone because I respect your accomplishments and know you're under stress. However, I have my orders, and if you want them countermanded, you need to see Chief Brown. You shouldn't even be in this office. Please step out so we can resume our work."

Sinclair took a step toward Farrington. Braddock tugged him back. Farrington reminded him of the Pillsbury Doughboy—soft and chubby. His tough talk was a joke. If he didn't have rank on him, Sinclair would've knocked him on his ass. Sinclair turned his back and stepped into the doorway.

"And Sergeant," Farrington said, "the officers in the unit have been ordered not to talk about any active or past intelligence case without checking with me, so if you'd like to question them about anything, I'd like you to do so in my presence."

Once Farrington closed the office door, Sinclair faced it and raised his middle finger.

★

Lieutenant Maloney listened intently and jotted a few notes on a yellow pad as Sinclair briefed him on his interaction with Farrington. It took every bit of self-control—and Braddock's calming presence and firm grip on his arm—to keep from busting back into Phil's office and kicking Farrington's ass. The asshole had to know what he was doing was wrong, but people like him never questioned an order from a superior. Sinclair felt himself calming down a notch by the time he finished.

Maloney set his pen on his desk. "Despite what we all think about Farrington, he's only obeying orders. You need to be careful around him. He has no qualms about initiating an IA complaint himself when he sees a violation of department rules and regulations."

"He'd look like more of a dick than he already is," Sinclair said, "making a complaint against the investigator assigned to find a cop killer."

"Farrington was acting unnecessarily righteous," Braddock said. "Cops on the street all know Matt's the best one to handle the murder of a fellow officer."

"Yes, and that's why Farrington probably won't make a complaint," Maloney said. "But let's focus on the issue at hand. The chief is obviously concerned that something Phil was doing will get out. We need to assure him that our only concern is finding out who murdered Phil."

"I kept his little secret about Preston Yates—what more proof does he need?" Sinclair asked.

City Councilmember Yates had become a suspect in the murder of Dawn Gustafson, the first victim in the so-called Thrill Kill Murders that occurred last December. Dawn was an escort who became Yates's mistress and got pregnant with his baby. Sinclair had initially suspected that Yates killed her to protect his secret and to stop her from shaking him down for more financial support. When Sinclair discovered the motive for the murders had nothing to do with Yates, Chief Brown told him to drop that part of his investigation. Although he personally thought the public should know the kind of man they elected, Sinclair agreed that playing politics was better suited to the chief and buried the details of Yates's extracurricular activities.

"You did," Maloney said. "And I'll bring that up when I see him. In the meantime, what other avenues can you pursue while we're waiting for the chief to open up Phil's case files?"

Braddock leaned forward in her chair. "Fletcher said Phil might've been working with people at the DA's office or some Feds on cases they weren't privy to."

Maloney rubbed his temples. "Okay, but tread softly. I don't want it to look like you're going behind the chief's back to find out what Phil was working."

"Which is what we would be doing," Braddock said.

"I'm good at playing dumb." Sinclair smirked. "We're merely looking into anything Phil was working that might have been reason to kill him. If we stumble into something the chief was trying to keep from us but happened to be the motive for the murder, should we ignore it? The chief would look pretty stupid if he told us to drop it."

"Keep me informed so I can run interference," Maloney said. "Phil was my friend too."

"Has the chief notified his wife yet?" Sinclair asked. "We still need to talk to her."

"The chaplain called just before you came in. She handled the news as well as one could expect but said there was nothing in Phil's personal life that could be a reason for someone to kill him. She'd like twenty-four hours before you contact her for an interview."

Sinclair got up from his chair. "I'll start reaching out to my Fed contacts."

"And I'll go upstairs and beg for an audience with the chief," Maloney said, "and try not to get myself fired in the process."

Chapter 9

Sinclair's watch read nine o'clock as he munched on the last of the granola bars he kept stashed in his desk drawer. It wasn't the dinner he had planned a few days ago, but Alyssa understood when he texted her in the afternoon to cancel their date. Two hours ago, Maloney had stepped into the homicide office and addressed his ten investigators. A few were on the phone or computers, but most just sat there waiting for something to break—a call to action. Maloney told everyone to go home—they could get a fresh start in the morning. Sinclair was prepared to stay there all night. It didn't matter that there was nothing productive to do and he was already fatigued from the 2:00 AM callout; it was his case, and he would work around the clock until Phil's killer was behind bars. Sinclair and Braddock had spent the previous hours calling every federal agent in their contacts lists, but no one knew what Phil was working. If Phil had been gunned down in a gang-related murder, the entire unit would have hit the streets and kicked down the doors of every gangbanger in the city. Having no place to direct their wrath was frustrating. Sinclair had walked out the door with his lieutenant and fellow investigators, only to circle back and return to his desk where he reread the reports, looking for something he had missed.

Sinclair pulled out his phone, went to his favorites list, and pressed *Alyssa Morelli*. This was the third time they tried to make a go of a relationship. They went out a few times ten years ago, but Alyssa cut it off. Looking back, Sinclair knew she was smart for doing so. He was a long-haired narc back then, living a crazy life fueled by adrenalin and booze. They'd both gone their separate ways, her marrying a doctor and living the country-club lifestyle for seven years, until she realized she couldn't be the kind of housewife her husband wanted her to be. Meanwhile, Sinclair had married a beautiful, successful prosecutor in the DA's office. That marriage ended shortly after he returned from his Army reserve deployment to Iraq, when his wife couldn't handle his excessive drinking and emotional paralysis. He and Alyssa went out a few times after Braddock reunited them last December, and Sinclair had felt an intense connection between them. Then Sinclair's life literally blew up. He stopped a group of anarchists in the midst of a school massacre plot, saving Alyssa, along with numerous students and teachers. But he was lucky to have survived the bomb blast that killed his attackers.

Once Sinclair recovered from his injuries, Alyssa received a call offering her a nursing position with a nonprofit organization that was providing medical services for the thousands of refugees fleeing the war-torn regions of the Middle East and Africa. Although he outwardly supported her decision to take the assignment, he secretly resented that she'd left just as they were trying to kindle a relationship.

She had just returned from Italy last week. Having been gone for half a year, she'd spent the weekend getting settled into her old life. She'd only had time for a quick coffee the day after she got home. Her olive skin was more deeply tanned than usual after her time in Italy and looked even richer against the white sleeveless shirt she wore over her short skirt. They'd made plans to see each other several times after work this week and to spend all of Saturday together, at which time Sinclair was sure he'd finally get lucky. "I'm glad you called," Alyssa said. "I can't even imagine what it must be like to be responsible for solving the murder of your former partner."

His emotions were so jumbled, he didn't even know how he felt. "I try not to think about it," he said. "We have a job to do, and people are depending on us to do it."

As soon as he said it, he knew it sounded too much like Clint Eastwood, not the kind of man he wanted to be around Alyssa. But he didn't know how to backtrack. "I really hate screwing up our plans for this week," he said.

He pictured her grabbing a handful of her sleek dark hair and tossing it over her shoulder and across her chest. "There's no timetable that we need to abide by, Matt. I'm not going any-where, and I'll still be around when you solve this case."

"It's not too late. Do you want to come over to my place for a while?"

When they had dinner last December and Sinclair suggested their evening continue beyond the restaurant parking lot, she made it clear she wasn't the type to sleep with a man on the first date. He wondered if after being apart for the past months, Alyssa set the date clock back to zero.

The line was silent for a few beats. When she finally spoke, her voice was soft and sweet. "I want our first time to be special, to wake up next to you in the morning and not have to rush off to work. Or have you leave in the middle of the night when a lead comes in on this case."

★

On the short drive home, Sinclair thought about what it would be like to spend all day in bed with Alyssa, her small, sleek body next to him, under him, on top of him. As pleasant as the thoughts were, his attention kept jumping back to the case and what he needed to do first thing in the morning: see if the crime lab had any results from the scene and autopsy evidence, arrange to meet with Phil's wife, follow up with the

Intel officers concerning outside agency investigators Phil had contact with, and get a one-on-one meeting with the chief if Maloney hadn't had any luck with him. He'd also have to remember to fill out his overtime slips: six hours on Jankowski's case and then three hours on Roberts's murder. There was nothing worse than completing your time sheet on Friday morning and trying to reconstruct all the overtime you worked.

A thought came to him. He pulled out his cell phone, scrolled through his recent calls, and pressed the number for Fletcher.

"Hey, Sarge, what's up?" Fletcher yelled over loud background noise. He sounded drunk.

"What do you guys do with your overtime slips?"

"What do you mean? We fill them out, turn them in to our sergeant—"

"I mean Phil's overtime—"

"Sarge, I can't hear you, can you speak up?"

"Where're you at?" Sinclair asked.

"Over at the Warehouse, toasting a fallen warrior."

"Stay there," Sinclair said and ended the call.

Chapter 10

Ten minutes later, Sinclair parked his car in a yellow zone on Webster Street, halfway down the block from the bar. Located in the old warehouse and produce district of Oakland, an area now filling with trendy restaurants and high-rent condos, the Warehouse had been the department's unofficial cop bar since the mideighties. Before Sinclair quit drinking, he'd spent many nights there.

A few dozen off-duty cops congregated on the sidewalk and street outside the front door smoking cigarettes and cigars. When they recognized Sinclair, they picked up their drinks and beer bottles from the curb. Normally, the off-duty cops policed themselves and didn't allow open containers outside, but tonight wasn't a normal night for Oakland officers. A muscular man with the typical patrol officer's crew cut asked, "You're the primary on Sergeant Roberts's murder, right?"

"Yeah," Sinclair said. "But everyone in homicide's working it."

The cop took a long pull of his beer. "You know who did it?"

"Not yet, but I will." Sinclair scanned the faces in the crowd and, before another half-tanked cop could pepper him with more questions, asked, "Anyone seen Kurt Fletcher?"

"He's holding court at the big table inside," a stocky female officer said.

Sinclair pushed through the door. The jukebox was playing a country-western song Sinclair didn't recognize. Every seat and barstool was taken but one. Thirty more people stood in the area between the bar and tables. Sinclair recognized most of them, although he didn't know many of the younger officers by name. He spotted Fletcher sitting at one of the large round tables with his three other Intel officers, along with Jankowski, O'Connor, and Larsen from homicide. In front of an empty chair were eight full shot glasses.

Jankowski said something to a young officer at the next table. The officer stood and slid his chair to Jankowski, who pulled it to their table. "Buy a round and join us," he said to Sinclair.

Affixed to the wall behind the mahogany bar were hundreds of patches from police departments around the world, as well as plaques and other police memorabilia. Sinclair recognized the bartender, Joe, one of the owners.

"Sorry for your loss, Matt." He glanced at two stools at the end of the bar. "I poured you and Phil many a drink here."

Sinclair nodded. Not too many years ago, two of these barstools had practically had his and Phil's name on them. If someone was sitting there when they came in, a bartender or one of the regulars told the patron those seats belonged to the top two homicide detectives in the Bay Area. "The table wants a round of shots, Joe. What're they drinking?"

"Because Phil drank single malt Scotch, that's what the guys wanted. But they'd go broke the way they're pounding them down, so I'm pouring the house label. None of 'em can tell the difference." He arranged eight shot glasses on a tray and filled them. He then grabbed another shot glass, filled it from a bottle under the bar, and placed it on the tray in front of Sinclair. "Ginger ale, my friend."

"Thanks, Joe." One of the few advantages of having had your drinking problems splashed all over the papers was that everyone knew you were an alcoholic, so Sinclair didn't have to hide it or explain why he no longer drank, as did many of his friends in AA.

Sinclair pulled two twenties from his wallet and held them out. The bartender took one and said, "Police discount."

Sinclair set the tray on the table and took his mock drink. Fletcher slid one shot in front of Phil's empty chair, and everyone else raised a glass. Sinclair said, "To Phil, a partner, a friend, and a cop's cop." Sinclair downed his ginger ale and watched as the others swallowed their shots. Sinclair listened as the cops at the table told tales of Phil's career, some hilarious, others terrifying. It took him back to the numerous nights when he'd swapped stories here with fellow officers over numerous beers, the stories becoming more embellished the drunker the storyteller got. Legends were born at the Warehouse.

When one of the Intel officers began telling the same story for a third time, Sinclair pulled a Macanudo Robust from the inside pocket of his suitcoat and said to Fletcher, "I'm going out for a smoke. You wanna join me?"

Fletcher grabbed his Budweiser bottle and followed him out the door. Sinclair led them down the sidewalk away from the crowd congregating by the front door and pulled out his lighter.

"You don't see those often." Fletcher gestured toward Sinclair's Zippo. "You really are old school."

"Bought it in Baghdad about six years ago," he said, puffing on the cigar until it was lit. "It's a reminder of some brother soldiers who didn't come home."

Fletcher shook a Marlboro from a pack and lit it with a disposable lighter. "Yeah, I forgot you were there. Marines, right?"

"Army. I was in the reserves, and they called me back for a year." Sinclair took a few puffs of his cigar, drew a mouthful of smoke into his lungs, and exhaled. "I was thinking that maybe

Phil wrote what he was doing on his overtime slips and maybe you guys keep copies of them."

"If we're working a straight investigation, we complete the slip just like the rest of the department does, with the RD number and all the necessary details to justify the overtime," he said. "If it's one of our Intel cases, we write our OT slips vaguely because everyone and his mother sees them before they end up in the accounting section. So we just list our Intel number and a few words of what we did, such as surveillance or preparing a warrant. We leave out all names and locations. Anything that could compromise a case."

"Do you maintain a log of case numbers?" Sinclair asked.

"Sure, in a set of books in the office."

"What about copies of your OT slips?" he asked, knowing that the CID admin made copies of all overtime slips and time sheets every Friday for homicide, robbery, and the other investigative units in the division before delivering them to the accounting section.

"Yeah, the sergeant makes copies of everything and files them. Accounting is always screwing up and losing shit, so we need to keep our own copies."

"I'd like to take a look at what you have."

"Now?" Fletcher asked.

"Unless you're doing something more important than solving Phil's murder."

★

Five minutes later, Sinclair followed Fletcher into the intelligence section office and watched him punch a code into the alarm panel by the door. Fletcher pulled a hardcover record book with a green canvas cover from a bookshelf in the main office and opened it where a ribbon marked a page. In the left column was a sequence of numbers preceded by the letter *E*. Following the number were columns for the date; the investigator's name; the general category, such as drugs, gangs, or terrorism; the location; and additional information.

"What's the *E* stand for?" Sinclair asked.

"That's the letter for this year. There's no rhyme or reason for it other than that's how it was done back in the fifties when the intelligence section created a filing system. The first case that year was *A-1* and the first case the next year was *B-1*. When they got to *Z*, they started all over again."

Sinclair chuckled. "While the rest of the department went to a multimillion-dollar law records management system, you continue to record information in a ledger just like the ancient Romans."

"When the department created LRMS, they bragged about firewalls and all that stuff, but the reality is, people who didn't have the need to know would be able to access our information, and if the wrong people did . . . well, you get the idea. We have some info that's computerized, but often the old system works just fine."

Sinclair didn't need convincing. Too many people in the department insisted on progress all the time. Quite often, it wasn't progress at all, merely change for the sake of change that only created confusion and additional bureaucracy.

Fletcher flipped back a page in the ledger, showing an entry that read, *E-11, Fletcher, Gangs/Guns, 50th Ave & Bancroft, Mongols MCC reportedly selling guns.* "This is an example. I initiated this case number based on a tip from a Southern Cal PD. They had an informant who said the Mongols motorcycle gang was establishing a foothold in Oakland around Fiftieth and Bancroft to sell guns to Hispanic gangs in the area."

"And all your work is documented in a case file somewhere?"

"Sure. On that tip, I conducted surveillance on the area, worked with informants, checked real estate records, and all kind of other stuff to eventually determine the info was bogus. The paperwork is filed in one of our locked unit file cabinets, and electronic files are on my computer."

Sinclair scanned the log, looking for cases with Phil's name. He found one from March. It read, *E-24, Roberts, S.* "This must be one of Phil's cases, but there're no details listed."

"He normally assigns cases to us, so he's not usually listed as the case officer, unless it's one of those secret ones I told you about. I'll bet this is the parks and rec thing I mentioned. Hang on and I'll tell you for sure." Fletcher sat at his desk, started his computer, and clicked through some files. "Yup, here's a surveillance log I did when I followed that knucklehead around one night. Same case number."

Sinclair tried to turn the doorknob of Roberts's office door. "Who's got a key to his office?"

"I've got one because I'm the acting sergeant when he takes a day off." Fletcher pulled a key ring from his pocket and fitted a key into the lock. He jiggled it, but it wouldn't turn. Fletcher slammed his hand on the door. "That motherfucking Farrington changed the locks."

That didn't surprise Sinclair. "Can I see the overtime files?"

Fletcher removed a file folder marked with last week's date. Sinclair removed Phil's time sheet. He'd worked eighteen hours of overtime. The last slip was for four hours on Thursday. It listed a case number, and the only description of the overtime worked was, *Meeting.* Sinclair read off the case number to Fletcher, who scrolled through the case log.

"That's the umbrella case for the joint terrorism task force. They have a meeting in San Francisco once a month, and Sarge goes along with our JTTF officer. After the meeting, the Feds go to a local bar. That's where the real interesting stuff gets discussed."

"Sipping scotch at time and a half," Sinclair said. "I guess that's why everyone wants to work Intel." Sinclair went to the next slip. "Tuesday, four to ten, surveillance, D-eighty-four."

Fletcher flipped back a few pages in the ledger. "That's one of Sergeant Roberts's S cases. No date when he initiated the case, but the sequence indicates he recorded it December last year."

"Any idea what it was about?"

"The number doesn't ring a bell."

"Who would know, if it's not in the log?"

"The *S* means it's secret or sensitive. Maybe the assistant chief since he has to sign off on Sergeant Roberts's overtime. The chief for sure."

The last overtime slip attached to that weekly time sheet was on the previous Friday from four to midnight and listed the same case number. The notation read, *Meeting.*

Sinclair pulled the previous week's folder and found an over-time slip for a meeting on that Friday and another four-hour surveillance with the same case number. The time sheet and overtime slips for the previous week showed the same.

"Looks like he's been meeting someone after work every Friday and conducting a surveillance during the week on this sensitive case."

"Most of the guys try to get out of here early on Fri-day to beat the traffic. I had no idea he was working every Friday night."

"Can I get copies of this?" he asked Fletcher.

"How about I make you copies tomorrow when my head's a bit clearer?"

"If Farrington figures this out, these files could be gone by then."

It was nearly midnight by the time Sinclair had copied all the overtime paperwork and dropped Fletcher back at the Warehouse. The crowd had grown as evening shift officers got off work. Sinclair knew in his heart he couldn't drink, but he missed the ability of the alcohol and camaraderie of the bar to numb his feelings about the passing of a brother officer. And the reminder that it could easily have been him.

Chapter 11

Sinclair woke at first light, showered, and shaved. Dressed in a Brooks Brothers navy-blue suit, he was out the door with his travel mug filled with French roast at a quarter to six. He started his car and crept down the driveway from the estate's guesthouse, where he'd been living ever since the Bus Bench Killer firebombed his apartment two years ago. He passed the main house, an eight-thousand-square-foot mansion set on the most exclusive street in Piedmont, a wealthy enclave in the center of Oakland, and continued down the driveway. Just before he reached the sensor that would open the front gate, he saw Walt walking toward the house with two newspapers under his arm and a dog on a leash.

Walt Cooper and his wife were the caretakers of Frederick Towers's estate. Sinclair met him at his first AA meeting out of rehab, but it wasn't until he nearly picked up a drink six months later that Sinclair began to accept Walt's support and friendship. Walt had been one of the top psychologists in the Bay Area until his drinking and prescription drug abuse nearly destroyed his life when he was in his forties. He served prison time for insurance fraud and lost practically everything. But as Walt had said in meetings for more than twenty years, as long as he had his sobriety, he had everything he needed. Walt had met Fred Towers seven years ago and took him to his first AA meeting. A year later, after his wife and daughter had died in a drunk driving accident and his son from an OD, Fred was living alone in the massive house and asked Walt to move in and take care of the estate. When Fred asked Sinclair to move in, Sinclair expressed his discomfort with Fred's generosity, but Fred shrugged it off, saying it was actually selfish because having a third sober alcoholic in the house would make it twice as difficult for him to pick up a drink.

"You're getting an early start," Walt said as Sinclair stopped alongside him.

"Who's your friend?"

The yellow Lab sat at Walt's left side as Sinclair exited his car.

"This is Amber, a new member of the household."

Sinclair bent over and ran both hands over the Labrador's head until his fingers found the spot behind her ears. Amber stood and wagged her tail so hard her butt shook from side to side. "Hi, Amber. You're exactly what this place has been missing."

"You remember Dean from the Friday night meeting?"

Amber dropped to the ground and rolled over on her back. Sinclair squatted and scratched her belly. "The guy who's been going through the messy divorce?"

"Right. The divorce was finalized last week, and Dean took a job in New York. His wife is moving into her parent's house, and neither can take a dog, so Fred volunteered to take Amber."

Fred Towers was the CEO of PRM, one of the largest corporations headquartered in Oakland. "I never pictured Fred as a dog person."

"Back in his previous life," Walt told him, referring to those days before the death of Fred's wife and children and before Fred's drinking nearly took his own life, "he had a Labrador retriever that looked a lot like Amber, except she was a chocolate. There's a beautiful family photo in his bedroom taken in front of a Christmas tree in the living room with the dog when his children were small."

Sinclair stood. Amber rose too, only to sit in front of him, her eyes begging for more attention. Sinclair patted her on the head.

"Dogs are a good judge of character," Walt said. "I'm guessing you grew up with dogs."

Sinclair smiled as he remembered the small puppy his mother brought home when he was twelve, a few months after his brother died. The tiny ball of fur had been the only bit of happiness that existed in his house after his brother's murder. Until that, too, was taken from him the day his father returned from the vet and told him his dog was too sick to save. "Yeah, but not for long enough."

★

The office was empty when Sinclair arrived and started the coffeemaker. As he ate a thick slice of banana-nut bread Walt's wife had handed him as he drove away, he sorted the pile of overtime slips and time sheets he'd gathered from the Intel office the previous night. He printed out monthly calendar pages and began entering Roberts's overtime by date, looking for a pattern.

Jankowski shoved the door open a little before seven. From across the room, Sinclair noticed his bloodshot eyes and flushed cheeks. "Sinclair, how the hell are you this morning?" he bellowed.

"Rough night?"

"I left about two. No OPD brass came around, which meant the Warehouse could continue serving its medicine to the troops." Jankowski poured himself a cup of coffee, brought the pot to Sinclair's desk, and filled his cup.

"I hope everyone made it home in one piece."

"I'm gonna do my damnedest to clean up this biker murder today so I can help out on Roberts," Jankowski said as he plopped into his chair and started his computer.

Braddock came through the door a few moments later. Even though her and Sinclair's normal start time was eight, he knew she'd be in early too. Once she had her coffee, he filled her in on his midnight foray to Intel with Fletcher.

"You seem pretty sure his murder was over one of these sensitive cases," she said.

"I'm not sure of anything, but when people try to hide shit from me, it only makes me look for it harder." He was accustomed to the direction of murder investigations changing frequently in the first few days. Investigators who weren't agile and flexible often grabbed onto one lead and ran with it while ignoring other possible leads. Right now, it felt like the most promising motive stemmed from a case Phil had been working.

She nodded, but Sinclair couldn't tell if she agreed or was merely humoring him. As she went about her morning routine of listening to voice mails and checking e-mail, Sinclair began reading the technician's report from the crime scene. The techs had searched and processed the scene thoroughly. Even though they went over an area the size of several football fields with a metal detector, they'd found nothing they could connect to the crime. The dry ground and pine needle–covered forest wasn't conducive to footprints, but they had photographed areas of disturbance in the ground cover, which may have indicated one or more people shuffled from the road on the other side of the gate to the gravesite. That was consistent with carrying a heavy load, such as a body, in the darkness.

Sinclair was on the last page of the six-page report when John Johnson, the veteran police beat reporter for the *Oakland Tribune*, dropped a copy of today's paper on his desk. "Anything new on Phil's murder?" Johnson had known every sergeant that worked homicide during the past fifty years, and he was one of the only reporters they trusted.

Sinclair shook his head.

"We were nearing deadline when OPD released his name last night, but I'll be doing human interest stories about Phil over the next week. I'd like to talk to both of you later on," he said, referring to him and Braddock.

They both agreed. Sinclair picked up the paper. The head-line read, *Body of Oakland Police Sergeant Found in Shallow Grave.* The article had no more details about the murder than those he'd included in his vague press release. It was important to keep certain details from the public so that if he was fortunate enough to interview those responsible, Sinclair could be sure the suspect wasn't regurgitating information he or she had read in the paper.

Johnson wrote that the department was especially tight-lipped about their investigation, inferring the motive may have stemmed from some of the sensitive work his section was involved in, such as terrorism, gangs, and narcotics. The remainder of the article talked about Phil's long assignment in homicide and some of the major cases he solved. It also discussed the investigators he'd trained, mentioning Sinclair and Braddock by name. Below the fold was the beginning of an article titled, *Motorcycle Gang Member Killed in Biker Bar Shooting.* Had it not been for Phil's murder, that story would've probably been the headline.

By eight o'clock, all the investigators were at their desks, and Maloney stepped out of his office. "Listen up, everyone. I don't need to tell you that Phil's murder is our top priority. Sinclair is primary, so anything he wants, do it. You don't need to ask for permission to work overtime, but no all-nighters unless we have the suspect in our sights. I'll handle media inquiries. No discussing this case with anyone outside this office. I'm meeting with the chief and the OPOA later today," he said, referring to the Oakland Police Officer's Association. "I imagine there will be a full line-of-duty funeral, probably early next week."

Sinclair tasked four investigators to pull all of Roberts's homicide cases and go through them to find anyone with enough of a beef to kill him. It was a long shot, they all knew. He tasked another team with going through all recent crimes and police activity in the area where the body was found, just in case Phil had stumbled upon a crime in progress. That was even more of a long shot. He didn't believe Phil was killed anywhere near the PAL camp, and he doubted someone who killed Phil during a chance encounter would take the time to bury him, but he had no better direction in which to point his fellow investigators. Phil being buried at a camp operated by OPD wasn't lost on him. It could've been the work of someone pissed at the department—there was no shortage of them—but nothing else so far indicated the burial site had any meaning to the killer other than being an isolated place to bury a body.

Braddock wheeled her chair next to him. "I hear you and Alyssa talked last night."

She and Alyssa were close, so it didn't surprise Sinclair that Braddock knew the most recent scoop on his love life.

"Just talk. Nothing happened."

"Just because you didn't get laid doesn't mean nothing happened."

"Come on, Braddock. You know that's not all I'm after with Alyssa. But still, we've been dating since before Christmas."

"And she's been gone most of that time. She's back to getting to know you."

"Jeez, she's known me most of her adult life." Sinclair put down his pen and turned to Braddock. "Except for my time in a combat zone, this is the longest I've gone without since I was sixteen."

"Sixteen?" Braddock raised her eyebrows. "So you've been a man-whore that long."

"I prefer the term male slut." He grinned.

"Are you saying you were faithful when she was gone?"

He was accustomed to Braddock's protectiveness over Alyssa, but he was in no mood for it this morning. "Even if I wasn't, it's not like we made some kind of promise before she left. How do I know she was, off in Europe with those French doctors and spending her down time in her grandparents' little village with a bunch of horny Italian men running around?"

"You know Alyssa's not that kind of girl. She really cares about you, but you need to give her time. She's been through a lot working in the refugee camp." Braddock plucked several short yellow hairs from his pants.

"It's dog hair, Braddock."

"It looks good on you." She smiled. "You're always dressed so perfectly with your nice suits, pressed shirts, and freshly polished shoes. It's nice to see some blemishes. They make you more human."

Sinclair's desk phone rang. *Criminalistics* appeared in caller ID. "Sinclair."

"Good morning, Sergeant. We examined the trash bag for DNA yesterday and collected some samples. It'll be a day or so before we know if we have anything beyond the victim's we can submit. We fumed the bag for prints and recovered a number of latents. We entered all of them into the system and got a hit on three of them. I'll give you the name and PFN when you're ready."

He picked up his pen. "Go."

"Last name of Gibbs. First name, Shane. DOB—"

"I've got his info. He was murdered last night in a biker bar. You're sure about this?"

"Positive match."

Chapter 12

Maloney, Sinclair, Braddock, Sanchez, and Jankowski sat at one end of the small conference table in Chief Brown's office. When Maloney finished his briefing, Brown clasped his hands behind his head and stretched. He then leaned forward and pulled down his monogrammed cuffs so that his gold cuff links faced outward. "This is great work. Let me see if I've got this straight—Gibbs was killed at the bar last night by a fellow Savage Simba gang member named Reggie Clement, known as Animal. Gibbs murdered Sergeant Roberts, meaning Roberts must have been involved in some sort of investigation into the motorcycle gang. He apparently got too close, so Gibbs killed him."

"We can speculate that's the scenario," Maloney said. "But Animal didn't waive his rights, and no one else in the club is talking."

Brown jotted some notes on a pad. "It doesn't matter. What's important is we know Sergeant Roberts was killed in the line of duty, and we can give him the funeral he and his family deserve. We have our murderer."

"All we have is a man's prints on the garbage bag," Sinclair said. "If we took a case like this to the DA, he'd laugh at us."

"But Gibbs is dead, so there's no reason to present this to the DA. You still have that clearance, called *Death of the Offender*, don't you?"

"Yes, sir," Maloney said. "But the standards are identical. We must have the same degree of proof to close a case whether the offender is dead or alive."

Brown waved his hand as if he were shooing away a fly. "Nonsense."

"There're still too many unanswered questions," Sinclair said. "For all we know, Gibbs handled that garbage bag days ago and had nothing to do with the murder. Even if Roberts's body was in it when Gibbs handled it, it doesn't mean he did anything more than transport a body. It took more than one person to move and bury Roberts, so even if Gibbs was one of them, there's still another suspect out there. And we've got nothing saying Roberts was investigating the Savage Simbas. To the contrary, Officer Fletcher, who's the outlaw motorcycle gang expert, says *he* would've been the case officer if there was an investigation."

"What about other physical evidence that can corroborate this?" Brown asked.

"The lab's doing a rush on the gunshot residue kits from Gibbs and Animal," Sinclair said. "If the kit from Gibbs's hands test positive, it's something, but it only means he fired a gun or was near one that was fired, not that he fired the shot that hit Roberts. If Gibbs was involved, I need to know what Roberts was doing that night that put him into the path of the Savage Simbas."

Brown began to speak but stopped. Sinclair could tell he was rethinking his push to close Phil's murder by pinning it all on Gibbs.

"There must be some clue as to what Roberts was working in his office—maybe in his desk, his files, or his computer." Sinclair knew the moment he continued talking he should've kept his mouth shut. "But there's some IA lieutenant sitting in Roberts's office invoking your name and keeping me from investigating the murder. If that happened any place else, I'd slap cuffs on the person for one-forty-eight PC, obstructing and interfering with an officer in the performance of his duties."

Brown glared at Sinclair. "Are you challenging my orders, Sergeant?"

"I never heard you give an order, Chief. Only some pencil-pushing LT said it was your order."

Brown locked eyes with Sinclair for a few seconds, then turned his attention to Maloney. "I'll make my orders clear. Lieutenant Farrington is the acting commander of the intelligence unit. He is working directly for me, and anything he discovers that might be connected to Sergeant Roberts's death will be conveyed to you, Lieutenant Maloney, immediately. I trust him explicitly to carry out my orders."

"What are you afraid I'll find in his office?" Sinclair asked.

Brown leaned in closer to Sinclair, as if his size and proximity would intimidate him. His lips tightened. He then smiled slightly and turned to Maloney. "I previously inquired as to whether Sinclair was too close to lead this investigation. You assured me he was the best one for the job. Your own future might be dependent on that assessment."

Maloney nodded without saying a word.

"Do you know which of the departmental values I prize the most in my subordinates?" Brown's eyes swept from Braddock to Jankowski to Sanchez to Sinclair to Maloney. When not one of them spoke, he said, "Loyalty."

Sinclair shot back, "Loyalty along with duty and selfless service are values I learned in the Army, and I can assure you of my loyalty to the department, the city, and our police profession."

Brown grinned. "The department's leadership seminars say loyalty must be earned and never demanded by leaders. However, in the real world, workers who aren't loyal to their leaders are lucky to keep their jobs."

★

An hour later, Braddock, Jankowski, and Sinclair stood on a West Oakland street corner, a block from the old Amtrak station. A hulk of burned metal, upholstery, and rubber that had once been Roberts's car was still dripping from the thorough soaking courtesy of the Oakland Fire Department. A uniformed officer wrote notes on his clipboard while an evidence technician took photographs.

"I still can't get over the arrogance of that prick," Sinclair said.

"Jeez, Matt." Braddock sighed. "You've got to stop fighting with the chief. You can't win with him, and when you piss him off, he'll get you for it."

"We were officers together in patrol," Jankowski said.

"You mean for the minute he was in patrol before he became a building rat and got promoted?" Sinclair said.

"He's not the only person in the command ranks who figured out that the way to the top required taking assignments outside of patrol and investigations," Braddock said.

"He didn't take an ounce of pride in handling the calls on his beat and didn't do shit proactive," Jankowski said. "Dudes could be slinging dope hand over fist on his beat and he wouldn't even get out of his car and talk to them."

"If you never do anything, you never get in trouble," Sinclair said.

"It wasn't just that," Jankowski said. "You'd think someone his size could handle himself out here, but he'd make sure he was the last car to arrive on a hot call. The fight was always over by the time he pulled up."

"Unlike the macho guys who race to calls at double the speed limit, sometimes wrapping their cars around a telephone pole on the way, just so they could show everyone how courageous they are by being the first one on the scene," Braddock said.

"Why are you defending him, Braddock?" Sinclair asked.

"He didn't get to where he is by being stupid. He decided early in his career that he wanted something more than pushing a beat car and handling radio calls for twenty years. You must give him credit for knowing the system and gaming it to succeed."

"I still can't believe his crap about personal loyalty," Sinclair said.

"Believe it," Jankowski said. "And watch your back. He's a vindictive motherfucker."

Sinclair's cell rang. A male voice identified himself as a fire captain. "We don't send out arson investigators on vehicle fires."

"That's what your dispatch said," Sinclair replied. "Then I told them this was the car that belonged to our officer who was murdered two nights ago."

"Was his body in the car when it was torched?"

"No, he was shot and dumped in the hills." Sinclair repeated the same story he told dispatch.

"Listen, Sergeant, our policy is to only investigate arsons when the dollar value is significant or when the structure or vehicle is occupied."

Fire departments' rank structure was top heavy compared to most police departments. Sinclair knew the authority and responsibility of a fire captain was only slightly greater than that of a police sergeant. "No, you listen, Captain. If you don't have the authority to make an exception to your policy for a line-of-duty death of a cop, put someone on the phone who does. If you won't send your people out here to help our tech process the car for evidence and determine the cause and origin of the fire, I guess I'll have to call the county fire marshal or ask ATF to send out one of their teams from Washington. I bet they'll be glad to help out us, especially since a cop might've been murdered in this car."

The line was quiet for several beats. "Okay, I'll approve the dispatch."

Sinclair hung up and walked upwind of the car. The smell of burned rubber and gasoline and the fumes from the toxic mix of plastics and fibers were starting to get to him. "Anything on the caller?" Sinclair asked the uniformed officer.

"It was a trucker who was passing by and saw the flames. Didn't see anyone on the street and no vehicles. He just dialed nine-one-one and went about his way."

The uniformed officer had been dispatched at the same time as the fire department. Once the fire was out, the officer thought the remains could've been a Dodge Challenger, the model of Phil's undercover car. He called for a tech and notified homicide once he located the VIN and saw it matched the information in the communications order on Phil's missing vehicle.

Sinclair walked around the car again, peering into the burned rubble.

"I don't know if we'll find anything in there after the fire," the tech said. "The firefighters on the scene said they smelled gas even though the gas tank hadn't leaked or exploded, which means someone doused it with gasoline."

"I don't know either," Sinclair said. "I've got someone from the crime lab coming out. Get the arson investigators to do the grunt work of going through every inch of the car and let the criminalist decide if anything you find has evidentiary value."

The tech nodded. "If there's anything left in the car, we'll find it."

Chapter 13

Sinclair and Braddock spent the remainder of the morning and early afternoon at their desks reviewing the reports and statements in Jankowski's homicide packet. They couldn't deny the evidence showing Gibbs was involved in Phil's death, but there were too many unanswered questions, the main ones being why Gibbs would want to kill him and what Phil was doing that put him in the path of the Savage Simbas.

Sinclair was mulling those thoughts over when his desk phone rang, showing a familiar 916 area code. His mother's cell phone, which she hardly ever used. He felt the walls come up around him, that protective shield he'd developed as a kid. He listened. She wanted him to drop everything and rush to Sacramento. He told her about the case and why he was needed here. She begged him. He said he'd try, but he had no intention of doing so.

He stared into the empty space in front of him and tried to pretend the call hadn't happened. Braddock's voice snapped him back to the present. "Matt, what's wrong?"

"Ahh, nothing."

"Bullshit. I heard your side of the conversation. That was your mom. What's going on?"

"My father had a heart attack."

"Jesus, is he okay? How serious was it?"

"I don't know. He was rushed to Mercy General in Sacramento. They bypassed the ER and took him straight to the angioplasty department."

"What did they find? Does he need surgery?"

"I don't know. I don't think my mother even knows yet."

She placed her hand on his arm and gently swiveled his chair to face her. "You need to be there." They'd talked about their respective relationships with their fathers at length in the past, and she knew that he and his father hadn't spoken in years.

"Why?"

"Because he's your father, Matt."

For a long time, Sinclair had hoped his father would die. Walt and other people in AA had urged him to consider forgiving his father, for his own benefit if for no other reason. But he couldn't. He wouldn't. In the last year or so, he had finally reached a place where he no longer cared what happened to his father. As far as he was concerned, he didn't exist. Sinclair could never figure out why his mother stayed with him. She knew what he was and that he would never change. "So?"

"If not for him, then for your mother. She needs you right now."

He pulled a report from the pile on his desk and began reading it.

"Matt, you need to go."

"I have a case to investigate. The murder of one of us. One of our brothers. This is my family, and this is where I need to be."

Braddock picked up her cup and headed toward the coffeepot without saying another word. He went back to the report and tried to focus on his mission.

A few moments later, Maloney called his name. Sinclair slumped into a chair across from the lieutenant's desk. "Cathy told me about your father. I want you to leave your desk exactly as it is. Braddock and Jankowski will pick up the case until you get back. There's nothing you're doing that they can't handle."

Braddock wasn't satisfied with just meddling in his love life; she had to stick her nose into his relationship with his parents as well. "There's nothing more important than solving Phil's murder. You said that yourself."

"There's nothing more important than family," Maloney shot back.

"You don't know my family."

"What I do know is that if your father dies and you're not there, you'll never be able to change that. Your mother called because she needs you. Your relationship will never be the same if you aren't there for her."

Sinclair knew he was right. He was so focused on his hatred toward his father, he hadn't considered what his mother must have been going through. While Sinclair should be feeling sadness for his father's condition or fear that he might die, all he felt was anger. Anger that his father would do this to him at a time like this. "Okay, but I'll be back first thing in the morning. By that time, he'll either be out of the woods or dead, and if he's dead, there's nothing else I need to do there."

★

Sinclair jockeyed his Mustang GT through the stop-and-go traffic headed toward the Caldecott Tunnel. The clock on his dash read 4:04, and he knew the only fast way to get to Sacramento at this time of day was by helicopter. It would take at least fifteen minutes to travel the mile to the tunnel. He'd then speed along until the traffic screeched to a halt as it entered Lafayette. It would pick up again until he approached the 680 Freeway, where it would be stop and go for ten miles. What took less than an hour and a half without traffic could be a three-hour drive at this time of day.

Braddock had driven him home, where he gave her the Crown Vic. He changed out of his suit and into jeans and a polo shirt, gave Amber a belly rub when she showed up and barked once to be let in, and headed out the gate in his Mustang.

Although he still missed his old Mustang, a month after the Bus Bench Killer firebombed it along with his apartment, he had test-driven a new one. The redesigned Mustang was a vast improvement over the old model with its archaic solid live axle, and the body looked more like the classic Mustangs from the sixties. The salesman tried to convince him to get the automatic, saying its performance matched the six-speed manual and would save his clutch leg in Bay Area traffic, but sports cars were meant to be shifted by the driver.

The thermometer read seventy-three degrees as he left Oakland and picked up speed entering the Caldecott Tunnel. It would be twenty degrees warmer by the time he reached Sacramento. Sinclair pressed a few buttons on the steering wheel. The ringing cell phone sounded through the car's speakers. "Any news yet?" he asked.

"The doctor just came out." Her voice was surprisingly calm. "He said there were some major blockages that would require surgery. They'll be moving him to the OR in a few minutes." Sinclair had been on plenty of heart attack calls. Many heart attack patients were treated with balloon angioplasty and stents right in the hospital cath lab, so open-heart surgery meant this was serious.

"What happened anyway?"

"He got home from work and was in the bedroom changing clothes. I heard a crash. I ran in and there he was, lying on the floor, breathing fast and complaining of chest pain."

"So you knew?"

"I fix him oatmeal for breakfast and then find out he stops for sausage and eggs on the way to work. If I make something healthy for dinner, he'll put a steak on the grill. He still smokes, and well . . . you know about his drinking. I've been expecting this."

"You did all you could."

"I called nine-one-one. The paramedics shocked him with the defibrillator on the way there. I don't know why because he was still breathing."

"I'm sure he's in excellent hands."

"I have to go. They want me to sign some paperwork. When will you get here?"

The GPS said he'd arrive in an hour and ten minutes. "It's rush-hour traffic, Mom, so at least two hours. Is anyone with you?"

"A lady from work, but she'll have to leave by dinner time."

His mother had become quite an entrepreneur in the last few years. Born in California's Central Valley to a mother who came from Mexico as a migrant worker and a father who managed a small farm, she'd worked as a hotel maid until Sinclair was born. When his youngest brother started school, she began working part time as a domestic so she could arrive home before Sinclair and his brothers got home. She then cleaned their house, did laundry, cooked dinner, and helped with homework while his father sat in front of the TV drinking beer. Now she ran her own house-cleaning business with twenty employees and a full-time office manager. "I'll be there as quick as I can."

★

It was past nine o'clock when a nurse finally led Sinclair and his mother into the ICU. With her smooth skin and dark-brown hair cut stylishly short, his mother appeared much younger than her sixty-two years. Sinclair got his dark eyes and complexion from her, but while she was clearly of Hispanic descent, few people guessed he was anything but white—or maybe part Italian. She hung tightly on his arm as they stepped into the room.

A breathing tube was taped in place over his father's mouth, and an assortment of tubes and wires ran under his blanket from IVs and machines arranged on one side of his bed. Monitors showed numbers representing his pulse, blood pressure, and other vitals. He looked frail and small, nothing like the man Sinclair had feared for years.

The last time Sinclair had seen his father was more than ten years ago. Sinclair was lying in a hospital bed in Oakland after being shot during an undercover drug deal that went bad. His father didn't say a word to him that day. Just shook his head.

Sinclair grew up as the oldest of three brothers. Although his father always drank, his habits got worse when Sinclair's little brother was shot and killed when Sinclair was twelve. As a teenager, he hated the hours between his father getting home from work and falling asleep. He grew to fear each slam of the refrigerator door, knowing that one of them might signal his father's nightly visit to his room where he and his brother did their homework—or pretended to, anyway.

Everything changed one Friday evening, as Sinclair sat on his bed listening to music and beating himself up over dropping a pass that would've been the winning touchdown for his freshman team. His mother was making dinner. He heard the yelling, first about dinner being late, and then about how Sinclair embarrassed the family on the football field. A moment later, his bedroom door banged open, and his father, drunk, loomed in the doorway. He wanted to tell him about the three passes he caught, not expecting praise from his father—that never happened—but to lessen his anger.

"You're no Sinclair," his father yelled. "You're a pussy—a girl." He pulled back his hand. Instead of waiting for the slap as he had for years—slaps that were never so hard to leave a mark but nevertheless left deeper wounds—Sinclair stood and raised his arm, blocking the blow. His closed fist struck his father's forearm with such force that he felt the shock up his arm and into his shoulder.

His father pulled his hand back again for another strike. Sinclair raised his fists in a boxer's stance. "Come on! Try it!" he growled.

They stood like that for what seemed like an eternity. Then his father simply turned and walked away. After that, his father never uttered a word of praise or criticism to him again, not when he broke a school record with five touchdown receptions in one game, not when he graduated from high school, not when he got married, and not when his life crashed and burned due to his own alcoholism. In his youth, Sinclair had vowed he'd never become like his father, but he had in too many ways, especially the way he drank.

Chapter 14

The ICU didn't allow overnight visitors, and the nurses urged Sinclair's mother to go home and sleep, telling her that the bypass went well and her husband was sedated and would sleep through the night. Still, she wouldn't leave the hospital. Sinclair sat next to her in the waiting room, dozing for a few minutes at a time until the sun blasted its morning rays through the window a little after 5:30. Sinclair wandered the hospital maze and returned with two coffees and pastries. They ate silently until a nurse came in.

"Your husband is doing well," she said. "His vitals are good and he's resting comfortably. The doctors expect to see him this afternoon, and I suspect they'll allow him to wake up and then remove the breathing tube."

His mother jumped up and hugged the woman, spilling half of her remaining coffee on the floor. The nurse patted her on the back and gently pulled away. "Now would be a good time to go home, maybe take a shower, and get some rest. I'll call you if there's any change."

Sinclair's phone vibrated. He moved to the other side of the room and said, "Good morning, Braddock."

"How's your father?"

Sinclair summarized the nurse's report.

"I'm glad," she said. "I left a message for Phil's wife last night, and she just called. She's available to talk at eight this morning. I'm headed into the office to meet Jankowski and take him with me to interview her."

"My mother's going home to rest for a while and there's nothing for me to do here. I'll meet you there."

On the walk to his mother's car, Sinclair asked, "Have you heard from Jimmy?"

She shook her head. "I left messages at every number I have for him. You know your brother."

Jimmy was a year younger than Sinclair and had been in and out of treatment centers since he was eighteen for oxycodone and heroin addiction. The last he heard, Jimmy was living in Seattle and working as a cook at a neighborhood coffee shop. "You want me to try to find him?"

She pursed her lips. "I'm sure he got the message. I'm just glad one of my sons came."

Interstate 80 was only a mile away. As he left the hospital, he put the convertible top down and felt the wind and warm sun on his face as he cruised down the freeway and wound through the rolling hills to the Green Valley Country Club.

Sinclair hoped Phil's wife would be able to shed some light on his work activities, but Phil might've been as good at keeping secrets from her as he was at keeping secrets from his coworkers. He followed his GPS's directions through a well-established neighborhood with spacious yards to an older sprawling ranch-style home overlooking the twelfth green of the golf course.

Braddock was waiting in their Crown Vic. "How was traffic?" he asked.

"Piece of cake. Going against the commute."

A slender woman with honey-colored hair and a porcelain complexion answered the door. Sinclair already had her particulars from the DMV: Abigail J. Roberts, 47, 5'8", 135, blonde, green. A two-year-old BMW SUV registered to her, with Phil listed as the "and." She was the "and" behind Phil on a four-year-old Corvette and a ten-year-old Harley. Makeup did a poor job concealing the dark circles under her bloodshot eyes. She forced her thin lips into a smile. "Matt, Cathy, I so regret the conditions under which we're finally meeting."

Sinclair put out his hand, but Abby ignored it and embraced him and Braddock.

"Me too. I'm sorry for your loss," he said, unable to think of anything else to say.

"Come in," she said with a hint of a British accent. "I have coffee waiting."

They followed her through a formal living room to a great room with large windows overlooking a patio and a large backyard with pool. Beyond it was a small stand of trees and the golf course's expanse of green grass. She poured coffee into three cups resting on saucers, added cream and sugar to two, and set them on a round glass table in the kitchen. She slid one toward Sinclair and one to Braddock. "Black and cream and sugar, right?"

Some Oakland officers fully integrated their spouses into their police lives, brought them to off-duty functions, and socialized primarily with other police couples and families. Others kept the two separate. Sometimes it was the officer's spouse who wanted to shelter the family from the horrors and dangers their husband or wife experienced daily. Sometimes it was the officer who kept his work at work to protect his family from worrying about him. And sometimes, it was a psychological defense mechanism, where officers flipped a mental switch as they drove out of Oakland after their shifts. Sinclair didn't know much about Phil's personal life. He seldom talked about his wife and kids, and Sinclair hardly ever asked during the years they worked together. He had always thought Phil wanted to keep his private life private, but Sinclair hoped that Phil didn't think he didn't inquire because he didn't care. Now he felt bad that he never asked.

He knew that Phil had met Abby in high school when his father was stationed in England with the Air Force, but after his father's tour, they returned to the States. When Phil returned a few years later to attend Oxford, he and Abby began dating. She earned a degree in civil engineering and got a job with a San Francisco construction company when Phil joined OPD. A few years after their second daughter was born, she took a job with Caltrans, the huge state agency that constructed and maintained all the state's highways and bridges, so they'd bought the house in Fairfield, halfway between Oakland and her Sacramento office.

"Have your girls made it back yet?" Braddock asked.

"My oldest came home from Boston yesterday. We were up late last night, so she's still sleeping. My youngest, who's going to school in London, arrives tonight."

Braddock took a sip of her coffee. "Has the department talked with you about the memorial service?"

"Yes, we're meeting again this afternoon. I'd prefer a private family affair, but I understand this huge production is necessary. Your chaplain explained how other officers, even those who had never met Phil, need to know that if they die in the line of duty, their lives will be honored and their death won't be in vain." She wiped a tear from her eye. "I never wanted Phil to be a policeman. Did you know that at one time he wanted to be a writer?"

"I knew he majored in English at Oxford," Sinclair said.

"English literature," she said. "But he loved police work, and because he loved it, I supported him. He told me many times that there was no other career where a man could make such a difference, where he could touch so many people in such a positive way."

"That's one of the many things that he passed down to me and Matt," Braddock said.

"When I was pregnant with our first child, Phil and I decided to keep that world separate from our family's. We didn't want our children to be exposed to the violence that existed in his world. I didn't want them to worry every time he left for work that he wouldn't come home. He rarely discussed his work, and I never asked about it. But he talked about the people he worked with. He adored you both and thought of you like a younger brother and sister. He was in awe of your courage—how you both rushed toward danger to save lives of people you didn't even know." She looked at Braddock. "I know you drink your coffee with cream and sugar and that Hannah, who was only four at the time, felt left out when you read a Harry Potter book to Ethan at night, so for six months, you let her lie in bed next to Ethan when you read his bedtime story."

"I always thought I drove Phil crazy talking about my kids when we had murders to solve," Braddock said.

Abby smiled at Sinclair. "Although we never met, I knew you through Phil. You were the homicide detective he always wanted to be—one who would stop at nothing to achieve justice. I don't know what happened, but Phil mentioned that he felt like he let you down recently. What Phil liked most about police work was the people he worked with. From his days at Oxford, he always had a way with words. He described his coworkers as ordinary people thrust into extraordinary situations and, as a result, transformed into heroes."

"You're not at all what I expected," Sinclair said.

Abby laughed. "I first went out with Phil to shock my parents. My mum was a stereotypical British aristocrat, except she was born a generation too late. When I brought Phil, an American black man, to dinner the first time, I thought for sure she was going to choke on her beef Wellington. He pretended he didn't notice how incredibly stuffy they acted, and by the end of the evening, he had them both laughing more than I'd seen in years. They had wanted me to marry someone whose ancestors owned a castle and had a title, but when Phil asked my father for my hand in marriage, he was thrilled."

"When did you last see him?" Sinclair asked, trying to steer the conversation back to the present.

"Monday morning. He leaves for work at six and always brings me coffee in bed before he goes. He called later that day, probably around five or so, and reminded me he was working late."

"Did he call you here?"

"He called my cell. I think I was on my way home."

"Did he call from his office?"

"From his cell. We always talk cell to cell these days."

Sinclair knew of no way to ease into the question, so he asked it outright. "Do you have any idea who would want to kill him?"

She looked lost. "I assume it had something to do with his work."

"We have to look into everything, so please excuse me if what I'm asking you is uncomfortable."

"Ask away, but no, there's no one from his family life who would want to hurt him. He still works long hours, although not as much as in homicide. We both have long commutes, so we only have a few hours together most nights. But he's mostly home on weekends now. We try to golf together once a week with other couples from the club. I've never seen him even have cross words with someone."

Out the window, Sinclair could see a golf cart stop in the middle of the fairway, and a man wearing a turquoise shirt and madras shorts got out, hit a ball, and sped off in the golf cart. "What about social activities on Friday and Saturday nights?" Sinclair asked.

"He's had a regular work engagement for months on Friday evenings, but we often have dinner with friends at the club or someone's home on Saturdays."

"Any idea what work thing he does on Friday nights?"

"Like I mentioned before, he never shared what he does at work."

Sinclair nodded. If Phil's murder wasn't work related, Sinclair had to rule out the other most common reasons for murder. "Have you ever suspected Phil of being involved with someone else?"

"Gosh, no. Matt, I know you're no prude, so I'll be direct with you—we had a very good relationship, emotionally and physically. Other women my age complain about their love lives—how one or the other lost interest in sex. Phil and I never had that issue."

Sinclair looked away awkwardly.

"I'm so sorry your marriage didn't work out," she said. "When Phil told me about your divorce, he was heartbroken. He was old-fashioned in that way. He would've never been unfaithful."

"Are you having any financial problems?" Sinclair asked, glad to get off the topic of sex and marriage.

"To the contrary, Phil planned to work for six more years for his maximum pension, and I would work a few more years after that, until I turned fifty-five. My state pension would be almost as much as his. We paid off our mortgage two years ago. My parents are paying for our youngest's college tuition. Of course, all our plans have changed now." She wiped her eyes with a tissue.

"Any recent influxes of cash or unusual expenses?"

"Not that I know of." She smiled at Sinclair's puzzled look and continued. "My parents are rather well-to-do, and I'm in line to inherit a sizable portion of their estate, so they insisted we sign a prenuptial before we married and suggested we keep separate accounts. At first, it was uncomfortable, but we found that we like it. Each month, most of our salaries go into a joint account, from which I pay all our living expenses. What we had left was our own, to do with as we wished. Last summer, Phil treated us to an Alaska cruise for our twenty-fifth wedding anniversary. For Christmas, he bought me a diamond tennis bracelet. I paid for a week in Barbados in April for the girls and us. So, to tell you the truth, I don't know if Phil spends whatever he has or if he has significant investments."

"This might feel intrusive, but I normally search a murder victim's home and go through their financials. I sometimes find things that tell me the motive for the murder and who did it. Other times I just learn things about my victim that can help me later on in the investigation. Phil would expect me to do this."

"I think you're wasting your time. I can't imagine there is something in our home that will tell you who killed my husband."

"Phil would've done the same if Matt or I were murdered," Braddock said. "And we'll treat your home with the same dignity and respect as Phil would've with ours."

Chapter 15

A few hours later, Sinclair waited for the heavy wrought-iron gate across the driveway of the Towers's estate to open. While he'd taken a quick shower and changed into a suit, Braddock spread the files they collected from Phil's home office on his kitchen table and went through them. They had found nothing noteworthy in Phil's house until they reached the fourth bedroom, which he and Abby used as a home office. Matching cherry desks faced each other in the small room. A closed laptop sat on Phil's desk. The organization Phil demonstrated at work carried over to his home desk. Two desk drawers contained labeled file folders filled with neat papers organized in chronological order. Sinclair asked if they could borrow those that dealt with his finances: bank statements, money market, deferred compensation plan, personal credit card, and mutual funds. After a little persuasion, Abby also gave them Phil's laptop for a few days. Sinclair found a list of his passwords taped to a slide-out shelf and took a photo of it with his phone.

"As far as Abby's concerned, Phil was the perfect husband and father," Braddock said as they drove out the gate and turned onto Sea View Avenue. "She could not imagine him having an affair, everybody in their community loves him, and it doesn't look like he had any money problems."

"I didn't suspect we'd find the motive in his personal life," Sinclair said. "But, then again, Phil's a master at keeping secrets, so if he was hiding something, his wife wouldn't know."

"Did you call Alyssa last night?" Braddock asked.

"I forgot—got busy with my mother and the hospital stuff."

"When you're going through a family tragedy like that, you're supposed to call your girlfriend so she can support you."

"I was okay."

"You always think you're okay. Alyssa knows how to be a girlfriend, but you need to tell her what's going on so she can be one. That is, if you really want a girlfriend."

"Okay, okay, I'll call her."

"When?"

"As soon as I can get some privacy from a meddling partner who's trying to run my love life."

★

When Sinclair and Braddock entered the homicide office, the other investigators were hanging up their coats and filling their coffee cups. "Where've you guys been?" Sinclair asked Jankowski.

"Did a search warrant on Animal's momma's house."

"Find anything interesting?"

"A bunch of bills and paperwork," Jankowski replied. "He used his mother's house as his mailing address. I also found a stack of pay stubs from Eastman Security."

"Animal worked as a security guard?"

"Most of the Savage Simbas had straight jobs. Believe it or not, Animal had no conviction record and only a few minor arrests. When I ran him in the state license database, I found he had a state guard card and a firearm card for armed security."

"The nine-millimeter Glock he just happened to have at the bar was probably his duty weapon," Sinclair said. "I'll bet the Simbas made pretty formidable security guards. Did Eastman employ other club members?"

"I was gonna head on over there and ask. Wanna join me?"

Sinclair left Braddock analyzing Phil's financials and rode with Jankowski to the East Oakland address where the state license bureau showed Eastman Security's office. Although his gut still told him that he and Braddock were on the right path looking into Phil's sensitive investigation, he couldn't ignore the obvious link to the Simbas. But connecting the motorcycle gang to a security company raised numerous questions, the answers to which might tell him why Phil was killed. They stopped at a storefront on International Boulevard that matched the address. A sign in the window read, *Latasha's Nail Salon*.

A heavyset black woman with bright-red lipstick and black braided hair sat behind a counter next to a cashbox. "We're looking for Eastman Security," Jankowski said.

An index finger with a long red nail tipped with silver beads pointed to the back of the shop. Sinclair followed Jankowski past six workstations, all occupied by manicurists and their clients. A short hallway led to a back door covered by metal bars. On one side of the hallway was a bathroom, and the other had a door with a sign that read, *Eastman Security*. Jankowski pushed open the door and stepped inside.

A sixtysomething black man with nappy gray hair sat behind a beat-up particleboard desk that looked like a reject from Goodwill. He put a phone receiver down and looked up at them. Jankowski reached over his huge belly and pulled his badge off his belt. "We're looking for Silas Eastman, the owner of Eastman Security."

"That's me."

"Tell me about Reggie Clement," Jankowski said. "A Savage Simba known as Animal."

"I'm sure you know he's one of the partners here. You got him in jail. That's why you're here, huh?"

Jankowski stepped out of the doorway to allow Sinclair to squeeze into the tiny office. "Tell me about the partnership of Eastman Security."

"I'm not at liberty to say without talking to the other partner."

"You're the only one listed on the license," Jankowski said.

"Nothing illegal about having financial partners. I'm the managing partner."

"And the partners work security gigs," Jankowski offered.

"Not me. I'm too old for that. Why you askin' if you already know?"

"How many guards work here?"

"I gotta clear that with my partner. Don't seem like your questions got nothin' to do with your investigation. You two are homicide, not the people that polices security guards."

"I could call a buddy of mine at the Bureau of Security and Investigative Services and see what he thinks about a private patrol licensee that doesn't cooperate with the police," Jankowski said.

"And you make sure you tell him old Silas answered all your questions about the subject of your investigation but ensured he protected the privacy of his employees and clients."

Jankowski's face began turning red. Sinclair stepped forward and said, "Look, Mr. Eastman, we don't want to make you any trouble. Please talk with your partner and see what info you can give us. In the meantime, we need to investigate Animal. We can't change what happened. All we're doing is searching for the truth."

Eastman pulled a Swisher Sweet cigar from a package on his desk and stuck it in his mouth. He chewed on it for a minute. "Whatcha wanna know?"

"What were Animal's duties as a partner?" Sinclair asked.

"He got new accounts and sometimes worked them himself."

"Which accounts are these?"

"Main one was B&J Liquors down the street. They wanted an armed uniformed guard Friday and Saturday night from six to closing. Animal usually did it himself."

Sinclair jotted some notes into his notebook. "What else?"

"The other account he worked was a funny one." Eastman pulled a folder from his desk. "Still don't know exactly what he did for this client. Woman works in a big company in the city. Animal billed her four or five hours two or three times a week. She always paid her bill on time. He was supposed to be working on that account Monday night. Maybe if he was working, none of this nonsense would've happened."

"You have a name and address for this client?" Sinclair asked.

Eastman chewed on his Swisher Sweet and opened the folder. "She's got a home address in Oakland, but we use her office address in San Francisco for billing. Her name's Maureen Yates."

Chapter 16

"Maureen Yates, the wife of Councilmember Preston Yates?" Braddock asked.

With a Simba connected to Phil's murder, the Simbas connected to Eastman Security, and Eastman Security connected to Yates, Sinclair wondered if his focus on Phil's sensitive work had distracted him from the right path.

Now back at the office, Sinclair grabbed the handwritten case log from a homicide packet in his desk drawer. "Same home address that I had on Preston from Dawn's murder. I listed Maureen's name in the work-up I did on Preston back then. She was ten years older than him and not particularly attractive. It made sense to me that Preston was stepping out on her with escorts. She owns a big ad agency in San Francisco."

"Why would she hire a mean-looking black biker for security?"

"Eastman didn't know, or else he was a good liar." Sinclair filled his coffee cup and stood next to Braddock's desk. "We also don't know why Animal wasn't working for her that night. Jankowski assembled the pieces from different witness statements from the bar, and it looked like the Simbas began showing up around four in the afternoon. It turned into a spontaneous birthday party for Animal. As the night wore on, more arrived and everybody got drunker."

"If Animal was supposed to be working for Maureen, maybe he called in and said he couldn't make it."

"Or he got someone else to fill in for him," Sinclair said.

"We need to talk to the other guards at Eastman."

Sinclair took a big swallow of the bitter coffee and winced. "I have a funny feeling they don't keep real tight records and might even work under the table whenever they can get away with it."

"You're saying that whoever might've filled in for Animal wasn't necessarily an employee of Eastman with all the right permits?" Braddock asked.

"I wouldn't doubt it. I know who can tell us exactly who, if anyone, worked for Maureen Yates Monday night."

"Are you crazy?" she shouted as the muscles on her neck jutted out. The other investigators in the office turned and looked at her. She lowered her voice. "The chief told us last December in no uncertain terms to leave Councilmember Yates alone. Even if we gather compelling evidence showing he committed a murder, we've got to get permission before we talk to him."

"They never said anything about his wife."

"Come on, Matt. I like my job."

Even though Yates hadn't been directly involved in Dawn's murder, Sinclair hated how he used her and then discarded her when she became pregnant. He'd been close to proving the connection between Sergio Kozlov, the multimillionaire developer, and Yates when the police chief and the Feds shut him down. If allowed to pursue the investigation, Sinclair was sure he could have proven Kozlov paid for the apartment where Dawn was set up as Yates's mistress. In exchange, Kozlov would receive Yates's vote and support that would award him a huge contract to develop the former Oakland Army Base. What pissed Sinclair off even more is that now Yates was so favored to win the mayoral election in November that a recent *Oakland Tribune* editorial suggested the other candidates should save their money and drop out of the race.

Sinclair was lost in his thoughts when he noticed Braddock staring at him. "What?" he asked.

"I know what you're thinking," she said. "We need to work around the edges of this Yates connection. We can't just go at them head on."

"Okay," he agreed. As much as he wanted to get Yates, Braddock was right. Absent some stronger link, they should continue collecting information and leave the high-risk/high-gain interviews for later. "Did you come up with anything while I was gone?"

"The lab called and said Gibbs tested positive for GSR."

Although the chief would view that as corroboration to Gibbs's fingerprints on the garbage bag, it actually didn't prove much. Someone could have gunshot residue on their hands if they fired a gun, handled a gun that had been recently fired, or was in close proximity to a fired gun. They already knew that Gibbs had been up close and personal to Animal when he fired the fatal round.

Sinclair's cell buzzed. "One of ATF's CIs knows where Tiny will be later on tonight," Fletcher said.

Tiny was another person who had answers to Sinclair's questions. Whether he would give them up in an interview room was uncertain, but the only way to find out was to get him in one. "Great, can you put a team together to grab him?"

"It's more complicated than that. If uniforms roll in there, we'll burn the CI, and there's no way to surveil the location without being made. But it wouldn't be out of the ordinary for me to show up there on my bike. I might be able to find out where he's laying his head at night. If he's there, I can try to jaw with him as a fellow biker."

"If you're gonna talk to him, I want to be there," Sinclair said.

The phone was silent. Sinclair looked at the screen to make sure he still had a connection. Finally, Fletcher said, "There's only one way that could work."

"Whatever it takes," Sinclair replied.

"You used to ride a Harley, didn't you?"

Chapter 17

Sinclair downshifted the Harley Heritage Softail Classic as he exited the 242 Freeway, allowing the engine to help brake the ten-year-old motorcycle. He followed Fletcher on his two-year-old Street Glide through a left turn. When Sinclair had been a young officer in the special operations section, a bunch of the older guys rode, so he picked up a used Road King and joined them on short rides on their days off and occasional overnighters. Some of the off-duty cops he rode with were motormen—OPD officers who rode Harleys in the traffic division. They'd taught him riding skills few civilians ever learned. When he made sergeant and got married four years later, he no longer had enough spare time to ride, so he sold his bike. Although it had been years since he'd ridden, once he ran the Heritage through the gears a few times and leaned it into some turns, everything came back to him.

An hour ago, Sinclair had met Fletcher at his house in Pittsburg, one of a string of blue-collar cities in eastern Contra Costa County that run along the delta of the Sacramento and San Joaquin Rivers between the Central Valley and the San Francisco Bay. Fletcher told him that he and Phil began riding together off duty when Phil transferred to Intel. Fletcher had changed the oil and filter on Phil's Heritage for him last weekend, and it was still sitting in his garage waiting for Phil to pick it up.

Sinclair felt strange sitting in the wide leather saddle of Phil's Harley with the large V-twin engine rumbling between his legs; biker code included never sitting on another man's bike. He and Fletcher rode side by side as they passed through downtown Concord. The sun, low in the sky, shined into their rearview mirrors. They took a side street and slowed in front of a brick building with a sign reading, *No Colors Motorcycle Shop*. When Irish Mike opened the shop fifteen years ago, he declared it a neutral zone, a place where bikers from any club could bring their Harleys for repair or service as long as they don't wear their vests with club patches. Over the years, it also meant that bikers of any race—black, white, brown, or yellow—were welcome, which wasn't always the case with many nondealer Harley shops.

The front doors were closed and locked. Sinclair followed Fletcher down an alley and through an opening in a chain link fence to a parking area behind the building. About ten Harleys stood in a neat row. Behind them, a dozen men sat on old car seats and lawn chairs drinking beer. Fletcher and Sinclair backed their bikes alongside the others, lowered the kickstands, and turned off the engines.

Fletcher pulled off his helmet and shook out his long hair. He stuck a cigarette in his mouth, lit it, and opened his saddlebag. Sinclair hung his helmet on the mirror, stepped off his bike, and pulled a black Harley baseball cap over his matted-down helmet hair. He'd worried about standing out with his clean-cut appearance, but that quickly evaporated when he saw the mix of men. Three were black, two Hispanic, one Asian, and the rest white. A few had long hair like Fletcher, while others had haircuts that would fit in at an accounting firm. The only commonality was their biker uniforms of boots, jeans, and black T-shirts.

Fletcher pulled a six-pack of Bud from his saddlebag, removed one from the plastic ring, and walked toward the group. Two men rose and grabbed a beer, and Fletcher set the remaining cans on a white plastic table. "My friend just bought this Heritage and is thinking about some performance work."

A ruddy-faced man with stringy red hair sticking out the sides of a black-and-orange Harley Davidson hat stood and grabbed one of the beers. "I seen you around," he said to Fletcher. "You show any colors or mention an affiliation, you're eighty-sixed from here."

"I know the rules, Mike," Fletcher said.

Sinclair wondered if Irish Mike thought Fletcher was with the Hells Angels or knew he was a cop. Maybe he mistook him for someone else, or maybe he just gave the warning to any nonregulars.

Irish Mike stood around five ten, and although he had to be close to sixty, his biceps bulged like those of a gym rat half his age. He limped toward Sinclair's Heritage Softail, partly dragging one leg that was a few inches shorter than the other. "How many miles?" he asked Sinclair.

"Thirty-two thousand."

"Not much for an oh-six. The engine stock?"

"Yeah. It's got some slip-on pipes, more for sound than performance, but that's it."

"You mind?" Irish Mike asked, pointing to the big chrome switch above the gas tank.

Sinclair nodded his okay, pulled a small cigar from the saddlebag, and lit it with his Zippo. Mike turned the switch and thumbed the starter. The engine turned over and settled into the typical Harley rumble. Mike revved the engine to three thousand RPM, then slowly increased it to redline.

Irish Mike turned the bike off. "Engine sounds strong. It all depends on what you want to spend. I can do a stage one for around a grand. That'll give you better airflow and make it run more efficiently. Might give you ten, fifteen percent more power. Add a big bore kit and we can turn your eighty-eight-inch engine into a ninety-five or one-oh-six. There's other things I can suggest, but truth is, unless you absolutely love this bike, you can easily put more money into it than the cost of a new bike after your trade-in. And new ones have better suspension, brakes, a six-speed, and, of course, bigger engines."

"What would you do?" Sinclair asked.

Mike pulled a shop rag from his pocket and wiped the dirt from the front fork. "You've got a leaking front fork seal, so first thing I'd do is get that fixed. Then I'd figure out how much money I want to put into my bike and come by when the shop's open. I can work out exactly what you can get to give you the most bang for your buck."

"Who you got helping you these days?" Fletcher asked.

"Hector does basic service, and Tiny helps me out with the performance work and rebuilds, but I oversee everything."

"Haven't seen Tiny around lately," Fletcher said.

"Not if you're looking in Oaktown," Mike said. "He was here a bit ago. His old lady works at the barbecue joint on Clayton Road. I'm sure he's stuffing his face down there right now."

Sinclair and Fletcher thanked Irish Mike, swung their legs over their bikes, and started them up. Fletcher led the way, cruising through side streets to Clayton Road. When Sinclair pulled alongside him at a stop sign, Fletcher said, "I know the place he's talking about. We'll cruise by. If his bike's there, we can call Concord PD to pick him up."

Sinclair pulled off behind Fletcher. A few blocks ahead, a red chopper roared out of a parking lot and headed their way.

"That's him," Fletcher yelled to Sinclair and pulled a U-turn across a double yellow line. Sinclair downshifted to second and made a fast U-turn, scraping the floorboards as he leaned the bike into the turn.

Tiny looked over his shoulder and accelerated. The scream from his straight pipes told them he was making a run for it. Fletcher's transmission clanked as he downshifted and took off after him. Sinclair did the same, accelerating to fifty in second gear before shifting into third and twisting the throttle again.

Fletcher pulled away, and Sinclair realized he couldn't keep up with the newer Harley with its more powerful engine. The red chopper swerved around cars, braking hard and accelerating into open gaps in traffic.

Sinclair concentrated on not crashing as he blew past cars, going twice their speed on the four-lane divided road that was flanked by houses on both sides. If he went down at this speed, he'd be lucky to survive. He braked hard behind two cars traveling abreast at thirty miles an hour. When there was enough room between them, he split the lane, squeezing between them, and rocketed forward.

Fletcher split the traffic lanes like a pro, weaving his eight-hundred-pound bike from one lane to the other and maneuvering between cars in the two lanes of traffic. A block behind, Sinclair tried to do the same, pressing the handlebar in the direction he wanted the Harley to turn and shifting his weight to make the bike dance from side to side like a slalom skier racing through the gates.

Red brake lights flashed on cars in front of him. The red chopper braked hard, locking its oversized rear tire with an angry squeal of rubber on asphalt. Fletcher braked hard too, but the ABS on his bike prevented his tires from losing traction. A small gray car behind him tried to swerve around the slowing traffic and sideswiped Fletcher's Street Glide. Still traveling about twenty miles an hour, Fletcher's bike wobbled back and forth for a few seconds. Sinclair thought Fletcher would be able to stay upright and ride it out until the back end suddenly bounced to one side and Fletcher went down.

Cars screeched to a stop. One rear-ended another. Fletcher's Harley slid about thirty feet with Fletcher still on it. Sinclair weaved through the stopped cars on his bike until he reached Fletcher, who was picking himself up off the ground and trying to right his bike.

"I'm fine," he yelled. "Don't lose him."

The red chopper disappeared down a side street two blocks away. Sinclair twisted the throttle and dumped the clutch, leaving a black ribbon of rubber on the road behind him. He speed-shifted into second gear and flung the bike into the right lane to pass cars slowing to enter a left-turn lane. He weaved back into the left lane, raced forward, and braked hard before turning right across the right lane of traffic. He leaned the bike hard, trying to keep his body as upright as possible. Car horns blasted behind him. Angry drivers he had cut off. He felt the right floorboard grating against the asphalt through the sole of his boot, but the tires stuck and he made the turn.

He rolled on the throttle as the chopper made a quick left turn ahead. Sinclair held second gear, the Harley engine near red line, then pressed the brake pedal while yanking the front brake lever with his left hand. Once he scrubbed off enough speed, he pressed the left handlebar forward to throw the bike into a sharp turn. Once again, the floorboard scraped the pavement, but this time, Sinclair was more under control than his previous reckless right turn in front of cars. The scraping sound became his barometer of how far he could lean the bike.

He rolled on the throttle. His bike came out of the turn onto another residential street. The chopper raced through the neighborhood of single-story ranch houses, the roar of its custom engine work announcing its horsepower advantage over Sinclair's older stock bike. But choppers were built for looks and straight-line performance. Their fat rear tires, skinny front tires on extended forks, and ape-hanger handlebars made them corner about as well as Toyota minivans.

The chopper made another turn and then another, and Sinclair gained distance in each corner. He was so close after the last turn, he could finally make out the rider for the first time, confirming that he fit the physical of Tiny, a six-foot-six man weighing around two-eighty. It made no sense that Tiny would attempt to lose him by making quick turns when his bike's advantage lay in the straightaways. But cops only caught the dumb crooks, as many of Sinclair's police buddies were fond of saying.

Tiny made a right turn and accelerated down a narrow street. Even though he was afraid to take his eyes off the road for a second to look at the speedometer, Sinclair still knew he was approaching seventy—insane for a residential area. Ahead, numerous cars crisscrossed in front of him on a busy road. Sinclair didn't know the streets of Concord like he did Oakland, but he recognized the street ahead as Kirker Pass Road. Instead of making a left that would've taken them over the pass and through the uninhabited brown hills to Pittsburg, Tiny turned right. Sinclair slowed at the stop sign and raced after him.

When Sinclair saw the red lights and flashing strobes of the first police car behind him, his first through was, *What took you so long?* He slowed slightly, expecting the police car to pass him and pursue the chopper, but the marked car stayed on his tail. He wished there was some way he could continue riding his motorcycle at double the speed limit while pulling his badge from his belt to show the pursuing officers. Since that was impossible, he wasn't about to pull over until Tiny did.

Tiny blew through the intersection with Clayton Road and snaked through the Lime Ridge Open Space into the city of Walnut Creek. A second and third police car pulled behind Sinclair. The chopper began approaching a wide, sweeping right turn ahead. Tiny was too upright to take the sweeping turn at the speed he was traveling. He tried to lean the bike by throwing his body into the turn. He then made the mistake of pressing the rear brake pedal too hard. Braking hard in a turn when the bike is leaning is a recipe for disaster. The fat rear tire skidded on the pavement, and the bike slid out from under the rider.

The chopper slid into a center median. Sinclair pulled his bike to the right side of the road. Tiny got up, shook himself off, and ran across the road toward an open field, beyond which lay a gas station and car wash. Sinclair dropped his Harley to its side stand and leaped off the bike, preparing to give chase.

Behind him, he heard the unmistakable slick-slick sound of a shotgun's slide racking a twelve-gauge round into the chamber, followed by "Police! Freeze!"

Chapter 18

Sinclair took a few puffs on the Rocky Patel Churchill and looked across the pool to the main house, which was dark except for a few night-lights inside. "By the time they proned me out, patted me down, and found my badge, Tiny was long gone. I can't blame the officers. I would've handled it the same way. Fletcher had called it in, but the info didn't make its way from the CHP nine-one-one dispatcher to the different police jurisdictions we were passing through in time. They assumed the bad guy was the one chasing the other one."

"And your friend," Walt asked, "Officer Fletcher. Is he okay?"

"Only his pride was hurt. His motorcycle is banged up a bit, but it's repairable."

Walt took a sip of his coffee. "How's your dad?"

"They'll probably move him from ICU to a cardiac care floor tomorrow."

"Will you go up and see him?"

Amber rose from the grass where she was lying, picked up a tennis ball, and dropped it on Sinclair's lap. He threw it across the yard and watched her sprint after it. "I'm more than a little busy right now."

"I understand." Walt took another sip of his coffee and watched as Amber scooped up the ball in her mouth at a full run.

"Besides, my visiting him last night was more than he deserves."

"So you're not ready to forgive him yet?" Walt grinned.

Amber returned and dropped the ball at Sinclair's feet. He picked it up and held it. She sat down in front of him, watching the ball intently.

"Shortly after I got sober," Walt said, "I was harboring serious resentments against a lot of people. I blamed everyone else for my predicament. I was wasting a great deal of emotional energy on hating people. I knew I needed to make amends—apologize—for my part to a number of people. It wasn't as if some of them didn't do things to me that weren't right, but I needed to focus on what I'd done. Once I'd made apologies to most of these people, it sometimes opened a dialogue, and I started feeling differently toward them. I had begun forgiving them for what they'd done to me."

Sinclair threw the ball again. "And what if I don't want to forgive him?"

"I'm just sharing my experience. You don't have to do anything you don't want to."

★

Sinclair had been waiting in the PAB's jail sally port since 6:30 AM. If this were a regular commercial building, this is where a loading dock for supplies and maintenance would be located. But a police station had additional needs and requirements. The vehicle entry door, located on Sixth Street, rose fifteen feet, high enough to accommodate the bus-like mobile command post and SWAT vans, which loaded and unloaded their equipment alongside a freight elevator that went to the basement, where the shooting range and storage rooms were located. A pedestrian door led from the open parking area to the rear door of the jail. Prisoner vans—called paddy wagons in the old days—parked there to unload arrestees. Another pedestrian door led to the first floor of the PAB, directly into the rear of the bureau of field operations, the uniformed division of the department. Powered, rolling metal doors could be lowered over the vehicle entrance and exits to seal off the sally port area, useful when moving a large group of prisoners into the jail or when loading the tactical operation team's vehicles out of sight of the public. In addition to parking spaces for special-purpose vehicles, five spaces were reserved for the highest-ranking brass in the department: the police chief, the assistant chief, and three deputy chiefs.

At 6:40 AM, a black unmarked sedan pulled into the space marked *Assistant Chief*, and a broad-shouldered white man with close-cut gray hair got out. Charley James turned fifty last year, a fact that he made known to everyone at City Hall, reminding anyone who considered messing with him that he could retire tomorrow. Unlike the others at the "chief" level, who spent most of their careers working IAD and OIG, the office of the inspector general, James worked his way up through the uniform ranks—patrol at the officer, sergeant, lieutenant, and captain level and a member of the tactical operations team as an officer, sergeant, and lieutenant. Chief Brown elevated him to the assistant chief position and made him responsible for the day-to-day operation of the department because, as much as he didn't like James's old-school mentality, he needed someone on the eighth floor who understood police work.

Sinclair's best memory of James was when Sinclair was a member of the SWAT entry team years ago and was going after a murder suspect holed up in an apartment. It turned out the suspect wasn't there, and his family members made a complaint to IAD and the CPRB, the citizens police review board, accusing the entry team of unlawfully entering a house without a warrant or probable cause. James, who was the tactical commander and the lieutenant of the special operations section at the time, marched down to IAD. He demanded that the officers be removed from the complaint and that he be named as the subject officer since he ordered it, and he insisted that officers such as

Sinclair were merely following orders. The CPRB held a hearing, viewed as a kangaroo court by OPD, and suspended James
for three days. Although it took a year for his suspension to be
overturned once it was shown the entry was legal, the officers
in the department never forgot the lieutenant who was willing
to sacrifice his career for his men.

"Shouldn't you be investigating a murder instead of hanging
around in the bowels of the PAB?" James asked.

"I was wondering if you had a minute to talk."

"Famous last words." James removed his suitcoat from the
back seat and slipped it on. "I come in early so I can lock myself
in my office and get work done before everyone arrives and
wants a minute."

"Sorry, Chief, but it's important."

"I'm just busting your balls, Matt. Do you want to come
upstairs?"

"I thought it might be best if you weren't seen with me."

"Maybe it's actually the other way around, but go ahead.
What's on your mind?"

"I'm trying to figure out what Roberts was working when
he was killed, and I'm hitting a brick wall."

"One erected by my boss?"

"I don't want to be insubordinate."

"That's one of your best qualities," James said in his grav-
elly voice. "The chief didn't bring me into the loop when he
assigned Farrington to Intel."

"They're hiding something," Sinclair offered.

"Some units report directly to the chief. IAD and Intel
are two of them. I get involved with most of the IAD cases
since they generally involve officers assigned to patrol and other
operational units. I also get involved in most of what Intel's
doing because it's related to operations, but there are some investigations or inquiries I'm not privy to."

"Such as Intel case number D-eighty-four?"

"How do you know about that?"

At that moment, Sinclair feared he'd made a huge miscalculation. James was the number two in the department after all. He owed his position to Brown and thus his total loyalty. "Look, Chief, I'm just searching for the truth—trying to find out who killed one of our own and why—but they're shutting me out."

"You didn't answer my question."

He couldn't squirm out of this. If James told Brown he was disregarding the order to leave this alone, he was finished. But he needed to trust someone. "Roberts wrote the number on his overtime slips citing surveillance and meetings every Friday night and usually another evening for the last few months."

"You obviously don't want me to mention that you know about D-eighty-four, do you?"

"No, sir."

"Then I never said what I'm about to tell you."

Sinclair nodded.

"I met with Phil once a week or so, usually when he delivered his unit's time sheets and overtime slips to my admin. I asked him about the case since I noticed all the overtime he was submitting on it. He said it was one of the top-secret-I'd-have-to-kill-you-if-I-told-you cases, and if I preferred, he could submit his overtime directly to the chief. I told him I'd ask the chief about it myself. When I did, the chief told me the investigation was between him and Roberts, and he would tell me about it when the time was right."

"And the time hasn't been right yet?"

"Guess not," James said. "What makes you think this has something to do with his murder? I thought the Savage Simbas were responsible."

"We have one likely suspect based on fingerprints, but there's no motive. Besides, if Phil was working some investigation involving them, Fletcher would've known about it."

"Unless Phil was doing something deeper on the Simbas and that's what D-eighty-four was about."

"I guess that's possible, but if so, why would the chief with-hold that information from me? Would he really let a cop killer walk?"

James studied his shoes for a moment. "The chief is a lot of things, but not that."

"I've been doing this long enough to know that people lie and withhold the truth for all kinds of reasons. One of those is because they're responsible for the crime. I'm not saying the chief's responsible, but he might be withholding a key piece of the puzzle without even knowing it."

"I'll ask him again about D-eighty-four. On another note, I've been asked to give the main speech—I guess they call it the eulogy—at Phil's funeral since I was his day-to-day supervisor. That is, after all the political ones by the mayor, the chief, the attorney general, and anyone else from Sacramento that shows up. You two were partners for a long time, so I thought you might like to say a few words."

"I don't think so," Sinclair said. "I want to devote all my focus to solving his murder."

"Understood. And, Matt, I know no one will prevent you from looking under all the rocks to find the truth." James slammed his car door. "Just don't kick the rocks over and cause a rockslide if you can quietly peek under them when no one's looking."

Chapter 19

Braddock arrived in the office shortly before eight. Once she sat down at her desk with a cup of coffee, Sinclair told her about his motorcycle chase and his conversation with Assistant Chief James.

"It looks like we have an ally," she said.

"I'd like to think so," Sinclair said, "but you don't keep the number-two job in the department by going against the chief of police."

"Is that what it's come down to—me and you against the police chief and figuring out which side everyone else is on?"

"It seems that way."

"You're scaring me, Matt," Braddock said. "I used to think everyone with a badge was one of the good guys. Do you think we can trust him?"

"He puts on the knuckle-dragger, former-SWAT-cop facade, but he's politically savvy. Has to be to survive at his level. But I think he'll do what's right if it comes down to it."

"Sort of like you," she said.

"The only difference is I really am just a knuckle-dragger. It's not a facade."

"And your idea of playing politics is telling superiors no offense intended before you tell them they're assholes."

Sinclair went back to typing up his investigative follow-up report. It was a constant battle trying to stay caught up. The more work he did on a case, the more he had to document. It almost made him reluctant to run down new leads and interview more people, knowing he'd have to spend more time pecking away on his keyboard.

At nine o'clock, Jankowski rushed into the office out of breath.

"Damn, Sinclair," he bellowed. "I heard that fat fuck Tiny outran you last night."

"Looks like you've been doing some running of your own," Sinclair replied.

"Just got a judge's signature on a search warrant. I'm headed over to our favorite security company to ruin someone's day."

"I thought Eastman and his partners would want to help out their local police."

"I got tired of waiting. We'll see how their tune changes once I take their computer and all their files."

"Have you had any luck talking to any of the other Simbas?"

"Sanchez and I are still dragging them in and grilling them when we can, but nobody's saying anything about Roberts's murder. Either they really don't know anything and Gibbs acted on his own and killed a cop for some reason that didn't involve the club or they're great liars."

"Do you need me to come along?"

"No, I'm sure you've got plenty to keep yourself busy. San-chez and I can handle it. All we're gonna do is bring a shitload of paperwork back here and go through it to see if something jumps out at us. I'm mostly interested in their employee roster and what kind of work they were doing for the wife of your favorite city councilman. We might find something to pressure someone to talk."

Sinclair's phone rang. It was the assistant chief's adminis-trative assistant, who said James wanted to see him. He and

Braddock took the elevator to the eighth floor, where the admin waved them right into James's office.

"Close the door and grab a seat." Once they were situated in the two guest chairs in front of his desk, James said, "I got a call from someone at City Hall asking what I knew about Eastman Security."

Sinclair didn't know how much James knew about Eastman's connection to the Savage Simbas murder. Maloney typically briefed the CID captain on normal cases, and the captain would brief the DC Investigations, the deputy chief responsible for criminal investigations if they were important enough. The DC would brief the chief and assistant chief on big cases or those in which the media was interested. But this was different. The chief was bypassing the chain of command and going directly to Maloney for updates, which probably left those in between out of the loop. Sinclair couldn't determine if James was fishing for information or if he was trying to be helpful. "What did you tell him?"

"What I normally do when it's obvious someone's trying to use the department to eliminate a business or political rival—I asked if there was something I should know."

Sinclair grinned. Although James had never been a major crimes investigator, he thought like one—gather information from people without giving up any more than necessary.

James continued, "This person said we should speak to Mrs. Hattie Armstrong, the owner of SFBay Security, who would be able to tell us about Eastman Security Company being responsible for a recent murder. Does any of this mean anything to you?"

Even if James was out of the loop, there was no reason to withhold this information from him. "Animal, the Savage Simba sergeant-at-arms who shot Shane Gibbs in the bar, worked for Eastman Security and was probably a part owner."

James slowly nodded, as if he already knew. Or maybe he wanted Sinclair to think he knew. "What do you know about SFBay Security?"

Sinclair glanced out the window, the same view as from the police chief's office, just through a smaller window. The sun illuminated the tops of a few of the high-rise buildings. In a few minutes, the ground fog would dissipate enough for the sun to bathe the entirety of the buildings in light. "Is there something about them you'd like me to know?"

James chuckled. "Smart ass."

"I never heard of them until a few years ago when all of a sudden there were new shoulder patches on the security guards at City Hall and other city properties," Sinclair said. "That's really all I know."

"Years ago, the city contracted with the large national security companies for uniformed security at city venues. Then came new city contracting rules to help disadvantaged companies. Those bidding for city goods and services got a bid discount or credit if their company was female owned, minority owned, or locally based. It was cumulative, so if a company was owned by a black woman with an Oakland address, they could overbid another company, maybe by as much as ten percent, and still get the contract."

"Quite an advantage," Braddock said.

James leaned back in his desk chair. "One would think that if a newly formed Oakland company had no experience in this particular field, it could never win the contract; however, some people in the know said it often made no difference. Once the contracting and purchasing department did their due diligence on new contract bids, they would submit their recommendation to the city council for large contracts such as this, and they would vote on it."

"I take it the head of the contracting and purchasing department is appointed by the mayor," Sinclair added.

"Actually, by the city administrator, who's appointed by the mayor," James said. "Of course, there's supposed to be no political influence involved in the issuance of contracts."

"Of course," Braddock said. "But how could someone with no security experience actually run an operation like that if they did happen to win the contract?"

"As soon as they're selected, they hire a security manager, such as the one that had the previous city contract."

"I imagine that since the security guards with the old company would be laid off as soon as the company's contract expired, the new company could hire those people," Sinclair said. "They already know how to do the job, so there'd be a seamless transition."

"So the same people are doing the same work, only a new person at the top is making a greater profit," Braddock said.

"Now you understand city of Oakland contracting one-oh-one," James said. "It's a lot more involved, but that's the basics."

"Are you're telling me that's how SFBay got their contract?" Sinclair asked.

"All I know is shortly after our current mayor took office three and a half years ago, the city council approved their contract."

"Who is this Hattie Armstrong?" Sinclair asked.

"A very pleasant woman," James said. "She's been very responsive and cooperative to the department. From what I understand, she was a teacher's aide at one of the middle schools in Oakland years ago. After that, she was a paid children's advocate for a nonprofit organization that the school district hired to tutor children in reading. Early in the mayor's political career, he was on the school board and took notice of Mrs. Armstrong's program. The board gave her a position in the district office running after-school reading programs for children."

"From teacher's aide and tutor to directing security for City Hall." Braddock shook her head in disbelief.

"What do you want us to do?" Sinclair asked.

"I have no dog in this fight. If you think Hattie might know something useful, talk to her."

"Can I trust what she says?"

"We all know that come November, there'll be a new mayor. When that happens, alliances will change. Department heads will jockey for position with the new mayor. City councilmembers will form new voting blocs. People with sizable contracts like Hattie are jockeying for position already. If they can knock out some of their competitors before the new mayor comes in, they have a better chance of continuing their gravy train."

"Why is she worried Eastman Security might win the city contract?" Sinclair asked.

"In a perfect world, it would be because they're the best and least expensive company for the job. But this is Oakland, so you need to look at the people who make up the company and find out who's connected to someone in the contracting and purchasing department or the city councilmembers who will control the voting bloc next year."

Chapter 20

After researching SFBay Security and Hattie Armstrong, Sinclair and Braddock walked two blocks to SFBay Security's office, located in one of the restored Victorian buildings between the PAB and City Hall. Floor-to-ceiling glass walls separated Armstrong's private office from the outer room that contained six workstations, half of which were occupied.

Her driver's license information showed her to be fifty-eight, five foot six, and one hundred sixty pounds. Stuffed into a black knee-length skirt and white blouse with ruffles, she looked like two pounds of sausage in a one-pound casing. "I never imagined Chief Brown would send two of his detectives so quickly," she said.

She offered them chairs at a round conference table in the corner of her office and slowly lowered herself into one of the chairs. Sinclair recognized the play of showing your visitors they were equals by leaving your desk and sitting with them. He felt the need to make it clear she didn't have the power to pick up the phone and have two detectives summoned to her office. "We work homicide, Ms. Armstrong. If you have information about a murder, we're interested."

"No Ms. for me, sergeants. I'm proud to be a married woman, so call me Mrs. Armstrong, or better yet, Hattie."

"Very well, Mrs. Armstrong," Sinclair said. "What can you tell us?"

"The gentleman who killed the young man in the bar, Reginald Clement, is a member of the Savage Simbas gang, and he not only works as a security guard for Eastman security but also is one of the owners."

"The state private patrol license says Silas Eastman is the owner."

"Do you think the Bureau of Security and Investigative Services would approve a licensee who was in their organized crime files as a member of an outlaw motorcycle gang?" she asked.

"I'm just a homicide investigator," Sinclair said. "You probably know more about that than I do. How do you know Mr. Clement is an owner?"

"Just like police officers, good security officers are trained observers and listeners. They need to be to prevent crime at places like City Hall. They also pick up other tidbits of information. If you were to go to City Hall and look at the city business permits, you might find Mr. Clement's name on the business permit for Eastman Security, along with a young lady named Tina Freeman."

"Who is Tina Freeman?" Sinclair asked.

"I'm surprised that name doesn't mean anything to you." She sat up straight in her chair and pulled her shoulders back. "She's what bikers call an old lady. She's the old lady of Pops, the president of the Savage Simbas."

Sinclair let it sink in for a moment. It was interesting, but his first thought was, *So what?* Although Mrs. Armstrong was trying to paint all members of the SSMC with a broad criminal brush for being a member of the club, the truth was most of the members, according to Fletcher, had regular jobs, and few had criminal records. That didn't mean they weren't involved in illegal activity. Law enforcement agencies suspected most motorcycle gangs were involved in drugs, guns, or other criminal activity in one way or another. But unless they could show club members had committed crimes, they couldn't prevent them from working as security guards or even owning the company.

"Interesting piece of information," Sinclair said, "but how's that connected to the murder?"

"I don't want to spread gossip. It would be very unprofessional, but you must assume my people hear a great deal of the goings-on at City Hall. Suffice it to say, Eastman Security is up to no good."

"I appreciate your assessment, but we need to make conclusions based on facts," Sinclair said. "I can't rely on rumors and hearsay. I need to talk directly to people who know something firsthand."

"You know that's not possible," she said. "I can't say where this information came from. Even though he's employed by my company, he works for the mayor, and anything he sees or hears is privileged information, just like the Secret Service with the president."

★

"Did you know that the Oakland mayor was once assigned a police officer as his driver?" Charley James asked Sinclair and Braddock as they once again sat in the guest chairs across from his desk.

Sinclair didn't want another Oakland politics 101 lesson. He already felt like an errand boy who'd been sent out to pick up a message, only to return and sit before his master and await his next task. James could've given him all the information he'd uncovered and the necessary background, especially the key fact that the mayor's driver worked for Armstrong's security company as a bodyguard with one of the very few concealed weapon permits the police chief handed out.

Sinclair shrugged, and James continued. "As long as anyone can recall, the department has assigned a police officer to drive the mayor. In the old days, he wore a uniform and drove the mayor in a marked car. I think the title might've even been chauffer. About the time of President Kennedy's assassination, the department realized those duties needed to include more than just driving. The officer was trained in protective service and began dressing in plain clothes. It was a very coveted job for an officer even when I came on in the mideighties. The officer had a brand-new unmarked car, his own desk right outside the mayor's office, and unlimited overtime. Even the police chief knew not to screw with the officer who had the mayor's ear. The officer usually picked the mayor up at his house in the morning, brought him to City Hall, and sat outside his office all day. If he went to a meeting, the driver took him. After city council meetings or social affairs, which the driver accompanied him to, he took him home. Fourteen-hour days were common."

"Sounds more like being an aide than personal security," Sinclair said.

"I'm sure that was part of the job. The last officer we had in that assignment was when Mayor Lionel Wilson was in office. I believe the officer's title was City Hall security, but he was the mayor's personal security officer and driver. When Elihu Harris was elected mayor in the early nineties, he wasn't comfortable with the cozy relationship Wilson had with a member of the police department. Harris had been a member of the state assembly for years and wasn't known for being pro–law enforcement to say the least."

"So he didn't want a cop with him who might report back to the police chief about what he said and did," Sinclair said.

"It was a reasonable fear. Although the officers assigned to the mayor were expected to maintain confidence, they still worked for OPD, so I wouldn't be surprised if information useful to the chief got back to him a time or two. Mayor Harris had such bad eyesight, he was legally blind. Since he couldn't drive, he'd had a driver of his own for years. In addition, there were rumors—rumors only, mind you—that Harris had a number of female acquaintances he liked to visit at night, some of whom had a fondness for certain illegal substances."

"That would've put an officer in an awkward position," Braddock said.

"Damn straight. Knowing of his reputation, the chief didn't object when the city manager suggested the city authorize a civilian position of driver to the mayor's office and allowed the mayor to appoint whoever he wanted without regard to civil service hiring rules."

"When did these clowns start toting a gun?" Sinclair asked.

"At some point, the chief at the time issued Harris's driver a concealed carry permit. That was like twenty-five years ago. When Jerry Brown was elected mayor eight years later, everything changed."

Jerry Brown was the mayor when Sinclair came on OPD. While previous mayors were mostly ceremonial and had little more authority than other city councilmembers, Brown was the first strong mayor. The city charter changed from a council/city manager form of government to one where the mayor was the chief executive instead of the city manager. Brown was a very hands-on mayor and a frequent sight around the PAB and local watering holes that were popular with cops. "I hear he didn't take no for an answer very well," Sinclair said.

"Right, so when he wanted Jacques, whatever the hell his last name was, to get a concealed weapon permit, the chief said, 'Yes, sir.' No one even knew what Jacques's position was in City Hall, but everyone knew the crazy Frenchman had been Brown's confidant and sort of aide-de-camp since the seventies, so no one messed with him. After Brown, the mayors' drivers were either city employees, part of the mayor's personal staff, or paid by the city as part of the City Hall security contract. Whoever it was got a concealed weapon permit, signed by the chief."

"And the current driver?" Sinclair asked.

"He's on SFBay Security's payroll. Rumor has it, he's a personal friend of Armstrong and totally loyal to both her and the mayor."

"It sounds as if Hattie is a lot more than merely one of many company owners doing business with the city," Braddock said.

"It's been said that whoever controls the palace guards knows the secrets of the kingdom," James said. "I doubt Hattie was expecting the mayor to end up with medical problems and leave after one term. The mayor, like anyone in a position of power, made enemies, and some of those will see his supporters as a threat. I'm sure Hattie's feeling vulnerable."

"And whoever becomes the next mayor might be able to influence the process and bring in his own security company," Sinclair said.

"Ahh, you now see the big picture," James said. "By the way, I asked the chief about D-eighty-four, without mentioning you, of course. He said it was nothing I needed to be concerned with."

"In other words, he wasn't about to tell you shit," Sinclair said.

James grinned and dropped his eyes to the stack of papers on his desk, signaling their meeting was over. They left through James's administrative assistant's office, and Sinclair was about to step into the hallway that led to the elevators when Braddock stopped dead in her tracks and raised her arm to stop him. Standing in front of the desk of Chief Brown's executive assistant were FBI Supervisory Special Agent Linda Archard and US Attorney Jack Campbell. A moment later, Chief Brown met them at his office door and escorted them inside.

Chapter 21

The sight of San Francisco's skyline on the approach from the Bay Bridge never failed to amaze Sinclair no matter how many hundreds of times he had driven into the city. To his left, the Transamerica Pyramid jutted 853 feet into the sky. To his right, a cluster of more traditional buildings, topped by 555 California Street with its fifty-two floors of prime office space, looked as if they rose from the waters of the San Francisco Bay.

They'd been traveling in silence for most of the drive. Braddock had voiced her objections to his plan, but eventually, she acquiesced. It was the next logical step. All the evidence pointed in this direction. The person who absolutely knew who killed Phil, Shane Gibbs, was dead. Sinclair suspected Animal killed him over something having to do with Phil's murder, but Animal lawyered up and wouldn't be talking. If Tiny hadn't gotten away after the crazy motorcycle chase, he might've been able to shed some light on the murder, but Sinclair couldn't sit on his ass waiting for him to be caught. Pops, the SSMC president, had already told Jankowski to shove it when they tried to interview him, and it was futile to try to talk to him again unless they had a hammer over him to induce him to talk. Even then, Pops might not know anything about Phil's murder.

If Animal was supposed to have been working security for Maureen Yates the night Phil was killed, she could tell Sinclair what kind of work he was doing for her and why he didn't show up. It might have some connection to Phil. Assistant Chief James was nudging Sinclair in this direction. The fact that SFBay Security was worried about Eastman Security grabbing their lucrative city contract and Animal was working an East-man security job for Maureen Yates, the wife of the likely new mayor, wasn't lost on him. Although Sinclair didn't believe Phil was murdered over something as minor as a security contract with the city, he'd seen his share of senseless killings in Oakland over much less.

The sight of Archard and Campbell entering the chief's office had caused his stomach to twist in his gut. The last he saw them was when he'd been lying in a hospital bed after nearly being blown to bits at the Caldecott Academy last December. Archard was a mystery to him. She first appeared when Sinclair had done the escort service sting. It had been obvious that she and Phil had been working together for a while, but she didn't work gangs for the FBI as Phil claimed. Sinclair had talked to the gang units at every Bay Area police department, and none had heard of her. The US attorney for Northern California was an important man—a presidential appointee with enormous power. If he wanted to talk to Oakland's police chief, he could summon him to his palatial office in San Francisco's federal courthouse. Him going to the police chief's office made no sense. Although Campbell had congratulated him as he lay in the hospital bed last year, Sinclair remembered vividly Camp-bell's warning a few days earlier to back off from his pursuit of the escort service angle. Warning? No, it was without question a threat.

Braddock understood as well as he did that they were headed into the same career-ending rabbit hole as before, only deeper. They both wondered if James would rescue them if they went too far or if he would merely kick dirt over their graves. Although

Braddock had suggested they bring Maloney in on what they were doing, they both knew this had gone well above the lieutenant's level. All Maloney could do was stop them himself or pass it up the chain of command for permission, which would never be granted. It was best to keep him out of it, if for no other reason than him maybe surviving the shitstorm they were about to start if Maureen Yates decided to call the chief.

Sinclair parked their Crown Vic in a yellow zone on the side of the glass-and-steel office building, hung the radio mic from the mirror, and placed his business card on the dash. Posters of ad campaigns for Wells Fargo Bank, Bechtel Construction, Del Monte Foods, Gap, and Pottery Barn adorned the walls of the lobby of Yates Associates. When the receptionist told them Mrs. Yates never sees people without an appointment, Sinclair insisted she tell her Sergeants Sinclair and Braddock needed to talk to her about a series of murders. Five minutes later, a tall, thin woman dressed in khaki pants and a cotton sweater guided them past open workstations interspersed with conference tables to a glass-walled corner office.

Maureen Yates came around her desk, a huge plate-glass table with two oversized computer monitors on one side and piles of papers, photos, and posters covering the rest. Although Sinclair's research showed she was ten years older than Preston's forty years, she looked even older. She had a small chest, wide hips, and a long face with shallow cheeks. Her hair hung limply to her shoulders, looking as if someone had tried to either add body to her straight hair or straighten her curly hair.

"What a pleasant surprise," she said in a flat voice. "Every time I think of your heroic actions at that school in Oakland, I get goose bumps."

"Thanks for seeing us," Sinclair said.

"I wish you would've called first."

Sure she did, so she could be unavailable or have time to prepare herself for their questions. "Homicide cases move so fast, it's easier for us to just pop in on people and hope they can make time for us." Sinclair smiled.

"Can I get you something to drink? Coffee? Water?"

The offer was an indication she didn't intend to rush them off in a minute or two. "Coffee would be great," he replied.

She waved to someone outside her office and then shuffled them to a circle of teal upholstered chairs in one corner. She grabbed a chair by the window. Sinclair and Braddock sat on either side of her. "Preston talks of you frequently. He's quite enamored by you, Sergeant Sinclair. He also speaks quite highly of you, Sergeant Braddock."

Sinclair wanted to laugh aloud. Her husband hated his guts because he wanted to unveil all of Yates's secrets for the voting public to see. "We got very lucky during that situation," Sinclair said.

"I think more than luck was involved. You saved numerous lives, and Preston and the rest of the city are forever in your debt."

A slender thirtysomething man dressed in dark slacks and polo shirt brought in two mugs of coffee and an assortment of sweeteners and creamers. Braddock began picking through the packets while Sinclair took a sip of his coffee. "How goes your husband's campaign?" Sinclair prompted.

"I'm happy to say there isn't much campaigning left to do. Our latest poll shows he has over fifty percent of the votes and the next closest rival is under twenty."

"Wow, his campaign contributors must be happy."

"Preston has many supporters in Oakland and on this side of the bay. They'd all be glad to donate more money if it was necessary, but yes, I'm sure they're pleased to not have to."

Maureen glanced toward Braddock, who had finally doctored her coffee to her liking. "I doubt you came here to discuss my husband's mayoral campaign."

"We're investigating the murder of a motorcycle club member by the name of Shane Gibbs," Sinclair said. "He was killed Monday night by another member, named Reggie Clement."

Maureen twisted the cap off a water bottle and took a gulp. "I've heard."

"Clement also worked security for Eastman Security Company," he said.

She took another gulp of water.

Sinclair continued, "He worked a security account that was in your name."

She twisted the cap back on the bottle and set it on her lap. "Yes."

Sinclair met her gaze, waiting for her to say more. She sat there quietly, alternating between looking at him and her water bottle. Most people couldn't stand silence, and by allowing the silence to build, Sinclair usually got some kind of response without saying another word. After two minutes, he knew it wasn't working with her. "Yes what?" he asked. "Tell me about what Reggie did for you."

"It was a private matter," she said.

"Private for you or for your husband's campaign?"

"Where are you going with this line of questioning?" she shot back.

"To be frank with you, Ms. Yates, I'm going wherever the truth takes me. Mr. Clement was scheduled to perform some sort of security services for you Monday night. But he didn't. Instead, he was in a bar shooting Shane Gibbs. I'm trying to figure out why."

"What does this have to do with me? I wasn't there. Mr. Clement clearly wasn't working for me that evening, and I wasn't at that bar. I've never stepped foot in it."

Sinclair turned in his chair to face Maureen directly. "What were you doing Monday evening?"

"Am I a suspect?"

"I don't know what you are, Ms. Yates, other than someone who's hiding something from us."

Her jaw muscles tightened. "What time are you referring to?"

"Well, let's begin at five o'clock and go from there."

"I was at the office at five," she said.

"After that?"

"I don't remember."

"We're only talking four days ago."

"I was at home."

"What time did you leave the office?"

"Six o'clock."

"Let's go step by step." Sinclair felt like a lawyer cross-examining an uncooperative witness who'd been instructed to answer only the question asked and nothing more. "Did you go directly home?"

"I commute with three coworkers. We leave at six o'clock. If traffic cooperates, that gets me home around seven. I went directly home that night and didn't go out again until I left for work Tuesday morning."

"We'll need the names of those you carpool with."

"I need to speak to them and get their permission before I do that. I'm not about to drag friends into some sort of police vendetta without their approval."

"What sort of police vendetta are you talking about?" Sinclair asked.

She glared at him and asked, "Are you satisfied with my alibi for the murder?"

Maureen didn't provide a way to verify her whereabouts. Sinclair had found over the years that friends often lied for friends, and allowing a suspect to speak with potential alibi witnesses first makes them more likely to lie. But he wasn't about to accuse her of involvement in the murder without some sort of evidence. "I don't believe you committed the murder, but since you brought it up, was your husband home when you arrived around seven?"

"I don't remember."

"It was—"

"I know, it was only four days ago. Listen, Sergeant, Preston does much of his work in the evenings. That's when his constituents are home, that's when the city council and many of the committees meet, that's when he has dinner or drinks with donors and associates. Most evenings he gets home by nine, but sometimes the city council meetings last until midnight in our crazy city. I don't remember what time he got home Monday."

People who went to great lengths to explain why they didn't know something were usually lying. And like most normal people, lying didn't come easily to Maureen. She wasn't good at it. If he'd had her in an interview room back in homicide right now, he would've pushed her harder. She would've gotten all indignant over being called a liar, but he would've persisted. Eventually, she would've cracked. But people lie for all kind of reasons, and they cover for people who might have no involvement in the crime. This was neither the time nor the place to confront her. Knowing she was lying was enough for now. When he knew more, they'd talk again. Maybe then, he'd have enough to get her into an interview room.

"If you want to know where Preston was Monday night, why don't you ask him?" Maureen said.

Sinclair thought about it. "Maybe we will." The second he spoke, he knew he'd paused too long before responding.

Maureen sat up straight in her chair and puffed out her chest. "He doesn't know you're here, does he?"

"The city council is not in our chain of command, Ms. Yates."

"Does Chief Brown even know you're here?"

"He's in charge of more than a thousand people. He doesn't concern himself with what every officer is doing every minute."

She stood. "I think we're through here."

Sinclair and Braddock got up.

"By the way, Sergeant Sinclair, I know all about Preston's little indiscretion with that woman years ago. He has told me everything, and I have forgiven him. I'm sure you've been wondering who's paying the child support and funding the college trust fund for that woman's daughter. You'd like it to be some sort of evil cabal so you can justify your vendetta against my husband. Well, it's been me."

Chapter 22

Sinclair was at his desk eating a chicken breast sandwich he'd picked up on the way back from San Francisco when his phone rang. "What were you talking to Maureen Yates about?" Lieutenant Maloney asked.

"A murder," Sinclair said. "That's what I normally talk to people about."

"Don't be a smartass, Sinclair. I'm sitting in the police chief's office, and he's the one asking."

Sinclair took a deep breath. "Animal worked for Eastman Security on a security account in Maureen Yates's name. Animal was scheduled to work Monday night on that account. Obviously he didn't because he was busy killing Gibbs. That leaves me with lots of questions."

"What kind of security work?"

"I don't know. Eastman said he didn't know, but he might've been lying. Mrs. Yates would only say it was private."

"She said you were trying to implicate the councilmember in the murder of Gibbs," Maloney said.

"That's bullshit. Braddock was with me, and she can vouch for that being bullshit."

"She said you were demanding an alibi from them both for Monday night."

"I didn't demand anything, Lieu. I was just trying to find out what went on Monday night that required a Savage Simba biker for security but later didn't require him because he was in the bar when Gibbs came in. I don't think it was a coincidence that that's when Phil was killed. So if I'm being accused of trying to determine what people were doing around the time Phil was killed, I'm guilty."

"Okay," Maloney said. "Don't leave the office. I want to talk with you when I'm done here."

The line went dead, and Sinclair gently replaced the receiver.

"Was he pissed?" Braddock asked.

"He was with the chief, so he was probably trying to show how cool he is under pressure."

Jankowski and Sanchez walked into the office with a muscular black man dressed in a dark-blue security guard uniform. They escorted him to an interview room and shut the door. Jankowski stopped at Sinclair's desk and told him and Braddock they'd collected a box of files and a computer from Eastman Security and the man they had in the room was an Eastman security guard. While Sanchez continued bringing up boxes of evidence from their car, Sinclair told Jankowski about their meeting with Maureen Yates.

Just as he finished, the office door banged against the wall and Maloney entered like the point man on a drug house raid. He scanned the room, pointed at Jankowski, Braddock, and Sinclair, and waved them into his office. Maloney removed his coat and dropped into his chair. He wiped the perspiration from his red face with a handkerchief.

"All three of you knew of Maureen Yates's connection to the security company, right?"

They all nodded.

"And none of you saw fit to tell me." Maloney was fighting to keep his voice low enough so those outside the office couldn't hear. It was causing his face to get redder.

"My fault, boss," Jankowski said. "It was my case, but I didn't think it was a big deal."

"I'm the one responsible," Sinclair said. "I made the decision to interview her."

"I knew better," Braddock said. "I should've told you."

"She tried to talk me out of it," Sinclair said.

Maloney raised his hand for silence. "I don't want to hear any of this *all for one—one for all* crap."

"What did the chief say?" Sinclair asked.

"What do you think? 'Who's running the homicide unit, Maloney?' 'Is there anyone controlling Sinclair, Maloney?' 'What was he thinking, Maloney?'"

"I didn't realize she was off limits," Sinclair said.

"Sinclair, don't act dumb with me. You were told to leave Councilmember Yates and the escort service client list alone. You knew damn well jamming up the councilmember's wife would get back to the chief."

"So I guess we're not supposed to pursue a lead in the murder of a cop because someone might call the chief and complain," Sinclair said.

"You know I'm not saying that. I want to find Phil's killer as much as anyone. Am I missing something here?" Maloney asked. "Do we think Yates killed Phil?"

All three of them shrugged.

Braddock said, "There's something funny going on with Eastman Security. Why would Maureen Yates hire a motorcycle gang member for security?"

"The guy she hired is the biker who killed the dude we're pinning Phil's murder on," Jankowski added. "That's too convenient."

"Are you three plotting to pick up Councilman Yates to try to force a confession or something?" Maloney asked. "Please tell me no."

"No," Sinclair said. "We're not that stupid. Not only do we have nothing on him right now, I know from our last dealing with him he'll lawyer up in a heartbeat."

"Okay." Maloney took a deep breath, exhaled, and wiped his brow again. "If that changes, if you even think about arresting or even talking to Yates—or any other city councilmember, for that matter—you have to see me first."

Braddock and Jankowski left the office, and Sinclair hung in the doorway for a minute. "He must get a huge hard-on bullying people," Sinclair said. "I don't know how you put up with it."

"That's the job of a lieutenant—take shit from the bosses and try to keep it off your people so they can do their jobs."

Sanchez was busy setting up Eastman's computer on an empty desk, running cables and power cords to an old monitor that had been sitting atop a file cabinet. Normally, investigators sent computers seized as evidence to a contracted computer forensics lab for examination. One problem with them was their speed. A rush job meant investigators might get information back in a week, and that was if the lab knew what they were looking for and where in the computer the data might be. Sanchez was the closest thing to an IT guru the unit had. As long as he wasn't shut out with passwords or other security measures, he could conduct a basic search of a computer a lot faster than the forensics lab.

The cardboard box on Jankowski's desk contained a stack of file folders two feet thick. Most had handwritten subjects written on the tab. Sinclair opened a few folders and found a mixture of computer-printed sheets of paper, handwritten notes, and scraps of paper.

"Yeah, it's obvious Eastman doesn't have the best organizational skills," Jankowski said. "Whenever he had a piece of paper he didn't know what to do with, he scribbled something on a file folder and stuck the paper inside. I looked in the one marked *Guard Cards*. That was the closest thing to a list of employees they had. A copy of Animal's state card and one for Pops and this guy, Jamal Pelletier, were there. There was a file on Pelletier with some time sheets showing he worked at a market in East Oakland, so we stopped there and picked him up."

"Any idea what he knows?" asked Sinclair.

"No, but seems like a good kid. I'm thinking we let Sanchez do his computer stuff, Braddock can go through the files, and me and you will talk to him."

"Sounds like a plan," Sinclair said.

Just as Sinclair was gathering up his notebook to join Jankowski for the interview, a thirtyish woman dressed in a pair of stretch pants and a loose top entered the office and called his name.

"Look at you!" Braddock hugged her, avoiding her protruding belly. "How far along are you?"

"Seven months"—Officer Julie Decker patted her bump— "but I feel like I'm ready to pop any day now."

"I've wondered why I haven't seen you on the streets," Braddock said.

"They've got me working in personnel until I deliver. That's another good reason to drop this kid early. I need to get back to real police work." She massaged the small of her back and faced Sinclair. "They asked me to hand-deliver this to you."

She gave Sinclair a copy of the department's emergency notification form. OPD developed this form years ago after a series of awkward mistakes when officers were injured or killed on duty. One time, a watch commander went to the address they had on record after an officer was involved in a serious car accident to break the news to his wife only to have the woman say they'd been separated for a year and was sad to hear her soon-to-be ex was still alive. When another officer was shot and killed on duty, his sergeant cleaned out his locker. After turning in the department equipment, he delivered everything else from the locker to his wife. Unbeknown to him, among the years of accumulated papers was a stack of love letters from a woman the officer had been having an affair with for a decade.

Sinclair scanned Phil's form. It listed Sinclair as the person to make required emergency notifications to his wife. Sinclair knew Brown was privy to this information when he decided to handle it personally. Phil also requested that Sinclair be the family liaison and clean out his locker if he were killed in the line of duty. The form contained several lines at the bottom of the form for special requests. In this area, officers were known to write things such as, *I leave my long baton, with its thirty notches, to Officer Jones. Use it well, Jonsie.* A few years ago, after three years without a pay raise, scores of officers wrote, *If I die in the line of duty, don't let the asshole mayor speak at my funeral.*

Written at the bottom of the form in Phil's handwriting was, *If I'm killed in the line of duty in one of those whodunits that we in homicide always love, I want Matt Sinclair to be assigned the investigation. If that really happens, let my old Traffic Div. partner, T. Kelly, be the family liaison so Sinclair can find my killer.*

Six years ago when they were partners, Phil and Sinclair had both filled out new forms and listed each other as their family liaison and the one to investigate their death. They figured their boss or someone in personnel would chuckle and make them redo the paperwork, but no one did. Damn Phil for not updating the form when he left homicide. Damn him again for not updating it after their falling out last year. He studied the form more closely. Next to Phil's signature was last month's date.

Sinclair handed the form to Braddock and looked up at Decker.

"He had quite a sense of humor, didn't he?" Decker said. "I'm sure that has no bearing on you being assigned his murder, but it is sort of ironic . . ."

"What does the family liaison duty entail?" Sinclair asked.

"You really can't do both. Family liaison is an eighteen-hour-a-day job from now until after the funeral. I ran this by the personnel manager when I learned you caught the case, and he said we would use Officer Kelly. I guess those two rode Harleys together in traffic years ago. Since it was specifically requested, you should be the one to clean out his locker. Not much to it. Turn in his handgun and other safety equipment to the range master, turn in other department equipment to the appropriate unit, and box up all of his personal effects for his wife. You're allowed to screen out anything that's not appropriate for his family, if you know what I mean."

Chapter 23

Jankowski had Jamal Pelletier sit in the center of the small metal table, leaving the chairs at either end for the investigators so they could triangulate on him. Sinclair had already looked at what the police databases revealed about him. Not much. A valid driver's license showed he lived in the flatlands of East Oakland, was twenty-eight years old, and drove a four-year-old Toyota. He'd never been arrested, which was a rarity for a young black man in Oakland. His state guard card was issued three years ago, and his only police contact was for a speeding violation two years ago.

Sinclair slid his legal pad from his leather folio to take notes while Jankowski took the lead. Jankowski led him through his basic information: name, address, phone numbers, employment. Pelletier answered the questions politely. Sinclair watched his facial expressions and body language for signs of deception.

"Do you know why we asked you to come down and talk with us?" Jankowski asked.

"I imagine it's about the murder of Shane Gibbs."

"That's right. Did you know Shane?"

"Sure, we were both members of the Simbas."

"How long have you known him?" Jankowski asked.

"A few years. He joined the club just after I did."

"Were you both full-patch members?"

Pelletier's face tightened. "Sergeant, so you don't get the wrong idea, I know what you probably believe. That the Simbas are a black version of the Hells Angels—a motorcycle gang that deals in drugs and runs prostitutes or something like that. We're not. We're a group of men who like to ride and socialize around our love of motorcycles."

"How would you compare yourselves to the East Bay Dragons?" Jankowski asked.

"They're an old-school club. They've been around for over fifty years, and most of their members are my grandfather's age. They do more drinking and socializing than riding."

"All your members are African American?"

"That's the way it is. Folks have been trying to integrate the races for generations. Still, it's human nature to want to hang with people like you. I think the only club that says they won't allow people of another race are the Angels. I'm not a board member, but if I were and a white or Latino wanted to join the Simbas, I'd have no problem."

Sinclair had expected a response like he'd heard too many times in this room—about how blacks needed to band together against the still blatant discrimination in the world. It was clear Pelletier wasn't a product of the Oakland streets.

"How well did you know Animal?" Jankowski asked.

"Better than most. He tried to help the new guys stay out of trouble with the law, find employment, go back to school."

"But he couldn't do that himself, could he?"

Pelletier took a deep breath and exhaled. "I don't know what happened. He must've just flipped. I'm sure alcohol fueled it. What happened that night was an embarrassment to the club."

"Were you there?"

"Not when it happened. I worked until five and went to the bar afterward for about an hour. They told me it was a surprise birthday party for Animal and we should all show up. I'm more into the gym than the bar scene, so I had a beer—yes, one beer—and went home. I have a wife and a young son."

"Why'd Animal shoot him?"

"I have no idea. People are saying Shane did something that disrespected the club and took a swing at Animal. That's all I know."

"We brought a bunch of club members in that night," Jankowski said. "Every single one said nothing—seemed like the code of the club to not talk with police."

"They were scared shitless that night. I heard about it. Police crashed down doors and treated the brothers like they were terrorists."

"We recovered a bunch of guns and some drugs."

"Whoever had drugs needs to go to jail. The club doesn't condone it. Possession of a firearm in one's home or a private establishment like the clubhouse isn't illegal. At least not yet in California."

Jankowski nodded to Sinclair.

"What's your club name, Jamal?" Sinclair asked. "The name on your vest."

"Rock."

Pelletier's biceps stretched the sleeves of his short-sleeve uniform shirt, and the extralarge shirt was tight across his chest. "Because of your physique?" Sinclair asked.

"They gave me the nickname when I was a prospect. I began lifting when I was in the Air Force. Found it to be a great stress reducer."

"How long were you in the Air Force?" Sinclair asked.

"Six years."

"Thank you for your service," Sinclair said. "I was Army. Actually, I guess I still am because I'm still in the reserves."

"Any deployments?" Pelletier asked.

"A year in Iraq," Sinclair said. "What about you?"

"The Air Force has shorter deployments than you guys. I did four months in Afghanistan and another four in Kuwait. Both on air bases, so not much risk."

"Just being there carries a risk," Sinclair said.

Pelletier smiled. "Thanks."

"Why'd you get out?"

"Wanted to put down roots. I was at Travis when I met my wife. We wanted to raise a family and not move our kids every few years."

"Why Oakland?"

"It's where we both grew up. The city's changing—getting better."

"How'd you come to work for Eastman?"

"A bunch of veterans work security, so I had no trouble getting hired. I worked for a few of the big companies. One day, I met Animal in the gym. He was a powerlifter and was impressed with what I could lift. We started talking motorcycles, and he invited me to take a look at the Simbas. Last year, he, Pops, and Mr. Eastman started up their own security company. He had big plans for expansion. Expecting some major corporate and government contracts after November. Animal liked my work ethic and the way I carried myself. Said he wanted me as a supervisor and later as part of the management team of the company."

"He sounds like a dreamer," Sinclair offered.

"I guess I am too. He said he made some great contacts with influential people in Oakland who'd hook him up."

"Any idea who these influential people were or what contracts he was talking about?"

"He said he had to keep it top secret to prevent other companies from knowing our business plan, but once he negotiated the contracts, we needed to be ready to hit the ground running. I trusted him."

"What about now?"

Pelletier shrugged. "I don't know. I can always go back to my last employer."

Sinclair changed the subject. "Do you know Bobby Richards?"

"Tiny? Sure. One of the best wrenches in the state."

"We hear he was with Shane before he got killed."

"I heard the same," Pelletier said.

"Do you know where they were or what they were doing?" Pelletier shook his head.

"Where would we find him now?" Sinclair asked.

"I haven't been back to the club or hardly talked to anyone since this thing happened. My guess—Tiny got spooked and went into hiding."

"Spooked over what?"

"If you believe the stuff you see on TV about motorcycle gangs, you'd think the club could be coming for you next."

"Would they be?"

"No way. Maybe the HAs do hits on members who break a club rule, but we're not the Angels."

"Where was Animal planning to get guards from if he won these big contracts?" Sinclair asked.

"He'd hired people away from other companies, but he was also trying to take care of the Simbas. He was handing out state guard paperwork to members and telling them when guard training classes were scheduled."

"Was Shane one of them?"

"I don't know. He could've been."

"What about Tiny?"

"No way. He's a good dude, but he's a fat slob. That's not the image Animal wanted to present."

"Who in the club would be likely candidates for him to recruit?"

Pelletier mentioned the names of fifteen club members who Animal might consider. Sinclair copied down the names and said, "I really appreciate your cooperation. If you hear anything, I'd appreciate a call." He handed him his business card. "Have you ever thought about applying for OPD?"

Pelletier smiled. "I'd love the pay and benefits, but it's not worth it. People on the streets hate you. No offense intended, but you've got to be crazy to be a cop in Oakland."

Chapter 24

Sinclair stood on the landing outside the back door of CID and lit a short Oliva, a mild cigar with a light Connecticut wrapper. He slipped on his sunglasses and looked at the list of voice mails on his phone. He called the number he most dreaded first.

"Hi, Matt," his mother said. "How's your big case coming?"

Sinclair never told her much about his work beyond how busy it kept him. "Haven't cracked it yet, but I think we're making headway."

"I've been reading the papers. Not much else to do when you're sitting around a hospital. It's so sad about your friend being murdered."

Sinclair heard in her voice, *It could've been you.* The papers were printing article after article about Phil and his family. Anything that stirred up emotions sold. The only thing that sold more papers was a scandal. Reporters would love to get their hands on information about his murder having resulted from a confidential investigation with political implications. "Yeah, Mom, that's why they need me here."

"Your father's awake and doing better. They get him up and make him walk a bit every few hours."

"That's probably a good thing."

"I know you're busy, but if you could make time, I'm sure he'd like to see you."

"Did he say that?"

The line was silent for a few beats. "No, but you know your father doesn't talk about his feelings much."

"How much longer will he be in the hospital?"

"They might transfer him to a rehab center in a few days or even let him go home."

"Sounds like he's in good hands. How are you doing, Mom?"

"I'm doing fine."

Sinclair called Alyssa's cell next. Since she left her phone in the nurses' breakroom when on duty, they mostly traded voice mails when they were working. She'd called when he was interviewing Pelletier, but he couldn't exactly tell Jankowski and his witness he needed to excuse himself to take a call from his girlfriend.

He told her voice mail that he didn't want to keep her on the hook for tonight. As much as he wanted to see her, he knew he wouldn't be getting off until late. If she didn't mind the possibility of being stood up again on Saturday, he'd like to take her to dinner around seven, he said to the recording. With twenty-four hours to plan it, he figured he could arrange for a two-hour break, unless they picked up a hot lead or something. He almost slipped and ended the call with *Love you.*

He didn't know where that came from. Hell, they hadn't even slept together yet. It had been a long time since he said the L word to a woman, and it wasn't a word he said lightly. When women heard a man say he loved her, they pretty much held their breath waiting for, "Will you marry me?" It was probably the stress of the case and the lack of sleep that almost caused the slip.

"You got another one of those?" Jankowski asked as he stepped outside.

Jankowski was famous for mooching food, drinks, or smokes from everyone in the unit. Sinclair handed him the cigar he'd pocketed a few minutes earlier in anticipation of Jankowski's visit. He eyed the label carefully before he clipped off the end and lit it. "You know, Sinclair, you moving in with that rich guy in Piedmont sure improved the class of cigars I smoke."

"Why do you still put up with this bureaucratic bullshit?" Sinclair asked. Jankowski hit thirty years with the department three years ago and could've retired with ninety percent of his salary. If you took away his overtime pay, he was nearly working for free.

"What am I gonna do, sit home all day with ole what's-her-name? I've got no hobbies. I'm already tired of the stupid TV shows I end up watching at night. I read one mystery after another about crooked cops who frame innocent people—it's enough to make me throw most books against the wall. Thousands of murder cases across the nation every year. One or two of the people we arrest are innocent, and they make it sound like it's an epidemic. Besides, my retirement check wouldn't include all the OT I pull in by looking at dead bodies and talking to liars in the wee hours of the morning. Without that cash, what's-her-name wouldn't be able to buy more clothes she never wears or replace all the faucets in the house again because the ones she put in two years ago are dated now."

A few years ago, a seventy-five-year-old sergeant retired from OPD with forty-five years of service, most of it working in uniform as a street supervisor. The man loved what he did. Even though Jankowski constantly complained, he loved the work. Sinclair doubted he'd stay a day after he turned fifty, assuming he survived the politics that long. He puffed on his cigar and watched the warm breeze carry the smoke toward the street. After a few days of the high barely hitting seventy—normal for June in Oakland—the forecast called for highs in the low eighties over the next several days. "What did you think of Rock?"

Jankowski positioned the cigar in the corner of his mouth and said, "The kid sounded righteous."

"If all the Savage Simbas aren't outlaws, maybe we should try to approach them again."

"I was thinking the same thing." Jankowski's cigar bobbed up and down as he spoke. "Of the names Rock gave us, we interviewed six of them Tuesday morning after our raids, and they said nothing. But we came down hard on them at the time because we figured they were major badasses. We might've had better luck with a softer approach."

Sinclair wanted to tell Jankowski what Assistant Chief James told him about the infighting between security companies, but he promised James he'd keep his name out of it. This case had too many secrets. Only James, Sinclair, and Braddock knew about the security guard company situation at City Hall, and Sinclair couldn't even say anything about it to Maloney. When he tried to keep Maureen Yates's involvement secret long enough to get the truth from her, that bit him in the ass the moment Brown and Maloney found out. He didn't know how Phil was able to work Intel, where just about everything he did was secret.

"I'm thinking that's the best direction," Sinclair said. "We do a work-up on the remaining nine and talk to them. Do you or Sanchez have a problem with working late tonight?"

Before he could answer, Braddock pushed through the heavy door carrying a pile of loose papers in her hands. "I found something interesting in the files. Eastman isn't as disorganized as we thought, or maybe his disorganization makes sense to me."

Braddock found a form in a folder titled *Yates* that had been filled out in handwriting that looked like Animal's. The form included Maureen Yates's name, home and business addresses, and three phone numbers. *Driver/Bodyguard* was written in a box labeled *Services* and *$50/hr.* in the box for *Rate*. Location read *Varied*.

Braddock held up a pink telephone message form. "I found hundreds of these in different folders. It looks like any time Eastman received a phone call, he wrote it down on a message slip. He then wrote some cryptic notes about what action he took and stuck it in a file folder. For instance, here's one dated Monday at three fifteen. It shows a call from Rosina Lopez, a phone number, and a note saying, 'Tonight, pickup seven sharp.' At the bottom of the form is written, 'Called Animal—OK.'"

"Who's Rosina Lopez?" Sinclair asked. "Name sounds familiar."

"I thought so too, so I did an online search." She handed him a printout.

Sinclair read a short article that appeared in the *Oakland Tribune* two months ago:

City Staffer Resigns to Run Mayoral Campaign

Rosina Lopez, the chief of staff to City Councilmember Preston Yates for the past three years, has taken a leave of absence from her city position to assume the duties of campaign director for Preston Yates's bid to become the next mayor of Oakland. Early polls show Yates as the favorite to win the election, taking place November 8. Prior to becoming his chief of staff, Ms. Lopez worked in a variety of positions for the city of Oakland and the Port of Oakland. Mr. Yates's campaign headquarters will operate out of his council district's community outreach office on Telegraph Avenue. When reached for comment about her future prospects, Ms. Lopez said, "The only thing I'm focusing on at this time is helping the citizens elect the man who will lead Oakland into its rightful place as the safest and most business-friendly city in the nation."

Chapter 25

Braddock crossed her arms and stared at Sinclair. "Assuming she was willing to talk to us, what would you ask her?"

"Who she wanted Animal to pick up at seven, where they were going, and what they were doing."

"And what if she gave a perfectly logical answer, like to pick up Maureen and take her to a fund raiser in Walnut Creek?"

"Then we verify the event happened and ask why Animal didn't show up."

"And she says Maureen had a headache and decided not to go."

"We can play this fucking game all day long, Braddock. There might be a perfectly reasonable explanation, but there's something here that doesn't smell right. And until we get people to tell us the truth, we won't know what it is."

"Animal knows the truth," Jankowski said.

"And he's sitting in jail on a murder charge with an attorney of record," Sinclair shot back.

"You want this to be about Preston Yates," Braddock pressed.

"I don't want anything other than the truth," Sinclair said. "I'd be lying if I said I didn't think Lopez's call was a request for Animal to pick up Preston Yates."

"And what?" Braddock asked. "Take him to a bar where a bunch of outlaw bikers were hanging out?"

"We'll never know if we don't ask her." Sinclair took a few puffs on his cigar. "Did you run her out?"

Braddock pulled the papers against her chest.

"Come on, Braddock, hand them over."

She shoved the papers toward him. Sinclair read through the LRMS printout, which showed Lopez was the reporting person on several crime reports, once for vandalism to the community office, once to report threatening phone calls directed at Yates, and once to report a burglary at her home. She had no arrests but had an atrocious driving record, with a half dozen moving violations over the past three years. The last page showed a thousand-dollar warrant for failure to appear for 14601 VC, a vehicle code violation for driving on a suspended license. "What have we got here?"

"Matt, the woman didn't pay some parking tickets, so they held up her vehicle registration and wouldn't renew her license until she did. She was stopped and ticketed."

"And she didn't show up for court, so the judge issued a warrant."

"If she walked into the department and turned herself in, they'd just give her a new court date and release her," Braddock said.

"The warrant calls for her arrest," Jankowski said. "We've been looking for a hammer to hold over one of these folks' head. This is it. She comes down to homicide and talks to us or we walk her to the jail in handcuffs."

"The chief will blow a gasket," she protested.

"Our orders didn't say shit about not talking to someone just because she has a connection to Yates," Sinclair continued. "Hell, he's a councilman, he knows everyone. Does that mean we can't talk to anyone he might know?"

"You've got the murder that matters, Sinclair," Jankowski said. "It's your call."

"We've been dicking around on this case for four days and gotten nowhere," Sinclair said. "We need some answers before

Phil's funeral. His family and thousands of cops from around the state will be there, and we can't say all we've got is a dead biker's fingerprints on a garbage bag." Sinclair crushed out his cigar in the pedestal ashtray by the door. "If she did nothing wrong, she should have no problem talking to us. That's what good citizens do. But this could go bad, real bad, and I don't want to take either of you down with me. I can handle this woman alone."

"I've got more time on the job that any of them fuckers on the eighth floor," Jankowski said. "What're they gonna do to me, put me back in uniform? Let's go pick her up and toss her in a room."

"Damn it, Sinclair!" Braddock bit her lip and stamped her foot. "I didn't hesitate to follow you into that motel room where a bullet was waiting for me. I was right behind you going into that school, even though we knew assault rifles and bombs were waiting for us. I'm your partner, so Jankowski needs to find something else to do."

★

Sinclair and Braddock reentered room 201 and took their respective seats on either side of Rosina Lopez. The last hour had gone as planned. Lopez had been sitting in the back room of the storefront community center turned campaign office in North Oakland when Sinclair and Braddock barged in on her. She resisted their invitation to accompany them downtown until Sinclair presented her with the alternative—ride in the back of a patrol car to the jail and sit with real criminals until she was processed. Once he settled her into room 201, the three of them then spent a half hour chatting and getting to know each other like people who had just met at a dinner party—except there was no food, the table was tiny, and the room needed serious updating. Just as Lopez was getting comfortable, they left her alone in the room for fifteen minutes.

Lopez was a tall, slender woman of forty with thick shoulder-length hair and a flawless complexion. She had a Spanish accent that she could turn on and off at will. "I know you're both very busy," she said, "but so am I, and I don't appreciate being locked up all alone."

Braddock smiled. "Sorry about that, Rose. We had to check a few things before we finished up talking to you, and since there are a lot of confidential investigations being conducted in our office, we can't leave the door open."

"How much longer will this take?"

"Not much," Sinclair said. "Since we're dealing with a murder investigation, it's necessary that we read you your rights. Is that okay?"

"Whatever. Councilmember Yates and I are both strong proponents of law and order."

Sinclair read the Miranda warning from the OPD form. Once she signed, he said, "I'm sure you're aware that we spoke to Maureen Yates."

She stared straight ahead, deadpan. By not denying it, she confirmed Sinclair's suspicion. He slid a photo of Animal in front of her.

"Do you know this man? His name is Reggie Clement. His nickname is Animal."

"I heard he killed another man, a member of a biker gang in a West Oakland bar."

"Everyone who watches the news or reads the paper knows that," Sinclair said. "My question is—do you know him?"

Lopez turned to look at Braddock, who was taking notes on a legal pad. Braddock met her gaze. If she was looking for a friend or ally, Braddock's blank face made it obvious she wasn't it. She turned back to Sinclair. "No."

Her first lie. Sinclair spent a minute paging through his notes, acting as if he was looking for something, but all he was doing was allowing the tension to build. "Mr. Clement worked as a security officer and driver for Eastman Security. Have you had any dealings or contact with Eastman Security?"

She stared at Sinclair, obviously trying to determine what he knew, and, therefore, how little she could get away with saying. Sinclair knew his face gave away nothing.

"Not that I can think of," she replied.

Her second lie. A soft lie where she could later say she had contact with him but it just slipped her mind. Sinclair placed a photo of Phil Roberts in front of her. "Have you ever seen this man?"

"I recognize him from the TV news. He's the police sergeant who was murdered."

"My question was have you ever seen him."

"Not in person," she shot back.

He placed another photo in front of her, this one of Phil lying in an unzipped body bag next to the shallow grave. She looked at it for a few seconds. Then she pushed it away.

"We have information that indicates you placed a phone call to Eastman Security on Monday shortly after three o'clock." Sinclair removed two forms from his notebook, filled out a few lines, and slid them in front of her. "This is a consent-to-search form, authorizing us to look at your cell phone. The second one authorizes the phone company to release call data on your home and office phones."

"Why should I sign these?"

"You said you had no contact with Eastman, yet I believe you did. Signing these will allow us to determine if you're telling the truth."

"I'm not about to let you snoop through my personal phones or those at the campaign headquarters. Who we speak to during this campaign is highly sensitive."

"The information will be kept in the strictest confidence."

Lopez's eyes moved upward and to her right. "I have nothing to hide."

For years, interview and interrogation consultants taught investigators eye movement up and right was a sign of deception. Sinclair never believed it. Determining when a person was lying or telling the truth wasn't an exact science. Eye movement, polygraphs, and voice stress analyzers had all been used with varying degrees of success, but none was perfectly reliable. Other studies showed that experienced police investigators, those who had spent thousands of hours interviewing deceptive people, could detect deception as accurately as the artificial devices. Sinclair didn't know if it was the way Lopez shifted in her seat, the way her eyes moved, the crack in her voice, or something else, but she was definitely lying when she said she had nothing to hide.

Sinclair smiled. "If you have nothing to hide, let's get your cell phone from my partner's desk, where we left it with your other personal items, and look at your call registry for the twenty-four hours beginning Monday at two o'clock."

Her eyes danced around the room. He had her backed into a corner. She had to either allow them to look at her phone or admit she was lying. Miniscule beads of sweat formed on her upper lip. She looked at him but couldn't maintain eye contact. She pushed her chair back and jumped up. "This is bullshit. You can't force me to do this."

Sinclair lowered his voice to a whisper. "You're right. We can't force you to give us consent, but we can and will keep your phone and apply for a search warrant. That way, we'll be able to download everything on it—phone calls, texts, e-mails, and GPS locator data."

She crossed her arms and snapped, "How am I supposed to function without my phone?"

"I think our murder investigation trumps any inconvenience to you."

"Do you know who I am?" she shouted. "I demand you release me immediately."

Sinclair had to struggle to keep from laughing. In this room, he intimidated people for a living. He had the power to control her freedom. He smiled. "Ms. Lopez, do you think you have diplomatic immunity or something like that because you work for a politician? Do you think your position gives you the legal right to lie to me? Do you really think that I'm scared of you?"

She spread her feet shoulder width apart and put her tiny fists on her hips. "I want to see an attorney."

Sinclair pulled a consolidated arrest report from his notebook and began filling it out. "How tall are you?"

"Five feet ten inches. Why?"

"And your weight?"

"One thirty-five," she said. "What do you need that for?"

"For the arrest report I'm completing. You asked for a lawyer, so we can't talk anymore unless you change your mind. Since you decided not to cooperate with our murder investigations, I have no reason not to book you on the warrant."

Chapter 26

Sinclair and Braddock exited the city jail, walked through the sally port, and opened the door that led into the back of the patrol division. Day shift workers were gone for the day, and the area was quiet except for a uniformed officer examining a red journal, known as the OTA book, searching for an open slot for an extra day off he could take in exchange for all the overtime hours he'd compiled.

They made their way into the front lobby. The patrol desk officer waved at them from behind the twenty-foot-long counter at the front of the kiosk.

"Do you think she'll change her mind and call?" Braddock asked.

Sinclair thought Lopez's resolve had cracked when she walked out of the elevator into the women's booking area. Female prisoners shouted from the cells down the hall. Others cried and wailed. The stench of urine and unbathed bodies filled the air. Lopez had looked at Braddock, as if pleading for her to intervene. Braddock slipped her business card into Lopez's pants pocket and reminded her that all she had to do was tell the jailer she wanted to talk.

"I was hoping the walk over would do it," Sinclair said. "If she makes it through the first hour, she'll gut it out until she's released."

"I wish she hadn't called our bluff."

"She did this to herself. All I asked for was the truth."

Sinclair stopped and looked at the black marble wall to his left. Below the oversized OPD badge, a seven-point silver star, high on the wall were the words, *In Tribute to Oakland Police Officers Who Have Given Their Lives in the Line of Duty*, etched into the marble. Names of fifty-one officers and their end-of-watch dates were engraved in the wall below those words. Six names had been added to the wall since Sinclair joined the department fifteen years earlier. He knew them all, worked with them, and even drank a beer or two with most of them. In the ten years before that, six more officers died in the line of duty. Soon, Phil Roberts would be added to the wall.

A black stand with the OPD shield on the front sat between the American and California state flags. On top of it was a leather binder containing summaries of how each officer was killed. Sinclair had read them all many times. Another page would be added. It would include a photograph of Phil in his uniform. It was up to Sinclair to ensure there was something to write beyond the fact that Phil was found buried in a shallow grave and investigators were still trying to determine how he got there.

Braddock squeezed his arm and gave him a knowing glance. They crossed the lobby to the staircase that led to a balcony, a sort of open hallway that overlooked the patrol desk kiosk and memorial wall. Sinclair trudged up the stairs. He'd been so hopeful that they could flip Lopez—that she would open the door to the secrets surrounding Phil's murder. Even if a judge signed a warrant for her phone, it might take the computer forensics lab a week or more to access the data, assuming they could unlock her password. From there, he might need to enter search-warrant hell, where he'd have to write warrants to get phone number subscriber information, wait ten days for the phone companies to respond, and then write more warrants to get call and locator information. He'd seen it take months and thirty or forty hours of work to track phone calls one or two levels out from the target phone.

They passed through the double glass doors that led onto the second floor. The sliding window where the Criminal Investigation Division receptionist sat during duty hours was closed for the day. They followed the hallway to the right and through the door to the homicide unit. Jankowski and Sanchez sat at their desks. Jankowski's face said, "Oh, shit!" and Sanchez's said, "Run for your life."

Sinclair took two steps inside the room and saw the reason for his coworkers' panic standing in Maloney's office. Even though his back was to them, there was no mistaking Chief Clarence Brown. Maloney stood behind his desk, a look of utter defeat on his face. He waved them in.

Brown waited until they crowded into the small office and then shut the door. "This feels like déjà vu," Brown started. "Didn't I tell you to leave Councilmember Yates alone months ago?"

"Sir, I—"

"I don't want to hear it, Sinclair. You're going to tell me that you're following the leads as they take you and this is murder—the ultimate crime—and you have some sort of God-given mandate to do whatever is necessary. I don't buy it. You've been out to get this man forever. Now you're harassing the people close to him to get at him."

"That's not true," Sinclair said. "Ms. Lopez is smack-dab in the middle of this."

"I don't care. I made it clear to your lieutenant that you were to get permission for any interviews or arrests of the councilmember or those in his circle from us. Did you not make that clear to him, Lieutenant?"

"I told him the councilmember—" Maloney said before being cut off.

"What part of 'This murder is solved' don't you understand?" Brown asked.

"But it's not," Sinclair said. "A man's prints on a garbage bag doesn't make him a murderer."

"Then you should have been pursuing the real murderer among his fellow motorcycle gang members rather than harassing city officials." Brown turned to Braddock. "And you, young lady—I expected better from you."

"It was my idea," Sinclair said. "She tried to talk me out of it."

Brown looked at Maloney. "Did you know what Sinclair was up to?"

"No," Sinclair said without hesitation. "I didn't tell him we were picking up Lopez."

"When this is all over, we may need to review your position as well," Brown said to Maloney. "This unit needs a strong commander—someone who can control this bunch of prima donnas."

"You can't do that," Sinclair said. "This isn't his—"

"I can't? This is my department. Sergeant Sinclair, you are hereby relieved of duty."

Sinclair's jaw dropped. He half expected the chief to pull him off the case, but not this.

"I am placing you on administrative leave with pay, pending the completion of an investigation for insubordination, for failing to obey orders from your superiors. Surrender your ID, badge, and pistol to Lieutenant Maloney."

Sinclair removed his police ID card from his wallet, pulled his badge clip from his belt, and placed them both on Maloney's desk. He swept his coat aside and gripped his Sig Sauer. "This is my personally owned firearm."

"I don't care," Brown said. "You no longer have police powers and can't carry a gun, so turn it over. If your lawyer wants to get a court order forcing us to return it, so be it."

Sinclair drew his gun, pressed the magazine release, and set the magazine on the desk. He racked the slide, caught the chambered round in his hand, and placed it and the gun on Maloney's desk.

Chapter 27

After Braddock dropped him off at home, he changed into jeans and sneakers and sat by the pool for a while, a thousand regrets swirling around in his head. He was pissed. Pissed at whoever killed Phil. Pissed at Yates, Lopez, and all the bikers who'd lied to him. Pissed at Brown for suspending him. Pissed at Phil for whatever the hell he did to get himself killed. But most of all, Sinclair was pissed at himself.

He didn't know if he thought he was bulletproof, that not even the chief of police could hurt him because he'd survived so many political squabbles or that because he'd always produced results on the big cases, they'd let him slide this time too. When Brown called the homicide unit a bunch of prima donnas, he wasn't too far off. Everyone in the unit certainly had an over-inflated opinion of themselves at times. To even want to work homicide, you had to. You had to believe you were up to the most difficult and important task in law enforcement. He didn't know where to draw the line between confidence and arrogance, but he'd defiantly crossed over to the arrogance side on this case. He'd heard people in AA describe the personality of a typical alcoholic as an egomaniac with an inferiority complex. That was exactly how Sinclair felt right now.

As he was sitting by the pool, his phone buzzed every few minutes with calls from Braddock, Jankowski, and Maloney. He listened to their voice mails. They all wanted to make sure he was okay. They probably wanted to make sure he didn't dig out one of his off-duty guns and stick the barrel in his mouth. Alyssa called too, wanting to know how he was doing. He sure wished Braddock would stop feeding his personal business to her. He didn't care if Alyssa and Braddock were best friends—they needed to find another subject to talk about other than him. At least when he told Walt he didn't want to talk about it, Walt respected it and left him alone. His only meddling was handing him Amber's leash when he headed out the driveway for a walk.

Sinclair didn't know how long he'd been walking, but the sun had disappeared below the trees. Amber was a perfect companion for the mood he was in. She heeled perfectly at his left side and sat whenever he stopped. She didn't care that he was angry or sad, as long as he walked and allowed her to stop and sniff things occasionally. And she never asked him how he was feeling or tried to fix him, unless she was intentionally trying to make him smile when she looked up at him and wagged her tail every few minutes of their walk.

He left her outside the Peet's Coffee Shop in Montclair and went inside to get a large decaf. When he returned, Amber was lying on her back receiving a belly rub from a young couple.

"What a great dog!" the woman said. "What's her name?"

"Amber," Sinclair said.

Amber rose and sat at his side. She looked up at him as if awaiting his next command. The man went inside and returned with a bowl of water. Amber lapped up half of it. "Bye, Amber," they said in unison as they walked down the street.

Sinclair sat on a wooden bench in front of the coffee shop. Laughter from groups of people seated outside a Greek restaurant next door filled the air. He smelled grilled meat from a burger place next to it. It was well past dinnertime, but he wasn't hungry. By the time he finished his coffee and got up, a closed sign covered the coffee shop's door.

He wandered through the streets, watching people on their way to restaurants and bars. Friday night and no one seemed to have a care in the world. He stopped in front of Crogan's. He had dinner with Alyssa there on one of their first dates. People his age and younger sat at the bar on the other side of the window. Well-dressed, professional-looking people, talking, laughing, and drinking. He wondered what it would be like to sit at the bar and have a few drinks and conversation with normal people—people who didn't know he was a cop—letting all his problems dissolve in a tumbler of bourbon. It had been more than two years since he'd had a drink. He'd come to grips with the fact that he was an alcoholic, that he would always be an alcoholic. At the end, he was either drinking, recovering from drinking, or obsessing over his next drink. He knew what would happen if he drank again. But at that moment, he didn't care.

Amber sat down, leaned against his leg, and looked up at him with her dark-brown eyes. He couldn't exactly tie her leash to a parking meter outside while he went in and got drunk. He reached down and scratched her behind her ear. The thought of having a drink vanished as quickly as it appeared. "Come on, Amber," he said, starting the two-mile walk home.

Chapter 28

It was 7:00 PM Saturday when Walt parked the Mercedes by the side entrance of the mansion. They'd just attended an AA meeting in Concord, where Sinclair heard exactly what he needed to hear. There were more tattoos and fewer teeth on the people at this meeting than he was used to, but the message of recovery was every bit as strong. The speaker, a large, gruff white man who had done time for manslaughter, said he learned he had a choice whether to live in the problem or in the solution and could either sit on his own self-constructed pity pot the rest of his life or take action to improve his situation.

Sinclair had been sitting on his pity pot for too long. Last night, he sat by the pool smoking cigars and thinking until midnight. He couldn't sleep and was outside with his morning coffee and another cigar when the sun rose at ten to six. He found a book that looked interesting in the mansion's library, but after twenty pages, he couldn't remember what he'd read. He flipped through the hundreds of TV channels but couldn't find anything that held his attention for more than ten minutes. Around noon, he called everyone who had left messages for him, apologizing for not calling earlier and thanking them for their concern.

Calling Alyssa was tough. He explained that he needed to be alone, but she didn't seem to understand. He told her he wouldn't be good company because he was too distracted by his thoughts. She said she didn't care. But he wouldn't change his mind. He cancelled their dinner date and said he'd call when he was better. He didn't want to lose her but was already feeling smothered by this relationship that wasn't even a relationship yet.

Amber was his constant companion. As Sinclair sat in his recliner, surfing through the various sports channels, she lay on the dog bed Walt had brought over yesterday. Every thirty minutes or so, she'd get up, walk across the room, and rest her chin on his knee. After he patted her on the head, she went back and lay down on her bed in the corner of the room. By midafternoon, he was done. He'd felt sorry for himself long enough. He couldn't change the past. On Monday, he would call the legal defense firm the OPOA contracted with and let the lawyers deal with his situation.

He changed his clothes and took off on a run. When he finished one lap of his three-mile route through the residential streets of Piedmont, he figured he hadn't punished his body enough, so he did a second lap. He followed it with reps of push-ups, sit-ups, and burpees. After a shower and change of clothes, he told Walt he was ready for a meeting.

After they returned from the meeting, Sinclair got out of the car and followed Walt inside the main house. When he smelled Betty's roast chicken, he was glad he had accepted Walt's invitation to join the two of them for dinner. He stepped into the kitchen, and Amber bounded over to greet them.

When he looked up from petting Amber, Alyssa was standing next to Betty in front of the long kitchen counter. She removed an apron to reveal an orange print halter sundress that gave her tanned skin a golden glow. Her long brown hair covered most of her bare back. "Hi, Matt."

His first thought was, *What the fuck are you doing here?* Instead, he said, "I guess you were also invited to dinner."

She stood on her tiptoes, and he leaned down to kiss her, feeling his own hesitation as their lips touched briefly.

"Since you cancelled your dinner date with Alyssa tonight, I figured we'd invite her to join me and Walt," Betty said.

"And then on the way back from the meeting, you agreed to join us," Walt said to Sinclair.

Neither Walt nor Betty tried to hide their conspiratorial grins.

"Alyssa came over just after you boys left and helped with the cooking," Betty said. "She sure knows her way around a kitchen."

"I grew up in a big Italian family." She shrugged. "Girls learn to cook out of necessity."

They ate at one end of the long table in the formal dining room. Walt poured water into crystal goblets and offered Alyssa wine, which she declined. Roast chicken, wild rice stuffing, green beans, and homemade rolls. It was the first time Walt and Betty had seen Alyssa since around the holidays, when she'd left for Italy. The conversation centered on her adventures attending to the medical needs of the masses of African and Middle Eastern refugees who had fled the chaos of their former countries. Sinclair enjoyed watching her face light up as she talked about the miraculous improvements made by some of the small children who were near death from disease, malnutrition, and dehydration when they first came off the crowded boats. It seemed like any joy or sense of satisfaction he'd felt from his job was eons ago. Everyone knew better than to ask him about his work.

After dinner, he tried to help clear the dishes. "No you don't," Betty said. "Walt and I will clean up."

Walt pushed back his chair. "There's a peach pie cooling on the counter that I understand Alyssa helped make."

"Take it over to your house," Betty said as she stacked the plates together and collected the silverware. "Go, you two. Scoot."

It was barely light enough to make their way down the flagstone path and across the verdant back lawn without turning on the lights. He cradled the pie with one hand and held Alyssa's hand with the other. They made their way around the pool in silence. The last time Alyssa was at his place was when she watched over him after he was released from the hospital following the explosion. To say he wasn't thinking about sex at the time would be a lie—he was a man, and as long as he was breathing, he thought about sex. But splitting headaches came and went for a week, and every muscle in his body ached. She never offered, and he never made a move. And then she left for Italy.

His plans fell apart with Phil's murder. Tonight, he had planned a romantic dinner, after which he would invite her to his place. But there was nothing romantic about the evening so far. He could only imagine what Betty said to Alyssa about his emotional condition when she invited her to dinner.

Sinclair liked women. When he was with a woman, she felt like she was the most important person in the room, because in Sinclair's mind, she was. But tonight, Alyssa had company in his head with the murder and his suspension. She had to notice his distraction. No woman wanted to be with a man who wasn't emotionally present, and Alyssa had told him too many times how she wanted their first time to be perfect. Besides, he wasn't about to risk rejection tonight on top of everything else. They'd have their pie and talk for a while. Then he'd walk her back to her car and get a good-night kiss.

They walked around the pool and through the French doors that led into the main room of the guesthouse. He set the pie on the kitchen counter. "Can I make you some tea or coffee?" he asked.

"Maybe later." She kicked off her shoes and sat on the sofa. "Betty's adorable. Reminds me of my mother."

"She's sweet and tough at the same time," Sinclair said. Alyssa knew of Walt's past as a psychologist and his time in prison, but Betty seldom talked about herself. "She divorced him when everything he had done came to light and raised their two sons alone. Ten years later, she saw the man Walt had become after he got sober and they remarried."

"I wish the kind of love they have for each other could be bottled." She sighed.

Sinclair sat on the end of the sofa, trying to figure out if he was supposed to respond, if she was trying to lead him into a conversation about love. The cool night air drifted into the room through the open French doors. Low-voltage landscaping lights popped on outside, as they did at dusk every night, accenting trees and shrubs and lighting the footpaths.

"I hope you didn't mind me showing up." She pulled her legs under herself and turned to face him. "I was a willing pawn in Betty's plot to drag you out of your isolation."

"I'm used to going off alone and licking my wounds when I'm hurt."

"And I'm used to surrounding injured friends or family members with people and nursing them back to health."

"I should feel fortunate to have friends in my life who care about me."

She slid toward him and kissed him. "I remember how hard it was for you to let me take care of you after you were hurt in that bomb explosion."

"I wasn't the best patient?"

She kissed him again, this time longer. "What's it like being so tough that you never need anyone?"

"Ask John Wayne. Bet he'd say it comes natural to us tough guys."

She laughed and touched his cheek. She put her hands around his neck and pulled him into her, kissing him again. He wrapped his arms around her, feeling the warmth of her bare back. Lean, yet soft and smooth. Her tongue entered his mouth, exploring, while her hand snaked under his shirt and rested on his chest.

Suddenly she stopped and pulled away. "Can I use your restroom?"

He nodded. She bounced up and disappeared into the powder room. So that was it. That was as far as she planned to go. She'll use the bathroom and ask him to walk her to her car. He cut himself a large slice of pie and returned to the couch.

She came out of the bathroom, shook her head, and smiled. "Do you like it?"

"I figured you didn't want any, so . . ."

"Can I have a bite?"

He handed her the plate. She cut a piece of the crust with his fork, speared a peach slice, and put it in her mouth. "Not bad."

She set the plate on the coffee table, climbed onto his lap, and kissed him on the mouth. She ran her fingers along his neck and into his hair as their lips met again in a longer kiss. She shifted her position until she was facing him and straddling his thighs. She reached behind her head and untied the halter-top, letting the front of her dress fall away.

"Looks like you're missing a bra," he joked, running his hand across her small, firm breasts.

She giggled and squirmed deeper into his lap. "Yeah, I think I'm missing my underwear too."

"I thought you were waiting for the perfect time and all that."

"Oh, Matt, shut up and kiss me."

Chapter 29

Sinclair had been sitting in the upholstered wing chair since the sun's first rays filtered through the bedroom curtains, alternating between surfing the net on his laptop, drinking coffee, and watching Alyssa sleep. Her dark hair was splayed across the pillow, and her face resonated with tranquility and peace. She was curled on her side, facing the window. When he was still lying in bed watching daybreak approach, she was spooned against him. That's when his mind began racing.

Because she had resisted sleeping with him for so long, he had begun to think maybe she didn't like sex. Nothing could have been further from the truth. On the couch, they acted like two horny teenagers in the back seat of a car. For a moment, Sinclair had tried to slow things down to savor the moment, but they'd soon reached the point of no return. Afterward, he looked down at her, propped up on his elbows as if his weight would crush her. She laughed. A deep belly laugh that was so genuine and uninhibited that he felt alive for the first time in months. He carried her to the bed, and she lay in his arms as they talked about their first date ten years ago and all the what-ifs that didn't happen because they both needed to travel separate paths to bring them together at that moment. His worries about being distracted didn't materialize. He was fully present with Alyssa, with no regrets about the past or worries about the future.

As he watched her sleeping in the early morning light, he still couldn't figure out how a woman could have a body so strong from her fitness regimen yet so soft, how her figure could be so athletic yet so feminine. They had made love twice more that night, each time more slowly, getting to know each other's bodies, needs, and desires. It was past two when they finally drifted off, and although he only got four hours of sleep, it was the deepest and most restful sleep he'd had in ages.

Her eyes blinked open. "So this wasn't a dream." She smiled.

"If so, I don't ever want to wake up."

"Why aren't you in bed?"

"I was restless and didn't want to wake you," he said. "Besides, I like watching you sleep."

"That's sweet. What've you got there?" She nodded toward his coffee cup.

"I'll get you a cup. How do you take it?"

"You don't have soy milk, do you?"

Sinclair laughed. "Afraid not. Regular milk or powdered creamer."

"Milk will work. What time is it anyway?"

"Eight twenty-one," he said, reading from the bedside clock.

She threw the covers off and jumped up. "Okay if I use your shower?" She didn't wait for an answer before scurrying across the room and into the bathroom.

Sinclair made a fresh pot of coffee, fixed a cup with milk, and placed it on the bathroom sink. He tried not to stare at her through the frosted shower door, her face under the shower spray. He got a clean towel and a new toothbrush out of the closet, placed them on the sink, and returned to his chair in the bedroom.

A few minutes later, she came out of the bathroom wearing just a black thong and strapless bra. "Sorry to rush off, but I promised I'd take my great aunt to mass this morning." She stepped into her dress and tied the strap around her neck. "I know, I said I wanted to lie around in bed with you all day, but—"

"I was the one who cancelled our date last night."

"Even if we had our date, I wasn't planning on this happening yet." She kissed his neck. "But I'm glad it did."

"You never mentioned you were a churchgoer."

She took a sip of coffee. "My family is, and my aunt loves to show off her nieces to her friends at church, so my sisters and I occasionally indulge her."

"You can go like that?"

"I guess you haven't been to Catholic Church in a while. People wear shorts and flip-flops in the summer. I didn't want to wash your scent off me so soon, but I doubt my aunt would approve of me coming to church smelling of sinful premarital sex."

"She'd probably have to go to confession for being related to such a sinner." Sinclair placed his hands on her hips and kissed her. "I see you found the toothbrush I left for you."

"Yeah, is it okay to leave it here?"

"Do you mean, 'Will you have an anxiety attack knowing a girl left something at your place?'"

"Something like that."

"I'm good," he said, kissing her again. "You can leave your thong behind too."

She slapped his shoulder playfully. "After church, there's some kind of family get-together. You can come over if you want."

"I think I'll pass, but can I call you later?"

"You better."

He walked her to her car, kissed her again, and watched as she drove off in her red Miata. He ate a large slice of peach pie for breakfast and was just getting ready to climb in the shower when his cell rang, showing the homicide number.

"Matt, this is Carl Maloney."

"Good morning, Lieutenant. I see you're working on a Sunday."

"I met Jankowski, Sanchez, and Braddock here early this morning to see if there was anything we needed to do that couldn't wait until Monday."

"And?"

Maloney hesitated, obviously deciding whether he should reveal details of an investigation to a suspended officer. "Jankowski and Sanchez are heading out to Santa Rita," Maloney said, referring to the main county jail. "They plan to interview a couple of informants and several Simbas who are in custody out there, and Braddock's going to finish bringing your case log up to date."

"I wish I was there to help."

"You doing okay?"

"As well as can be expected."

"Hang in there," Maloney said. "Cathy told me that you were listed on Phil's emergency card to clean out his locker and personnel gave you his spare locker key."

"Yeah, do you want me to bring the key to you?"

"The whole purpose of the emergency card is for a friend Phil designated to handle this. Cleaning out a locker doesn't require police powers, so your suspension doesn't prevent you from doing it, as long as you're willing."

"No problem. It's not like I'm doing anything else."

★

A half hour later, Sinclair sat on the wooden bench in front of Phil's metal locker. He unlocked the padlock. Unlike when he was a uniformed officer and changed into his uniform before shift and back into his civvies at the end of shift every day, Sinclair no longer spent much time in the locker room. He used it a few times a week to shower and change after working out in the gym or to change into a fresh shirt after pulling an all-nighter on a murder case. Some plainclothes sergeants and command officers probably didn't open their lockers for years.

Patrol officers didn't have a desk, and their patrol cars were shared with officers who worked the beat on other shifts, so their lockers were the only personal space they had and were often used to keep whatever was of value to them. Sinclair still kept his passport and personal papers in an accordion folder next to his boots on the bottom shelf instead of paying a monthly bank fee for a safety deposit box. He knew fellow officers who kept cash from off-duty jobs in their lockers, as well as expensive watches, jewelry, and boxed handguns they'd bought but never fired.

Sinclair arranged three empty boxes on the bench. Into one, he placed Phil's duty gun, ammunition, gun belt, Kevlar vest, and other safety equipment. He pulled a box for a Glock Model 27 from the top shelf. Empty. That was the gun Phil carried when in plain clothes, the one that normally resided in the empty holster they found strapped to his body. He pushed a uniform and the dress jacket to the side. He would keep that in the locker for Officer Kelly, the family liaison, to deliver to the mortuary for Phil's funeral. He folded the other uniforms and a few items of civilian clothes that hung in the locker and put them in the box destined for his wife.

Sinclair couldn't figure out why Phil hadn't removed his name from the emergency form. On his own form, Sinclair kept Phil as his family liaison for a year after they were no longer partners. Phil was his closest friend and one person who had never let him down. But after their falling out last year, Sinclair changed it to Braddock—someone he could trust.

Sinclair removed three cigar boxes stacked on the top shelf. The first one contained hundreds of mug shots—suspects that were wanted for a variety of offenses ranging from burglary to robbery and murder. Some dated back more than twenty years, when Phil worked patrol. Phil had written notes on the back, documenting dates and locations where he searched for the suspects and car license numbers associated with them. Many had notations of the date and location he had arrested them. Sinclair had a stack of similar mug shots in his locker—trophies of criminals he'd bagged in the urban jungle.

The second box contained dozens of pocket-sized spiral notebooks filled with notes from when Phil was in uniform. The most recent was fifteen years ago, when he made sergeant and transferred to CID. Sinclair recognized the last box from the day they solved the murder of a twelve-year-old boy who'd been killed by a stray bullet fired by a drug dealer in a drive-by shooting. Phil had splurged on that three-hundred-dollar box of Padrón cigars to celebrate.

Sinclair opened it. A stack of hundred-dollar bills lay on top. He counted eight thousand dollars. Sinclair removed a spiral notebook from the cigar box and paged through it. It was some sort of ledger, an accounting of money spent and received that went back five months. Weekly entries showed a thousand-dollar payment to *Sheila,* and other payments included *Hotel* and *Meal.* On the first of every month, entries marked simply as *In* were followed by dollar amounts in the thousands. The last entry showed five thousand dollars on June 1.

A sheet of paper lay at the bottom of the box. Sinclair unfolded a color picture printed from a computer of a gorgeous woman wearing a thong bikini, her skin the color of the lattes Braddock drank. She had straight, black shoulder-length hair and looked to be in her late twenties or early thirties. Scrolled lettering at the top of the page read, *Special Ladies Escorts—Sheila.*

Chapter 30

Sinclair and Braddock sat in the passenger seat of their Crown Vic in a parking lot on Embarcadero overlooking the Oakland Estuary. Sailboats and small fishing boats bobbed at the dock in the wake of a passing powerboat. Sinclair took a swig of his Diet Coke.

Braddock stared at the stack of cash in the cigar box and the photo of Sheila. "We have to report this."

"And say what? That Sergeant Roberts, the head of OPD's intelligence unit, was having an illicit affair with a call girl and paying her through some sort of bribery or protection scheme? That he was probably murdered by an organized crime syndicate or maybe by a pissed-off former lover of his hooker? Or maybe by his wife when she discovered his extracurricular activities?"

The connection to Special Ladies Escorts had caused Sinclair's stomach to tighten the moment he saw the photo in Phil's locker. It took him back to the Thrill Kill Murders last December. Dawn Gustafson, a former prostitute who was shot and hanged naked from a tree, had worked for that same escort service. It was on this same case that the rift between him and Phil began when his former partner sided with the Feds and police chief to keep the extensive client list and database of escorts from him. Even after Sinclair ended the lives of the killers during a shootout at a school, the police chief and Feds continued to withhold the information about the escort service's clients. Although Sinclair still held city Councilmember Preston Yates and business CEO Sergio Kozlov partly to blame for Dawn's death and had strong evidence showing political corruption ties between them, the chief had ordered him to drop it.

"We don't know any of that," Braddock said.

"What's another explanation?"

"Maybe she's a source."

"It takes an act of god to get a couple of hundred bucks from the department for an informant. And why would he hide the money in his locker? If you're running a confidential source, you document everything in a file, which you lock up in your office. The Intel unit is about the most secure place in the PAB. Not even his officers had keys to his file cabinets. No, whatever he was doing with this woman didn't involve police work."

Braddock glared at him. "I wouldn't expect *you*, of all people, to be so judgmental about someone's sex life."

"I couldn't give a shit about the affair. That's between a husband and his wife. It's the money. Women like this Sheila don't give it away for free, and Phil wasn't paying her from his sergeant's salary. He had to be doing something else to get the money, and I'm sure there's no shortage of crooks who'd pay big bucks to have the head of Intel in their pocket."

It wasn't entirely true when he said he didn't care about Phil having an affair. He had looked up to Phil. When Sinclair was struggling with a marriage that wasn't working, dating a TV reporter everyone knew wasn't right for him, and going out with a succession of women in search of something that was missing inside him, Phil was going home each night to his wife and kids. His family life seemed perfect, unlike the family Sinclair had grown up with.

Booze, broads, and bills. According to the academy, those were the reasons cops went bad. In Phil's situation, it appeared sex was the catalyst and created a need for money. Officers working vice, narcotics, or intelligence had plenty of ways to make extra money, and none of them were good.

"So you're in agreement that we need to tell the lieutenant," Braddock said.

A sea gull landed a few feet from Sinclair's open window and looked up at him as if asking for a handout. "This could be the worst scandal to rock the department in decades. They won't go through with a line-of-duty funeral if this comes to light."

"I loved Phil as much as you did, Matt. He dedicated his life to the city and department. I want to see him get the hero's funeral he deserves, but we'll all look like fools if it comes out that Phil died because of some off-duty love triangle or as a result of corruption and graft."

The last Oakland officer funeral Sinclair attended was for the four officers killed in one tragic day seven years ago, the year Sinclair transferred to homicide. Two motorcycle officers had stopped a man for a routine traffic violation when the guy, who was a parolee at large, shot them both. A few hours later, the parolee emptied an AK-47 into two SWAT officers as they entered the apartment where he was holed up. At the time, it was deadliest incident for the police since 9/11, and ten thousand law enforcement officers from across the country and more than twenty thousand people total filled the Oracle Arena, the home of the Golden State Warriors, for the memorial. Although Phil's funeral wouldn't be that large, thousands of police from across the state and many more thousands of citizens would certainly flood whatever venue the city selected for the memorial.

"Then we better get to the bottom of this before the funeral is set in stone and impossible to stop," Sinclair said.

Sinclair put his phone on speaker, called Fletcher, and asked how their unit tracked confidential informants.

"We've formalized the procedure since the NSA's been around," he said, referring to the federal negotiated settlement agreement, which stemmed from a series of lawsuits for false arrest, excessive force, and misconduct against the department fifteen years ago. "We have to initiate a CI file on anyone who we pay for information or who we use as a CI in a search warrant affidavit. Sergeant Roberts maintains the files in his office, so he knows the identity of all the informants in the unit."

"I take it those files are in one of the locked file cabinets that only Farrington has access to," Sinclair said.

"That would be right, but we each keep records of our own CIs."

"What about if you pay a CI for info? How's that handled?"

"The same as with you guys in homicide or in narcotics. We fill out the little slip when we want money, take it to Sarge, and he gives us the cash. At the end of the month, Sergeant Roberts hands out the little slips, and we fill out the big one-page form, which he then turns in to accounting with his paperwork to re-up our cash. We don't put the CI's name on it because it goes to accounting and too many people have access. Instead we just list our CI number and case number."

Since Sinclair was sure Farrington wouldn't allow him to see the CI files, he asked, "So accounting would have copies of the monthly reports?"

"I guess so."

"Do you think you could get copies of those reports for the last six months? Tell them some bullshit like you'll be handling this until the unit gets a new sergeant." Sinclair thought for a moment. "I'm trying to find out if Roberts was paying any informants. I'm looking for significant money, not just twenty or thirty dollars here and there."

"I'll ask to look at the reports we submitted, saying I can't remember if I claimed an expense or if Sergeant Roberts did. I'll jot down any CI payments he claimed for, let's say, fifty or more."

"Sounds good," Sinclair said. "Does that cute little Asian girl still work weekends in accounting?"

"Susie, yeah, I think so. I'm in the office working on a project for your partner. You want me to do this now?"

"No time like the present."

"Okay, and tell Sergeant Braddock the other stuff she asked for just came in. I'll print it out and sort it as soon as I get back from accounting."

Sinclair hung up and turned to Braddock.

"I was looking into Phil's financials yesterday on the off chance that he was killed over something in his personal life," Braddock said. "One thing stuck out, so I asked Fletcher to do a little research for me. I figured it was probably nothing, but with what we just discovered, it's all starting to make sense."

"What are you talking about?"

"In addition to his deferred comp, Phil has close to a hundred thousand in a family of mutual funds and money market. Any money that went into the funds came out of his checking account, so everything appeared on the up and up. Unless he has some secret account somewhere."

"He always struck me as a saver rather than a spender."

"I used his bank password, went online, and downloaded his checking account transactions for the past year. His OPD paycheck was deposited into his account every two weeks. Once a month, there was an automated transfer of five grand into their joint account. Assuming Abby matched that, I'd think ten grand a month could easily handle their living expenses, especially without a mortgage. Six hundred dollars went to the credit union for a car payment, probably on his Corvette. There were a bunch of small miscellaneous checks, electronic transfers, and an ATM withdrawal every few weeks for a few hundred dollars, probably just spending money."

"No big cash deposits or withdrawals?" Sinclair pushed, hoping there'd be something that explained the cash he found in his locker or the money to pay for his weekly visit with Sheila.

"One monthly electronic payment had me baffled. He made a payment to Wells Fargo on a Visa account every month. Sometimes it was only for fifty or so, but recently it's been for more than a thousand. Just before the payment, there was a cash deposit and a deposit of another city of Oakland check, much smaller than his paychecks. When added together, it was the exact amount of his Visa payment."

Sinclair was tempted to interrupt Braddock and explain what was obvious to any officer who'd worked an undercover assignment, but he wanted to see if she came to the same conclusion.

"I had a hunch and called Fletcher," she said. "As I guessed, their undercover credit cards are issued by Wells Fargo, and most of the guys submit their undercover expenses in time to get paid just before their credit card bill is due."

"That's a lot of money to put on your UC credit card," Sinclair said. "When I was in vice narcotics, some guys used their cards when their personal cards were maxed out or to hide expenses from their wives."

"Was that permitted?"

"As long as we paid off our balance every month, no one cared what we used the card for."

Braddock's cell phone chimed. She looked at the screen and quickly typed a message with her thumbs. Sinclair had resisted texting for years and still hated it except for quick messages he could peck out with his index finger. "That's Fletcher," she said. "He has the last year of Phil's UC credit card statements and wants to meet us away from the PAB."

Chapter 31

They sat at one of the classic red vinyl booths in the back of the Claremont Diner, a fifties retro building not far from the Berkeley border. "I hope you guys don't mind coming way up here," Fletcher said. "I wanted to make sure we wouldn't be seen together by any of the IA rats that scurry around all the downtown eating joints."

"I appreciate the risk you're taking," Sinclair said.

"Hell, I think we're all in deep shit if they find out what we're doing. First of all, I checked in accounting, and Sergeant Roberts didn't claim any CI expenses in the last six months."

With that, what little hope Sinclair had held onto that the payments Phil had made to Sheila were legit had vanished. The waitress brought coffee for them, and Fletcher ordered breakfast. After she sashayed across the black-and-white tile floor to the kitchen with their order, Fletcher slid a file across the table.

Sinclair pulled the stack of credit card statements from the folder, and as he and Braddock scanned the top one, Fletcher explained, "Everything looked normal until about mid-January. Beginning then, a dinner charge for fifty or sixty dollars started showing up every Friday night for different restaurants in Napa and a hotel charge for the same night. Beginning in March, there was only the hotel charge, but it was higher than before and varied by ten or twenty dollars."

"He probably ate at the hotel and charged the meal to his room," Braddock said.

"My thought exactly," Fletcher said. "Ever since March, he stayed at the same place, the Chardonnay Spa and Resort in St. Helena. Their website lists their cheapest room at two-sixty a night, which would explain a charge for close to four Benjamins after taxes and meals."

"Unless you're willing to stay at a Motel 6, that's not all that expensive for Napa Valley," Sinclair said. "I spent twice that for a room during a weekend last year." Out of the corner of his eye, he saw Braddock's furrowed eyebrows. He was about to add that it was before Alyssa but then decided to leave his partner guessing.

"It looked nice in the photos," Fletcher said. "A few blocks off the main drag, so it would be a good place to stay if you're looking for privacy from the tourists and San Francisco weekenders."

Or a good place for a clandestine affair, Sinclair thought as the waitress brought a huge plate of corned beef hash, eggs, toast, and fruit, placed it in front of Fletcher, and filled their coffee cups. He took a sip of his coffee and explained Braddock's discovery of Phil's cash deposits and city check that matched his credit card bills.

"Guys handle their bills different," Fletcher said between bites. "When I first came to the unit, I did everything by cash to avoid comingling my UC expenses with my personal money. When I received my reimbursement check, I'd cash it at Citibank, where the city check was drawn. I'd then assume my undercover identity, walk over to Wells Fargo, and pay my UC credit card bill. After a while, I realized how ridiculous that was."

"Do guys still sometimes use their UC credit card for personal stuff?" Sinclair asked.

"I never did. Too confusing trying to keep everything straight, but I know some guys do."

"How'd you get copies of Roberts's credit card statements?"

"I called the guy at bank security that we deal with. He already heard about Sergeant Roberts and was glad to e-mail the statements so we could take care of his affairs." Fletcher put his fork down and stared beyond Sinclair and Braddock, obviously trying to come up with a way to ask the obvious. Finally, he said, "I have no idea why Sarge was at that hotel every Friday night. He claimed overtime for Friday nights, but I doubt whoever signed off on his overtime questioned what he was doing. If it was for a case he was working, why didn't he request reimbursement from the department?"

The obvious answer was that Phil was submitting overtime that he didn't work, which wouldn't be the first time an Oakland officer did so, and the logical reason to hide dinner and hotel charges on his UC credit card was to hide an illicit affair from his wife. Fletcher surely had the same suspicion, even though he wasn't privy to what Sinclair had found in Phil's locker.

Braddock pushed her coffee aside. Looking across the table at Fletcher, she said, "I know things look plenty suspicious right now, but I'll bet once we find the answers to this, everything will make total sense."

Chapter 32

The picturesque part of the Napa Valley that most tourists asso-ciated with the famous wine-producing area actually began just beyond the city of Napa and continued north to Calistoga. On sunny weekends, the roads there were packed with convertibles cruising between winery tasting rooms, restaurants, and over-priced shops. It took Sinclair and Braddock almost two hours to reach the Chardonnay Spa and Hotel.

Before deciding to make the trek to Napa, Sinclair had called Bianca Fadell, the attorney who represented Helena Decker, the madam of Special Ladies Escorts. After they had arrested Decker last December, the organization shut down and their website disappeared. He wouldn't be surprised if she had started up again under a new name, but if he were to start inquiring within those in the law enforcement community who would know, the word would get back to those who had told him to leave it alone last year. Even though Bianca had her own agenda, which didn't coincide with the police's, she had felt partially responsible for what could've been the worst school massacre in the nation had Sinclair and Braddock not intervened in time. Besides, Bianca had made it clear she had the hots for him, and he wasn't above using that to get what he needed. But both her cell phone and her private office phone had messages saying she was out of the country for several weeks and was only checking voice mail infrequently. Nevertheless, he left a message.

With no other way to identify Sheila and figure out what Phil's relationship was with her, Sinclair suggested they go to the hotel. Braddock was rightfully reluctant, knowing that if she were discovered pursuing this lead, especially with an officer under suspension, without informing the chain of command, she'd suffer the same fate as Sinclair.

They parked on the quiet street and walked up a flagstone walkway and through a small garden to the steps leading to a wide front porch lined with rocking chairs. A thirtysomething woman wearing a white shirt and black skirt greeted them from behind a reception desk. "Checking in?" she asked.

Braddock smiled and swept her blazer aside to show her badge. "Afraid not. We're looking into a guest who's been staying here every Friday night for several months." Braddock pulled the most recent credit card statement from her folio and showed it to the receptionist. "His name's James Farron."

"The name sounds familiar." She began typing on her computer. "Has he done something wrong?"

Sometimes the best way to convince average people to cooperate was by letting them know they weren't looking into something as minor as a stolen car or forged check. Dropping the "H-bomb" normally did the trick. "We work homicide in Oakland. Mr. Farron is dead," Sinclair said, using Phil's undercover name.

She stopped typing. "Jesus! What happened?"

"That's what we're trying to figure out," Braddock said.

She looked at the monitor. "Yes, he checked in a week ago Friday at nine twenty and checked out at eight fifty the following morning."

"Was he alone?" Braddock asked.

"No, he had a guest." She continued to type and said, "You're right, he's been staying here just about every Friday night—a room for two—all the way back to March."

"Does it show the guest's name?" Braddock asked.

"No, only the person whose name the reservation was made in."

Braddock showed her a photo of Phil on her iPad. "Is this James Farron?"

"Sorry, but I never registered him. I get off at five, and it appears he checks in after that."

"Do you work on Saturday when he checks out?"

"I come in at eight. I see that he's checked out after that time most days, but that photo doesn't look familiar. Maybe his guest turns in the key."

Braddock pulled up another photo from her iPad, a headshot of Sheila, cropped to eliminate the sexy swimsuit.

"Oh, yeah. I remember her. I just didn't associate her with Mr. Farron. She's a sweet girl and always thanks us for a nice stay."

"Who would've been on duty when he checked in?" Braddock asked.

"Friday nights, that would be Karen. She's off today, but she'll be here tomorrow. Our statements show they ate at the restaurant when they were here. Maybe someone there would recognize him."

Sinclair and Braddock made their way through the small lobby into the restaurant. A dozen empty tables stood in the back of the large room, while the tables in the sun-splashed front of the room overlooking the porch were all filled by couples dressed in shorts and sneakers. A slender man with shoulder-length hair wearing a black apron greeted them with two menus. "Inside or out?"

That was the trouble with a female partner; everyone assumed he and Braddock were a couple. Braddock flashed her badge. The waiter said he only worked lunch, but Tess, who was busy serving customers on the patio, worked dinner hours. He seated them on the patio under a big umbrella and brought Braddock water with lemon and Sinclair a cup of coffee so he could maintain his caffeine level. A woman with short brown hair and a sun-weathered face smiled at them as she hurried back and forth with plates of food and pitchers of water and ice tea. Finally, she stopped at their table.

"I understand you want to know about a customer?"

Braddock showed her the photo of Phil.

"Oh, yes, Mr. Farron. A weekend regular. Veal picatta or the rib eye. And his"—she paused, searching for the right word—"ah, companion, normally has fish."

"What can you tell us about them?" Braddock asked.

"Not much, other than what they order."

"Do they have a favorite table?"

"Mr. Farron prefers a table in the back. Always inside."

"How do they interact with each other?" Braddock asked.

Tess scrunched up her nose in a puzzled look.

Although Sinclair was letting Braddock take the lead since she was the only one with a badge, he needed to get to the point. "Were they lovey-dovey, or did it look like they were having a business dinner?" Sinclair asked.

She was silent for a moment. "I shouldn't really be saying."

"Tess, Mr. Farron is dead," Braddock said. "He was murdered in Oakland a few days ago."

She gasped, covering her mouth with her hand. They waited for her to compose herself.

"I guess it was somewhere in between. They didn't arrive together but usually met in the bar. Their conversations seemed to start off serious, but by the end of dinner, they were laughing and having a good time together. With their age difference, I first thought she could be his daughter, but as I overheard their conversations, it was clear they weren't related. So I assumed . . . well, you know."

"What did you overhear?" Braddock asked.

"I try to be friendly with my customers, especially those I see regularly. It's not like I eavesdrop or pry, but one night I asked her, just trying to be friendly, what brought them to Napa.

She said that her grandfather was in a nursing home up here and she visited him Saturday mornings."

"From that you concluded they weren't related?" Braddock asked.

"Yeah, well, she didn't include Mr. Farron in the statement. He sort of ignored what she was saying as if it didn't concern him."

"Anything else you can think of?" Braddock asked.

"Not really. Mr. Farron always took the chair facing the door. His eyes were always moving, but not like he was looking for anyone in particular. More like he didn't want anyone to recognize them."

She handed the waitress her card. "If you see the woman again, please call. We really need to talk to her."

They returned to their car, where Sinclair asked, "What do you think now?"

"Tess said they didn't seem to be intimate."

"Open your eyes, Braddock. Phil wasn't the kind of man to act all kissy-poo or grab boobs in public. We've got him getting a room for two in romantic Napa Valley, having dinner with a woman we know was an escort, and then checking out the next morning. Other than a video of their bedroom activities, what more do you want?"

"What's an escort charge for an overnight?" Braddock asked. "The one we caught in the sting operation said two thousand dollars for eight hours, right?"

Braddock was referring to the woman from Special Ladies Escorts who came to Sinclair's hotel room when they were trying to make an inroad into the escort service to find out who killed Dawn. "A girl might charge portal to portal, which would be more like sixteen hours. Or she might charge less for a regular, especially if a nice meal and hotel room is included."

"So a thousand could be reasonable," Braddock said, referring to the thousand-dollar notations in Phil's pocket notebook. "With the room and meal, Phil would need to come up with close to fifteen hundred dollars a week—six grand a month—to see her. He didn't pull it from his savings. Where would he come up with that kind of money?"

"Maybe the question we should be asking is what would he have to do to get it?" Sinclair replied.

Chapter 33

They pulled into the fifth assisted-living facility on their list. Braddock had found twenty-nine of them in the Napa Valley. Sinclair knew several people from AA who got sober at one of the many treatment centers in the area, most of which ironically overlooked acres of vineyards. It seemed drinking, stopping drinking, and warehousing the elderly were the major industries in the area.

They'd shown Sheila's photo at the first four facilities, but no one recognized her. Sinclair was losing hope. They didn't even know if Sheila was her real name, and without her full name or the name of her grandfather, they were relying on someone recognizing her as a visitor—if what she told the waitress was true, that is, and not something she just made up to avoid saying, "The reason I come to Napa every Friday is my client prefers I screw his brains out up here instead of in Oakland where someone might recognize him."

Sinclair and Braddock entered an office marked *Director* at Golden Years Retirement Home. After identifying themselves, Braddock showed a gray-haired woman sitting behind the desk Sheila's photo.

"Sure, I recognize her," the woman said. "Sheila Harris. I wish all our guests had such dedicated and regular visitors."

"She visits her grandfather?" Braddock asked.

"Yes, Melvin Harris."

"Do you have an address and phone number for Sheila?" Braddock continued.

The woman tapped a few keys on her computer, jotted down a phone number on a scratch pad, and handed it to Sinclair. "Only a phone number. She's one of Melvin's emergency contacts."

"What else can you tell me about her?"

"Nothing much. She's been a weekly visitor since Melvin arrived about a year ago. Very pleasant woman. She brings small gifts to the staff and occasionally orders pizza at lunchtime. Usually stays for three or four hours, which must be very hard, considering."

"Considering what?" Braddock asked.

"I can't provide any information related to the medical condition of a resident, but you're free to visit Mr. Harris. He's in nineteen."

They walked down the hall to room nineteen. The facility was clean and absent the normal odor of urine and disinfectant that permeated many nursing homes. A light-skinned black man dressed in a long-sleeve shirt, sweater vest, and slacks sat in a recliner watching TV. Braddock approached, got his attention, and said, "Hi there."

"Hi there, yourself," Melvin said.

"I'm a friend of Sheila," she said.

"Who?"

"Sheila, your granddaughter."

"I have a granddaughter?" His eyes opened wide in amazement. "Do I know you?"

"My name's Cathy. What's your name?"

He smiled again and after a pause said, "Mel. What's your name?"

A dresser topped with photographs stood against one wall. One showed a younger Sheila, probably in her early twenties, standing on a beach. Sinclair used his phone to take a picture of it. A few magazines sat on a table next to Melvin's chair: *Sports Illustrated, Motor Trend,* and *Hilton Head Monthly.*

Sinclair picked up the *Sports Illustrated.* "What's your team, Oakland A's or San Francisco Giants?"

"Oakland," he said without hesitation.

"Who's your favorite player?"

"Ricky Henderson, the man of steel."

Sinclair showed him the photo of Sheila on the beach. "She's a pretty girl. What's her name?"

Melvin's face contorted as if the effort of trying to remember was too great. He took a deep breath and sighed. "Dennis Eckersley was the best pitcher to ever play the game."

Sinclair handed him the *Motor Trend.* "I drive a Ford Mustang. What kind of car do you have?"

"Cadillac Eldorado. Four-twenty-nine cube V-eight. Front-wheel drive." He smiled broadly. "What a car!"

Braddock picked up the last magazine. "Do you drive it in Hilton Head?"

Melvin looked at her, puzzled. "Of course not, silly—that's too far. We take a plane."

They spent another ten minutes with Melvin, but his thoughts gradually became even more scattered. When they returned to the facility administrator, she asked, "Was he able to help you at all?"

"He didn't even recognize Sheila but knew who played for the Oakland A's thirty years ago and what car he had in the late sixties," Sinclair said.

"That's not unusual for some patients."

"You said Sheila was one of his emergency contacts," Braddock said. "Can we get the names of other family members?"

"I don't want to violate any privacy rights, but the other emergency contact is his daughter-in-law, Charlotte Harris." She wrote a phone number on a pad and handed it to Braddock.

"If you want any more information, you'll need to have her contact me and authorize it." She paused and said, "You never did tell me why two detectives would drive all the way from Oakland to talk with a man who can't remember much from the last several decades."

"A man was murdered, and we believe Sheila might know him," Braddock said.

"If Sheila comes back to see her grandfather, would you like for me to call you?"

Braddock slid her card across the desk. "Without tipping her off."

★

Braddock turned the ignition and ran the air conditioner at full blast to cool down the car. "Should we call Sheila and see if she'll meet with us?" she asked.

"If she refuses and demands to know what we want to talk about over the phone—which she probably will—we'll never get her to tell us the truth. Plus, if she's involved in the murder, we've just played our hand."

"I can call the office. If Jankowski's back in, he can run her out for us and maybe get us her address so we can catch her by surprise at her home."

The police department consistently remained at least half a decade behind the rest of the world in technology, so they didn't have computer access to the department's crime networks outside the PAB. "Do we really want to involve someone else in this?" Sinclair asked.

"The longer we wait to tell the lieu, the more trouble we're going to be in," Braddock said.

Finding Sheila was important. She held the key to many unanswered questions. If they discovered Phil was on the take, they'd have to decide what to do with that discovery. But they first needed answers. "I'll work this angle alone if you want."

"That's not what I'm saying, Matt. I just think Phil might've been involved in something we need to inform the boss about."

"So you now think he was having an affair with a hooker and paying her with money he got from some crooks?"

"Come on, Matt. You heard the way Phil spoke about us to Abby. Yet you're still mad at him because he wouldn't support you instead of the police chief and the Feds on a case?"

"He taught us that we in homicide were the ones who spoke for the dead, that no more profound duty is ever imposed on police officers than when we are entrusted with the investigation of the death of a human being. But he let politics and his comfy position in Intel trump his duty as a cop."

"He's dead, Matt. Forgive him."

As a kid, Sinclair had looked up to his father, but his father had let him down years ago. There was no one in the department who he had looked up to more than Phil. But he too had let him down. "It doesn't matter how I feel about him," Sinclair said. "It's not like I refused to work a case when the victim was a dope dealer or a hooker. We'll do what we always do on a homicide—collect all the facts and see where they point."

"He's not just a victim. He was our friend—our partner."

Sinclair stared straight ahead and said nothing. He was mad at Phil for betraying him and betraying the badge. Why could he ignore the conduct of other victims—even ones who were killers themselves—when they were victims of murders he was assigned to investigate but couldn't set aside what Phil had done? It was their duty to bring killers to justice, because if people were allowed to kill with impunity, society would collapse. It was even more important that people couldn't be permitted to kill a cop and get away with it. Corrupt or not, the peacekeepers and law enforcers had to be off limits to the criminal element. He needed to shift his anger from Phil to those responsible for his murder.

"You're right," Sinclair said. "What do you want to do about Sheila?"

"I don't know what to think. She visits her grandfather every weekend and, according to everyone who met her, is a sweet girl." Braddock pulled her iPad out. "Heck, I know escorts are regular people with regular lives. Being a sex worker is just something they do. But this whole thing with Sheila and Phil just doesn't feel right."

"If Phil was a regular murder victim, someone you didn't know, would you feel the same way?"

She was quiet for a moment. "Probably not."

"So there's a real possibility no one knew this side of Phil."

As they sat in their car, Braddock dug up what she could about Sheila online. Melvin Harris was too common of a name to find anything meaningful. The phone number for Sheila Harris came back to a Verizon cell phone out of Oakland, but the white pages and other searches for a Sheila Harris around thirty years old turned up no matches. The phone number for Charlotte Harris showed a Sprint cell phone out of Detroit. Braddock found a fifty-eight-year-old Charlotte Harris who lived in Birmingham, an affluent suburb of Detroit. Another website showed a sixty-one-year-old Melvin Harris at that same address. Possibly the son of the man they'd just met.

Braddock put the car in drive and headed south toward Oakland. It felt strange having Braddock drive their car, carry the only badge between them, take the lead on interviews, and call the shots on what was his case. "What now?" he asked.

"I drop you off at your car and you go home, where every officer on suspension is supposed to be."

"What about Sheila?"

"I'll run her out, and if I can ID her, I'll do a full background and figure out the best way to approach her."

"By yourself?"

"Hell, Matt, I don't know. This is all uncharted territory for me. I don't know what to do. If I get caught working with you, I'm done. I sure as hell can't go driving around Oakland with you looking for Sheila."

"We can still—"

"Don't you get it, Matt? There's no *we*. You're no longer a cop. It's just me."

He sighed. "You're right. It's your case now, but if word leaks, I'm sure the chief will cancel the department funeral. Even if we later find out Phil did nothing wrong, his reputation will be tainted forever."

"Isn't it better for it to come out now rather than later?"

"I think it's best if it never needs to come out. Talk to Sheila. If Phil's murder has nothing to do with her or the money, maybe this doesn't have to become front-page news."

"I don't know, Matt. You're gone, and I'm all alone on this thing now. The funeral's Wednesday, and if I can't make sense out of what we found in Phil's locker, I have to tell someone."

"Can you talk to me before you do that?"

"Expect my call Tuesday morning," she said.

Chapter 34

Braddock dropped him off at his car and drove back toward the PAB. As Sinclair put his Mustang in gear, his phone rang.

"Hey, Uppy, what's up?" Sinclair said, noting the name of Upton Bellamy on his caller ID. Uppy was one of the few FBI agents Sinclair considered a friend. After years as a Detroit cop, he was hired by the FBI and spent his first ten years in the New York field office. He came to Oakland two years ago and was assigned to the bank robbery squad, where Sinclair worked with him on a murder connected to a string of bank robberies the bureau was investigating.

"Matt, we need to talk."

"What about?"

"About Phil's murder."

"In case you haven't heard, I've been suspended, so you'll have to talk to a real police detective. One who's allowed to work homicide cases."

"I have heard," Uppy said. "And that's why we really need to talk. I can be at your place in twenty or thirty minutes. If you don't like what I've got to say, kick me the hell out."

"You know my address?"

"I'm the FBI—we know everything."

Sinclair called Walt to make sure the library was available and headed home. He parked his car in the circular driveway at the front of the house, opened the door, and stepped into the entry hallway. Walt was coming out of the library. "Your guests are inside. I'm getting coffee."

Standing in the middle of the wood-paneled room were Uppy, Linda Archard, Jack Campbell, and a balding white man in his late fifties who looked vaguely familiar. Sinclair stood by the doorway and said, "What the fuck, Uppy? You sand-bagged me."

"Sorry, Matt, but you need to hear them out."

He didn't trust Campbell or Archard as far as he could throw them. They'd done everything in their power to conceal from him information he needed during the Thrill Kill Murders. Why the US attorney would come to visit him at his home—and on a Sunday, to boot—baffled him.

The bald man extended his hand. "Sergeant, I don't believe we've met, but my name is Bruce Davis. I'm the US marshal for the Northern California District."

Sinclair had read about Davis when he took the position. The US marshal for a particular region of the country, like the US attorney, was a presidential appointee, and Davis spent a career with the Santa Clara Sheriff's Department before being appointed to his position two years ago. He was in charge of all the deputy marshals in the northern part of the state and responsible for court security, federal prisoners, fugitive apprehension, and the enforcement and investigation of a wide array of federal laws.

Sinclair shook his hand. Before he could ask what this was all about, Walt reentered carrying a tray of cups and coffee fixings.

"Will your guests be sitting, or shall I set this up on the bar?" he asked.

Sinclair's first thought was to keep them standing because they'd be leaving in a minute, but he was too curious about their agenda. "We'll sit."

Walt set the tray on the coffee table in the center of the room and placed one cup on the end table next to the club chair at the head of the furniture grouping. "Your coffee, Mr. Sinclair," he said. Everyone took a seat on the leather sofas behind their cups of coffee, and all except Uppy removed cream and sweeteners from the tray. "Will there be anything else, sir?"

Although Sinclair had seen Walt serve Fred and his guests at dinners and parties before, it felt weird having Walt wait on him. He wanted to tell him to knock off the "sir" shit, but he understood Walt was performing for his benefit, even setting him up in the position of power around the table. "Thank you, Walt. That will be all."

Once Walt left and closed the door, Campbell asked, "Was that your butler?"

"He's more of a caretaker for Frederick Towers's estate. I'm just a guest here."

Campbell smiled. "Fred and I are acquaintances."

The sense of déjà vu hit him. This felt just like when he was summoned to the private room at the Scottish Rite Temple by Campbell. That too was a room of old wood and leather and powerful men. Back then, it was Campbell who dismissed the waiter so they could talk, and when Campbell was finished, he dismissed Sinclair. The four visitors chose their seats based on their understood pecking order. Campbell and Davis sat closest to Sinclair, Archard sat on the sofa next to Campbell, and Uppy sat at the far end of the sofa on which Davis was sitting. Uppy leaned back and took a drink of his coffee. He acted as if he was supposed to stay out of the mix now that his job of getting them to Sinclair was finished.

"I'll get right to the point," Campbell said. "Sergeant Sinclair, we'd like you to work with us."

Sinclair leaned back in his chair and crossed his ankle over his knee. "Doing what?"

"Among other things, helping us find out who killed Phil Roberts."

If that was intended to get Sinclair's attention, it worked. "There're a few special circumstances that make murder a federal crime, but they don't apply here. Why would you be interested in who killed an Oakland cop?"

Campbell rubbed his chin. "I'm interested because I'm part of the law enforcement community in the Bay Area, but besides that, let's just say we have a common goal."

"And what goal is that?" Sinclair asked.

"I'm not at liberty to say at this time," Campbell said. "We'd like to know what you've learned so far about what happened to him. Do you have a suspect or any leads at this time?"

Sinclair stood. "I played this fucking game with you last year. We told you everything we knew and you didn't share shit in return. How do I know if you're really interested in who killed Roberts or if you're just concerned with what political toes I'm getting ready to step on?"

Uppy leaned forward and looked at Campbell. "No disrespect meant, but I told you Sinclair wouldn't go along with this. He's not some kind of snitch you can pump for information and walk away from. If you want his help, make him part of the team."

Campbell nodded to Davis across the coffee table. Davis said, "We have records of you being sworn in as a special deputy US marshal in the past." He reached in his briefcase and removed a folder and a large envelope.

When Sinclair worked vice narcotics eleven years ago, he was assigned to a federal narcotics task force and sworn in as a special deputy so he could access information the DEA had collected through federal subpoenas. Four years later, he and Phil worked a series of drug-related murders, and he was sworn in again so he could hear wiretap recordings and follow the investigation outside California, where otherwise they'd have no law enforcement powers.

"I've always done this as a sort of ceremony at the federal courthouse, but this is a special situation," Davis said as he pulled a credential case from the envelope. Affixed on the outside was a five-point star set inside a ring. The badge said, *Special Deputy, United States Marshal.*

"Please stand, raise your right hand, and repeat after me. I, Matthew Sinclair, do swear or affirm . . ."

Sinclair completed the oath and signed a special deputization form.

Archard spoke for the first time. "We're giving you the creds for a very limited purpose. You cannot tell anyone outside the task force of your involvement with us. Everyone—and I mean everyone—at OPD must be kept in the dark. They need to think you're still suspended."

"How am I supposed to investigate a crime in Oakland and make sure no one from OPD sees me doing it?"

"You'll be working with me," Uppy answered. "We'll mostly be in the task force headquarters looking through the information that's been compiled so far. We're hoping you'll be able to connect the dots that have so far eluded the analysts."

"How can this happen if I'm still suspended?" Sinclair said. "I hope no one forgot that."

"If OPD finds out you're working for us, they'll probably fire you on the spot," Campbell said. "Legally, you're in a gray zone right now as far as special deputization goes. Being on administrative leave from your department doesn't prevent us from deputizing you, but if it becomes known that you're working with us, this entire thing can blow up in our faces."

The same icky feeling he had when he sat with the Feds in Phil's office last December returned. He wondered if the Feds had said the same words to Phil and if that was why he was forced to betray his old homicide partners. But Sinclair needed to remain involved with the investigation one way or another. He owed it to Phil. "I understand."

Campbell handed Sinclair a two-page document. "Good, there's one final thing. This is an agreement of nondisclosure and acknowledgment of confidentiality. You will have access to information that may be classified or law enforcement sensitive.

You'll see information obtained from wiretaps and other electronic intercepts and may listen to active wiretaps. You'll see information obtained through federal subpoenas, search warrants, and grand juries. From this point forward, you cannot share information about this investigation with anyone outside the task force or without our permission."

Sinclair read the paper. "Let me get this straight—if I look at some of this stuff you've compiled and figure out who killed Roberts, but you decide you're going to continue your investigation to look for bigger fish for the next year, or two years, or five years, I can't say shit to anyone."

"I can't imagine that happening," Campbell said.

"But it could. And this form says I understand I could be prosecuted under Title Ten, US Code, section . . . whatever."

"Technically, that's right."

"You can take your badge and shove it up your ass."

"Sergeant, you're making a big mistake," Campbell said. "We can help you accomplish what you've been after."

"I'm not about to trade working for a police chief who tells me what I can't pursue or talk about for a bunch of Feds who want to do the same." He walked out of the library and opened the front door.

Davis gathered up the badge and creds and followed the others to the door.

"This isn't what you think, Matt. We can make it work," Uppy said as he walked out the door.

Sinclair wanted to tell Uppy how ashamed he was to see how he'd forgotten his cop roots, but he kept his mouth shut. He'd probably said enough already. Sinclair suspected that the Feds either needed him because of what he knew or desperately wanted to keep whatever he knew from getting out.

Chapter 35

Sinclair plopped back into the soft leather chair in the library. Amber stood in front of him and rested her head on his leg. Walt filled his coffee cup. "How did your evening with Alyssa go?"

Very little went on within the estate that Walt missed. He probably knew exactly what time Alyssa's car exited the front gate. Sinclair smiled.

"That well?" Walt said. "Good for you, Matthew. She's an exceptional young lady, both Betty and I agree."

In more ways than you might imagine, Sinclair thought.

Walt collected the empty coffee cups and put them on his serving tray. "Your guests left rather suddenly."

Sinclair patted Amber on the head, and she lay down on the Persian carpet at his feet. "Yeah, I'm afraid they didn't get what they wanted from me."

"Is there anything Fred or I can do to help?"

"No, I think this has to be up to me."

"Fred will be out of town for a few more days, so feel free to use the library to work."

Walt knew him well enough to know that despite being on suspension, he wasn't about to stop working.

"What's a good rule of thumb for when we should keep a secret that could harm someone's reputation?" Sinclair asked.

"Sounds like a trick question," Walt said. "In AA, people say things in meetings and to one another in confidence. With few exceptions, we should never repeat it. I think it becomes more complicated when you're talking about secrets you discover in your job. It's your duty to uncover people's secrets and report them, so you have different obligations there."

"What if a man's dead and I discovered things that would hurt his reputation and harm his wife and family?"

"You're obviously talking about your friend. People used to say we should never speak ill of the dead. If a man's dead, is there a need to share his sins? Courts don't try dead people for criminal offenses."

Sinclair took a sip of his coffee. "What if, by protecting the secret, someone else will get away with a serious crime?"

"You answered your own question. You need to determine what's more important, one person answering for his crime or the secret being buried with the dead."

"I'm asking someone else to keep this secret too."

"Secrets are harder to keep when more people know. And it makes you beholden to them. Have you ever been asked to keep a secret that made you uncomfortable or destroyed a friendship?"

Sinclair nodded, leaned back in his chair, and stared at the ceiling.

Walt closed the door behind him.

Sinclair's life had revolved around secrets when he was drinking. Not mentioning to a friend's wife that his buddy was at the bar. Asking the friend not to tell Sinclair's wife that he was there. Not telling the boss when a coworker went home early. Hoping no one told the boss when he sneaked out early to hit the Warehouse. Hiding his drinking required a lot of work. Now that he was sober, he didn't have as many secrets in his personal life. But asking Braddock to keep this secret was destroying their friendship.

Work was different. There he lived in a world of secrets. Suspects and witnesses all had secrets, and it was his job to discover what they were so he could determine the truth surrounding a murder. While he forced others to reveal their secrets, murder investigations required him to withhold information from the public, from witnesses, and from suspects.

He had no qualms about keeping secrets to maintain the integrity of a case. But the secrets he'd uncovered surrounding Phil's murder were different. It was as if Phil had left him a note on the emergency contact form asking him to keep his confidences from his family and the department. And it pissed him off that Phil would ask him to do this when he'd kept secrets from Sinclair last year.

But keeping secrets was sometimes necessary. Keeping a secret to maintain the integrity of a homicide investigation was right. Keeping a secret and ordering others to keep a secret for one's personal ambition was wrong. That's why it irked Sinclair when Brown ordered him to stand down on his investigation into Yates and Kozlov. Yates's extramarital affair was none of Sinclair's business. Heck, a US president had an affair and remained in the oval office afterward, so who was he to judge a man's fitness for a city position who had done the same? But payoffs for political favors were wrong and shouldn't be buried. Brown was obviously willing to ignore them to ensure he kept his chief of police badge when the next mayor took office.

Sinclair wondered if the money in Phil's locker came from Kozlov. Kozlov had paid Yates's expenses to keep Dawn. What would Phil have had to give Kozlov in return for the money it took to keep Sheila?

A primary reason for keeping secrets during an investigation was so he could determine the entire truth. That was Sinclair's goal after all. If they told Maloney about the money and Sheila, it would spread like wildfire through the department. The case would be ripped from homicide's hands and turned over to IAD. The important issue—who killed Phil and why—would become irrelevant. He needed to uncover the entire truth and the motive behind it before that happened.

The question of how Sheila Harris was connected to Phil was still foremost in his mind, but the more direct route to the mystery of his death lay with the Savage Simbas. He knew Jankowski and Sanchez were pursuing that route, and if the answers were there, they would find them. But something had been nagging at him ever since he and Fletcher visited the motorcycle shop. He remembered keying on the light-blue shop rags at the coroner's office when dark-red ones were more typical. As he recalled Irish Mike pulling the rag from his pocket to wipe the dirt from his bike, he knew what had been nagging at him.

Chapter 36

Sinclair parked his Mustang in front of the No Colors Motorcycle Shop in Concord. A sign on the door said they were closed on Sundays, but he checked the door anyway. Locked. He peered through the window. Lights off—no activity. He didn't have much of a plan. If Irish Mike was there, he could tell him he was in the neighborhood and stopped by to talk more about doing performance work on his bike. Maybe Mike would let him in and he'd see something that further linked the shop to Phil's murder. If the word had filtered back to Mike about two bikers chasing Tiny just moments after he and Fletcher were at the shop asking about him, Sinclair would have to do some fast-talking.

Sinclair pounded at the door in case Mike or someone else was inside working. When no one came after a few minutes, Sinclair drove down the alley to the back of the shop. The chain link fence gate was locked with a heavy chain and padlock. The lawn chairs and old car seats at the back of the shop were unoccupied, and the space where a row of Harleys had been parked was empty. He looked around for cameras, alarms, or signs of a dog but saw nothing.

People who install a fence and a locked gate have a reasonable expectation of privacy. Absent exigent circumstances, police would need a search warrant before entering the shop yard. But

Sinclair was no longer a cop according to Chief Brown. If the Concord police caught him going over the fence, they'd arrest him for trespassing or, more likely, for attempted burglary. Telling the officers he was an Oakland cop suspended from duty wouldn't help one bit.

He pulled himself to the top of the ten-foot fence, swung his leg over, and dropped to the ground on the other side. He waited for a few seconds. If someone inside poked his head out the back door, he figured he could get back over the fence and flee. The absence of a gun digging into his right hip felt strange. But it was the absence of his police badge and the authority that accompanied it that was the most unsettling. He scurried across the cracked asphalt surface to the back of the building. He tried the back door, but it was locked. He looked in through a dirty window but saw no movement. Under the overhang and scattered among the car seats and lawn chairs were two trash cans and a few plastic bins filled with old motorcycle parts.

He reached into the first trash can and dug to the bottom, looking for anything of interest. He did the same to the second one, wishing he had gloves on as he searched through used oil filters and cigarette butts. The first bin contained two engine pistons inside a broken-down cardboard box. Sinclair yanked the cardboard from under the heavy pieces of metal and saw several filthy and badly worn light-blue shop rags.

Sinclair retraced his steps, climbed back over the fence, and got into his car. He drove to a McDonald's a half mile away, where he washed his hands and ordered a large ice tea. He wiped the grease and dirt off his steering wheel with a handful of napkins and pulled out his cell phone.

"I was wondering if Jankowski and Sanchez had any luck out at Santa Rita today," he said.

"Not really," Braddock replied, "but they're whittling away at the list of the Simbas who have guard cards or are in line to get them. No big revelations yet."

"Have you seen any more of the US attorney, Archard, or other Feds?"

"No," she said. "And I tried to talk to Assistant Chief James. He kinda hung you out to dry. But he's not returning my calls. You doing okay?"

"Yeah. I'll call an LDF attorney tomorrow. Even if they sustain me for insubordination, what's the worst they'll do? Give me a couple days of suspension? I can handle that."

"If IAD sustains the complaint, the chief will transfer you out of homicide. What will you do then?"

Sinclair hadn't fully considered what might happen to him professionally. He'd weathered so many IA complaints, he figured he'd survive this one as well. But Braddock was right—Brown wouldn't let him off this time. He couldn't dwell on that, however.

"You haven't told anyone about Sheila Harris and the money, have you?"

"I still don't know what I should do. I did a work-up on her and might know where she lives. I went by an address, but there was no answer. I'll try again first thing in the morning."

"Where does she live?"

"Matt, you need to trust me to handle this."

Giving up control and trusting others was not something Sinclair did well, but if he pushed any harder, he risked Braddock totally cutting him off from the investigation. "The real reason I called was I just remembered I forgot to put something in my notes."

"That's not like you."

"Do you remember the color of the shop rags in the garbage bag?"

"Yeah, baby blue," she said. "We have photos of them."

"When Fletcher and I did the UC visit to the No Colors Motorcycle Shop, the owner, Irish Mike, had one in his pocket, and I saw a bunch of old, greasy ones in a plastic bin filled with old parts around the back of the building."

Braddock was quiet for a few counts. "You're just telling me this now?"

He felt a bit guilty about manipulating Braddock, but he couldn't exactly tell her he had to jump the fence and do an illegal search to confirm the color of the rags. Besides, they might find something else inside the shop or get someone there to talk. "We were pretty fucking busy after visiting the shop, in case you forgot. And then poof—I was no longer a cop. I was intending to have you and Jankowski go back there, badge the guy, and ask to look around. I didn't want to do it myself because it would've burned Fletcher and his informant."

"How uncommon are those rags?"

"I've only seen that color twice—at that shop and with Phil's body."

"So that means Gibbs probably got them from the shop," she said. "Does he have any connection to the place?"

"Not that I know of," Sinclair replied. "But we know Tiny came into the bar with Gibbs that night. Half of CID probably takes office supplies home. Tiny worked at the shop. Wouldn't a mechanic take shop rags home?"

"And use them to wipe his bloody hands after he murders someone," she said. "First thing tomorrow, I'll take Jankowski and Sanchez out there, collect some of those rags as evidence, and question everyone who works there. It will also give us something to hold over Tiny's head should we ever get him into an interview room."

"Exactly my thought. Are you still in the office?"

"Just leaving," she said. "We're fried, so Jankowski, Sanchez, and I decided to call it a day and start at six tomorrow morning."

★

A half hour later, Sinclair parked his Mustang a few blocks west of the PAB and walked down Seventh Street to the side door leading to CID. He was glad they didn't take his key card and that no one thought to delete him from the system. The only people working Sunday evenings in CID would be homicide if there'd been a callout. The lights were off in homicide, so there hadn't been a fresh murder. Sinclair unlocked the door and went to his desk. He started his computer and did the same for Braddock's.

While they were warming up, he took the Roberts homicide packet from Braddock's desk and paged through it. He went to the copy machine and made copies of his handwritten log and the additional notes written in Braddock's handwriting. He copied some other papers that wouldn't be in the computer, such as Phil's overtime and expense paperwork and criminal history printouts. By this time, his computer was up. He copied all the files related to the Roberts case onto a flash drive. He signed into Braddock's computer with her password and copied all the files she had on the case as well. Once finished, he shut down both computers, slipped the thumb drive into his pocket, and returned the case packet to Braddock's desk. He removed the cigar box he'd found in Phil's locker from where Braddock had stashed it in the back of her top drawer and made a photocopy of the spiral notebook pages. He then replaced it in the box and relocked the box in her desk. Braddock's deadline was on Tuesday, when she would take the box to the lieutenant. He had until then to find the truth.

Sinclair made it out the side door and back to his car with only a few uniformed officers seeing him. He doubted they even knew he'd been relieved of duty or would think twice about seeing a homicide investigator on a weekend.

Sinclair returned to the mansion and set up his laptop in the library. He inserted the flash drive and read through Braddock's investigative follow-up report and notes to reconstruct what she and Jankowski had done since Friday afternoon. On Friday, they interviewed two Simbas who were among those identified by Pelletier. Both said Animal approached them at the clubhouse one night and asked if they'd ever been arrested. When they said no, he suggested they take a training course to become security guards and promised he would soon have a lot of work for them. That was about all they knew about it.

Braddock's handwritten log indicated that about an hour ago, she'd run Sheila Harris in LRMS and other databases. She discovered Sheila had no presence on the web, which didn't surprise Sinclair. If a girl was going to be an escort and didn't want any of her clients to learn her true identity, she'd have to keep a very low public profile—no blogging, YouTube videos, Twitter, Facebook, or other social media. She had never been arrested and had no contacts with the Oakland police, not even as a crime victim or witness. Sinclair was beginning to think Sheila Harris wasn't her real name until the next entry in Braddock's report indicated she found a similar name in DMV records.

A driver's license in the name of Sheila Harris included identifying information for a woman thirty-two years old, five foot ten, and 135 pounds, with black hair and brown eyes and an address on Lee Street. Sinclair thumbed through the papers he had photocopied and found a black-and-white copy of her driver's license photo. She was without a doubt the same person in the photo he'd found in Phil's locker. A four-year-old Honda Accord was registered to her, but there was nothing else in the DMV file on her—no citations, previous addresses, or other vehicles.

Next, Sinclair went to the photos. Since the evidence techs posted scene photos onto a central server that investigators had access to, there was little reason for investigators to download all the images onto their personal computers. But Sinclair had gotten into the habit of doing that in case he might need to access them when out of the office. Braddock was much more computer savvy than Sinclair, and she often downloaded an assortment of photos to her desktop computer, and from there she'd e-mail them to herself so she could view them on her iPad when they were in the field. Sinclair found the photo of Sheila that Braddock had manipulated from the sexy swimsuit photo, e-mailed it to himself, and also printed a copy.

Chapter 37

The Adams Point neighborhood was one of the more desirable areas for young, single people to live in Oakland. A hundred apartment buildings, most plain concrete or stucco boxes, dotted the hill north of Lake Merritt. A mile from downtown and close to mass transit, shopping, restaurants, and nightlife, the cheapest one-bedroom apartments in the area started at $2,000 a month, with two bedrooms another thousand higher.

Sinclair cruised by Sheila's DMV address on Lee Street looking for parking. Since he didn't have a police car, he didn't dare park in a yellow or red zone. Not only didn't he want an eighty-three-dollar ticket, he didn't need any official record of his car in this area. He cruised the area and eventually found a place to park a block away.

He pressed the buzzer for 206 and waited. No answer. If he had his badge, he would've buzzed the apartment manager next, but he couldn't come up with a plausible story to convince him or her to give out information on a single woman living in his complex. He took out his cell phone, pressed it to his ear, and waited. About ten minutes later, a thirtysomething hipster-looking man came out the door. Sinclair continued to carry on his conversation with the imaginary person on the other end, caught the door, and said, "Yeah, yeah, I'll be right up."

He took the stairs to the second floor and followed the open walkway around the inside of the building. Below was a lush courtyard filled with plants and small trees in large pots and a few small tables. He pressed the doorbell on apartment 206 and knocked. He waited a minute and knocked again.

A door opened behind him and a voice said, "She's not home."

Sinclair turned and faced a plump blonde in her late twenties. "Yeah, I see that. I'm a friend of Sheila's from Napa. I was in the area and thought I'd surprise her."

"From Napa?" Her voice indicated she wasn't buying it.

"I'm Matt," he said, giving her his best smile, the one Braddock said caused girls to get weak-kneed. "I had dinner with Sheila last weekend in Napa. She hasn't mentioned me?"

"Oh, we're not that close. But I've wondered where she's been going every weekend."

Sinclair winked, hinting that he and Sheila might be more than just friends.

She stepped out of her doorway onto the balcony. "I think she left on vacation or something."

"Maybe that's why she's hasn't answered her phone." Sinclair looked down at his feet. "I guess I'm making a fool of myself, but I thought we had something."

Her eyes softened, obviously understanding how it felt to be rejected. "Sheila's really hot, but she's nice too. I don't think she'd lead you on."

"When did you last see her?"

"It must've been last Saturday or Sunday. She just got back from Napa."

"That was our weekend," Sinclair said, looking down again.

"No, wait, I saw her at the bus stop Monday morning."

"Going to work?"

"Yeah, I often run into her at Perkins and Grand. We both take the number twelve and get off at Twelfth Street. I get on

BART and head into the city. She must work somewhere down-town because I see her walking in the opposite direction."

"I seem to know so little about her," he said. "I don't even know what she does for a living."

"I think she's in business administration. Maybe an office manager or something. She always dresses very professionally."

"Any idea where she was going on vacation?"

"My roommate might know. She's watering her plants while she's gone."

"Is your roommate around?"

"No, she's out with her boyfriend." Her look said she wished she had a boyfriend to be out with on a Sunday evening.

"Do you think you could ask your roommate where Sheila went and if she knows when she'll be back?" Sinclair shuffled his feet and looked at her with his best awe-shucks look. "I hope you don't think I'm a stalker or something, but I really like her."

"A guy like you doesn't need to stalk women," she said. "What's your number?"

Sinclair gave her his cell number, which she entered into her phone. "Call me so I can make sure you got it right."

A second later, his phone buzzed. "Hi, this is Matt, who's this?"

She giggled. "Lori."

Sinclair entered her name into in his phone. "Well, thanks, Lori."

"If things don't work out with Sheila, and you wanna . . . you know—"

"I've got your number."

Sinclair walked back to the staircase, feeling Lori's eyes on him as he walked away. He continued down the steps to the underground parking garage. He spotted a Honda Accord and verified it was the same license as the one registered to Sheila according to the DMV printout. Although he wanted to go door to door and talk to other neighbors, if Lori saw him, it would blow the story he'd concocted and any chance she might pass on something her roommate knew. Besides, this was Oakland, and someone would call the police after they saw him knocking on multiple doors. He'd be in a world of shit if he was discovered working the case while on suspension. As he was walking back to his car, he wondered how much more successful Braddock would be with Sheila's neighbors and the manager by showing her badge.

He drove down Van Buren Avenue, passing cars parked bumper to bumper on both sides of the street. A dark-green sedan followed about a block back. He'd noticed the car parked a few buildings down from Sheila's apartment when he came out and thought he'd spotted it sitting in a yellow zone when he went inside. Too far away to be sure, but it looked like two men inside. He turned right on MacArthur Boulevard. The car turned behind him, remaining about a block back. Probably nothing—plenty of people live in this area, and it wouldn't be unusual for someone else to be leaving by the same route.

Sinclair stopped at the light at Grand Avenue. The green car had slowed to let two other cars get in front of it. A classic surveillance technique. Definitely two people in the car. Looked to be a Chevy Malibu. His first thought was that the FBI was tailing him to see what he was up to after he rejected their offer. If so, he was getting sloppy because they had to have picked him up at his house and been following him ever since. He should've noticed the tail earlier. But he crossed out that possibility since they wouldn't have been sitting in front of Sheila's apartment when he got there. If he was working, he would've gotten on the radio and had a patrol unit stop the car and check them out. But that wasn't an option. Before he did anything else, he'd have to be certain he was being followed and not just being paranoid.

At the next block, he made a left onto Lakeshore Avenue. If it wasn't the FBI, he didn't want to lead them to his house, so he put on his left turn signal as he came out from under the freeway and made a quick left onto Lake Park Avenue. The Malibu drove past him. He turned left onto Grand Avenue and made another left to get back on MacArthur Boulevard. If the car was in fact following him, he had lost it.

He heard a squeal of tires through his open window. In his rearview mirror, he saw the Malibu come off Grand and make a left, pulling into traffic a few cars behind him. It must have made the block past him when he turned on Lake Park, raced through the residential streets, and caught up with him. Now there was no doubt it was tailing him, and Sinclair needed to figure out his next move.

If it was the FBI or another federal agency and they were conducting a solo surveillance, it was amateurish. It was impossible to follow someone who was surveillance conscious without a team of at least three or four cars. But if it wasn't the FBI, then who could it be? Was someone else looking for Sheila? Maybe the same people who killed Phil?

If he had a gun, he might take them on. He could lead them into a dead end, block their car from escaping, and take them out of the car at gunpoint and identify them. But he wasn't even a cop anymore.

The light turned green, and instead of turning left, Sinclair went straight and took the freeway on-ramp. The green car followed.

He drove slowly up the ramp. Being Sunday, the traffic was light. He merged onto the freeway, still going forty. A few cars whizzed by at seventy. The Malibu remained about a hundred yards back. He punched it. At sixty, he shifted into third and popped the clutch. The Mustang lurched forward. Pressed back in his seat, he turned the steering wheel a tad to the left and cut across the four lanes. When the tachometer hit redline, he shifted into fourth. Ninety miles an hour. He kept the gas pedal floored. The two left lanes ahead were clear. The high-performance V-8 was still pulling.

The Malibu had made it into the left lane but was falling far behind. Sinclair continued to accelerate and shifted into fifth at 110, just shy of redline. The freeway curved slightly to the left, and Sinclair let his speed climb to 130. He lost sight of the Malibu as he passed Thirty-Fifth Avenue. A mile later, he still couldn't see it. As he approached Seminary Avenue, he braked hard, cut across the four lanes, and took the exit. He made a series of left turns and got back onto the 580 Freeway, going in the opposite direction. He caught a last glimpse of the Malibu speeding past the Seminary exit.

Chapter 38

Sinclair stretched out his legs and accidentally kicked Amber, who had taken up residence under the library table. She nuzzled his foot and resumed her position on the plush Persian rug. He went back to reviewing the papers he'd copied from the case packet when his phone buzzed.

"Hey, you," Alyssa said.

"How'd church go?"

"I might be going to hell because I was thinking about what you and I did last night instead of listening to the priest's sermon."

"I keep thinking about it too."

"I'm just leaving my parents' house. I still need to go grocery shopping and run a load of laundry. And I'm beat. You didn't let me sleep much last night. What I'm trying to say is, as much as I'd love to see you again tonight, I really should get to bed early for work tomorrow."

Amber sat up and looked at him. "I understand," he said to Alyssa.

"Let's talk tomorrow once I get a chance to look at my schedule for the week."

"That sounds fine."

"Did you do anything fun today?"

"Not really. You know, just hanging out."

"Think of it as extra vacation days," she said. "You should do something fun tomorrow."

"I will."

"Bye, Matt."

Sinclair set the phone on the table and patted Amber's head. Did she just brush him off? Was he sensing a tinge of regret in her voice about sleeping with him? Part of him was glad she was tired and busy tonight. Otherwise, he'd have to lie about what he was doing. But she sounded like she was glad to have a reason not to see him. It seemed real last night when they were together, but maybe to her it was just sympathy sex. She knew he was feeling down about his suspension and Phil's death, so she did it to cheer him up. In the early morning hours as he was watching her sleep, he could imagine falling in love with her and wondered if she was feeling the same. There was no way that he would have said that to her though. Now he didn't know how he felt. He definitely didn't want to fall in love with someone who didn't love him back. What the hell did he know about love anyway?

Sinclair went back to the murder investigation, something he did understand. He found the entry in Braddock's follow-up report that detailed their visit with Sheila's grandfather, Melvin Harris, at the nursing home. Sheila's cell phone number was in their notes, but he was reluctant to call it. He always preferred face-to-face interviews. It was too easy to lie over the phone. People could make an excuse why they couldn't physically meet, and if they didn't want to talk in the first place, they'd go into hiding as soon as he called. But he was out of options and running out of time. He dialed the number and held his breath.

He heard a recording saying the number was no longer in service. He dialed it again. Same recording.

Sheila was on the run. She'd left her apartment, and it now appeared she'd ditched her phone.

He went on the Internet and brought up one of the white pages websites. The phone number that Braddock had found at the nursing home listed for Charlotte Harris came back to a Sprint cell phone out of Detroit. Sinclair called the number.

"Hi, this is Charlotte."

"Hi, Charlotte, I'm a friend of Sheila's from Oakland."

"Yes," she said, drawing out the word.

"She hasn't been home for a few days, and her phone number is disconnected. Do you have a new number for her?"

"How'd you get my number?"

Sinclair thought. "One of her neighbors gave it to me. I guess Sheila gave it to her as an emergency contact or something."

"I don't know why she'd do that."

"I thought you were her mother," Sinclair said. "I'm just trying to reach her."

"Give me your name and number, and if I talk to her, I'll let her know you called."

Sinclair gave her his first name and cell phone number. He wanted to ask if she knew where Sheila was, but he was pushing the woman to even take down his name and number.

"What's your last name, Matt?"

He thought for a second. "Roberts, ma'am. Matt Roberts."

"I don't expect to hear from her, but if I do, I'll pass on your number to her."

"When did you last speak to her?"

"Are you sure you aren't a bill collector or a telemarketer?"

"No, ma'am, just a friend."

"Good-bye, Mr. Roberts."

With all the scam calls these days, it was no wonder people were suspicious. Fraud experts constantly told people not to give out any personal information over the phone unless you knew who you were speaking to. Maybe she detected Sinclair's scam—after all, everything he'd told her was a lie. For all he knew, Sheila might've been sitting beside Charlotte when she spoke to him. Nevertheless, it was a dead end.

He entered Melvin Harris into an Internet search engine, and 342 different Melvin Harrises in California popped up. No wonder Braddock had said it was too common of a name to pin down the right Melvin Harris. If he had access to his work computer, he could find him. Even if Melvin had no arrest record or contacts with OPD, he would run the name in DMV with an age range from seventy to ninety. DMV might show as many people with that name, but the age parameter would cut it down significantly, especially after eliminating those in Southern California. By looking at the height and weight of those Melvin Harrises remaining, he could eliminate at least half. He'd then pull up the driver's licenses of the remaining ones to find a photo that matched the man they spoke to.

But the Internet search engine had something DMV didn't. Since these websites compiled their information from credit reports and other public data, they listed relatives. Scrolling through the names, he found a Melvin Harris who was eighty years old with a relative named Melvin Harris Jr. Braddock's initial search for Charlotte Harris had shown a sixty-one-year-old Melvin Harris at the same address. The listing for this Melvin Harris showed an address in Berkeley and a phone number. He called the number but got a recording saying it was disconnected and no longer in service. He wouldn't find Melvin Harris at the address, but he wouldn't know what else he might find there unless he went and knocked on a few doors.

Chapter 39

The drive to Buena Vista Way, a half mile north of the University of California campus, took twenty minutes, including the extra turns to make sure he wasn't being followed. Sinclair parked in front of the rose-colored two-story stucco house and walked through the gate of the picket fence that surrounded the front yard. A white man with unkempt brown hair and dressed in khaki pants and a long-sleeve oxford opened the door before Sinclair could knock. He appeared to be in his midforties.

"I'm looking for Melvin Harris," Sinclair said. "I take it he doesn't live here anymore."

"We bought the house eight years ago. I believe that was the name of the previous owner."

Sinclair sighed. "My grandfather and Mr. Harris were old friends, but they lost touch years ago. He recently tried to reconnect, but the phone number he had for Mr. Harris is disconnected. He asked me to try to locate him."

"I never met him. We only dealt with his realtor, but I seem to recall his children handled the sale—Mr. Harris was quite elderly."

"Yeah, so is my grandfather," Sinclair said. "Can you think of anyone in the neighborhood who might've known him and maybe kept in touch?"

"You can try Dr. Lowenstein next door." The man gestured to his left. "He's lived here for close to fifty years."

Sinclair thanked him and walked up the sidewalk to a brown shingle house with a two-car detached garage next to it. He pressed the doorbell alongside the restored wood-plank door. A long minute later, a white-haired man wearing a rust-brown cardigan sweater opened the door. Sinclair introduced himself as Matt Roberts and repeated his story about looking for Melvin Harris for his grandfather.

"Melvin? Oh, sure. It's been some time since I've seen him."

"Do you know where he is? I think my grandfather's trying to connect with some of his old friends in his final days."

"Would you like to come in?"

Sinclair followed him inside to a large room with polished wood floors and a vaulted ceiling. "Beautiful house," Sinclair said.

"It was built in 1924, and we try to maintain it in its original form the best we can, allowing for modern conveniences and such. Can I get you a glass of wine?"

Sinclair declined and followed Dr. Lowenstein to a redwood deck on the back of the house. A teak table surrounded by four chairs took up most of the outdoor space. Through the trees, the San Francisco Bay and a foggy San Francisco was visible. Sections of the Sunday edition of the *New York Times* and *San Francisco Chronicle* lay scattered across the table. Lowenstein picked up a half-full glass of red wine and sat down, gesturing for Sinclair to do the same.

"How long did Mr. Harris live next door?" Sinclair asked.

"Oh, my, I think it was about thirty years ago when the university recruited him to take the department chair position. That's when he and Marie bought the house and moved in."

"He lived in Michigan before that, didn't he?"

"Oh, yes, he taught at the University of Michigan for years. He loved Ann Arbor but absolutely hated the winters there."

"I understand his children are still there. My grandfather spoke of them."

"I know Mel Jr. still lives back there. He and his current wife were the ones who moved Mel out when it was time."

"When it was time?" Sinclair asked, pretending he knew nothing about Melvin's current condition.

"I regret that I have some bad news for you to take back to your grandfather. Mel began showing signs of dementia some years ago. After the police picked him up for a second time wandering around and unable to tell them who he was, Mel Jr. arranged to move him to an assisted living facility in El Cerrito."

"That's too bad. Would I be wasting my time helping him and my grandfather reconnect?"

"I stopped visiting him when he no longer recognized me. That was about two or three years ago. I imagine he's worse now. How did your grandfather know him?"

"They met professionally," Sinclair said.

"Was he a painter himself or in academia?"

Sinclair thought quickly. Since he assumed the doctor title Lowenstein used meant he had a PhD and was a professor at Berkeley, he couldn't say his fictional grandfather worked there as well, because Lowenstein would know fellow professors. He took a gamble and said, "He worked for different museums. He was at the San Francisco Museum of Modern Art for many years. Did you teach at UC also?"

"I was a medical doctor." Lowenstein laughed. "Been retired a few years myself. Around here, most every doctor is a PhD."

"My grandfather said Mr. Harris often spoke about his granddaughter, Sheila. Did you know her?"

"Ah, I'll bet your grandfather talks about you too, Matt. But Sheila . . . she was everything to him. Do you have children?"

"Afraid not."

"Well, men often become fathers about the same time their careers are taking off. That was the case with Mel. I think he regretted not spending more time with his children. When Sheila was born, he had time and spoiled her rotten." Lowenstein smiled. "As a little girl, she'd come out and visit him and

Marie during the summers and even went on vacation with them. They were overjoyed when Sheila was accepted to UC and could move in with them full time. When she graduated, she got a job in the area and continued to live with them."

Sinclair pulled a copy of the photo of Sheila on the beach from his pocket. "I think my grandfather vacationed with Mr. Harris a few times. He gave me this photo to make sure I asked about Sheila."

Lowenstein removed his wire-rimmed glasses, wiped them on his sweater, and studied the photograph. "Such a beautiful girl. She was the spitting image of Marie. She must've inherited her island genes."

"Island?" Sinclair asked.

"I guess your grandfather didn't tell you much about the young Melvin. He was quite adventurous for an African American man coming of age in the fifties. After school, he studied art in Paris. There, he was inspired by the work of Paul Gaugin and moved to Martinique to paint the same scenes made famous by the French master. That's where he met Marie. Some of his most famous early paintings were portraits of her."

The breeze picked up, bringing a gust of cool air through the trees from the bay far below. "Where's Marie now?"

"Died about eight years ago. Cancer. Mel started slipping after that."

"I guess that's where they vacationed," Sinclair said looking at the photo. "Certainly a beautiful beach."

"Oh, no. After they married, Marie fell in love with America. She always said America had beaches just as beautiful as Martinique and then joked that they weren't filled with rude French tourists. They discovered Hilton Head Island back in the sixties, before the development really took off. Until Marie passed, they went down there for two or three weeks every June and for a week or so in December between semesters."

"Was there any special place they liked to stay there?"

"Jeez, I don't know. I just remember Mel talking about walking on the beach and sitting in the sun."

"I'm sure my grandfather would love to talk to Sheila. You wouldn't happen to have a phone number for her?"

He shook his head. "She got her own apartment when Mel was moved into the home. The last I saw her was at the facility in El Cerrito. We spoke about how dreadful a place it was, and she said she was going to move him to a nicer assisted-living home in Napa as soon as she could come up with the money to pay the difference."

Dr. Lowenstein would've talked all night if Sinclair let him, but he had what he needed. He thanked him for his hospitality and returned to his car. As he drove his Mustang around the eastern edge of the UC campus on his way home, his phone rang. He pressed the button on the steering wheel. "Hello."

"Hi, Matt, this is Lori."

"Hey, Lori. How are you?"

"Good. My roommate said Sheila's trip just happened all of a sudden, like she just got extra vacation days or something. She packed a suitcase and left Tuesday evening."

"Did she say where she was going?"

"Only that she didn't need a big suitcase, because all she needed was a swimsuit, shorts, and T-shirts."

"How long was she planning to be gone?"

"That's what was strange. Sheila told my roommate she didn't know when she'd be back."

"Her old phone's been disconnected. Did she leave a new phone number or any way to reach her?"

"That was weird too. She told my roommate she was getting a new phone and would text her the number. But she hasn't yet."

"If you get it, can you let me know?"

"Sure. Take care, Matt."

There was no doubt in Sinclair's mind that Sheila had gone into hiding. And he was pretty sure he knew where.

Chapter 40

Sinclair made himself a quick dinner of stir-fried vegetables and sliced chicken breast, which he ate at his kitchen table with his laptop in front of him. People hiding out from the police often flee to their parents' house or where they grew up, but after talking to Dr. Lowenstein and Charlotte, Sinclair got the feeling Sheila wasn't especially close to her parents. Besides, Sheila seemed more sophisticated than the average crook he dealt with and would know that would be the first place someone would look for her. June in central Michigan can be warm, sometimes downright hot, but nights sometimes dropped into the fifties, so it wouldn't be a place to travel to without a jacket and long pants. Although he'd never been to Hilton Head, he'd spent enough hot, humid summers in the south, courtesy of the Army, to know you didn't need a jacket come June in South Carolina.

People connected to homicide cases fled afterward for a variety of reasons. If they were a suspect in the killing, fleeing to someplace the police couldn't find them made sense. If they were a witness, the reasons got more complicated. It could be they just didn't want to get involved. Maybe they were a friend or business associate of the killer. Maybe they too were involved in some sort of illegal activity, which they wanted to conceal from the authorities. Or maybe they were hiding from the killer because the killer wanted to eliminate anyone who might testify against them. It was also possible the killer was out to murder other people for the same reason they'd killed the first victim, so they had to get out of Dodge to stay alive. Sinclair didn't know into which category Sheila fell.

Police fugitive apprehension units normally begin their search for perpetrators in locations where they had previously lived or visited because people felt comfortable in familiar places. Sinclair remembered a drive-by shooting case in West Oakland he'd investigated a few years ago. The shooter hid out at a cousin's house in East Oakland because no one knew him on that side of town. The shooter had never been more than twenty miles from Oakland in his life, so the other side of town was a world away to him. Needless to say, it didn't take Sinclair long to find him. Hiding out on the other side of the country was different. If he was still working and told Maloney he wanted to fly three thousand miles to look for a witness, the lieutenant would've kicked him out of his office. The department didn't have the budget to fly somewhere on a hunch, and the truth was, the tiny pieces of information he had that pointed to Hilton Head didn't amount to much more than that.

Sinclair perused several websites about Hilton Head Island. A barrier island just north of Georgia, it was a popular beach and golf destination and was connected to the South Carolina mainland by a bridge. The island had a population of 40,000, but with hundreds of resorts, hotels, and timeshares, 2.5 million people a year visited the island. Although Sinclair didn't know whether she was hiding out from the killer or from the police, if she was good at hiding her trail, she'd be hard to find on an island with that kind of transient population. If he were still a homicide investigator, he'd contact all the airlines and confirm she actually flew there. Then he'd contact the car rental agencies at the airport and check her name with alternate airport transportation, such as busses and shuttles. He'd then contact the local police for help. Police in tourist destinations often had contacts with the hotels and could send out a mass inquiry when they were looking for someone. They could also blanket the town with her photo in hopes that some waiter, hotel clerk, or bartender recognized her.

He called Braddock. "How's it going?" he asked.

"That was a great tip about the motorcycle shop. I called Jankowski, and he called a CHP buddy who works on a regional auto theft task force. There's a law that allows them to inspect any vehicle repair facility for stolen vehicles or parts without a warrant. When we showed up, Irish Mike and a few bikers were drinking beer around the back, so we detained them and searched the place. The task force officers found a hot engine, transmission, and some other Harley parts, which was enough to haul everyone downtown. We also found a case of brand-new light-blue shop rags. Mike said he orders those because no real man would walk off with them like they do with regular red ones."

"Except for Tiny," Sinclair said.

"We're taking a break in our interview right now, but Mike already said he'd gone to lunch with Tiny before in Tiny's van, which always had a bunch of his rags on the floor."

"I don't remember Tiny having a van."

"There's none registered to him," she said. "It's supposed to be an old gray Ford. Jankowski figures he bought it for cash and never registered it."

"What about others who might have some of his shop rags?"

"He says anyone who comes in the shop could pick one up, but why would they? My guess is, after our suspect killed Phil, he grabbed what was available to wipe the blood off his hands."

"Could the murder have happened at the motorcycle shop?"

"Nothing to indicate it," she said. "We have a few techs going through the place, so if there's any evidence there, we'll know."

"Which brings us back to Tiny." He sighed.

"Mike remembers Tiny getting a phone call sometime around eight Monday night and leaving all of a sudden in his van. That fits with when Phil was murdered."

"Do other Simbas hang out at his shop?"

"Not according to Mike," she said. "The Simbas are all pretty much Oakland guys, so unless you work there like Tiny did, there wouldn't be much reason to come out to Concord."

"Did Mike say anything about what happened Monday night?"

"I don't know if he's telling the truth or if it's his way of keeping himself out of it, but Mike said everyone heard about the bar shooting. When he saw Tiny the next day, he reminded him to keep all club business out of his shop."

"How convenient."

"He's pissed at Tiny right now," she said. "He hasn't seen him since the police chased him and Tiny dumped his bike. He thinks Tiny got into it with the Hells Angels or some other rival gang. It seems that Irish Mike thinks Fletcher is affiliated with the Angels, and we didn't let on any differently."

"He'll be happy to know his cover's still intact."

"We're gonna have another go at Mike, press him on the murder. If we get nothing, we'll probably call it a night."

"You find anything more on Sheila?"

"Been busy with this. I hope to get some time tomorrow to try to track her down," Braddock said. "What've you been up to?"

"Nothing much. Right now, I'm looking at vacation destinations on my computer. Have you ever been to Hilton Head?"

"No, if I wanted sun and sand, I think I'd go to Hawaii. It's an easier flight, and the weather's better."

"I wish I was with you guys right now."

"Me too, Matt. I'll talk to you tomorrow."

Sinclair hung up and called his mother. After the *Hi, how are you*s and *I'm fine*s, he bit his tongue and asked how his father was doing.

"We're in a cardiac rehab facility now. He's sitting up in his chair watching TV."

"That's good. Are you getting rest yourself, Mom?"

"They kick me out of here early every night and only let me visit for an hour or two at a time. They want him either resting or doing his exercises and say I'm an interference. Can you believe that? I'm an interference to his recovery!"

Sinclair heard a bark and saw Amber sitting outside the door. He opened the door, and she ran in with her tail wagging, then dropped to the ground and rolled onto her back. He crouched down and rubbed her belly. "It's probably good for both of you."

"Do you think you'll have time to come up and see your father?"

"I'm still pretty busy with work," he lied. "But I'll try."

He hung up and sat on the floor. Amber rested her head in his lap, and he thought about the puppy he had for too short of a time as a kid. A few months after his little brother, Billy, had died, his mother brought home a little black puppy from the shelter. Although Lucky was supposed to be for both him and his brother, Jimmy, Sinclair took on the responsibility of feeding and training him. His father made it clear that if he ended up having to feed him or pick up one piece of dog poop, Lucky was gone. That was no problem for Sinclair. Lucky filled a void left by his brother's death. The dog was his shadow from the moment he got home from school until he went to bed. They were always together, playing, going for walks, or just sitting together in his room while he did his homework.

Sinclair had checked out books from the library about dog training, and by the time Lucky was nine months old, he knew a dozen commands and walked at heel without pulling on the leash or straying from Sinclair's side. One night, he overheard his father and mother in one of their many arguments. This time it was over Lucky. His father scolded his mother for having spent money required by the shelter for shots and neutering, yelling angrily that a dog couldn't replace the son they had lost.

His mother, in one of her rare moments of standing up to him, replied that she didn't get Lucky to replace Billy. Instead Lucky was someone Matt and Jimmy could love that would love them back in return, something their father never did. The louder the arguing became, the tighter Sinclair hugged Lucky.

One day, just after Lucky turned a year old, Sinclair came home from school, but Lucky didn't meet him at the door. He found him lying on his bedroom floor with barely enough energy to raise his head and wag his tail. Lucky didn't touch his food that night or the next morning. His mother agreed they needed to take him to the vet, but when his father found out they were about to spend more money on a dog, his anger erupted. When he was a kid, his father said, they didn't waste money on sick or old dogs. They put them down and got new ones. Sinclair and his brother scrounged what money they had saved from mowing lawns in the neighborhood and promised they would pay their father back no matter what it cost to make Lucky better. Finally, his father relented, and Sinclair wrapped Lucky in an old beach towel and carried him to the car.

Sinclair and his brother were getting in the car when his father told them they couldn't come—he couldn't stand having two little boys crying in the car all the way to the vet. His father left with Lucky alone. He came back a few hours later without Lucky. He had said that Lucky was too sick to save and that the vet had to put him to sleep. Jimmy cried himself to sleep that night, but Sinclair never shed a tear. He was angry. Angry that he'd abandoned Lucky. If he'd been there, he could've convinced the vet to save him. The following day, he went to the family car to get the old beach towel and Lucky's leash. When he popped the trunk, he saw the towel, the leash, and a shovel caked with mud from down by the river where he used to take Lucky for long walks. At that moment, he knew his father never took Lucky to the vet. He took Lucky down to the river, killed him, and buried him there.

Chapter 41

The main cabin lights came on, and the flight attendant announced it was five o'clock, but Sinclair's watch and his body said it was two o'clock in the morning. Sinclair didn't like flying under the best of circumstances. Being stuck in a middle seat between an overweight man, whose bulk spread into Sinclair's already cramped space, and a young mother cradling an infant in her lap who cried continually from the time they took off made the flight even more miserable.

His back, neck, and shoulders were on fire from being crammed into a seat designed for people six inches shorter and with shoulders six inches narrower. When he tried to sleep, his head extended over the headrest. When he slouched down in his seat enough to support his head, his back ached within thirty minutes. When he actually dozed off for a few minutes, a six-year-old kid in the seat behind him kicked his seat and jarred him awake. Unable to sleep, he spent most of the flight signed onto the free Wi-Fi researching Hilton Head Island—where tourists stayed, what they did for recreation, and where they ate, drank, and shopped. He looked at hundreds of photos, trying to identify the buildings in the background of Sheila's photograph. Even though his laptop was small, when he opened the lid enough to see the screen, with the seat in front of him reclined, the laptop's keyboard was resting against his sternum. He didn't know how people actually typed on a computer in coach seats.

★

He breezed through the ultraclean Savannah airport terminal with his leather carry-on and out to pick up his rental car. His sunglasses immediately fogged over when he stepped into the humid air, which he tried to think of as tropical rather than sauna-like. He threw the leather duffle bag onto the passenger seat, dug out a portable GPS, and entered an address in the heart of Hilton Head Island. Traveling north on I-95, a huge sign welcomed him to South Carolina. He wondered where the industrial and commercial blight and sketchy neighborhoods he'd seen in every other city were. All he saw were lush green trees, flowering shrubs, new developments, and golf courses.

His stomach was growling so he scrolled through restaurants on the GPS. He saw a Cracker Barrel on the list and hit enter. He wasn't familiar with the chain—it wasn't a California restaurant—but figured it had to be better than Wendy's, which had also come up in the search. He passed a sign for Sun City Hilton Head, one of the many gated golf communities in the Bluffton and Hilton Head area he had read about. With seven thousand homes, three golf courses, swimming pools, tennis courts, and other amenities on five thousand acres, it was one of the largest communities in the area. Sinclair couldn't imagine himself living in a place like that. He pictured thousands of old people dressed in plaid shorts getting around on walkers, playing shuffleboard and bridge, and engaging in hour-long discussions about their medical ailments.

Every breakfast combination at Cracker Barrel seemed to include grits, so he ordered the one with scrambled eggs, bacon, and biscuits and told the waitress she could keep the grits. He was sipping his coffee and studying one of the tourist maps of Hilton Head Island he'd grabbed at the airport when the waitress returned with his food. "There ya go, honey," she said. "Visiting here for the first time?"

"Is it obvious?"

"I don't recognize you." She grinned. "And you dress like someone still working for a living."

He was dressed in khaki pants, a green polo, and sneakers among a crowd wearing shorts and sandals. Four men in their sixties and seventies wearing golf shirts and shorts sat at the table next to him. They were tan and looked fitter than most people Sinclair knew twenty years younger. On the other side of them sat six women about the same age dressed in tennis outfits.

"I guess I should be glad you didn't say I dress like a northerner," Sinclair said.

"'Visitor' is code for 'Yankee.'" She grinned again. "Truth is, there are probably more northerners living in the Hilton Head area than most places up north."

He pulled the beach photo of Sheila from his pocket. "I'm trying to find this beach."

She studied the photo. "I guess it could be South Beach down in Sea Pines, but I've never seen no buildings like that down there. Maybe Folly Field. That's where most locals go. There's lots of timeshares, hotels, and condos you can see from the beach. If you go down the beach to the left, you'll hit the Westin and some other resorts. The other way, you'll see more and eventually run into Palmetto Dunes."

"How long's the beach?"

"They say there's sixteen miles of beach on the island, but you find most of the people right next to the public access areas. If not Folly, try Coligny. That's where most tourists go."

Sinclair finished his breakfast and returned to his car. It wasn't quite eleven o'clock and the thermometer in his rental car showed it was eighty-eight. With the humidity, it felt like a hundred. He followed the divided highway past more gated communities, shopping plazas, and golf courses and over a bridge that crossed the Intracoastal Waterway, which separated the mainland from Hilton Head Island.

Sinclair couldn't get over how lush, green, and colorful Hilton Head was compared to the brown dryness of the Bay Area. Magnolia trees bloomed with white flowers, and Crape Myrtles with vivid red and pink flowers lined the road. Spanish moss hung from giant live oaks that were hundreds of years old. After walking more than three miles along Folly Field Beach, his pants and shirt were soaked with his sweat and he had no luck finding a building that matched his photograph. The light breeze had done little to cool the blazing heat.

Coligny Plaza was fifteen minutes down the road, past more golf courses, high-end resorts, and restaurants. He bought a pair of overpriced cargo shorts; a T-shirt that read, *Hilton Head Island, Laid Back Since Way Back*; a baseball cap; and a small backpack in a store that also sold surfboards and boogie boards.

He stripped off his hot, sweat-soaked clothes in a public restroom, stuffed them in the pack, and trudged across the street toward the beach. He passed a large splash pad, where laughing and screaming kids were running through giant sprays of water, and walked down a wooden boardwalk bordered by shaded arbors where people sat on porch swings.

This beach was a lot more crowded than the last one. People sat in beach chairs under umbrellas and lay on towels in the sun, while others waded and swam in the shallow water. Carrying his sneakers, Sinclair made his way toward the water. The coconut fragrance coming from sunscreen covering the mass of tanned female bodies in skimpy swimsuits distracted him for a few seconds. He turned right and walked along the water's edge. A small wave lapped over his feet. Warm water, unlike Northern California. A slender fortysomething woman wearing gym shorts, a bikini top, and wide-rimmed floppy hat walking the opposite way on the beach smiled at him. Her long, sun-bleached hair looked like it was styled by the salt water, sun, and wind. He wondered how Alyssa would look with sandy feet and wind-blown beach hair.

He looked across the sand toward a string of buildings, pulled out the photo, and studied it. Sheila stood in fluffy white sand wearing a conservative two-piece swimsuit. A few other people in swimsuits were in the distance. Past small sand dunes covered with wisps of sea grass was a large, brown stucco building with darker brown shingles on the sides. There were three rows of balconies, meaning it was probably a four-story building. On the right side of the roof was a raised structure, possibly some sort of penthouse. The corner of another building showed in the far right of the frame. It looked like a motel with rooms facing perpendicular to the beach. In the foreground of the motel-looking building was some sort of structure with a thatched roof that resembled a fake Polynesian hut.

He walked away from the water across the wet, packed sand and stopped to look at the scene in front of him. He was standing in the exact spot where Sheila's picture was taken.

Chapter 42

Sinclair made his way through an outdoor beach bar into a hotel café and to the front lobby. A sign on the front desk announced he was at the Holiday Inn Beach House Resort. "Hi, can you tell me if a Sheila Harris is staying here?"

"Sorry, but we can't give out guest information," the woman behind the counter said.

"What if someone called and asked to be connected to her room?" Sinclair asked.

"Then you'd be connected."

"Or told that she's not staying here," Sinclair said.

"Right," she said. "Sorry, but I'm just following the rules."

Sinclair stepped outside the front door, searched for the hotel on his phone, and called the number. "Beach House Resort, how may I help you?" replied a female voice.

"Can you connect me to the room of Sheila Harris, please?"

A moment later, the voice said, "I'm sorry, but we have no guest by that name."

Sinclair went out the back door to the outdoor bar known as the Tiki Hut and climbed onto a barstool. Twenty or thirty people sat around the bar and at nearby tables. There was a day when Sinclair could've vacationed for a week in a place like this, having his first drink after breakfast and his last one before returning to his room to sleep at night. But now, he'd take home more memories and see more sights than the inside of bars. The bartender was bald and in his late forties. "What can I get you?"

"You got ice tea?"

The bartender filled a plastic cup with ice and poured tea from a pitcher on the bar. Sinclair said, "Guess this place gets pretty lively at night."

"Sometimes," he said. "We have a band every night. A lot of partying."

Sinclair chugged the drink and slid the cup back toward him. The bartender filled it again. "I'm looking for a friend who's supposed to be down here, but her phone isn't working."

"Visitors are always frying their phones in the sun or drowning them in the surf."

"Her name's Sheila Harris," Sinclair said.

"I don't know visitors by name. They come and go too often."

Sinclair slid the headshot of Sheila across the bar. "Does she look familiar?"

"I never forget a pretty face. Frozen daiquiri drinker. She's been coming here for years. I just saw her a few nights ago."

"Any idea where she's staying?"

"There's gotta be a thousand hotel rooms and villas within walking distance. Could be anywhere."

"What's a villa?"

The bartender laughed. "A fancy name for a condo unit. Most are individually owned and rented out by one of the rental companies or on VRBO—that's vacation rental by owner, a website."

"Was she with someone?"

"It was busy, but I think she was sitting at a table with a couple of other cute chicks about her age. Stayed for a few drinks, then left."

"Where else would cute chicks like her go?"

"Man, the island is one big party spot. Grab one of the magazines and you'll see places all over with music and alcohol."

"If you see her again, can you call me?"

"We're pretty busy here, guy."

Sinclair pushed a fifty across the bar. "The rest of this is your tip."

"Gimme your number."

Sinclair wrote his number on a page from his pocket note-book, handed it to the bartender, and headed back to the beach. The next complex was Ocean One Villas. Sinclair spoke to a couple as they were exiting the building. They said all units were rented by individual owners, so there'd be no master list of guests. After passing four or five additional condominium complexes, he came to a Marriott resort. He didn't even try going to the desk but called the number he found on the website. The operator who answered the phone said they had no Sheila Harris registered there. He talked to the bartender at the pool bar, but he didn't recognize her photograph.

Sinclair walked back down the beach, the sun high overhead beating down on him. The beach had been mostly vacant until he got closer to Coligny Park. He eyed the women as he walked by, hoping Sheila would be one of them. But no such luck. As he walked by the showers, he wished he was in a swimsuit so he could wash the sweat from his body but instead opted for rinsing off his feet before he slipped his sneakers back on. As he continued, he stopped in a flatbread restaurant and a few other places to show Sheila's photograph. He then crossed the street to the plaza, where he went from shop to shop showing her photo and leaving his number with anyone who would take it.

By four o'clock he felt hot, tired, and hopeless. He got his laptop from his car and entered a casual café that had air conditioning and Wi-Fi. He plugged his phone into his computer to charge it while he worked and ordered a Diet Coke. He searched for the nearest hotels and began calling them. Four had told him Sheila wasn't registered there when his phone buzzed, showing Braddock in caller ID.

"How's it going?" he asked.

"Fine. How's it going with you?" she said in a singsong tone that said something was wrong.

He ignored it and asked, "Any luck locating Sheila?"

She hesitated for a few beats and then said, "I went to her apartment, but there was no answer. The manager wasn't much help. Said she moved in with a roommate who was the one that completed the rental application. The roommate moved out two years ago, and the manager never had Sheila fill out any paperwork, so he knows nothing about her other than her name and cell phone number, which, by the way, is now disconnected. I canvassed the building, but it's a working-class place, and everyone's gone during the day. I took a chance and called the number we had for her parents. Spoke to Charlotte, who is her stepmother. She said Sheila lives her own life and talks to her husband—Sheila's father—about once a month. She doesn't even know anything about where she works other than it's somewhere in Oakland and it has something to do with the business undergrad degree she received at Cal."

"That's too bad," he said.

"Charlotte wondered why other people were looking for her daughter. She got a call a few days ago from Sheila's work wondering if she was all right. Before you ask, no, she didn't get a name or even the name of the company. Then yesterday, she got a call from someone named Matt Roberts. Coincidentally, this man has the same cell phone number as you."

"Cathy, I can explain."

"What the hell are you doing, Matt? You're on admin leave. If you're caught working this case, you can kiss your job good-bye."

"I can't just sit around doing nothing."

"A few hours ago, Uppy called. He asked if I knew where you were and what you were doing. At that time, I was able to tell him honestly that I thought you were taking it easy at your house. He seemed worried that you were about to extend yourself so far out on a limb, there'd be no way down."

"I'm just trying to track down Sheila before your deadline."

"Oh, make me out to be the bad guy because I won't cover up police corruption."

"I'm not saying that. We both want the truth. Either Phil was a good cop, or he went bad at some point. Even if he was dirty, if he wasn't killed over whatever he was involved in, he still deserves a police funeral, and we don't need to ruin his reputation."

"It's all black and white to you," she said. "Last December, when we finally determined Councilmember Yates had nothing to do with Dawn's murder, you still wanted to publicly shame him for hiring an escort and getting her pregnant. But you'll give Phil a pass."

"That's different." He searched his fatigued mind for the rationale. "Phil's dead. If he was still alive and taking graft, I'd report him in a heartbeat. You know I won't tolerate crooked cops. But he's dead. What would be gained from dragging his name through the mud?"

"If we conceal this and it turns out to have something to do with his murder, we'll have tainted the investigation so badly, they'll never be able to prosecute the killer."

Braddock knew which buttons to push. There was nothing more important to him than bringing a murderer to justice. "I wish I never told you about the cigar box in his locker."

"Why, so you could decide how to handle this based on Matt Sinclair's rules of right and wrong?"

"No, so I could've avoided dragging you into this. You know my opinion, but this is your case now, so the decisions are yours. Just be aware of the consequences of whatever choice you make."

"Are you going to tell me where you are and what you're doing?" she asked.

"It's probably best you don't know. That way you won't have something else you need to hide."

He didn't blame Braddock. Deciding whether or not to reveal Phil's activity was tough for anyone. It shouldn't have to be made by police sergeants. If the department had a chief with the courage to make the right decision, he'd have no problem pushing it up the chain of command. But Brown made decisions based on what was best for himself. He'd always take the safe way out. And the safe decision meant telling the city administrator and mayor, both of whom would do whatever best ensured their political survival. They'd cancel Phil's funeral and release the information to the press so they could tout how transparent they were on police misconduct and corruption.

Chapter 43

Sinclair took several gulps of his Coke and returned to his computer. After searching for Hilton Head rentals and coming up with hundreds of options ranging from one-bedroom condos for a thousand dollars a week to an eight-bedroom house on the beach for twenty-eight thousand, Sinclair remembered Dr. Lowenstein telling him that Melvin Harris had been coming to Hilton Head since the sixties. If Sinclair planned to vacation at the same place year after year, he'd consider buying a timeshare or even a condo that he could rent out the rest of the year.

It took Sinclair a few minutes to figure out how to navigate the Beaufort County assessor's website and enter a search for property tax records in the name of Melvin Harris. One entry popped up: a two-bedroom, two-bath villa owned by Melvin Harris, trustee, with a mailing address for the property tax bill in Birmingham, Michigan. Sinclair entered the address in Google Maps. A six-minute walk away. He slid his laptop into his backpack and rushed out the door, through the parking lot, and down Forest Beach Drive. He jogged through the parking lot and followed signs directing him to the unit. An elevator with glass sides provided a view of lush lagoons and tennis courts as it took him to the third floor. He followed an open concrete landing to 315 and knocked.

A white man in his late forties wearing knee-length swimming trunks and a baggy tank top advertising the Crab Shack Restaurant opened the door.

"I'm looking for Sheila or Melvin Harris," Sinclair said.

"You must have the wrong villa. We're the Hodges."

"Who's there?" a woman yelled from inside.

"No one," he yelled back. "A man's got the wrong unit."

"Who's he looking for?" she yelled.

"Sheila or Melvin Harris," Sinclair said loud enough for her to hear.

A few seconds later, a full-figured woman wearing a long cover-up over a swimsuit appeared in the doorway. "Excuse my husband," she said. "He's an idiot." She turned to her husband. "How long we been coming here? The Harrises are the owners of this villa. The black family." She turned back to Sinclair. "They're usually here this week and we rent another unit, but for some reason it was available, so we got it. When you come the same week year after year, you get to know other people in the building because people stick with the same weeks."

"Do you know Sheila?"

"Sure. Mr. Harris's granddaughter. She used to always come with her grandfather and usually her parents or an aunt and uncle."

"When did you last see her?" Sinclair asked.

"She left when we moved in on Saturday. She's staying with some friends in another villa until we leave. Unless it's rented at the last minute, she'll move back in."

"What unit is she staying in?"

"Three-oh-nine, down the hall. Tiffany and Rob are the couple who're renting there. Tiffany's sister stays with them. Those two have been hanging out down here together since they were teenagers."

Sinclair thanked them, went down the hall, and knocked on 309. An athletic man about Sinclair's age answered the door. A baseball game was on a TV inside. "Is Sheila here?"

"Who are you?"

"Matt, a friend of Sheila's from California."

The man eyed Sinclair up and down. "Girl's night out. She went with my wife and her sister for drinks and maybe dancing."

"Where at?" Sinclair was losing patience, but if he pushed too hard and too fast, he'd get nothing.

"They said they were starting at the Boathouse, something about happy hour from four to seven."

"When did they leave?"

"Maybe half hour ago. But it's supposed to be just the girls—my wife is obviously married, her sister's engaged, and Sheila—well, Sheila's sworn off men for a while."

"No problem," Sinclair said. "We're just friends."

Sinclair strolled down the hallway. When he heard the door shut, he began running. He bypassed the elevator and bounded down the staircase two steps at a time. He sprinted through the parking lot and turned onto the sidewalk, breaking into an easy run that covered the distance rapidly without attracting undo attention. He started the car, searched for the Boathouse on his GPS, and took off while it calculated the route.

He had noted the Boathouse Restaurant when he studied the map earlier. Along with the Charthouse and Hudson's, it was one of three restaurants on Skull Creek, which was not a creek at all but actually part of the Intracoastal Waterway. Past the Boathouse lay Hilton Head Plantation, a huge gated community that encompassed the northern corner of the island.

At a sign for the Boathouse, he turned down a long driveway with parking stalls on both sides. A gigantic metal building fifty feet high stretched the length of a football field on his right. Inside, boats of all shapes and sizes were stacked on racks to the ceiling, to be removed and placed in the water with a special forklift when the boat owners called. He parked near the street and jogged down the driveway.

Past the boat storage building, the driveway ended and the restaurant was to his immediate left. A line of people waited to give their names to a woman standing outside at a hostess podium. Avoiding the crowd around the restaurant, Sinclair walked to the right of the pier where a sign read, *Beer Garden*. Wood chips covered the ground under huge live oak trees, and a young woman was setting up speakers and running cables on a raised bandstand in front of a bunch of large picnic tables. He scanned the faces of the people sitting at the tables and standing in line for a beer but didn't see anyone looking like Sheila.

Sinclair skirted past the hostess stand and waded through an outdoor seating area filled with diners surrounding huge plates of fish and crab and smaller plates of hamburgers and salads. The aroma of fried fish filled the air. He weaved through the tables toward a covered rectangular bar surrounded by people laughing and talking. Three bartenders scurried back and forth with drinks and bottles of beer. Large fans above made the thick, muggy air almost bearable.

Sinclair scanned the crowd around the bar. Thirty people on barstools and twice that many at small tables around the bar and sitting on chairs facing the water. Many were in their twenties and thirties and dressed for the weather, with men in shorts and T-shirts, polo shirts, or Hawaiian-style shirts, and women in sundresses or shorts and tank tops.

Around the far end of the bar, Sinclair spotted the back of a tall, slender woman with long jet-black hair talking to two attractive blondes dressed in loose, sheer tops over bright-colored sports bras. He made his way through the crowd to the other side of the bar.

He maneuvered where he could finally see her face. She glanced at him, smiled, and looked away, probably used to men's eyes looking and lingering too long. A second later, she caught his eye again. Her face showed a flash of fear followed by surprise or confusion. He pushed through the crowd toward her.

"Hi, Sheila, my name's Matt Sinclair."

Her face relaxed. "Hi, Matt." She smiled. "I've been expecting you."

Chapter 44

Sinclair bought two cans of Diet Coke from the beer garden bar and sat on a picnic table across from Sheila. Except for the band setting up and a few people at other tables, they had the area to themselves.

"You look like—what's that cowboy saying?—you've been ridden hard and put away wet," Sheila said as she poured her soda into the cup of ice.

Sinclair removed his baseball cap, noticed a white salt ring around its rim, and ran a hand through his greasy hair. He'd been on the go for the last twenty-four hours with one objective in mind. He wished he could bask in the glory of mission accomplishment for a while and take a long shower, drink a gallon of water, and lie down for twelve hours of uninterrupted sleep. But how he handled the next hour or so would determine whether it was worth the effort or not. He had so many questions that he didn't know where to start. Sinclair preferred conducting police interviews from a position of advantage, where his knowledge of the facts and his authority left the interviewee uncomfortable, even a bit intimidated. Instead, he felt physically and mentally exhausted—beat up by the past few days, while Sheila looked rested, composed, and comfortable in his presence.

"How do you like Hilton Head?" She took a sip of her drink and waited for a response, as if they were on a first date and getting to know each other through small talk.

"Hot." He popped the top of his soda and poured it over the ice.

"You get used to it."

The ease with which Sheila carried a conversation reminded him of Dawn. He imagined that skill was even more important for an escort than her abilities in the bedroom. "You can probably imagine I've been through a lot to find you." Turning the conversation to her, he asked, "But how are you, Sheila? How are you doing?"

The smile and facade of false confidence left her face, and tears began to well in her eyes. He read in her face the journey she'd been on, one that may have been more arduous than his own. "I'm more scared than I've ever been in my life. I don't know what to do next and don't know who to trust."

Until he got a better feel for who Sheila was and what she knew, he would stick with open-ended questions. He had the feeling he wouldn't need to pry the truth out of her. "Why are you scared?"

She dabbed her eyes with a cocktail napkin. "Phil's dead. He was murdered. You, if anyone, should know that."

"When you first saw me, you said you've been expecting me. What did you mean by that?"

"The more I got to know Phil, the more he talked about himself and the people close to him. He said you were the best homicide detective in the world. He joked about how sorry he felt for those poor crooks that committed a murder when you were on call. When I ran, I figured someone would come looking for me. I didn't know if it would be the cops or . . . them. Then I read in the paper that you were assigned Phil's murder. If you were everything Phil said you were, you'd figure out who I was and find me."

Sinclair didn't know whether to feel flattered or be pissed that Phil was sharing things with his prostitute that he wouldn't share with a brother officer who'd had his back for years. "Sheila, please believe I'm not judging you. I know about your employment with Special Ladies Escorts, so that's where we need to start. Is that where you first met Phil?"

She tilted her head sideways with a confused look. She then began laughing. "Oh, my! You don't have a clue, do you?"

He really hated when the person he was interviewing had the upper hand. And he hated it even more when they gloated about it. He sipped his Coke and waited for her to get over herself.

"Phil wasn't my client. We weren't lovers. I was a source, his confidential informant, or, if you prefer, his snitch."

Sinclair did his best to conceal his relief. He felt like hugging Sheila and immediately calling Braddock to give her the good news. "Since I really don't have a clue, why don't you start from the beginning and fill me in."

She told him Phil showed up at her apartment, flashed his badge, and insisted they talk one evening just before Christmas. He had photos and records showing every client she'd serviced since working for the agency and how much money she'd made. He also knew everything about her, including her employment and family. He had enough evidence to prove numerous counts of prostitution and federal tax evasion; however, if she worked for him, he would forget all of it. She'd broken down. She wasn't proud of what she did but saw it as an easy way to make extra money. She'd wanted to move her grandfather into a nicer assisted-living facility, but her stepmother said there wasn't enough money in his estate to do so. Sheila's father had the power of attorney, but he delegated all financial matters to his new wife, a woman Sheila didn't trust at all. A friend introduced Sheila to the owner of the escort service, who assured her she could easily make two thousand dollars a month, the amount needed to move him into the Napa facility, with one or two calls a week.

Sheila wasn't naïve. She knew the men Phil was interested in were involved in criminal activity and could be dangerous, but she also knew she was in the unique position to provide him the information he needed, so she insisted she wanted more than immunity from prosecution. She wanted payment so she could keep her grandfather in his home. She insisted that Phil not reveal her identity to anyone at all, because she knew the men she was involved with had friends everywhere, including judges, prosecutors, and cops. She suggested they meet outside of the Bay Area, and when she told Phil she visited her grandfather every Saturday in Napa, they developed a plan where they could meet up there for a few hours every Friday and she could pass on everything she picked up the previous week.

"So you met in a romantic restaurant and spent the night in a bed-and-breakfast?" Sinclair asked.

"You would've preferred we sat in a parking lot for three hours eating McDonald's?" she retorted. "I was providing what a bunch of cops had been trying to get for years but couldn't. Phil's bosses must've known that because they had no problem with the expenses. And it was a good cover if someone saw us. I had a legitimate reason to go to Napa every weekend, and I could've explained him away as just a friend or a rich boyfriend, depending on who saw me. We had dinner and talked. Sometimes we continued talking in the room for an hour or two, but nothing ever happened. Phil was a gentleman, and I could tell he loved his wife."

Her story answered most of the questions that had bothered him since he discovered the cigar box. "Did he say who he reported to? Who gave him the money he paid you?"

She shrugged. "He was as worried as I was about who he could trust."

"So who were these clients of yours that Phil was so interested in?"

"It wasn't my clients. It was my day job. I was the office manager and executive assistant to the CEO and president of NorCal, Sergio Kozlov."

Chapter 45

The band was getting ready to play and people were filling the tables in the beer garden, so Sinclair and Sheila strolled down the wide concrete pier that jutted a hundred yards into the water. Three aluminum gangways led down to an array of floating docks where a dozen powerboats and a few sailboats in the twenty- to thirty-foot range were docked. A man dressed in white linen shorts and a silk shirt stepped off a seventy-foot yacht that was tied up on the left side of the pier followed by a woman dressed all in white wearing oversized sunglasses.

Sheila grinned. "Yachters love to mingle with us common folk." She leaned against the railing and looked across the water at the sun, still an hour or two above the horizon. Sinclair recognized the closest land less than a half mile away as Pinckney Island, a four-thousand-acre national wildlife refuge, one of a string of them along the South Carolina and Georgia coast.

"What kind of stuff about Kozlov did you pass along to Phil?" Sinclair asked.

"Everything. From payoffs to politicians to money laundering. I had to be careful to avoid getting caught when I downloaded documents and financials, but as long as I had a legitimate reason for accessing a file, I could copy it and upload it to my cloud and transfer it to Phil."

"Did you give him paper copies of documents or copy stuff to a flash drive for him?" Sinclair asked.

She chuckled. "You remind me so much of Phil. I thought he was going to give me a little spy camera like the CIA used during the Cold War. Do you understand cloud storage?"

A steady breeze ruffled an American flag atop a flagpole at the end of the pier. "Sure. I have my home documents, photos, and such on a cloud, so if I lose my computer in a fire or something, my files are still there."

"You're way ahead of Phil. All he knew was what his coworkers taught him, and that was mostly about the department's system. I helped him create a Google account under his fake name and set up Google Drive for him. I did the same for myself and set it up to share everything with him. When I download files at work to my drive, Phil could upload them to his own drive, which only he had access to."

"What kind of stuff did you give him?"

"As an example, I keep track of our corporate sports team seats. We have four seats for the Golden State Warriors three rows from the court. They're supposed to be worth about two thousand dollars per game. I keep track of who Sergio gives them to. It's done all the time, but you know someone on the Oakland city council can't legally accept a gift worth over a few hundred dollars. I gave Phil the list of everyone who received free game tickets for the Warriors, the Raiders, and the Oakland A's. When certain people appear over and over, you can be sure Sergio's getting something in return."

A blue heron walked along the mud flats at the water's edge and stopped occasionally to jab its beak into the water. "What else?"

"Cash; use of a house in St. Thomas; money contributed to nonprofits, which the nonprofits then turn into campaign contributions; the names of political action committees set up by Sergio for specific politicians; copies of e-mails between Sergio and political candidates discussing how that money would be spent. I managed all these executive accounts and perks, as he called them, and kept track of who got what. Sergio was anal about knowing exactly what he was giving so that whenever he needed something, he could remind the person how generous he'd been."

"Where'd he get the money for this stuff?"

"I'm not the CFO or an accountant, but he has a number of companies incorporated in Nevada with bank accounts in the Caribbean that aren't part of the official accounting. I remember when Sergio had me draw cash from the bank every day for a month. Always under ten thousand. The account I drew the money from was set up with a half million dollars, which, according to rumor, came from a kickback on a land deal that Sergio knowingly overpaid on."

"Did Phil have enough to take down Kozlov and the politicians?"

"Phil wanted the accounting for the entire company, including the shell corporations and Caribbean bank accounts. Although I knew Sergio's password, I had no legitimate reason to access that stuff, and Sergio would know about it the next time he logged in. The IT security people would confirm it came from my computer, and I'd be in big trouble. Phil's plan was that as soon as the lawyers said they had enough evidence, I'd download everything, and Phil would get me into witness protection. Then Phil would swoop in and arrest everybody."

It sounded as if Phil might've been exaggerating what he could do. Getting someone into witness protection was no easy feat, and taking down so many people at that level would require resources well above what the police department had. "Any idea when that was going to happen?"

"He kept saying it would be well before November."

If Phil was close to making a case, what he'd intended to ask Sheila to do would've been the coup de grace. But she got spooked after Phil was murdered. Kozlov would never trust her again, so whatever she could've provided was now lost. "I don't blame you at all for taking off," Sinclair said. "I guess I'll have to look at what you already gave Phil to see if there's enough."

"When Phil was murdered, I knew it was because he got too close, so I initiated our exit plan. I downloaded everything onto my cloud drive, left the office, packed, and flew here."

Professionalism be damned, Sinclair hugged her. "Phil would be proud," he said.

"I did it for him." She pulled her phone from her pocket. "What's your phone number?"

He gave it to her, and a few seconds later, his phone buzzed with a text message.

"That's my Google Drive account name and password along with Phil's account name. I don't know his password."

"What's ChloeLily539 stand for?" he asked.

"Chloe and Lily were my cats. My two best friends when I was a kid."

Sinclair pulled a sheath of folded papers from his pocket. He paged through the copies of Phil's spiral notebook. On the last page, he saw Sheila's account name and password written in Phil's handwriting. Below it was Phil's undercover name written as one word, followed by *MattCathy187*. The number 187 was the California penal code section for murder.

Everything he'd been thinking about Phil for the last six months was wrong. Although he didn't yet know who they might be, he had to get this information to the right people, people who wouldn't try to sweep it under the rug as Chief Brown did last year. Phil wasn't working this alone. The visit by Campbell, Archard, and Uppy was beginning to make sense.

"You thought you were in danger once Phil was dead. What makes you think Kozlov was involved in his murder?"

"That day, Sergio was going through the redevelopment proposal for the Howard Terminal, the abandoned shipping terminal that some businessmen and politicians want to develop into a new stadium. He added a meeting to his calendar for seven o'clock that night. My computer has a master calendar including all his events and appointments, so I spotted it. It didn't list names other than show CC-two, which stands for two city councilmembers; CS-one, which means one city staffer; and B-four, which means four people from the business community."

"He probably has meetings with people all the time." Sinclair was skeptical.

"But seldom at his house. He also had me get money from the safe to put five thousand dollars each into four envelopes. Phil told me before that he needed ways to corroborate the stuff I sent him, so I texted him about the meeting. Maybe he went there and got caught."

The entire time they had been talking, Sinclair was watching people come and go. Couples strolled to the end of the pier, hand in hand, looked at the water, turned around, and strolled back. Parents with kids running ahead of them came down the concrete pier, pointed at the shore birds, and admired the boats. Sheila's two girlfriends walked halfway down the pier, saw Sheila was okay, and sauntered back to the bar.

Two men walking toward them along the right side of the pier caught his eye. Their heads swiveled side to side as they checked out everyone around them. While everyone else wore beach-casual clothes, these men were dressed in long pants and button-front shirts with the shirttails out. Both were taller and more muscular than Sinclair, probably outweighing him by thirty or forty pounds. Both had dark hair, and one had the kind of scruffy look achieved by four or five days without shaving. But when Sinclair noticed one small detail about their appearance, the hairs on the back of his neck stood up and his heart rate jumped. They were both carrying guns.

Chapter 46

The right pants legs of both men hung about an inch lower than the left, signaling that both men wore heavy guns supported by thin belts that didn't properly carry the weight. It was the mark of an amateur, but one that Sinclair had also seen among off-duty cops who weren't used to carrying a gun in plain clothes.

"We need to go." He put his hand on the small of Sheila's back and gently pushed her toward the left side of the pier, away from the men and toward land.

The men turned toward them, blocking their path. They stopped ten feet away. The clean-shaven man looked at Sheila and said, "Sheila Harris, you will come with us." He had an accent that sounded Eastern European.

"Who are you?" Sinclair demanded. "Are you the police?"

The clean-shaven man stepped toward Sheila, stopping an arm's length away. The other people on the pier recognized trouble and began walking away. A few ran. "Ha ha, yes, police," the man said. "That is funny."

"You have this lady mistaken for someone else," Sinclair said. "So we'll just be on our way."

The man put his hand against Sheila's shoulder. "Come with us, now."

Sinclair stepped toward him, but before he could do anything, the other man grabbed him from behind in a bear hug, pinning both of his arms to his sides.

"This not your business." The clean-cut man glared at Sinclair. "You do not want our trouble." He grabbed Sheila by the arm and pulled her down the pier.

He couldn't allow them to take her. A brutal interrogation of Sheila flashed through his mind. Once she revealed what she did with the files, her body would be dumped in one of the many marshes in the area. They obviously didn't know who Sinclair was; otherwise, he'd be dead already. He stomped on the right instep of the man holding him, feeling the crunch of the small bones in the top of his foot. He then bent his legs, as if he were dropping into a squat, while simultaneously clutching his hands together and thrusting them above his head to break the hold.

The man wasn't prepared to hold up Sinclair's weight, especially after the raging pain in his foot. He released his grip, and Sinclair spun around and faced him. The man's face grimaced in pain and rage. He spread his legs apart into a balanced wrestler's stance. Without hesitation, Sinclair kicked him between the legs with his right foot as hard as he could. The man doubled over. When he looked up, Sinclair stepped forward and punched the man in the center of his face with his left fist, turning his hips to give it as much power as he could. The man collapsed in a heap onto the concrete.

The clean-shaven man stopped dragging Sheila down the pier when he saw Sinclair take down his partner. Sinclair covered the distance between them in six giant steps. The man pushed Sheila away and raised his fists like a boxer. She fell onto the pier, banging her head on the concrete. She lay there and looked up at them. Sinclair feinted with his left hand to the man's face. The clean-shaven man raised an arm to block it, opening up his body. Sinclair buried his right fist into the man's solar plexus.

He knew immediately his punch lacked the needed power to end the fight. But it knocked the wind out of his opponent and staggered him back a step. He quickly straightened and rushed at Sinclair, throwing a powerful roundhouse with his right fist toward his face. Off balance, Sinclair was unable to step back quickly enough to get out of range of the man's punch. Instead, he tucked his chin into his chest and leaned farther forward, raising his arm to try to deflect the blow. The man's huge fist struck Sinclair's forearm and glanced off the back of his head.

Dazed but still on his feet, Sinclair twisted to his right to allow the momentum from the man's punch to carry his opponent past him. The man quickly regained his balance and pulled up his shirttail with his left hand.

Once Sinclair saw the butt of the handgun, he pounced.

Sinclair had practiced drawing a handgun thousands of times on the range. Instructors had drummed into him the necessity of keeping your eyes on the target. You know where your gun is on your belt. You don't need to look at it. It's your opponent that will kill you. That's what you need to watch.

Sinclair's adversary obviously never had that training. He was looking down at his gun when Sinclair struck him in the temple with the back of his left fist. He followed it up by driving the palm of his right hand upward, striking the man under his nose. Blood spirted from his broken nose.

The taste of your own blood in your mouth and the blurry vision that accompanies a shattered nose was enough for most men to give up. But not this one. He fumbled at his waist and pulled out the gun.

Sinclair grabbed for it and got both hands on the barrel. He turned sideways to get out of the line of fire and simultaneously clamped one hand over the back of the man's hand. He twisted and pushed the barrel of the gun away from him with his right hand while holding the man's wrist with his left. He heard a squeal of pain as the man's tendons and ligaments popped and his hand opened.

With the pistol now in Sinclair's possession, he stepped back and pointed it at the clean-cut man. He dropped to his knees, groaning and holding his injured hand. Blood and snot dripped from his face. Suddenly, his eyes darted behind Sinclair, and his lips turned upward into a twisted smile.

Sinclair spun around to see the other man pulling a gun from his waistband. Sinclair swung his pistol toward him.

Sinclair had no time to determine what kind of gun he held in his hands. It felt similar to a Glock. A light polymer frame, a heavy slide.

He snapped it up to eye level and pulled the trigger. Two, three, four times. The man staggered back a step, the gun still in his hand. Sinclair fired twice more. The gun fell to the ground, and the man collapsed beside it.

Sinclair stuffed his pistol into his waistband and ran to Sheila. "Are you okay?" he asked.

She looked up at him and nodded. As he was helping her to her feet, the clean-shaven man scrambled past him toward his fallen comrade, scooped up his gun, and leaped over the side of the pier.

The cop in him wanted to give chase, but a fleeing suspect was not an imminent threat. Protecting Sheila had to be his first priority. She put her arm around his shoulder. He wrapped his arm around her waist and walked down the pier toward the restaurant. He saw his attacker trying to run through waist-deep water and muck away from the pier.

With his free hand, Sinclair pulled out his phone and called 9-1-1. It went directly to a recording. No doubt, many others were trying to call too.

A sea of people flooded out of the outdoor area around the restaurant and up the driveway. Cars trying to get out of the parking spaces blew their horns to try to clear the throng of people rushing toward the main road. A few people stood around the bar, stunned or not believing the gunshots they heard were real. A cluster of people stood outside the building, half of them with phones to their ears.

"Has anyone called nine-one-one?" Sinclair yelled.

A man said, "Yeah," and two women said they were on hold.

Sinclair pushed on the door to the restaurant. Locked. He saw people inside, many huddled under tables. "Let's get you out of here and somewhere safe," he said to Sheila.

Sheila held onto him tighter. He trailed the crowd of people heading toward the street. His car was a hundred yards away.

In front of him, the crowd parted. Two men walking against the flow of people pushed through. Both muscular with dark hair and dressed in long pants and button-front shirts. The same Eastern European appearance. Sinclair looked over his shoulder toward the restaurant. Jogging his way was the clean-cut man from the pier, now soaking wet and covered in mud. He held a gun at his side.

Chapter 47

With the path to his car blocked by two men who were undoubtedly armed and the clean-cut man cutting off any escape back toward the restaurant, Sinclair pulled Sheila between two parked cars on their right.

He crouched down, drew the gun, and looked it over. Springfield Model XD. The working mechanism was similar to a Glock, except with a grip safety. Springfield made excellent pistols—reliable and accurate enough out of the box. He popped out the magazine. Seven rounds of nine millimeter remaining. "Can you run?" he asked.

Sheila nodded.

A green chain link fence about five feet high separated the two parking lots. He boosted Sheila over it, then vaulted it himself. He landed in a thicket of small saplings, shrubs, weeds, and branches broken from the large trees above them.

Sheila cried out in pain as a sharp stick jabbed into her calf. Sinclair pulled it out. A trickle of blood oozed out of the wound. "It's not serious," he said. "You gonna be okay?"

She nodded. He grabbed her hand and pushed through the tangle to a strip of grass. Ahead was a parking lot filled with cars that ran between the Chart House restaurant fifty yards to their right and the main road a hundred yards to their left.

He led Sheila down a row of cars to a walkway that led to the restaurant. Sticks snapped behind him. He turned to see the two men crashing out of the thicket.

They saw him and Sheila at the same time. He dragged her behind a pickup truck as gunshots sounded and bullets pinged off the cars around him.

Alone, he could evade his pursuers, staying low and running and crawling around the cars until he got to the far end of the parking lot. But not with Sheila.

He leaned around the truck and fired two shots at the men as they approached the parking lot. They were too far away to hit, but his shots did what he intended. They took cover behind a car.

The Chart House restaurant was less than a hundred yards away. Although his attackers didn't seem to care about bystanders or witnesses who could identify them, they might hesitate rushing into a packed restaurant. Sinclair hated drawing gunmen toward a crowd of innocent people, but he was out of alternatives if he wanted to save Sheila.

"When I tell you to go," he said to Sheila, "I want you to run to the restaurant as fast as you can. Don't look back. I'll be right behind you."

She nodded, showering him with drops of perspiration as her head moved up and down. Sinclair gave their path one final scan. He saw movement—a man creeping toward them a few rows of cars to their left. The clean-cut man, holding his pistol at his side. He hadn't yet spotted him and Sheila, but he was between them and the restaurant.

The two other men left their position of cover and crept forward. Sinclair took aim and fired one shot. A half dozen bullets came their way in return. Sinclair peeked around the truck and saw one of the men dragging his partner, who was holding his leg, behind a car.

The clean-cut man fired several rounds. Sinclair fired one in return, forcing him to dive for cover. Three rounds left. One man wounded, but still a threat. Two still armed and mobile.

They couldn't stay where they were. The gunmen would eventually converge on them and catch them in deadly cross fire. Thirty yards behind them, past ten parked cars, was a driveway that led from the main road to Hudson's, the waterfront restaurant next to the Chart House. If they could make that driveway, the main road was a hundred yards away. Sinclair remembered a fire station across the road from the entrance to the Boathouse. That would be their destination. The 9-1-1 calls must have made it in by now. Police should be on their way. A fire engine should be staging, waiting for the police to secure the scene before they roared in with their paramedics.

With luck, they could make it to the driveway before their attackers could react. Most trained police officers couldn't hit a running target at that range with a pistol, so unless these men got off a lucky shot, they'd probably make it through. But once they saw Sinclair and Sheila running, they might give chase—the clean-cut man and the one who wasn't nursing a bullet wound in the leg. They should have enough of a head start to make it to the main road. It wasn't the best plan, but if they stayed where they were, they were dead.

Sheila clung to his left arm. She had lost her sandals climbing over the fence, and her feet left bloody prints on the asphalt where they crouched. He told her the new plan. "Can you do it?"

She nodded. Her eyes returned a steely determination.

"Go," he whispered.

She jumped up and ran. One of the two men rose from behind their car and aimed his pistol. Sinclair fired a shot at him. He missed, but the man ducked back down. That was the time Sinclair needed as a head start. He had two rounds left.

Sinclair sprinted across the parking lot and cut left onto the driveway. Sheila was going as fast as he could expect from a woman running in bare, bloodied feet. In a few seconds, he was alongside her. "Keep going," he yelled.

Over his shoulder, Sinclair saw the clean-cut man running forty yards behind them. The other man left his wounded partner, ran across the parking lot, and joined the chase, now neck and neck with the other man.

Sheila was breathing hard. Sinclair looked over his shoulder. Both men were gaining on them. Sheila was running as fast as she could, but it wasn't fast enough. In another few seconds, the men would be close enough to hit them.

Several contingencies flashed through his mind. Sprinting ahead of Sheila to get to safety for himself was not one of them. In two more seconds, the men would be fifty feet from them. If they started shooting, there was a good chance they could hit him or Sheila.

His only alternative was to have Sheila continue to run while he stopped and faced them. Fire one bullet at each one, ignoring any bullets coming his way. If he survived, he'd have to go hand to hand. He might get lucky and wound one of them with one of the shots. Maybe they'd lose their will to fight. Sinclair wouldn't. He'd have to rush them even if they were still shooting. As the military had taught him, when no other options remain, assault directly into the enemy. Don't quit even if you're hit. You can survive a gunshot wound. Attack with everything you have, with a ferociousness—a viciousness—that will either destroy your enemy or cause them to flee.

He glanced over his shoulder. They were still gaining. He and Sheila wouldn't make it to the main road. They were almost within range. They'd begin shooting any second now.

An SUV squealed around the corner from the main road and came barreling toward them. Forty feet away, it jerked to a stop. Both doors swung open. The driver jumped out with a gun in his hand. Dark crew cut, clean-shaven. A split second later, the passenger appeared.

Behind Sinclair, the two men were still coming.

Two rounds left.

Sinclair stopped dead in his tracks. He began to raise his gun toward the SUV driver when he saw the passenger raise his gun.

"Get down," Uppy yelled from behind the passenger door.

Sinclair tackled Sheila and pulled her to the ground. He shielded her body with his as a barrage of gunshots rang out in less than three seconds.

"Get in," Uppy yelled.

Sinclair pulled Sheila to her feet and ran to the SUV, where Uppy was holding open the back door. The SUV jerked forward before their door was closed, executed a three-point turn, and took off. Marked police cars and unmarked cars with blue lights flashing sped down the road. The SUV driver said over his radio, "We have Sinclair and the girl. Engaged two suspects. Unknown if we hit them. They fled northbound into the Chart House parking lot." He turned his head and said to Sinclair, "How many more suspects?"

Sinclair told him about the wounded man in the parking lot and the one on the pier. The agent relayed that information over the radio.

Sheila clung onto Sinclair as tightly as she could. Her chest heaved as she tried to catch her breath. Finally, she buried her face into his neck and sobbed hysterically. Sinclair put his arms around her and held her.

Uppy turned around to face them. "Are either of you hurt?"

"Just scrapes and bruises for me," Sinclair said. "Sheila cracked her head pretty good and has cuts and abrasions on her feet and legs."

"Do you need to go to the hospital, young lady?" Uppy asked.

Sheila looked up and shook her head.

"Where we headed?" Sinclair asked.

"The bureau has a resident agency office just on the other side of the bridge. Ten minutes away."

"Maybe get a paramedic to take a look at her there," Sinclair suggested. "Avoid a trip to the ER."

The agent driving nodded, said something into his radio mic, and whispered something to Uppy.

"There's a motel about a half mile from the RA," Uppy said. "We'll let you two get cleaned up and get you something to eat. Then we'll sit down and talk."

"It better be a two-way conversation," Sinclair said. "Because I've got a lot of questions for you. To start with, how'd you know where I was?"

"Matt, my brother warrior, I've been telling you for years— I'm the FBI, and we know everything." Uppy laughed and tossed something onto Sinclair's lap. "You must've forgotten this when you left Oakland in such a hurry."

Sinclair ran his finger over the special deputy US marshal badge on the outside of the leather credential case and leaned back in the seat for the remainder of the ride.

Chapter 48

Sinclair and Uppy sat outside the Comfort Suites motel puffing on cigars. "Not bad," Sinclair said, eyeing the Romeo y Julieta band around the brown tobacco leaf wrapper.

"Yeah, when you're the west coast super special agent who swings into town to save it from death and mayhem, people jump to fulfill your every desire."

"Right, buddy. One of your Feebee friends bought the cigars with your money, right?"

Uppy smiled. Sinclair had no complaints about how the bureau was treating him. The rooms were nothing fancy, but the shower was amazing. Actually, any shower with soap and water would've been amazing. By the time he finished half of the pizza they bought for him, another agent had arrived with his rental car and brought his bag with its clean clothes to his room. The agent told him Sheila was in a room down the hall and someone was picking up fresh clothes and toiletries from her villa.

"Don't worry, I'll come up with a way to expense them." Uppy laughed.

"I'm certainly not bitching about my rescue, but I'm curious how you found me."

"Archard and I figured you had a lead you were pursuing, so we put a loose surveillance on you."

"So that was you guys in the green Malibu that I lost on the freeway."

"What? No. We couldn't get a team on you for a while. The only place we tailed you was to the airport. When you headed there, we knew you were on to something. I couldn't convince the field office down here to surveil you right away, but we were able to get an emergency trace on your credit card account. I got on the first morning flight out of SFO. By the time I landed in Savannah, we knew you got a car at the airport, ate at a restaurant in Bluffton, and bought clothes at a store down by the beach. I didn't believe for a second you were on vacation. We were finally able to convince the local resident office to saturate the area."

"But you had no idea why I was here."

"The big mystery to everyone in the task force was the identity of Phil's informant. Archard never agreed with allowing Phil to keep her confidential. It's against bureau policy, but Phil wouldn't give in. The info she provided was amazing. With Phil gone, the task force needed to ID her and bring her in. I guessed you had a line on her."

"Why didn't you level with me about Phil being on this task force?"

"I didn't even know it until a few days ago when they asked me to join them. Sure, I suspected something big was going on back when we worked the Thrill Kill Murders, but I wasn't part of it."

"Until they needed someone I trusted to recruit me," Sinclair said.

"I didn't like the way they did that any more than you did. I asked them to just let me talk to you. If I laid it out to you, you would've jumped at the chance to be part of it."

"How'd you know I was at Skull Creek?"

"Agents were canvassing Coligny Plaza when they saw two marked sheriff's cars racing to a condo complex down the street. One of them checks it out and finds out the deputies are taking a report about two Russian goons beating the shit out of a man until he tells them his wife, sister-in-law, and a friend named Sheila Harris were partying at the Boathouse. And a guy fitting your description was inquiring about them earlier. By that time, I'm in the car with the agent who picked me up at the airport, so I tell him to go to Skull Creek. About five minutes before we arrive, the police radio goes crazy with multiple nine-one-one calls reporting a shootout. And I know that wherever Matt Sinclair goes, a shootout follows."

Sinclair took several gulps from his bottle of Gatorade. The temperature had dropped to the low eighties. Even with the humidity, it felt comfortable sitting in the breeze with a cold drink. "Any word on who the goons were?"

"Two were originally from one of the 'stans—Kazakhstan, I think—but they had Russian passports and were in the US legally with work visas. The other two didn't have papers on them. Right now, one's in the morgue and a second's under police guard at the hospital. The sheriff's deputies that swarmed the area arrested the two we shot at. They're on their way to our field office in Columbia. Agents there will try to interview them, but I wouldn't expect them to talk."

"Any ties to Kozlov?"

"Not so far, but give us time."

"Who else is your task force targeting?" Sinclair asked.

"You mean *our* task force. You're part of it now. There's probably about fifty people with varying degrees of culpability on the suspect list."

"Is Preston Yates one of them?"

Uppy puffed on his cigar a few times. "Matt, even though you haven't signed the disclosure form, you can't repeat what I'm about to tell you."

Sinclair made an *X* over his heart.

"He's number one on the corrupt politician list. The US attorney would like to have enough to charge him long before your mayoral election takes place in November."

"I think Sheila might've gotten what you need." Sinclair forwarded Sheila's text containing her cloud drive user name and password to Uppy and, over the next half hour, summarized what Sheila had told him. What he didn't tell Uppy was that when he was eating pizza in his room and waiting for the FBI to conclude their strategy meeting, he'd downloaded everything from Sheila's drive to his computer as well. He wasn't about to be kept in the dark again. He also didn't tell Uppy about Phil's cloud drive because he wanted to go through everything Phil had before he released it to the FBI.

"Damn!" Uppy said. "This is what they've been hoping for. I'll get this to the task force tonight. I'm sure it'll move up the timetable."

"Why's that?"

"If Kozlov had something to do with Phil's murder, he must suspect the police know something. Then Sheila disappears and he figures out she was accessing his files. Assuming he sent the goons to grab her, he'll soon know they failed. I don't know how much longer he'll wait before he starts liquidating assets and takes off to someplace from where we can't extradite."

"We need to keep what happened here out of the media," Sinclair said.

"Already in the works. The Beaufort County Sheriff's Office and the circuit solicitor—that's what they call the district attorney out here—have to investigate the shooting. We're cooperating with them and have already told them a special deputy US marshal working undercover as part of a secret task force was talking to a woman in witness protection when two armed men tried to kidnap her. That's all they'll know about you and Sheila—no names, nothing else. One of the assistant US attorneys from Columbia has been read in and will sit with you and Sheila during the interview. I'm sure they'll rule the shooting justified."

"And the media?" Sinclair asked.

"A federal agent was with a woman in the witness protection program when men tried to kill her. No innocent people were hurt, and the agent and witness are fine. The heroic agent, whose name must be withheld because of his sensitive assignment, drew the assassins away from the crowd, blah, blah, blah."

"After I'm done with the shooting interview?"

"The bureau will do their investigation. An assistant special agent in charge from the Columbia field office is here with a team. They'll be looking at whether your shooting was within policy, sort of what your IAD would do."

"Why do you Feebees need to investigate me?"

"Because you're a member of the FBI task force."

"I thought I told you guys yesterday to shove the badge up your ass."

"If you think about it for a second, Matt, you'll agree that it would be best for you and everyone concerned if you just remember being sworn in, issued your badge and creds, and sent off to work the case independently as you saw fit."

Sinclair took a few puffs on his cigar and watched the smoke linger in the thick air for a few seconds before drifting off as the breeze returned. Uppy was right. Police treat a normal citizen who killed someone vastly different from a law enforcement officer who used deadly force in the line of duty. Although he was confident the system would eventually work out in his favor, as a citizen, he would need to hire an attorney, probably have to stick around for a few days while they verified his story, and possibly sit through a grand jury or a coroner's inquest before it was ruled self-defense. "I need to tell Braddock something by tomorrow morning." He explained Braddock's deadline.

"I have to tell you officially that you can't say anything to her," Uppy said. "But if she was my partner and I trusted her completely, I'd tell her enough to satisfy her so she doesn't report Phil for shit he didn't do and screw up the funeral he and his family deserve."

"I'd like to bring her in all the way."

"You have to ask Archard. She's in charge of all the agents."

"She's a piece of work," Sinclair said.

"I know you two didn't hit it off well last year. There's no doubt she's known for being a hard-ass. But she's also one of the sharpest agents I've ever worked with. She was brought in specifically to head this investigation. A few years ago, she did a similar case in Baltimore. Before that, Chicago. Her attitude toward you will be totally different now that you're part of the team."

"I won't let Phil's murder get lost in all this political corruption bullshit you guys are working."

"Neither will we. Archard has some info that will help you. There're four AUSAs assigned to the task force. All good guys. They've even talked about taking Phil's murder federal. We can prosecute suspects in federal court for murdering a federal agent, and Phil qualifies since he was part of the task force. But we know it would be better to prosecute the killers locally, so everyone will be on board to help you make it happen. Don't forget, they all knew Phil and want justice as much as OPD does."

Uppy's phone pinged. He looked at the screen. "They're ready for you. Let's head on over to the office and get this over with."

Chapter 49

The officer-involved shooting interviews finally wrapped up around midnight. Although he was dead tired, the adrenalin from the gunfight and reliving it repeatedly in minute details lingered in Sinclair's body. The Beaufort County Sheriff's Office obviously knew Sinclair was more than what the Feds told them, but they never questioned who he was or what he was doing before the men tried to snatch Sheila.

When Sinclair slipped the comment "based on my training and experience," the AUSA immediately interjected. He said, "Although we can't go into details, suffice it to say the special deputy has extensive law enforcement and military training and experience, to include surviving more than one deadly force encounter against armed suspects." Sinclair wondered if his identity would ever be revealed to the sheriff's detectives or if they would forever think he was some kind of spook or covert operative who slipped into town, shot up one of their prime tourist landmarks, and was then whisked away by the FBI.

Once they concluded that interview, Sinclair sat down with the FBI team. They covered much of the same ground. When finished, they told him he was booked on a 5:15 AM flight out of Savannah and handed him his itinerary. He declined their offer to drive him the half mile back to his motel.

The temperature had dropped into the high seventies. The warm tropical air reminded him how long it had been since he took a vacation. With the time change, it was just past nine in California, so he called Alyssa. He had sent her a text when he landed this morning to say he was out of town but was looking forward to seeing her when he returned.

"Hi, Matt. Is everything okay?"

"It is now. I miss you." He was walking through a parking lot parallel to the main road that led onto the island. Unlike the Bay Area, where the streets buzzed with activity all night long, the area was blissfully quiet this time of night.

"I miss you too," she said. "Where are you?"

"I can't say, but I'll tell you all about it when I can."

"Fair enough. But you're okay?"

"I am."

"Were you in danger?"

Sinclair didn't know if she sensed something in his voice or was asking out of concern. Their relationship was new, but he didn't want to begin a pattern of lying to her as he'd done with women in past relationships to keep them from worrying. "I was for a while, but it all worked out."

"Were you able to save whoever you were after?"

He detected the crack in her voice as she spoke and knew she was thinking about her ordeal in the school last year when he rescued her, a number of teachers, and a classroom full of children. "I was."

He heard her sniffle—maybe fighting back tears. "I'm so glad. When are you coming home?"

He walked through a shopping plaza, past a Kroger store, small cafés, and shops, all closed for the night. "Tomorrow, but I might be busy with this thing for a few days."

"Are you still suspended from OPD?"

"It's complicated."

She laughed. "It often is with you."

He wondered if she was commenting on his work or the state of their relationship. "I don't know what will happen with the department, but I'm getting close to Phil's killers."

"Have you talked to Cathy yet?"

"I'm calling her next."

"She's worried about you."

"I better let you go then," he said.

"Matt," she started and paused.

Was she about to say, "I love you," or tell him that what happened Saturday night was a huge mistake? He held his breath and waited.

"I'm really glad you're okay. Call me when you get back."

He hung up and stopped in front of a closed restaurant. The menu in the window had plenty of dishes Alyssa would love. He continued toward his motel, which was situated at the far end of the plaza. With Spanish moss hanging from the large trees and wide walkways in front of the stores and shops, it felt so different from the shopping centers in the Bay Area, where they crammed as many stores and parking stalls that would fit into a given footprint. Things here seemed more inviting and relaxing and moved at a slower pace.

He continued walking and called Braddock's cell. "Are you home or still at work?" he asked.

"Just put the kids to bed. Getting ready to sit down and hug my hubby."

"I found her," Sinclair blurted out.

"Found who?"

"Sheila Harris."

She said nothing for a few seconds. "Where?"

"Hilton Head Island."

"Jesus, Matt, what are you doing out there?"

"She and Phil weren't having an affair. She was his CI."

"Are you just saying this so I don't tell the lieutenant everything tomorrow morning?"

"It's the truth."

"What about the money we found?"

"Look, if you repeat this to anyone, everything Phil did will be for nothing, and we may never get who really killed him."

"What's going on, Matt?" she asked. "This isn't making any sense."

"Phil was working on a federal task force investigating political corruption. We think he was going to a meeting the night he was killed."

"Who's we?"

"Me and Sheila," he said. "And the FBI."

"Is Uppy down there with you?"

"Yeah."

"Well, at least you have adult supervision." She sighed. "When are you coming back here?"

"Tomorrow morning."

"We need to meet as soon as you get in."

"I can't come to the PAB. No one can know I'm working this. Once I check in with the task force, I'll call you. Until then, I need you to trust me."

"When have I not?"

★

Sinclair sat at the departure lounge in Atlanta waiting for the flight that would get him into San Francisco at 10:09 AM. After he'd gotten off the phone with Braddock last night, he called Walt and gave him his flight information so he could pick him up at the airport. He said his good-byes to Sheila, who thanked him profusely. The FBI and US marshals planned to hide her until they arrested Kozlov and she was no longer in danger. Uppy had to attend a meeting with the local FBI supervisors in the morning, after which he would jump on the next flight to the Bay Area. Sinclair got about two hours of sleep before he had to wake up and get to the airport in time for his 5:15 AM flight.

The plane that took him from Savannah to Atlanta was in the air less than an hour, so even though he was in a middle seat, he coped. But he wasn't looking forward to the next five-hour flight shoehorned into another middle seat when he desperately needed a few more hours of sleep. The loudspeaker called him to the ticket counter.

He handed the agent his boarding pass, and she punched some keys on her computer. "You've been upgraded to first class, Mr. Sinclair."

"How'd that happen?"

"Your sky miles have been applied to the upgrade," she said.

Sinclair didn't even know he had a frequent flyer account with Delta. "I don't know how that happened."

She shrugged and said, "You can board now. Enjoy your flight."

Sinclair walked down the jet way and settled into a spacious window seat in the third row. A flight attendant offered him a glass of wine, but he settled for Fresca and opened his laptop. His phone buzzed with a text from Walt: *Hope the upgrade went through. Fred has so many miles, he'll never use them.*

Sinclair opened the folder where he had downloaded everything from Phil's cloud drive and scrolled through a hundred photos. Most were grainy pictures that looked as if they were shot with a telephoto lens. All were date and time stamped. Photos of people. Some he recognized. Several photos of Kozlov with Yates. One of Yates with Chief Brown. Sinclair wasn't so naïve as to assume a man's guilt by association, and he could expect a police chief would need to meet with a city councilmember. He sorted the photos by date and found nothing on the night of Phil's murder. If he took any photos that night, he never had the chance to upload them.

People were still filing into the plane's economy section as he looked at photos dated the week prior. One of Yates exiting the passenger side of a Toyota Camry as a black man with a shaved head dressed in a dark suit held the door. A second photo showed the man's face. Sinclair recognized Reggie "Animal" Clement, the sergeant-at-arms of the Savage Simbas. That answered his question about why Maureen Yates had hired Eastman Security. A photo showing the license plate of the Toyota followed. Sinclair jotted down the plate number in his notebook. A Camry wasn't exactly a limo, nor did it require a driver, but if Yates didn't want to alienate his constituents, he wouldn't want to be seen pulling up to community meetings in a luxury sedan. And what better way to appeal to the minority voters than by including minorities on his staff—an African American driver and a Hispanic chief of staff.

A gray-haired man dressed in a business suit dropped his briefcase on the seat next to Sinclair. A flight attendant took his coat. He sat down, acknowledged Sinclair with a nod, and pulled a *Wall Street Journal* from his briefcase. Sinclair went back to the photographs as the flight attendant brought the man a glass of tomato juice and ice and poured two small bottles of vodka over it. At times like this, Sinclair wished he could drink like a normal person. After all he'd been through, a complimentary scotch would taste wonderful, even if it was only eight in the morning. He wondered if normal people drank scotch in the morning when flying first class. He asked the flight attendant for another soft drink and went back to his work.

In addition to the photos, the folder contained about a hundred document files, each labeled by date. He opened the most recent one, which was dated the week before Phil's death.

1710—Surveilling Yates's car (Camry) outside City Hall. Man earlier identified as Clement, Reggie, arrives on foot and stands by car.

1722—Yates exits City Hall south door, walks to car, hands keys to Clement. Gets in passenger seat. Clement drives. I follow.

1741—Yates exits vehicle at Claremont Country Club, enters building. Clement stays with car. I walk through building, see Yates sit at table in dining room with Port of Oakland commissioner I know to be Jonathan Yee. Club is members only. I return to my car.

1935—Yates returns to vehicle, still driven by Clement.

1947—Vehicle stops at Yates's residence. Pulls into garage. Clement walks to street. Waits. Lights in right front room come on.

1958—Chev 2D gray pulls up. Vehicle previously identified as belonging to Gibbs, Shane. From my location, driver profile matches Gibbs, but I can't positively ID. Clement gets in. Car drives off.

2130—Light still on in right front room. No further activity. Ended surveillance.

So much for getting sleep. Sinclair asked the flight attendant for a cup of black coffee and opened another document, starting from the beginning.

Chapter 50

Walt picked Sinclair up at the curb in the big Mercedes. With morning rush hour over, it took less than an hour to make it through San Francisco, over the Bay Bridge, and to the estate. Sinclair had read half of the documents from Phil's cloud drive on the plane and was beginning to get a clear picture of Phil's investigative activities. While other members of the task force might have been focusing on other players, Phil was working Yates and contributing to the case against Kozlov with what Sheila was providing. He'd prepared an interview summary after every meeting with Sheila and completed a second, redacted version that he labeled *TF* with the same date. The task force version was sanitized of details that would identify Sheila, indicating Phil didn't fully trust the people on the team. Sinclair sometimes did the same with informants. When he worked narcotics, he was judicious about the details he included on search warrant affidavits, since including too many specifics could give away informants' identities, which could get them killed.

In a surveillance report dated months ago, Phil was following Yates from a meeting in Pleasanton, about a half hour from Oakland, when Yates ran a red light and hit a car broadside. Phil noted in his report that Yates was looking at his phone when he was driving, which Yates did frequently. A copy of the collision report was among the documents on the cloud drive, and Sinclair read that the responding officer cited Yates for distracted driving and use of a mobile device. In the next surveillance report, four days later, Phil noted that Yates's chief of staff drove him during business hours but that Animal drove him after hours. Phil had followed Animal several times after he dropped off Yates and connected him to the Savage Simbas and Eastman Security. He also saw Animal with Gibbs and Tiny on different occasions.

What most interested Sinclair were the unsanitized reports of Phil's meetings with Sheila. She had barely touched the surface of what she knew when they talked at the Boathouse. Over the months that she and Phil had met, she laid out extensive details of Kozlov's operation and his efforts to own Yates and other politicians. Kozlov provided the condo for Yates to set up Dawn as his mistress, paid all her hospital and doctor bills when she got pregnant, and established investment accounts through shell companies to pay Dawn after they broke up. If Maureen was being truthful when she told Sinclair she was now paying for Dawn's daughter's child support and college trust fund, he wondered where the money Kozlov was providing for that purpose was going.

Walt dropped Sinclair off at the back door of his house. He grabbed a diet soda from the refrigerator, noting that Betty had gone shopping and stocked his refrigerator while he was gone. He carried the can of Coke to his bedroom and dumped the contents of the duffle bag on his bed, throwing the dirty clothes into the clothes basket in his closet along with the clothes he was wearing. He dressed in jeans and a long-sleeve dress shirt and worked the combination to his safe. He removed his Kimber CDP II, a compact .45 pistol with an aluminum frame and tritium sights. The single-action semiauto didn't meet the specification for on-duty carry at OPD, but as much as he liked his Sig Sauer, if he had his druthers, he'd carry this gun instead. Super reliable, extremely accurate, and with its rosewood grips and two-tone finish, utterly beautiful. He threaded a holster onto his belt, loaded the Kimber with one round in the chamber and seven in the magazine, and pushed it into the dark-brown leather holster. He slid an extra magazine into the matching leather pouch on his left side and pulled a light-gray sport coat on over everything.

As he was adding his credentials, notebook, flashlight, and other tools to his pockets, he heard Amber bark outside. He opened the living room door. She bounded inside with her tail wagging and plopped on the floor at his feet. He bent over and rubbed her belly. "Did you miss me?" he asked.

She trotted into the kitchen and sat next to the sink. He filled a bowl of water and set it on the floor. She drank some and returned to the spot in front of the sink. He opened the cabinet doors and saw a box of dog biscuits in front of the soaps, detergents, and cleaners. "Looks like Betty bought you some goodies too," he said as he opened the box and gave Amber one.

He packed his briefcase and went out the back door to his Mustang with Amber at his heels. "I have to go to work, but I'll be back soon. You be a good girl while I'm gone." Amber trotted around the side of his house. As he drove down the driveway to the front gate, he saw her headed toward the mansion's kitchen door.

Once he got on the freeway, he called his mother. "Hello, Matt," she said. "Still busy with your big case?"

"Busier than ever. How are you doing?"

"I'm fine," she said, as she always did. That was the nature of their conversations, telling each other how fine they were. "They're allowing your father to go home tomorrow."

"Really? He must be doing better."

"He is. He'll still have to take it easy for a while, but he should make a full recovery as long as he does what the doctors told him."

"Let me guess—eat healthier, stop smoking and drinking, and begin exercising."

"You could've been a doctor," she said. "I think those were his exact words."

"Mom, I've got a question for you. Did Father really take Lucky to the vet that day when he was sick?"

"That's really coming out of the blue."

"The place where I'm living—the family just got a dog, and it got me thinking. Did he?"

"Yes, of course."

"How do you know?" he asked in the same cold and inquisitive manner he would ask a witness who claimed to know something about a crime.

"Your father said he did. Plus, I saw the vet's invoice and paid the bill."

"What exactly was wrong with him?"

"He had a large tumor that was pressing on his heart. The vet did an ultrasound and saw it. The vet said he was in pain, and even if he could've operated, the cancer had spread too far."

"All that was on the invoice?"

"Yes, and the shot to put him to sleep. I remember the bill was several hundred dollars. I told your father to never say a word about the money to you or your brother."

"What did they do with Lucky after they gave him the shot?"

"The vet offered to cremate him, but your father insisted on burying him. We talked on the phone, and I told him about the spot down by the river you and Lucky used to go, where you said you taught Lucky to swim."

"Really?"

"He buried him up on the bank and carried a bunch of river rocks up there and stacked them over the grave so that no animals could dig him up. After you and your brother left home, I had more free time and used to go for walks down there. The pile of rocks is still there."

Sinclair wiped his eyes with the back of his hand. "Why didn't you tell me?"

"You and your brother never asked, and I figured you didn't need to be reminded. I thought about getting another dog, but after Billy and then Lucky, I thought you boys had enough death to last a lifetime."

"And then I became a homicide detective," he said.

She laughed. "And then you became a homicide detective."

Chapter 51

Sinclair arrived at the address Uppy had given him, a nonde-script single-story building located in a nondescript business park on Capwell Drive five minutes from the Oakland Airport. A medical supply company's sign was on the suite at the front of the building. Sinclair followed the parking lot to the rear and saw number 107 on a reinforced glass door. He pushed inside to a small foyer with a reception counter at the back and a camera mounted on the ceiling looking down at him. A stocky man stepped out of a doorway behind the counter. "May I help you?"

"My name's Matt Sinclair, looking for Ms. Archard."

"ID."

Sinclair produced his special deputy marshal creds.

"Welcome, Matt. Hank Foster, FBI." He held out his hand. "We've been expecting you."

Sinclair followed Foster into a large room containing about thirty cubicles with four-foot-high partitions. Roughly half were occupied. Five women and the rest men, some dressed in jeans, others in suits.

Linda Archard rose from a chair in a cubicle near the front and approached him. She smiled—the first time he'd ever seen her smile. "Matt, call me Linda." Dressed in a black pantsuit, she was in her midforties and wore her brown hair cut extremely short. "Hell of a caper down there in Hilton Head. You're lucky to be alive."

"Thanks to Uppy."

"Yeah, it's nice having a real street agent on our team. Let's get you settled." She escorted him to a workspace in the middle of the room. "This was Phil's cubicle. We've gone through his computer and drawers. He didn't keep any personal items here, but if you find a pack of gum or a cigar, I'm sure he'd want you to have them. Let me introduce you to the crew."

There were no private offices at the task force. It didn't matter if you were an AUSA, a supervisory agent, a street agent, or an analyst—everyone got a cubicle the same size. The large room had a drop ceiling and florescent lighting, and the floor was covered with industrial-grade carpeting that looked so tough, you could probably play soccer on it and not see any wear. Sinclair met three assistant US attorneys, two FBI analysts, two deputy US marshals, and several agents from the FBI, homeland security, and IRS. Archard said he'd meet others when they returned from whatever they were doing in the field. She showed him a large conference room behind a closed door. Behind another closed door, two men wearing earphones sat behind computers with multiple monitors.

"This is the wire room," she said. "We have six agents assigned here, two on duty at a time."

"Whose phones are you up on?" Sinclair asked.

"Business, home, and cell phones for Kozlov and Yates and a few other outliers."

"Getting anything good?"

"We have enough for a RICO case on both of them with what they've said on the wire alone. Plus we've heard enough to seek grand jury indictments on a dozen other people who work for the city of Oakland and a bunch of other politicians and business executives."

"Any from OPD?"

She folded her arms across her chest. "We recorded conversations between your police chief and Yates where Yates promised to keep him on as chief if he's elected. Brown flatly refused some of Yates's requests, such as opening investigations on opponents and businesses when it was obvious their only crimes were being political enemies of Yates."

"What about shutting down my investigation?"

Archard pursed her lips and said nothing for a moment. When she spoke, Sinclair could tell she was choosing her words carefully. "We weren't up on the wire when he told you to leave Yates alone during your Thrill Kill investigation, so we don't know what transpired. But Yates called him last week after you visited his wife. Brown said he'd look into his complaint and called him back to say you were reprimanded. When you dragged his campaign manager in, Yates called him again, very irate that time, and said that if Brown couldn't control his officers, he'd find a chief who could when he became mayor."

"That's what prompted the chief to take my badge and gun," Sinclair said.

"It wasn't that simple. Brown told Yates that a homicide sergeant's never been fired for following a lead on a murder investigation and that with your history of awards and commendations, firing you would look very bad. Yates came back saying that Brown might need to decide whether you stay in homicide or he stays in the police chief's office."

"And then he came downstairs and relieved me."

"At that point we knew we could trust you."

Sinclair understood. "No talk about Phil's murder?"

"Brown asked Yates if he had any idea why you suspected his wife and campaign manager of having knowledge of Phil's murder." Archard led Sinclair from the wire room to a folding table inside the main room holding a coffeepot. "Yates said he didn't, that it had to be your continuing vendetta to destroy his reputation over your obsession with a dead hooker."

"Sounds like you've got nothing solid on the chief."

Archard poured coffee into a Styrofoam cup and handed it to him. "When we initiated this investigation last year, US Attorney Campbell and I met with your chief, told him we were looking into possible corruption at City Hall, and asked for officers for the task force. He assigned Phil. In our first sit-down, Phil agreed to keep his briefings to Brown about the task force's progress extremely vague."

"You're telling me a police chief, conspiring with a crooked businessman and politician to cover up Phil's murder for his own gain, will get away with it."

Archard smiled. "For now, let's focus on Phil's murder and taking down Kozlov and Yates."

Sinclair followed Archard to her cubicle, where he sat in a guest chair and sipped his coffee. "Uppy said I could continue working to find out who killed Phil."

Archard leaned back in her chair and crossed her right ankle over her knee. "I had one of our analysts pull together everything we know about the murder. That night, Shane Gibbs called Reggie Clement, who you know as Animal. Cell tower triangulation showed he was in the vicinity of Kozlov's residence in Oakland. We can only pin it down to within two hundred yards. A few minutes later, Gibbs called Bobby Richards, the man known as Tiny. If we believe Phil was at Kozlov's house and Gibbs either killed him or moved the body, then it's likely he got some help either for the murder or to dispose of the body."

"We know Animal didn't leave the bar," Sinclair said.

"That leaves Tiny as the likely accomplice. He only used his cell phone once since you chased him on that motorcycle."

"Jeez, you guys know about that too?"

"You have the knack of leaving a wake of destruction in your path, so you're not hard to track," she said. "Tiny called a Tyrone Hammond a few hours after the chase."

"That's T-bone. I arrested him on one of the Savage Simbas search warrants after the bar murder. He's back out?"

"Yeah, he bailed on the drug charges but didn't show up for his court date. One of our surveillance teams has eyes on him. We could pick him up if you want to interview him again to see if he'll tell you where to find Tiny."

"I'd like to have my partner with me on the interview."

"Uppy mentioned that. We've already vetted her, and Brad-dock's about as straight and narrow as they come. If she comes over, it's with conditions: I meet with her and feel her out first, she agrees to total nondisclosure, and we come up with a plau-sible excuse for her to be away from OPD without attracting attention."

"I'll set up the meet," Sinclair said.

Chapter 52

Sinclair ate the last bite of apple crisp pie and piled the plate on top of the one that had once held his double cheeseburger and fries. Denny's was only a mile from the task force headquarters, so it had become a regular lunch spot for the Feds. After operating on about four hours of sleep over the past three days, Sinclair's body needed fuel to keep going, and he wasn't particular as to the quality of it right now. As long as he pumped in enough coffee to get him through the sluggish feeling that accompanied this much food, he should be good to go for a while longer.

After they'd talked for forty-five minutes, Braddock said to Archard, "I'm in. I never use my kids as a work excuse, but this is an unusual situation. I'll tell Jankowski my daughter's really sick and I have to take her to the ER. He'll tell the lieutenant if he has to. Have the files Sheila stole been useful?"

Archard looked at her phone, scrolling through an e-mail, something she'd been doing every five minutes during lunch. "When Uppy sent me the link to her cloud drive last night, I immediately called in our IRS special agent and one of our bureau guys who understands financial crimes. All they could say after opening each file was, 'Oh, my god.' It would've taken them weeks to analyze everything Sheila provided, so I made a few phone calls and got a team of accountants and agents back in

Washington to work on this. The last update says we can show the money trail connecting every target of our investigation."

"So this isn't going to be one of your typical operations that goes on for years?" Sinclair asked.

"Sorry to disappoint you," Archard said, "but we'll have enough to make arrests, freeze assets and bank accounts, and hit a half dozen locations with search warrants by tonight if needed. I just don't want to jump the gun if it'll jeopardize your murder investigation."

"We could always continue to investigate after you make your case," Braddock offered. "Charging some of the Simbas or people at Eastman Security federally could motivate them to talk."

"That never works," Sinclair said. "They get an attorney, we sit in an office with the AUSA on one side and the suspect and his slime-bag attorney on the other, and the lawyers play *Let's Make a Deal*, but nobody ever gives up a murderer."

Archard snatched up the check the second the waitress put it on the table, waved Sinclair away, and put her credit card down. "Honestly, who do you think killed Phil?"

Sinclair preferred keeping an open mind and letting the evidence point him toward the right suspect. But the Feds needed to know what he was thinking if he expected their help. "I think Tiny might've been involved, but I suspect he and Gibbs were just the worker bees. The fact that Phil died from suffocation makes the issue of motive fuzzy. Kozlov and Yates had the motive to kill Phil to keep him from discovering what they were up to or to keep him quiet about whatever he already discovered."

"Do you really think they ordered the murder of a police officer?" Braddock asked. "They're crooks and all, but killing a cop?"

Sinclair held up his empty coffee cup to a passing waitress. Once she left he said, "I don't know, but I don't want to see a couple of foot soldiers take the fall if they're not responsible."

"I'll help any way I can," Archard said. "What's your plan?"

"Have your guys bring in T-bone," Sinclair said. "We'll see if he can lead us to Tiny. Then we see what Tiny says and go from there."

Archard looked at her phone. "He's waiting for you in an interview room. Shall we go?"

★

Two plainclothes deputy US marshals met them at the state parole office. Since the location of the task force had to remain secret, they certainly couldn't bring crime suspects or witnesses there, so they had an arrangement with the nearby parole office to use their interview rooms. Parolees filed into the office all day long to meet with their parole agents, so having a few additional seedy-looking people in the building was no problem.

They had decided that Braddock should begin the interview to avoid any legal issues arising later because of Sinclair's suspension. The interview room was larger and cleaner than the ones at the PAB, the tables were less scarred by graffiti, and the chairs were more comfortable. T-bone's eyes opened wide when they entered the room.

"Do you remember us?" Braddock asked as she and Sinclair sat down and opened their notebooks.

"Fuck yeah. You two are like a bad toothache that just won't go away."

"Remember when we talked last week and my partner here told you he wasn't much concerned about drugs and guns?" Braddock asked.

"And here I am. I was charged with drugs, and now you all arrest me because you say I missed my court date. My lawyer said he was gonna get it continued."

"Well, we're still not concerned with drugs," she said. "As a matter of fact, we're not even concerned about Animal having murdered Shane."

T-bone's face showed no surprise. Sinclair winked at Braddock.

"My partner will tell you what we're concerned with," Braddock said.

"The murder of a police officer," Sinclair said.

"I don't know nothing about that."

"Let's see," Sinclair said. "Harboring a fugitive. Accessory to murder. Do you know who those two men were that picked you up and brought you here?"

"They said they US marshals. And why they bring me here? I'm no parolee."

"You know what the US marshals do, T-bone?"

"They arrest federal fugitives and shit."

"That's right. Did you know the police officer you guys killed was also a federal agent?"

"I didn't kill no one," T-bone said. "What you mean, federal agent?"

"That's why the US marshals are working with us. This is a federal crime. And we're talking here so we can protect your confidentiality and not parade you through the police station or the FBI office."

T-bone nodded. Sinclair continued, "What we want to know is why you, Shane, and Tiny killed a federal agent."

"Whoa, whoa, whoa! I didn't kill no one," T-bone said. "And who's Tiny?"

Sinclair leaned across the table toward T-bone. "I can accept you denying the murder—that's what people do. But don't insult my intelligence by denying you know Tiny." Sinclair slid a photo of Bobby Richards in front of him. "This is the Savage Simbas Motorcycle Club member nicknamed Tiny. This is the man who I chased on a motorcycle in Concord last week. This is the man who called you after that to come and rescue him."

"Now I know you lying," T-bone said. "I know Tiny. 'Course I do. But it was two HAs chased him in Concord. Not the police."

"Maybe one of them was a Hells Angel. Don't you think the FBI has informants in the HAs? Don't you think we could get one of our informants in the Angels to introduce us to people who knew Tiny? And tell us where Tiny was eating barbecue? Then Tiny took off. The HA with his fancy bike crashed. I was the other guy, the one on the old Heritage Softail. The one who outrode Tiny on his high-powered chopper. The guy who caught up to him on every corner because Tiny can't ride. The guy who pushed him so hard that he lost control and dropped his bike and then ran off like a little bitch before the police came."

T-bone sat there quietly.

"I know Tiny told you all this, but he didn't know it was us chasing him," Sinclair continued. "If you can't see that you're mixed up in something way bigger than you, you're pretty dumb, T-bone."

"I didn't know Tiny was a federal fugitive when I came and got him."

"I can probably get the US attorney and the DA to believe that," Sinclair said.

"And I had nothing to do with that cop that was killed. I wasn't even there. It was an accident is what it was."

"A police sergeant working as a federal agent was shot in the head and it was an accident?" Sinclair asked.

"Lookie here. Shane is working for some white dude. Driving him and watching his back. Something happens with the officer—or whatever he was—and Shane's gun goes off. They can't just leave him there. Get the man Shane's working for in trouble. So he calls Tiny to come help him. Tiny and him load him in the van and go bury him. They didn't even know he was a cop until after he was dead. He was black. How they supposed to know he was police? Tiny said he had an Oakland police badge. Didn't say nothing about him being a federal agent."

"If you weren't there, how do you know this?"

"Tiny told me. When I picked his ass up in Concord, he tells me all this. Shane was supposed to get a bunch more money from the man for burying the officer and stuff and split it with

Tiny. Then he ends up dead. Tiny now shit out of luck. He gets nothing, and now he has to hide from the police, from the HAs, from the Simbas. From everyone."

Sinclair pressed him for another fifteen minutes, asking him where the shooting occurred, the name of the man Shane was driving for, and any additional details, but T-bone continued to deny knowing anything further. "The only person who can verify what you told me is Tiny," Sinclair finally said. "Where can we find him?"

"Oh, man. I ain't no snitch."

"Look, T-bone, everybody is in this mess because of the people actually responsible. They're getting away with it and leaving the blame on dudes like you. You didn't do shit but pick up Tiny and listen to his story. Tiny only helped a friend move a body. Shane shot the officer, and since Shane's dead, he can't take the blame. This man he was working for, who might be the one really responsible, is probably sitting at home watching TV with his wife, not a care in the world because everyone else is taking the fall for him."

"He's staying with his cousin, Crystal. Girl he grew up with out on Sunnyside."

Sinclair copied down Crystal's full name, her address, the description of her house, and everything T-bone knew about the house and occupants. They left the two marshals to babysit T-bone and drove back to the task force headquarters.

When they walked inside, Archard was sitting in her cubicle with Uppy, who had just arrived from the airport. Sinclair filled them in on T-bone's interrogation.

"These two dudes are for real, Matt?" Uppy asked. "T-bone and Tiny. You're not making up these names, are you? And T-bone is like two-fifty, yet a man named Tiny's the bigger one?"

Sinclair needed the laugh. "If I were gonna make up fake witnesses, I'd be more original."

Archard remained serious. "Do you believe him?"

"It fits with what we know," Sinclair said. "The round grazed Phil's scalp and probably rendered him unconscious. The doc said he could've appeared dead to a casual observer. Cause of death was suffocation, resulting from putting the garbage bag over his head. Shane saying it was an accident fits. But this is double hearsay. We've got Shane telling Tiny what happened before he got there, who then tells T-bone."

"If we pick up Tiny and he tells the same story, all we still have is hearsay," Archard said. "So aren't we just wasting our time?"

Sinclair shrugged. "We won't know until we talk to him. He might've given T-bone a line of shit. He might tell us he was there. Maybe he was even the one who pulled the trigger and Shane only helped move the body."

"Let's go and see if he's home," Archard said.

Chapter 53

They waited at the city park four blocks from Crystal's house in the 9200 block of Sunnyside. Sinclair and Braddock were in their OPD car, with Braddock driving. Uppy and Archard were in a bureau car driven by Uppy. Sinclair got out and stood outside Uppy's car, listening to him talk on the radio as another task force team fed him details of the house from his recon of the area.

Uppy gathered the four of them together for a briefing. Even though Archard was the supervisor, she didn't try to take over. She reminded Sinclair of Maloney in that way, both supervisors who knew their limitations and trusted their subordinates to do what they did best. Maybe she wasn't the bitch he'd thought she was last year and, like Phil, was just doing her job when she had iced him out when he was pressing her for information.

"We don't have a warrant, so it'll be a knock and talk," Uppy said. "If Tiny's in a public place or we're invited inside, we can arrest him on probable cause. We'll try to talk him into the back seat of a car rather than fight him. We don't want to advise OPD we're here, so let's not get into the shit where we need to call the cavalry out to rescue us. Linda and I will meet the other two agents in front of the house and go to the front door. Matt and Cathy, I want you guys out of sight in case OPD does come by. You'll take the back, just in case Tiny decides to squirt out when we put pressure on the front. Questions?"

They all nodded their understanding. "We're not anticipating trouble, but let's vest up just in case," Archard said.

Braddock popped their trunk, and he was glad to see she still carried his gear. They pulled on their vests and slapped the Velcro straps in place. Braddock was pulling on her OPD raid jacket when Archard came around the back of their car with two FBI windbreakers. "If anyone calls in, all I want them to be able to report is people in jackets with big yellow FBI letters. Remember, you're not OPD today, so practice in your head yelling, 'FBI, stop! FBI, drop the gun!'"

They pulled the windbreakers over their vests and trailed Uppy's car down the street. Sinclair had been in this neighborhood hundreds of times in his career. He'd handled several homicide scenes on this street alone over the years, every one of them drug related. As they crept down the street, he felt the eyes of the neighborhood watching them, wondering whose house they were going to hit, who they were going to haul off to jail, or whose drug stash they were going to seize.

The intersection of Ninety-Fourth and Sunnyside was empty, the street corner dealers normally camped out there long gone. If the dealers knew they were the FBI, they wouldn't have been concerned; the FBI doesn't hit corners and chase down drug dealers.

Uppy stopped behind the bureau car that was scouting the area. The four FBI agents got out and walked up to the house. Sinclair and Braddock followed with guns drawn. Like most houses in this neighborhood, a low chain link fence surrounded the front yard. As the agents walked toward the front door, Sinclair and Braddock peeled off and crept down the side of the small stucco house toward the back.

The rear door was covered with a metal security gate, and bars covered the windows. Three concrete steps led out of the house to the backyard, which was nothing but dirt and weeds with rusted bicycles and old car tires scattered about. Sinclair couldn't find any decent cover from where they could see the back door, so he knelt at the corner of the house, his gun trained on the back door. Braddock stood over him with her gun pointed in the same direction.

Sinclair heard the agents knocking at the front door and the buzz of an old-fashioned doorbell from within the house. Voices at the front door. Uppy and then a woman. "FBI? What you want? Tiny? Who's that?" Footsteps headed their way. Heavy footsteps.

The back door sprang open. A huge black man appeared in the doorway, every bit of the six foot six and two hundred eighty pounds that his driver's license indicated. He stood on the doorstep for a second. Blue jeans, leather boots, black T-shirt. No weapons in his hand, only a black duffle bag slung over one shoulder.

Sinclair wasn't concerned that this big man would be able to leap the back fence and lose him in a foot chase. Better to allow him to get all the way out of the house and fight him in open ground if that's how he wanted to go rather than let him slink back inside the cramped interior of the house. Sinclair ducked out of sight around the corner so Tiny would think he had an open escape route.

A few seconds later, the metal door slammed shut. Sinclair stepped around the corner with his gun up. Braddock followed at his side. Tiny stood ten feet away, halfway to the corner of the house where he thought his escape route was clear.

"Tiny, you're too big to fight," Sinclair said firmly. "So if you don't put your hands up right now, I'm going to shoot you."

Tiny dropped the duffle bag and put his hands in the air.

★

While Tiny sat in an interview room at state parole, Sinclair spread out his belongings on a desk outside. They'd searched him and removed a cell phone, wallet, and a ring of keys from his pockets. Sinclair went through the wallet but found nothing interesting. He missed the days when they could search a suspect's cell phone incident to an arrest, but the Supreme Court recently decided police now needed consent or a warrant. Another time-consuming hurdle to do their job. He unzipped the duffle bag and pulled out shirts, underwear, and socks. He removed a pair of jeans, laid them on the table, and unrolled them. Inside was a compact Glock pistol and an Oakland police sergeant's badge etched with Phil's badge number.

Braddock hugged him. Her eyes were welling up. "We got him, Matt," she said. "We got Phil's killer."

Sinclair wished it were that simple. They needed more. Sinclair got a pair of gloves and evidence bags from one of the marshals babysitting T-bone. Sinclair unloaded Phil's gun, noting it was still fully loaded and hadn't been fired. He placed the magazine and cartridges in a bag, the gun in another bag, and the badge in a third.

When they began working together two years ago, Sinclair would never have allowed Braddock to lead a suspect interview when the outcome was so critical. Her anxiety and apprehension would've been all over her face. But Braddock was no longer that rookie homicide investigator. They discussed their strategy for a few minutes and entered the room.

Tiny had moved a chair to the corner of the room where he sat facing the door. "Mr. Richards, would you stand up, please?" When he did, Braddock moved the chair back to the table, patted it, and said, "Please have a seat."

Tiny sat down, looked at Sinclair on his right, and turned to face Braddock on his left. She placed a tape recorder in the center of the table and turned it on, opened her notebook, and slid out a legal pad and a statement form containing the Miranda warning. Even though the room was cool, Tiny was sweating profusely.

"Mr. Richards, my name is Sergeant Braddock. I'm assigned to the homicide unit of the Oakland Police Department. This is my partner, Sergeant Sinclair, who is now assigned to an FBI federal task force."

"I don't—"

Braddock held up her hand, and Tiny stopped speaking. "There will be plenty of time for you to talk later, but right now we need to complete some formalities. I'll ask the questions, okay?" She smiled.

"Okay," he said.

She went through the standard routine: name, date of birth, address, and other questions. She slowly printed his responses on her legal pad and the statement form. She set her pen on the table. "Mr. Richards, you're being detained right now as a suspect in a homicide investigation. The murder of Oakland police sergeant Phil Roberts. You are not free to leave."

"I know you went through my bag and found his stuff," Tiny said. "I swear to God, I didn't kill him."

Braddock patted him on his huge forearm and smiled. "We want to hear what happened and how you came into possession of a murdered police officer's gun and badge, but under the law, we must first read you your rights. Is that okay?"

Braddock's smile and soft voice drew Tiny in. She conveyed empathy in a way Sinclair never could. She read him his rights and asked, "Do you understand each of these rights I have read to you?"

"Yeah, I think so."

"Is there any part you'd like me to read again or any part you don't understand that I can explain to you?"

"No, I understand."

She smiled again. "Having these rights in mind, do you wish to talk to us now?"

"I want to tell you I didn't kill your friend."

"And we'll be glad to listen. First I'd like you to place your initials on the form in these two places and sign your name here."

Chapter 54

Although their strategy had called for Sinclair taking over the interview once Braddock got Tiny to waive his rights, she'd developed such a good rapport with Tiny, he signaled for her to continue. She started with questions about his background to keep him relaxed and talking. People like to talk about themselves, and Braddock had a way of making people feel like she truly cared about getting to know them better. Tiny had started tinkering with motorcycles when he was twelve. He worked as a mechanic for Oakland Harley Davidson for a few years but left after he got into an argument with the manager. He went to work for Irish Mike part time while doing motorcycle service, repairs, and custom engine modifications for club members on the side. His goal was to save up enough money to open his own shop one day. Tiny had worked the afternoon of the murder at Irish Mike's shop. He quit at six o'clock, went out for dinner, and came back to drink beer with the guys when Shane called him around eight.

"Shane was talking a million miles a minute. Said he took Animal's place on some security job and there was a horrible accident. Shane called Animal, but he said it was his mess so he had to clean it up. Animal told him to get me to help."

"Did he say what the accident was?" Braddock asked.

"Not then, only to bring my van and some shovels."

"To where?"

"He texted me the address."

"Is it still on your phone?" Braddock asked.

"Yeah, I guess."

"Can we look at your phone to see?"

"Yeah, whatever it takes to prove I didn't do this."

Sinclair left the room and returned with Tiny's phone. He loved how smoothly Braddock had gotten his consent to search it. Tiny scrolled through his messages and handed the phone to Braddock. She looked at it and handed it to Sinclair. Kozlov's home address.

"What happened next?" Another open-ended question to avoid leading him in any given direction.

"I drove there. Parked on the street. Started walking up to the house. Fancy place. White neighborhood. Shane was on the side of the house. Yelled my name when he saw me. There, under some trees, behind some bushes, was a body. Shane said he saw this man sneaking around with a camera. Man was black, so he knew he didn't belong in the neighborhood. Shane pulled out his gat and grabs the man. The man and him wrestle and bang! Shane said it was an accident. Shane said people from the house came out when they heard the shot. They found his police badge and said he was dead."

"Why didn't they call nine-one-one?"

"Shane said he wanted to, but the white man said if they called an ambulance, the police would come and they'd all get in trouble. Besides, the bullet hit him in the head, so he was dead."

"When you got there, how'd you know he was dead?" she asked.

"He's lying there in the dirt, blood all over his head, not breathing."

"Are you sure he wasn't breathing?"

"It's not like I checked or nothing. But he ain't moving at all. I didn't see his chest going up and down. And Shane said he's dead."

"Who else besides Shane was there?"

"The white man I told you about and a Mexican lady. Both standing there by Shane."

"What did the man look like?"

"About forty, pale, like he never goes in the sun, small, skinny, dark-blond hair."

Braddock showed him a six-pack, a photo lineup of six white males.

"That's him. Number four."

Sinclair looked down at his notebook so Tiny couldn't read his face. He wrote in his notes that Tiny just identified Preston Yates. Braddock had him sign the back of the photo and calmly placed another six-pack in front of him.

"The lady is number three," Tiny said.

Braddock asked him to sign the back of Rosina Lopez's photograph. "Anyone else?" she asked.

"There were other people in the house looking out the window and two on the back deck watching us."

"What race were they?"

"It was too far away to be sure, but white, I think. Most people who live up there are white."

"What happened next?"

"The man starts giving orders. Tells me to back my van into the driveway and load up the body. I start thinking this should be worth something, so I ask what's in it for me. The man looks at me funny, like I should just be taking out the garbage for him or something. I get back in my van, make like I'm leaving."

"Nice negotiation strategy," Braddock said. "What did they do?"

"Shane begs me to come back. Then the Mexican lady says she'll give us a thousand dollars."

"What's Shane doing now?"

"He's just standing there all nervous and shit. I tell the lady a thousand each. She starts to say something, but the man says one thousand each is fine. He wants us to get a boat, wrap the dead dude in chains, and throw him out in the bay. Me and Shane look at him like he's crazy. Like he's been watching too many gangster movies."

"What happened next?"

"He said we could bury the body someplace that nobody could ever find it. Said he tried to work the officer's phone, but it had a password. He took the card from the officer's camera already but was afraid there might be stuff still on it, so he wanted us to throw the phone and camera in the bay, then take the body and bury it with his gun, badge, and everything."

"But you kept the gun and badge," Braddock said.

"Insurance, in case the man didn't pay Shane the two Gs."

"What happened next?"

"Shane picks up the feet, I grab under his arms, and we carry him to the van. I see hella blood coming from his head. Said I ain't getting blood all over my van. The lady goes in the house, comes back with garbage bags. The white man said to put him in the bags. But a man won't fit in a garbage bag. Me and Shane say all we gotta do is cover up where he's bleeding. Shane sits him up. Me and the man pull a garbage bag over his head, tie it around his waist. Then we put him in the van."

"If he was still alive, that would've suffocated him, huh?" Braddock said.

Tiny looked at Braddock, puzzled. "Yeah, but he was already dead."

Braddock wisely didn't pursue that line of questioning further. "What did you do then?"

"We drive to Lake Merritt, me in the van, Shane driving the officers' car. We throw the phone and camera in the water."

"Where at Lake Merritt?"

"Over by Grand where the big columns are."

"What did you do next?"

Tiny described how they drove into the Oakland Hills looking for a place to bury the body. They saw the road off Skyline
Drive leading to the PAL camp. Not knowing what it was other
than it being deserted, they carried and dragged the body off
the road and dug a hole. After about two or three feet, the soil
became too rocky, so they quit, put the body in the shallow
grave, and covered it over.

From there, they went to the bar where the Simbas were
celebrating Animal's birthday. Animal was drunk and angry
about what'd happened, not only because Shane killed a cop,
which could draw heat on the club, but because it likely ruined
the plans for his security company. Animal continued to berate
Shane, saying he was stupid and put the club at risk. After a few
minutes of being insulted, Shane punched Animal in the face.
Animal shot him. Afraid that he'd be next, Tiny left. Two days
later, he picked up Phil's car from where they left it by the lake,
drove it to West Oakland, and torched it.

When he finished, Braddock nodded to Sinclair. He asked,
"Have you seen or had any contact with that white man or the
Hispanic woman after that night?"

"I wanted my money, but that shit was too crazy. Shane was
dead. I didn't want to be next, so I let it go."

"Where's your van?"

"I parked it on the next street over, Olive."

"We need to examine it for evidence to verify what you told
us," Sinclair said.

"You got my keys."

"Who have you talked to about all this?"

"No one. I couldn't talk to Animal; the police arrested him
for killing Shane. I was gonna talk to Pops. Figure the prez
would know what to do, but then I figured if he wanted to talk
to me, he'd let me know. So I just forgot it all. Like it never
happened."

"I have no further questions," Sinclair said for the recording
and Braddock.

"I told you the truth," Tiny said. "Can I go home now?"

"Not yet, Tiny," Braddock said. "We'll let you know once we check a few things out."

Sinclair and Braddock calmly left the room and closed the door. Once outside, they gave each other a high five.

Chapter 55

Sinclair drained his second cup of coffee as the recording ended. He looked across the conference room table at Archard, Uppy, and the AUSA who was brought in to evaluate it. "What do you think?" Archard asked.

The AUSA said, "It's not the kind of case I like, but we could charge Tiny federally with murdering an agent. By putting the bag over Roberts's head, he killed him. The fact that he thought he was already dead is irrelevant. We have his confession, and there's plenty of evidence to corroborate it." He looked at Sinclair and Braddock and said, "I'm sure your DA would charge him with murder too, if that's the route we want to take."

"What about Yates?" Archard asked the attorney.

"We have one coconspirator naming another. We could possibly make this work in federal court if we gave Tiny a reduced sentence in exchange for his testimony. We have plenty of corroborating evidence—all circumstantial by itself—but combined with Tiny's testimony, it might be enough. Depends on the jury. However, we didn't do all this work to prosecute Yates for something best handled in state courts. Sergeant Sinclair probably knows better than I whether his DA would file on Yates."

"Not with what we have," Sinclair said. "I wouldn't even take it to a DA. One witness, who can only testify to what Yates said, isn't enough, especially when he's also a defendant in the murder. If we hit Kozlov's house with a warrant and find blood, a shell casing, and other evidence, it might help. Maybe we'll find someone who saw or heard something if we canvass the neighborhood."

"I'm not usually the pessimist," Braddock said. "But I agree with Matt. An Alameda County DA won't charge Yates with what we have."

"You have enough to arrest him on probable cause," the AUSA said. "You could also arrest Ms. Lopez and try to get a confession or play one against the other."

"I interviewed Lopez already, and she lawyered up," Sinclair said. "I've also dealt with Yates. There's no way he'll confess."

"Has there been any discussion about the murder over the wire?" the AUSA asked.

Archard shook her head. "There's been no reason for Yates or Kozlov to talk about it. They probably believe they cleaned it up. I'll bet Yates will be shocked to find out he helped kill a man by putting a bag over his head."

"Does anyone know where Kozlov and Yates are right now?" Sinclair asked.

Archard set her phone to speaker. "Location and status of your target?" she asked.

"Still in his office," a male voice replied. "He normally leaves around seven."

She called another number and asked the same question. A female voice said, "Just left the mayor's office and entered the council chambers for the rules and legislation committee meeting. By the way, Yates was invited to use the mayor's office while he's out for minor surgery this week."

"Copy that," Archard said. "We'll get up on the landline in the mayor's office. Any idea how long the committee meeting lasts?"

"Between an hour or two normally."

Archard hung up and looked at Sinclair.

"I have an idea," Sinclair said. "It'll sound crazy, but it just might work."

★

Sinclair pushed open the massive door to the city council chambers. Behind the semicircular dais at the front of the ornate room sat the five council members who composed the rules and legislature committee. About thirty people sat in the audience, a tiny crowd compared to a regular city council meeting. A woman dressed in a colorful flowing dress stood behind a podium at the front of the public area of the room addressing the committee about proposed legislature for a public housing project in the San Antonio district. As the committee chairperson, Preston Yates sat in the center of the dais, paying more attention to a computer screen in front of him than to the speaker.

Sinclair stood against the back wall for a moment. When the speaker finished and thanked the committee for hearing her statement, Sinclair staggered up the center aisle toward the podium. "I have a statement to make," he yelled as he approached the polished wood table.

A woman sitting at the side of the dais behind a sign that read *City Clerk* pulled her microphone to her lips and said, "Sir, you need to submit a speaker card and be recognized."

Sinclair grabbed the podium with both hands and spoke into the microphone. "I'll just be a minute," he slurred. "I came here to talk to Preston Yates."

"Sir," Yates said into his microphone, "you are out of order and must immediately vacate the council chambers."

"It's you who's out of order!" Sinclair shouted. "And I'm going to take you down for murdering Sergeant Roberts if it's the last thing I do. You tried to kill his source in Hilton Head. But I was there, and she's alive."

"If you don't leave immediately, I'll order you escorted out!" Yates shouted.

"Roberts was shot at your buddy Kozlov's house. Instead of calling paramedics, you ordered your goons to dispose of his body. But he wasn't dead. Until you pulled a garbage bag over his head." Sinclair swayed back and forth. "That's right. The cause of death was suffocation. You murdered him."

Mouths of the other councilmembers gaped open. They stared at Yates wide-eyed.

Yates screamed, "This man is drunk and a liar. Remove him immediately."

Sinclair glanced over his shoulder as Braddock and a uniformed OPD officer approached him. The officer grabbed him by one arm, and Braddock grabbed the other. They spun him around and escorted him from the podium.

"You won't get away with it," Sinclair shouted on his way out the door.

Chapter 56

Once they were outside, Braddock said to the officer escorting Sinclair, "Thanks, Bill."

Sinclair winked at the young officer and hustled down the stairs alongside Braddock.

Ten minutes later, they rushed into the task force headquarters. About forty men and women wearing nylon raid jackets emblazoned with FBI and other federal agencies' three-letter designations mingled around the front of the main room. They pointed toward the wire room's door. Sinclair and Braddock stepped inside.

Archard, Uppy, Campbell, and four other members of the task force stood behind the two agents wearing headphones. "I heard it was an award-winning performance," Campbell said.

"Has it stirred up anything?" Sinclair asked.

"Our agent in the audience reported the committee took a recess, and when they came back a minute ago, Yates announced he was postponing the remainder of the meeting until next week," Archard said. "Yates just entered the mayor's office with Lopez. Our team on Kozlov says he hasn't left his office."

"I have an outgoing call from Yates's cell," one of the agents wearing earphones said.

"I have an incoming call," said the other agent. "Into Kozlov's private business line."

"Put it on speaker," Archard ordered.

YATES: Sergio, I think we have a problem.

KOZLOV: What now?

YATES: Sinclair just came into a public meeting intoxicated, mentioning your name and saying I killed Sergeant Roberts.

KOZLOV: The ramblings of a drunk. So what?

YATES: He knows Roberts was shot at your house. He knows we put the body in a garbage bag.

KOZLOV: We? I recall you were the one who pulled the bag over him.

YATES: That damn fat biker trash didn't want blood in his old van.

KOZLOV: Maybe Sinclair was just guessing about this.

YATES: He said Roberts was still alive after the shot to his head.

KOZLOV: You said he was dead.

YATES: My driver told me he was.

KOZLOV: You didn't check? Now you're telling me you ordered a man buried alive?

YATES: It was your idea to move the body. You're so paranoid about the police knowing your business. This isn't Russia, Sergio. There's no KGB here.

KOZLOV: And you assured me your police chief could contain anything Sergeant Roberts discovered.

YATES: The chief told me Roberts had nothing in his office files about us. I'll have him get the autopsy report. Sinclair might be lying about Roberts surviving the gunshot.

KOZLOV: But Sinclair knew about my house.

YATES: Maybe he found the missing biker.

KOZLOV: I thought you had that handled.

YATES: The lawyer you hired for Mr. Clement is having the motorcycle club locate the biker so he can be reminded to keep his mouth shut.

KOZLOV: If he talks to the police, he needs to be handled.

YATES: Like you handled that girl who used to work for you?

KOZLOV: You should watch your tone, mister city council-man. I will take care of my house, but you need to get yours in order. What will you do about that homicide detective?

YATES: I had the chief suspend him, but Sinclair doesn't know how to obey orders. I can have the chief arrest him for that outburst tonight—drunk and disorderly, or something like that.

KOZLOV: You do that. And have your police chief announce publicly that the detective was drunk and everything he ranted about was a pack of lies.

YATES: Okay, I'll call you tomorrow.

KOZLOV: With good news. No more problems.

They both hung up, and the computer speakers emitted a low buzz.

Everyone in the room was smiling. Even Sinclair.

"Should we call your DA and see if this is enough to arrest Yates for murder?" Campbell asked.

"That's an advantage of being a local cop," Sinclair said. "Unlike my federal friends who need permission from lawyers to tie their shoes, we can make those decisions ourselves."

"Touché, Sergeant," Campbell said. "You earned this. My office will talk with your DA tomorrow and work out the prosecution details." He turned to Archard. "Are you ready to go?"

Archard stepped into the main office and cleared her throat. "You've all been briefed as to your assignments. We'll execute at nineteen hundred hours. I will accompany the team at Kozlov's office. Those hitting his house, make sure you call OPD to process the murder scene once you secure it. Sergeant Braddock from OPD will take custody of Yates. Transport everyone else to the Oakland office for interviews and processing. Questions?"

A man Sinclair recognized as a special agent with the criminal division of the IRS raised his hand. "We have all the court orders to freeze the designated accounts at all financial institutions ready to go out electronically. Who'll give the order to transmit?"

"Send at seven o'clock unless you hear from me otherwise," Archard said, then turned back to the others. "We have about thirty minutes, so let's get to our staging locations."

Chapter 57

Sinclair led the team up a side staircase to the rotunda. Braddock and Uppy were behind him, followed by five FBI agents. US Attorney Campbell and an AUSA brought up the rear. Everyone was in raid jackets except for the lawyers—Braddock's was marked *OPD*, the others *FBI*. They bypassed the grand entrance to the council chambers at the top of the marble staircase, turned left, and pushed through doors to the mayor's outside office. An unarmed security guard got up from his chair.

"Is Councilman Yates in the office?" Sinclair asked.

The guard nodded but made no effort to stop them. Sinclair pushed the double doors open with Braddock at his side, followed by the rest of the team.

Yates was sitting behind the mayor's massive mahogany desk. Lopez stood behind him. The wire room had warned Sinclair that Yates's second phone call was to Chief Brown, ordering him to report immediately to the mayor's office, so he wasn't surprised to see him sitting in one of the chairs across from the desk.

"FBI—search warrant," Uppy yelled. "Don't anyone move."

Sinclair and Braddock stepped behind the mayor's desk. "Mr. Yates," Sinclair said, "as a special deputy US marshal assigned to a federal corruption task force, I'm placing you under arrest for the murder of Phil Roberts, an Oakland police sergeant assigned to a federal task force."

Sinclair grabbed Yates by the shirt, pulled him from the chair, and spun him around. "Hands behind your back," he ordered.

As Sinclair handcuffed him, Braddock added, "And I'm placing you under arrest for the murder of Sergeant Roberts, a violation of section one-eighty-seven of the California penal code."

Sinclair dragged Yates away from the desk.

Braddock said to Lopez, "Stand and put your hands behind your back." Braddock handcuffed her and said, "Same charges—murder under both state and federal statutes."

Sinclair looked at Brown's face for the first time since entering. His lips were turned up in a slight smile, as if he knew he'd gotten away with it.

Two agents headed toward Yates's city council office to search it while two others bagged a laptop that was sitting on the mayor's desk and sifted through an assortment of papers and files.

"Follow my lead," Uppy said. "This is what we Feds do best." He headed down the marble stairs, through the ornate lobby, and out the front door. Sinclair and Braddock followed, holding their handcuffed prisoners with firm grips on their upper arms. A crowd of TV news vans and reporters were assembled outside City Hall's main entrance. All the cameras turned toward them as they came down the steps. With their mouths shut and faces void of any expression, Sinclair, Braddock, and Uppy marched through the throng of reporters toward the street where they had parked their cars. Sinclair glanced over his shoulder and saw Campbell and the FBI special agent in charge of the San Francisco field office surrounded by cameras.

★

Sinclair was operating on autopilot. The caffeine he'd been feeding his body was no longer working, and his thought process felt like molasses. As they suspected, Yates invoked his right to an attorney before they made it halfway to the PAB, so they drove him directly to the jail and booked him for murder, a no-bail offense.

He and Braddock cruised by Kozlov's house and watched as Maloney, the rest of the homicide unit, and a team of evidence technicians scoured the area where Phil had been shot. As much as Sinclair wanted to get involved, he knew it was best to stay on the sidelines given his fuzzy status and his even fuzzier brain.

Sinclair sat in the Crown Vic beside Braddock outside Kozlov's house and phoned Phil's wife. Calling the mother or wife of a murder victim to tell her he got the killer was normally one of his greatest joys. But when Abby answered the phone, Sinclair felt nothing but sadness. He told her how Phil died and that Yates, Lopez, and Tiny would stand trial for his murder.

"It makes no sense," she said. "A careless accident? And all they had to do was take him to the hospital? It's so senseless."

"I know," Sinclair said. Murder was essentially a senseless act. Yet people always wanted it to make sense.

Sinclair listened to her tears, her confusion, and her anger. She wanted answers that didn't exist. Phil's death made no sense. It never would. The network of spouses—police survivors—had already reached out to her. Knowing she was not alone was comforting, but the fact that there were so many other women and men whose spouses were killed in the line of duty was nothing if not disheartening. Sinclair promised he'd be there if she ever needed anything—even if it was to mow the lawn or fix a leaky faucet. He meant it, but he knew she'd never call. He wanted to apologize to her for how he treated Phil during the last six months. To make amends for doubting Phil's motives. For believing he'd forgotten his oath. But he knew he couldn't put that burden on her. Not now. Not ever.

Braddock drove their car to the Oakland FBI office. Archard told them agents had arrested Kozlov at his office along with several other executives. Lopez was in an interview room spilling her guts in an attempt to avoid prison. Teams of agents streamed in carrying boxes of files and other evidence.

At 11:35 PM, Sinclair trudged up the steps behind Braddock and into the homicide office. Maloney was sitting in the main office chatting with the homicide sergeants who'd just returned from Kozlov's house. Sinclair accepted handshakes and back-slaps from everyone and plopped into his desk chair.

"The techs are still at Kozlov's house," Maloney said. "We've verified Tiny was telling the truth. They found a shell casing, footprints, and blood, which I'm sure will match up with Phil's DNA. They also found security camera footage from that night."

"What?" Sinclair asked.

Maloney laughed. "Kozlov's wife, who looks like an old, worn-out Russian mail-order bride, had accused her neighbors of letting their dogs poop on her lawn. Without telling her husband, she had their security company add motion-activated cameras outside to try to catch them. It's not the clearest video, but it shows everything from the accidental shooting to them putting Phil's body in the van."

If he wasn't so exhausted, Sinclair would've laughed.

The door opened, and Chief Brown and US Attorney Campbell stepped inside.

Sinclair didn't know if it was the fatigue, the adrenalin, or that he just didn't care anymore, but he blurted out, "We got them, Chief. As hard as you tried, you couldn't keep me from getting Phil's killers."

Brown walked across the room, opened a large manila envelope, pulled out Sinclair's badge and police ID card, and handed it to him. He set the envelope on the desk and glanced at the Kimber .45 on Sinclair's belt. "Your gun's inside. I take it you had a spare one at home."

Sinclair stared at him, speechless.

"Chief Brown was the one who initiated this investigation more than a year ago," Campbell said to Sinclair. "He noticed an overly cozy relationship between Kozlov and Yates and requested the attorney general and FBI open a political corruption inquiry. Your cracking open the escort service's records was the catalyst we needed to get people talking. For this to work, Chief Brown had to play along with Yates, so Agent Archard and I were the only people who knew he was working with us."

Sinclair didn't know what to say. There was too much to process.

"What about Phil?" Braddock asked.

"We kept what Chief Brown and Phil were doing strictly compartmented," Campbell said. "In a sense, your police chief was working undercover, and you all know the importance of protecting the identity of an officer who's infiltrating a criminal enterprise. We knew Yates was buying it, and not even Phil was wise to it when he reported his informant overheard Kozlov bragging about having a police chief in his pocket."

"Were Assistant Chief James and Farrington in on your plan?" Braddock asked.

"No," Brown replied. "Lieutenant Farrington obeys orders without question. Every organization needs people like him. If there was anything in Phil's office about the task force, I needed to contain it. Chief James sensed something was going on and was starting to dig to figure it out. I've already briefed him on everything and apologized for having to shut him out."

"So that was the purpose of suspending me—to shut me out?" Sinclair asked.

Brown smiled. "Matt, you're like a bulldog that won't let go of his prey no matter what. We thought we had you under control after the Thrill Kill Murders when the US attorney and I both talked to you, but after Phil's death, you went after Yates with such determination, we knew of no other way to stop you from prematurely blowing months of work."

"When Yates called Chief Brown and demanded he do something about you, we had to act to show the chief was still Yates's stooge," Campbell said. "We later realized that if you believed Chief Brown was on the take, you wouldn't have

reported everything you were discovering, specifically the identity of Phil's CI, so we had to take a chance and ask you to join
our task force."

Sinclair huffed. "That worked well."

"I should've handled our little meeting better," Campbell
acknowledged. "Trusted you more."

"I'm sorry I had to treat you the way I did," Brown said.
"I've told the personnel manager to void any reference of your
suspension. It never happened. Amend your time sheets and
overtime reports to show you were on duty continuously."

Maloney stood and looked at his homicide detectives. "Is
anyone doing anything right now that can't wait until tomorrow?" When no one said anything, he continued, "Then get
out of here and get some sleep. We've got a funeral tomorrow."

Chapter 58

Sinclair, Braddock, and the other four pallbearers, wearing their dress uniforms, sat at attention on the raised platform on one side of the podium. Guest speakers and dignitaries sat in a row of chairs on the other side. Four members of the department's honor guard stood at parade rest alongside a flag-draped casket in front of the podium and dignitaries. A row of people in black suits and dresses sat directly in front of the casket—Abby, Phil's daughters, and other family members. Beyond them were row after row of men and women in the OPD dress uniform and white gloves. Gloved hands occasionally rose to their eyes. Beyond them were more rows of dress uniforms in many colors, representing officers from departments around the Bay Area and throughout the state as well as smaller contingents from major departments across the nation. Behind them were thousands of people in civilian clothing: investigators and agents from other agencies, judges, attorneys, probation officers, retired police, and nonsworn employees of the department and the countless agencies that worked within the criminal justice system, as well as thousands of citizens who never worked with Phil or knew him but were there to pay their respects for what he had done as a law enforcement officer.

After the opening by the department chaplain, they sat through speeches by the governor, the state attorney general, a US senator, and several local officials. Chief Clarence Brown eventually took the podium and spoke of the Phil Roberts his fellow officers knew. He told stories that brought laughter and tears about a man who dedicated his life to his family, friends, fellow officers, and citizens of Oakland.

"Before I conclude and turn this back over to the chaplain," Brown said, "I want to talk about what Phil considered the most meaningful assignment of his career—that of a homicide investigator. Last night, I was in the homicide office discussing the results of the extraordinary efforts by this department and our friends in the FBI and other federal agencies to bring to justice those responsible for Sergeant Roberts's murder. I was trying to come up with words to express what Phil did for many years in that unit and what the men and women still working there do every day. And there it was—on a plaque hanging on the wall. These words describe what Phil did and why he did it and embody the very essence of the homicide detective, like those who would stop at nothing to find Sergeant Roberts's killers."

Brown cleared his throat, turned to the next page of his notes, and read,

The Homicide Investigator's Creed

No greater honor will ever be bestowed on you as a police officer or a more profound duty imposed on you than when you are entrusted with the investigation of the death of a human being. It is your moral duty, and as an officer entrusted with such a duty, it is incumbent upon you to follow the course of events and the facts as they develop to their ultimate conclusion. It is a heavy responsibility. As such, let no person deter you from the truth or your personal conviction to see that justice is done.

★

Sinclair puffed on a cigar Jankowski had given him as he stood in a small circle of fellow investigators. The midafternoon sun beat down on them through a cloudless sky. About a hundred officers, all in civilian attire now, had formed conversation groups on the second-floor deck of the OPOA building, a few blocks from the PAB. Below, hundreds more congregated in the parking lot and the barricaded street. Sinclair and the other pallbearers had carried Phil's coffin to the waiting hearse several hours ago and watched as it left with a motorcycle escort for a private graveside ceremony a few miles from Roberts's house. A steady stream of officers returned to the PAB, changed out of uniform, and arrived at the OPOA office, where food and an open bar greeted them. In the past, Sinclair would've stayed there until well past midnight.

Braddock grabbed a beer from an ice-filled bucket and pulled Sinclair aside. "I'm sorry I didn't do more to defend you when Chief Brown suspended you."

"Are you crazy?" Sinclair flicked the ash off his cigar. "You needed to keep your head down exactly as you did so one of us could continue the investigation."

"When I discovered you were operating on your own, I didn't know whether to be pissed at you for the risk you were taking or envious of your courage to keep up the fight."

"I've walked that line between courage and stupidity a few times too many," he said.

She took a sip of her beer. "I'm really going to miss Phil."

Braddock found it so easy to apologize. He wondered why it was so hard for him to do the same. "Me too. I wish I could tell him how sorry I am for not trusting him during those last few months and for thinking the worst when I found the money and Sheila's photo."

"He knows," she said.

"You think?"

"Phil's smiling down on us right now, and he's really proud of what we did. I think he's sorry he couldn't tell us about the task force and grateful you were able to finish what he started."

"I'd like to think so."

"Big plans for your day off tomorrow?" she asked.

"Alyssa's off, so we were going to spend the day together."

Braddock smiled. "I'm glad."

He looked at his watch. "She should be leaving the hospital about now, so I think I'll call her."

Braddock returned to their coworkers as Sinclair turned away and called Alyssa.

"Is your funeral over?" she asked.

"I'm at the reception and getting ready to take off. Are we still on for dinner?"

"Sure, give me a half hour to shower and change. Maybe an hour if it's a fancy place. Where are we going?"

"I know a great little Italian restaurant in Old Town Sacramento. Traffic getting there will probably suck, and if you're okay with it, I'd like to make a stop on the way."

"I don't mind the traffic. It'll give us plenty of time to talk. Are we stopping to visit your father?"

Although Sinclair regretted some of the hatred he'd felt for his father for all those years because he thought he'd killed Lucky, he wasn't ready to give up the resentments he still harbored for everything else he had done. He didn't know if he'd ever be ready. But there was one thing he wanted to do that might be a step toward the healing he sought. "No," he said. "I want to take a walk along a river and stop at the gravesite of a childhood friend and say the good-bye I never had a chance to say before."

Acknowledgments

As my writing career progresses another year, my law enforcement career falls further into the past. I'm grateful to those active and retired police officers and other law enforcement professionals who help keep my stories and police procedures current as well as friends who give me advice on everything from heart attacks to security guard licensing: Bob Crawford, Wendy Cross, Tyrone Davis, Rich Fanelli, Harlan Goodson, Shawn Howard, Julie Jaechsch, Steve Mauser, Tony Morgan, Tim Nolan, Steve Paich, Tim Sanchez, and Rachael Van Sloten. If I missed anyone, I'm sorry.

I would not be where I am today without my wonderful agent, Paula Munier, who continues to offer encouragement, support, and a critical eye that makes me a better writer. Without Matt Martz and his amazing team at Crooked Lane Books, especially Maddie Caldwell, Sarah Poppe, Heather Boak, Dana Kaye, and Julia Borcherts, the Detective Matt Sinclair Mystery series would be nothing but a dream. They continue to amaze me with spot-on editorial advice and savvy marketing and publicity. Thanks also to my writers groups: Hilton Head Island Writers Network, Sun City Sunscribers, and WCSU MFA Grads. Your support, advice, and fellowship are invaluable.

Thanks also to my readers. It blows me away to realize that people around the country who don't even know me read my books and want to discuss Matt Sinclair's strengths and flaws and whether he and Alyssa will actually get together. And of course, thank you, Cathy, for your love and support. I know it's not always easy explaining to friends when your husband's unavailable for golf, dinners, and other events because he's busy killing people and trying to help Sinclair and Braddock figure out who did it.